Idée Vixe

or,
Лиса чёрного Леса
Lisá chornovo Lesa
(Black Forest///Fox)

RON COGAN

CONTENTS

NOTE –

The following text, the plot of a novel, was found in a drawer of a mahogany desk uncovered while reconstructing the foundations of a building in Freiberg, Germany. It is dated from November 1944 and is presented in full, along with some commentary made in 2014 by the editor, in footnotes and an epilogue.

Chapter I

> The first couple of chapters must needs be relatively dry, prior to the introduction of our heroine. I promise to try to keep it brief.
> WALTER SCOTT

St. Tropez was one of the sea-landings of the American 7th Army, whose assignment was to bring down the Vichy French government and rendezvous with the other armies in northern France.

It was an August day, and Tropéziens out on the shore could see the troops landing on the north side of the bay.[*] Côte d'Azur was not a region of strategic importance to Germany; thus there were only several divisions guarding it, just one of which was a Panzer division. The defenders were ill-equipped and easily overcome by the combination of troop landings, aerial bombings, naval fire, paratroopers, and French resistance activity.

The German army retreated, and in one month's time American and French troops succeeded in pursuing them through half of France. The army moved 700 kilometers in 30 days, one of the fastest ever sustained advances. The offensive finally came to an abrupt halt when the Americans ran out of fuel and supplies. Tanks by themselves can do nothing until all the logistics catch up. The Germans entrenched themselves in the Vosges mountains, just before the German border, and a stable front was established. It appeared that the armies would be spending the winter there.

*   *   *

Among the Americans was a Major, Karl Stevens, who commanded a mechanized company in an Infantry

---

[*] (Only 12 years before the bay became the famous setting for the films of Brigitte Bardot and Louis de Funès). – Editor's notes, 2014.

Division.[*] He was a commercial real estate agent from Chicago, but had decided to study law after he returned from the war. Karl was one of several officers who had a good knowledge of German. Thus he was part of a group assigned to go behind the front in the end of September to disrupt a German resupply and communication line going from Freiburg to Mulhouse.

He formed one platoon of 25 men from his company, chose two lieutenants, and left for the German lines at night with several amphibious jeeps. He had changed his field coat for a leather bomber jacket. At this point Alsace was part of the German Reich. As planned, Karl avoided the inevitable German troops near the front lines by crossing through a small, desolate portion of Switzerland illegally. Even if caught, the worst that would happen was that the Swiss, observing the rules of neutrality, would keep him prisoner at a ski resort in the Alps for the remainder of the war. (Their hotels were mostly empty due to lack of tourism).

Karl's platoon passed into Alsace, then crossed the Rhine slightly north of Basel. They were among the first American soldiers to enter Germany. A few times they were seen on the road, but there were no distinguishing marks on the jeeps to give any observer, at night, the idea that these were US soldiers. Before daylight the small convoy managed to reach the mountainous roads of the Black Forest, or Schwarzwald.

A setback occurred. The other officers' platoons were taking slightly different routes and at different times to avoid detection of a large movement. They were supposed to rendezvous with Karl and move north through the forest until they reached the line. Karl was told of delays and asked to wait a day. When the next day came, the commander transmitted via radio, "Some of the groups

---

[*] For reference, platoon < company < battalion < brigade/regiment < division < corps < army < front/army group.

were captured, some had to turn back. You happened to be lucky being the first to set out. You were the only one who made it across the Rhine."

"Do we go back then?"

"Unfortunately, that is impossible now. Our activity has alerted the Germans and the area between Basel and Mulhouse is heavily patrolled."

"How long should we stay here?"

"It's uncertain. German forces are quickly increasing their concentration in Alsace as they dig in against our offensive. We can't reach you by air either. You should count on staying there, concealed in the forest, until the front reaches you. There are not that many of you, so you might remain undetected. We will try to airlift supplies to you later."

Karl was dismayed. What a wasteful and poorly thought-out plan this had been. The situation of his platoon made it almost impossible for them not to be captured. The front was expected to be stationary for months. The 7th Army could not advance, and the armies in the north near Paris were still too far away. One insurmountable challenge would be obtaining food once their supplies ran out in a few weeks, if it could not be parachuted to them. In the event of depleting supplies, it would be better to try to cross the lines back again in the northern direction of Baden-Baden or to cross the southern border and surrender to the Swiss. Before considering these possibilities, Karl decided to try to find an isolated German house, and hold its owners hostage while staying there.

The group continued through the winding roads of the Black Forest on its jeeps. Karl sat with one of his lieutenants, Tom Landon, and remarked on the intensity of the forest growth. The trees were mostly pine and fir, with some oaks. Not only was the canopy dense, casting the road in deep shade, but the forest floor also: The bushes and occasional tall grass, various boulders, and rugged terrain rendered a poor range of visibility. It was desolate and appeared that it had been that way for ages; it almost seemed that a lookout should be kept not for German soldiers, but for some ancient trolls lurking behind the trees. The German philosopher Heidegger enjoyed the seclusion of the Black Forest, coming here to write about "being and time".

Reaching a higher elevation, there occasionally appeared, without warning, large fields covered with green grass, sometimes with one or several houses. None of these could be suitable to assail because of their exposure; they were looking for one more concealed. In a nice part of the wood further on, they found such a house. It was just barely visible from the road, being separated by a driveway. The sign on the road said "Marzell", the name of the estate. The house was large, with two stories, and made elegantly from light gray stone. The roof was a darker gray and above the second story it sloped down except where interrupted by triangular gables. The most favorable aspect of it from a strategic standpoint was a field to the side, which appeared to extend all the way behind the house and, if so, would be perfect for building tents for the troops.

Chapter II

> Soon, trembling in her soft and chilly nest,
> In sort of wakeful swoon, perplex'd she lay,
> Until the poppied warmth of sleep oppress'd
> Her soothed limbs, and soul fatigued away;
> Flown, like a thought, until the morrow-day;
> KEATS, *The Eve of St. Agnes*

The cars were driven right to the door, stopping in the circular driveway. Karl pondered, "Well, Landon, what do you think? This will suit us very well."

"Yes, I think so. Let's go in quickly before they recognize who we are, see–."

Karl rang the bell and the door was answered by an elderly housemaid. With his accented but tolerable German, Karl asked for the master or mistress of the house, making sure to enter into the foyer before receiving a reply. One of the sergeants also spoke German – Andreas Wurzer. He followed closely, as did Landon and a few others. The servant woman refused to answer anything and assailed them with reprehensions. She was told to be silent, and Andreas stayed with her while Karl stepped forward through the hall. There was a large drawing room exposed to view. Passing this, further along the hall and before a large staircase, there was another parlor, into which Karl turned.

A long, two-barreled hunting rifle faced him. Holding the rifle was a young girl.

She did not aim it in a particularly threatening way but could easily cock it within a moment. She looked 17 or 18 and had long black hair with side-swept bangs that went well with her vivid, resplendent blue eyes. Some eyeliner was visible and further enhanced her eyes. She wore a short yellow dress that was tightly fitted at her narrow waist, which suited her.

Karl was confounded by this paragon of beauty, and he lost his thoughts. As a commander who has led troops into battle, delivering orders in the midst of danger and variable conditions, he was accustomed to decisiveness and composure. However, this unexpected encounter threw him off balance.

The girl was not insensible to the danger she was in, with this incursion into her house of troops not even of her own Wehrmacht. Distressed, but not wishing to appear intimidated, she had seized the rifle when she first saw what was going on. She actually could barely lift the heavy gun, disliked weapons in general, and was terrified at the thought of using one for something other than target practice. She expected an immediately explanation but not receiving one, asked, "Who are you? What are you doing?"

Karl replied, "Fräulein, I deeply regret offending you with such an imposition, but we are soldiers of the American Army and have suffered some setbacks that cause us to look for some help."

The girl interrupted, "American? But how can this be? There are no American armies in Germany! Not even close."

"We came from the south of France. The front there is actually just a little over 100 kilometers from here. We have gone behind the lines on a reconnaissance mission."

This information bewildered and shocked the girl. Meanwhile the soldiers who entered with Karl were mostly standing behind him. Some still had their rifles slung on their shoulders, but some had them in their hands. The girl was glad to have her rifle, as it still afforded her some amount of influence in this situation, despite being outnumbered as she was. However, a revolver would have been more convenient to hold, as already the weight was becoming burdensome. Karl continued, "Who else is in the house? I must speak with someone."

"Nobody else is here now except me."

"Your parents?"

"They are away. I am alone here, except for my maidservant."

"Very well. What is your name?"

She hesitated to reply, and then said, "I cannot tell you my full name. You may call me Vixey."

"Alright, fräulein Vixey, my name is Karl Stevens; I am a Major in the US Army. I would not do this unless it was absolutely necessary. As you know there is a war going on, and we happen to be stuck behind enemy lines and cannot go back to our own side. There are 25 of us. Since we do not want to surrender to the Germans, we have decided to stay here and wait until conditions change."

"What do you mean, here?"

"I mean right here, in this house. The men can set up tents behind, and I trust you can find lodging for three officers inside."

Vixey looked away, finding this demand hard to swallow. She started to feel faint. There were many things she wanted to say but lacked the strength. She just said, "We should sit down."

"Of course. I was about to offer it myself," Karl said, moving with her to a nearby table in the spacious *salon*. The others entered further in as well, some silently taking seats, some leaning against the wall.

Karl continued, "We will compensate you financially, although I do agree it may be problematic – some aspects of our being here."

Vixey dropped the rifle on the table with a loud clatter and slipped into a chair. She brushed her hand through her beautiful hair and sat with her elbow on the table and head against her hand. It seemed to her there was nothing she could do. She used her other hand to wipe away tears. "'May be problematic', you said? I have guests coming the day after tomorrow! What do you expect me to do about that!"

"You have to cancel it!"

"Do you hear that, Annette," Vixey said, addressing her maid. "This is villainy!" Her eyes, shining with vexation and stifled tears, appeared all the more dazzling, like Alpine ice under a blinding sun.

"Mam'zelle," Annette replied, "I don't know what to do. You must telephone your father at once! He will be able to do something."

Karl interjected, and it pained him to impose such unfortunate terms on the young fräulein, but he explained that due to their dangerous situation trying to remain concealed in Germany, it would be impossible to permit her to have any kind of free contact with other people, or even to leave anywhere unescorted.

As the full picture of what it meant to quarter these enemy soldiers became evident, Vixey fell into a dismayed teary silence. At length she asked, "Doesn't this violate some kind of international laws?"

Karl said, "I don't think so. But even if it does..."

"Assuredly as soon as I can I'll inform the top authorities of the Reich of everything that you do– "

"*Chérie*, after we leave you can write to the Führer, Winston Churchill, or the Pope. After we leave. By the way, I have had an audience with the Pope in Rome recently, when we liberated that city, and I think he would take my side. But I give you my word that aside from what we do for absolute necessity of war, you won't be imposed on. And we will give you a fair compensation in dollars."

"I dislike Americans in particular. I'll tell you that," she said spitefully and suddenly.

"Why?" asked Karl, genuinely surprised. After his earlier experiences liberating Palermo, Rome, Lyon, and other cities, he became accustomed to a general good-will towards the Americans and British. He naïvely expected some of it to continue even in Germany, and was somewhat unprepared for enmity towards his whole nation.

"Your president Roosevelt is a barbaric brute intent on destroying Germany completely, out of spite, and handing over what's left to the Bolsheviks. You're doing everything you can to help Stalin... The British I respect. They are honorable and would not do such things. In fact, they would have made peace with us by now."

Karl tried to be diplomatic, "Well, I don't quite understand some of your points; maybe we can talk later. I seriously doubt anyone wants to deliver Germany to the communists. But I want to emphasize that I don't know what politicians do or why in this war. Some of our generals disagree strongly with our president and his staff. I hope that you won't be unfriendly based on politics."

Vixey was not convinced. She said, "Since we find each other on opposite sides with conflicts of interest, I don't see how I can cooperate at all."

"Can you try?"

"Well, can you at least say you don't support your country's politics?" she asked.

Karl thought that it should have been him asking her that question, to determine the degree of her complicity with the Nazi regime. He felt he had more of a right to be angry and suspicious at the other side in the conflict, having lost many good friends to German bullets and grenades. These were not just casual friendships made during the campaigns, but people he had known since his youth, many years before the war. Their absence will be felt severely when I am home again, Karl thought. But he wanted to calm Vixey down, not to vex her. He saw no harm in being agreeable with her. He said, "As long as I carry out my orders and uphold my country's interests, I can oblige you by disagreeing with whatever you convince me is unreasonable."

"Hmm," she said, thinking. "Alright; that's not such a large concession but I think it will have to do. We might be able to get along."

Karl hesitated over the right words when he continued, still trying to take into account her comfort. This was not how he originally imagined taking the owners of a German house hostage would take place. He said, "Fräulein, I cannot conceal that, despite the briefness of our meeting, I think highly of you... And I sympathize with your position. I want to offer you my revolver as a token of good will. You won't need it, but if for your contentment you would like to have it, you can." Saying this, he placed it on the table in between them.

Vixey smiled for the first time. Although it was momentary and only a partial smile, Karl noticed it and was left with a beautiful and tender impression that lingered the rest of the day whenever he thought of her or saw her. Vixey did not intend to carry the revolver around with her. However, she was certainly touched by the gesture, as it indicated not only that Karl lacked any malicious intentions or thoughts, but that he believed her to be a reasonable person, and believed himself to be worthy of gaining her good will and establishing amiable relations. Throughout the conversation, besides acknowledging that his behavior was cordial, she observed that he was not unfortunate-looking in appearance. The black leather jacket he had on was impressive and avant-garde, not a conventional style. *

Still, her first reaction on returning alone to her room was to cry for some time. She was struck by how suddenly and irrevocably everything around her changed. It seemed to her too awful to be true, and especially hard to endure was the future uncertainty. Her room was the one last thing left to her; everything else was gone for an unknown, long time. Her feeling of being so alone – the awful loneliness of being among unreceptive strangers – added much to the distress. She was lying on her side atop the soft covers of her bed, and tears kept crossing the bridge of her nose as they flowed from one eye into her other, and after that dropping to the bedcover.

At length she felt a little less of the shock and resolved to reconcile herself to the situation. She told herself that her conditions would probably be eased. Already, she thought, her charm helped her to secure the freedom to

---

* This was well before Marlon Brando and Arthur Fonzarelli.

have this firearm. Not through manipulative arts, but simply through the effect of the natural graces she knew she had, did she hope to soon demand anything else she wanted.

*   *   *

Karl informed his platoon of soldiers, most of who were still by the jeeps, of what had transpired. He directed them to the field in the rear of the house, where they started setting up camp. It was agreed that Andreas, the German-speaking sergeant, would accompany Annette the maid to town whenever she went to buy provisions. Vixey gave guestrooms on the second floor to Karl and the two lieutenants, Tom Landon and Cliff Fadiman. She showed that she knew English quite well, and thus was able to talk with any of the Americans.

All the day's business concluded, the three officers found it difficult to restrain their delight at the improvement in their fortune. They were in an elegant and comfortable country house, richly and tastefully decorated (except for some portraits of Hitler and various swastika paraphernalia). They had real beds for the first time in ages, and most importantly, a gorgeously charming young hostess. Of course the men expected her to inform the Wehrmacht or the police if she had a chance, and one of the duties of the constant 24 hour watch was to see if she's not up to something. The keys of the Mercedes in the garage and access to the telephone were controlled. Vixey's concern on relinquishing the keys was evident, as the car had the elegance of a work of art. It was a black 1939 coupe, of unmistakable Art Deco style.[*]

Karl proposed to have a drink. He called Vixey – who half-opened her door and stood by it – and asked her what kinds of wine she had.

---

[*] Indeed, even 70 years of progress in automotive design would do little to diminish its merits.

"You want to drink wine?" she asked.

"Yes, why not. A glass of wine will make you feel better."

"Me?"

"Yes. Have one with us.."

"I will check," she said resignedly.

They followed her downstairs, not without noticing (the lieutenants for the first time), that a *cat* also resided with them here. It came out of Vixey's bedroom and met them at the top of the staircase, a nice long-furred gray cat with some subtle black stripes and yellow eyes. It had an intelligent and august expression. They also observed an interesting architectural design in the ceiling above the staircase. The entire roof in that area consisted of a rectangular section of semi-translucent yellow and green stained glass. The colors formed an array of geometric patterns.

The kitchen had a wine cabinet, and Vixey told them the options – there was demi-sec Champagne, Prosecco, red Bordeaux, Vouvray, Dolcetto d'Alba, and a lot of various local Alsatian and German wines.

"We're in the Markgräflerland wine region of Baden, where we make our own variety," Vixey said. She spoke so softly that the three officers had to come closer to her to hear what she was saying. In her life she was accustomed to never having the need to raise her voice, not lacking any attention. "But it's more similar to the white wines of Vaud and Valais than it is to Riesling and Gewürztraminer. In fact, I would suggest a Riesling at this point."

"Alsatian Riesling? Isn't that the closest of that kind?"

"It's closer, but something from the German side further north would be better, since you're not eating anything. For the French, food is all-important – when making wine they typically think about how it will pair with food and so their Riesling is stronger and less sweet. In Germany, we like to drink wine by itself as well, so ours is sweeter and has more character. Especially the better ones, like these, from the Rheingau."

"Let's try that then," Landon proposed. Like most Americans, Landon was raised a beer and whiskey drinker and wine was foreign to him. But during the Italian campaign, there was only wine available so he gained a taste for it. He was fine with any sort.

Karl opened it and poured four glasses. Vixey did not feel like drinking, but she accepted because to go to such a degree of incivility as to refuse one single offered drink would have been distasteful to her.

"To your health, fräulein," said Karl. "Thank you for tolerating us in your home... I take it you won't be our enemy then, on a personal level?"

"Enemy! No."

"Very well... I'm glad."

She sat on a barstool and crossed her legs while the men remained standing. She looked out of place among these men in military field jackets. Karl observed that she had taken the opportunity to put on shoes with a higher heel and also tiered earrings, now that her house was occupied by people. They all lit cigarettes, but she declined, saying she almost never smokes.

"Why are you here alone, in this splendid house? With such an extravagant car too?" asked Karl.

"My father is away because of the war. My mother passed away a long time ago."

"Sorry to hear that. Does your father have an important position in the Reich?"

"In a way," she said, avoiding the subject. "I also have a sister. She lives in Munich at her husband's house. Nobody even thought there would be any danger from the war for me being here, not at this time."

"Are you in a university?"

Vixey leaned in a little closer to them, resting her elbow on her top-crossed bare knee, with her hand holding the wine glass in front of her face. Her bent arm and the leg it was touching formed similar cute acute angles. She took sips of the wine intermittently, "I'm supposed to start in Freiburg after next winter.. I would have already been there but there are certain 'national labor service' requirements that have to be completed before. I'll do them at the University, which would be the closest I can get to avoid that service work entirely."

Recalling some of her irritation at the inconveniences of the intrusion, she said, "None of you have obviously been in any decent house for a long time! Do you notice how much mud and dirt has covered the floor in just one day? Annette can't clean it as fast as it gets dirty. What do you expect me to do, seriously? Switch shoes every time I go in or out of my room? I can no longer walk around here in stockings. And what about my cat? She will get so dirty walking here!"

"Alright," said Karl. "We can clean our boots. We can also get some of the men to wash the floor every other day or so, if you require it."

"Do you realize," she added in a resigned tone, "by being here while I am here alone, the extraordinary degree of impropriety you are subjecting me to?"

"Yes. I apologize," replied Karl.

"It's possible that my reputation will be negatively affected if this becomes known. And I can't see how it might not become known... Although... Who knows what the country will look like after the war is over,– whether there will even be a country. Nothing might matter anymore."

There was an awkward silence. The wine did indeed make her feel better, as Karl had suggested earlier. But at this point she had to turn away and stifle some tears. Karl asked, "Do you believe the war will be lost then?"

"Yes, it will."

"It might not become known afterward that we were here, if there is no military activity in this area. But if there is and if it becomes dangerous here, we may be in a position to protect you, and your property, from other troops."

"Perhaps," she said, and at that moment one of her high-heel shoes happened to slip off the back part and remained suspended, being held by her foot at the vamp (the enclosed front part). This was noticed by Karl, although he did nothing to give away his fascination by this subtle event. She was also not wearing stockings. The shoe remained balanced like that, and the fact that she did nothing to correct it, he somehow interpreted as a favorable sign of there possibly not being any strong antagonism towards him on her part. He thought that if there was, she would be more reserved and not as relaxed.

When she finished her wine glass, the three Americans had another but she excused herself. She reached down to correct her shoe. Then, she did something else that bewitched Karl – she lifted slightly her right leg which was crossed over the left one, and put her hands in between her legs on top of her left knee. Despite the apparent innocence of her motives some damage was done. It was difficult to be insensible to her beauty,- which was exemplified in every small movement.

Some minutes later Vixey went upstairs to retire. Landon said in a quiet tone, "Well, gentlemen, what do you think of the doll, of our sylphic wench?"

Fadiman replied, "I would just say, to quote from O. Henry, 'She's the kind of girl you like to have reach across you in a car to pay the fare.'"

"Yep. That says it all," said Landon. "Do you remember when she talked of her reputation and how this all would look? You know what I was thinking? We should have told her that since her reputation would be affected anyway, she may as well do something to make it worth it, see–. What if we split her amongst the three of us!"

Karl interrupted, still whispering, "I am shocked and appalled by your remarks, Landon! You don't distinguish the refined character and taste of this girl?, her sensibility (which however does not make it difficult to reason with her); and her naturally trusting nature? How offensive even a remote hint of what you just said could be?"

"Enough, see–. Your solicitude for her is well explained, Major," Landon replied irritably, blowing out smoke and putting out his cigarette.

Karl laughed, "Alright Landon. I've always tolerated your rebellious manner, so I shouldn't be surprised at you."

They talked of other things and remained in good spirits. They had paid no attention to the Army's newly issued German non-fraternization policy. These rules superseded the more appealing draft version of guidelines for soldiers' behavior. The now-withdrawn *U.S. Army Pocket Guide to Germany* had suggested that men might converse with, or even marry, German nationals without violating military law. But under the new policy, any friendly contact with the enemy was forbidden as fraternization, and drinking wine would definitely fall into this category. The American officers' situation was obviously an exception to any rules, as they were concealed behind enemy lines and would need to pursue whatever actions best fit their needs.

Retiring, Karl was troubled about Vixey's influence and resolved to suppress the affinity from getting stronger, not just because she was loyal to the enemy during a war, but because he mistrusted women in general. Women are known to deviously mislead for nothing else but a little amusement for themselves, so why wouldn't they also mislead for some tangible benefit?

In the situation he found himself in currently, concealed in a German wood, responsible for 25 men, with a myriad of things that could go wrong, to give up a capacity for sober and clear evaluation would be much more dangerous than in ordinary circumstances.

Still, going to sleep the one thought that consumed him was how close in physical proximity to him she was sleeping. She was in the very next room. On the other side of that wall over there. Earlier this day, completing his inspection of the overall house, he had to enter her room and violate its privacy. She had forced him to take his shoes off – never allowing anyone in outdoor shoes to step on the soft rugs covering her lacquered wood floor. Entering, he saw the serene but watchful cat sitting on a corner of Vixey's bed and looking at him. The down *couverture* was overturned slightly, revealing most provocatively her chic red bedsheets. This is where she sleeps,- is the significant thought that arrested Karl. He saw the red pillowcase, the pillow where she sinks her charming head lying on soft hair.

The rest of the room consisted of some bookcases and a dressing table, writing table, and armchair. There were red curtains, and two doors, one leading to a walk-in closet, the order to a private washroom. The room was mostly minimalist, as opposed to the density of rococo ornamentation. Most striking to Karl were the superfluity of mirrors. In addition to the one at the dressing table, there were mirrors on two of the walls reaching from the floor to the ceiling. One of these covered almost half the length of the wall.

Vixey had large windows looking out on trees and forest in the room. There were some scattered military paraphernalia – for instance Panzer tank bookends with the cannon shaft against the book; a belt of heavy machine gun rounds draped over a hanging shelf on the wall. On the dressing table, among various cosmetics, stood a mint-green box shaped like an elongated pentagonal pyramid – probably a container for perfume. Also noticeable was a plush toy platypus on a bookshelf, although it was camouflaged with the wooden shelves.

The most beautiful thing in the room was a framed photograph of Vixey standing with a red parasol and red short skirt during a snowfall, probably a year or two ago. The spruce trees behind her were entirely white from the snow coating them and large damp snowflakes could be seen falling down and settling on the parasol, which had a triple line trim: black/white/black. Color photographs are expensive to obtain, but it was worth it in this case because of the vividness of the skirt and parasol standing out against the solely black or white colors of the rest of the picture.

On the way out, Karl felt something soft strike his ankle. He looked down and saw that it was the *cat*, which was attacking him- apparently playfully because its claws were not extended. The cat, for one, was not pleased he was leaving the room but he explained he had business to attend to and departed downstairs.

Vixey's thoughts that night in bed were also focused on the day's events. The terrible thought suddenly struck her that things could have been much worse. She could have been tied-up or locked away somewhere while schemes of plunder were underway. She was not even overtly threatened with this. Although she knew they had to be far better than Russians, she still did not believe American soldiers could be very magnanimous. She attributed most of her lack of misfortune to Karl.

*　　　*　　　*

To introduce myself, the author, I will just state that I am a citizen of Berne, where I work in a Swiss bank (Credit Suisse). I usually stay on my side of the border, but sometimes venture into Germany to observe happenings there. I am writing this in Fall 1944.

When Thomas Mann was still here in Switzerland I told him that he must have copied his banker personage in *Tonio Kröger* from me. It's not a character *per se* but a short vignette of a character. He replied that it's impossible, since he wrote it not recently, but all the way back in 1902. So it must be a coincidence, although the similarities are many, except for that banker being much older than me.

Hermann Hesse is still staying here during the war, and I see him often when I am in Lugano, but Mann relocated to Los Angeles. He's in a coastal suburb of LA near San Monica. It has indeed a great climate and some film industry, but what is there to do there, especially for a man of culture? Where would one find a *konditorei*, a *pâtisserie*, or even any kind of café? It is like choosing a tropical island over a city; it could be because I'm younger, but I would take the city – an island is too desolate and un-cosmopolitan.

On such an island one would be missing out on the top developments in *design* and fashion; one would be away from a more interesting and cultured set of people – the ones with discerning tastes who create the demand for more refined nightlife, culinary arts, and other cultural products. The majority of these people are in major cities, especially European ones.

Also, one would lack the business – the hum of street ambiance at all hours of the day that lets you know something is always open. And the bankers, lawyers, traders, and newspapermen gathering in the financial district. One would lack something like the rush hour intensity of the Zürich Hauptbahnhof or Gare du Nord. Everyone is fixed in a serious purpose – a different expression on peoples' faces than there is on a riverside promenade on a fine day. But one feels good from having the focus, being amidst other professionals who have the same, and being able to haughtily look down upon some dallying gawking tourists. There could be an espresso bar in a corner, able to function because of the high level of efficiency of both clients and servers. Everyone knows what they want and what the price is. Not a single word is wasted. They drink the single or double café and go. However, one befuddled small town visitor, or an American, is enough to upset the entire mechanism and build up a queue.

Chapter III

Charmants yeux, vous brillez de la clarté mystique
Qu'ont les cierges brûlant en plein jour; le soleil
Rougit, mais n'éteint pas leur flamme fantastique;
BAUDELAIRE[*]

Vixey had coffee and croissants for breakfast with Karl. Having a bit more eyeliner and black shadow than yesterday, along with blackened eyelashes and an amethyst necklace, her beauty was almost unbearable to look at, until one's eyes became slowly accustomed, like they do when suddenly opening the curtains of a dark room and flooding it with morning light. She frequently used winged liner, a practice picked up from her Parisian fashion milieu. (She often went to Paris, and had an apartment there). In order to balance the blackness around her eyes, she also added a little eyebrow pencil. In two words, she transcended art.

Vixey bit into one end of a croissant with her pure white teeth and pulled on it so that it ripped apart. Steam drifted up from the hot interior. These were German croissants, significantly moister than their dry, overly crispy French counterparts. She split the rest of it with a knife and applied some raspberry *confiture*, flipping back some strands of hair that fell over her shoulder. Vixey's hair was straight, but it had volume (*ne prilízanniye*), curling slightly with ringlets at the ends.

When Vixey awoke that morning she was uncertain of how to handle the awkward, new situation. She listened at her door but did not hear anything going on – no voices or footsteps. She needed to have breakfast, so she put on some pretty clothes, spent some time perfecting herself at her

---

[*] *Fleurs du mal*, Le flambeau vivant (The living flame). Quotations from non-English poems are not translated, since an exact translation of both style and meaning is not possible. This one is about a girl's bright eyes.

mirror, and left her room to go downstairs. Karl was already on the lower floor, but was waiting until she came down before getting anything to eat. He assured her again of repayment for her costs.

Karl tried some other *confitures* from Swedish and Finnish berries that he had never heard of before. The fact that during wartime privations and trade embargos, she had products not even seen in America, spoke to her belonging to the higher echelons of Third Reich society. Also, her refrigerator had a freezer component, a rarity in Germany at the time.

"Where did you get these Swedish things in particular?" he asked. They spoke in English more often because Vixey's English was better than his German. Her accent was halfway between a British and a standard English one. It lacked the coarseness and raspiness found in the voices of many American women.

"In Basel. It's actually the closest city to here. But even Switzerland doesn't have the same range of products it used to. The war has hurt their trade so much they officially have rationing. But there's also a healthy black market and I have money for that. In Swiss gold, not in Reichsmarks."

"Do you just need to show a passport to go there?"

"Now you also need a travel visa to go there and back. I have this and so does Annette. If not for this she would have to go to Mülhausen, where there's not much. In all Germany there is rationing and there are no longer any products from tropical places, which means no chocolate or coffee!"[*]

---

[*] And it was not until 1948 that Berliners would see chocolate again, when it was dropped with parachutes during the airlift that countered the Soviet blockade. The 'Chocolate Bombers' did this on their own initiative, a further addition to their already renowned heroism.

"Were there never any plans on annexing Switzerland?"

"No; Hitler, as an Austrian, would be of course afraid of the Wilheim Tell legends! So the Swiss remain in political isolation from everything around them. It's a center of espionage and safe banking activity."[*]

"What about these croissants and fresh bread? Where do you get that?"

"Oh, there's a local *viennoiserie* and a bakery down the road in the valley. Did you know that croissants are from Vienna? The legend is that the shape is from the crescent on the Turks' flag and it was created after the great victory in the 1600s."

"Hmm. I didn't know. What I remember from that battle is that it was the King of Poland who came with his army and saved the city with a massive cavalry charge. Then the Turks started to be pushed out of Europe."

"Poland saved us again, actually, quite recently... In 1920, Germany was almost being overrun with communists and Russia invaded to try to link up with them. And it was Poland who stood in the way and held them back. It's not the Turks anymore trying to take Europe, it's the Russians."

"The Russians? Well, some of our generals do say that the Russians might become a problem soon."

"They are right. The Russians are the biggest problem now."

Karl, thinking it was German aggression that was the impetus for the entire war, was about to say something, but in a rapid movement she leapt back from the table, pointing at it, stammering, "An ant!"

Karl saw the ant and calmly crushed it with a napkin, throwing the remains in the rubbish.

---

[*] In later decades this would become even more true, as Geneva became the world capital of espionage, swarming with Soviet agents making deals with Western sellers of technology.

Vixey said, "Thanks. I usually go get my cat or the maid when something like this happens." She was afraid of most insects.

"No problem," said Karl. Their breakfast being over, he said, "I noticed you have a piano. I'm going to go try it out."

Vixey went to the other room with him. She was wearing Chanel colors: a pure white chemise tightened by a black leather corset-belt, black opaque stockings, black 125mm stiletto court shoes[*]. Chanel's advice, which she often followed, was that black and white were a perfect harmony just by themselves. The platform heels and black stockings she was wearing were part of her simplistic signature look.

Her attire was usually too captivating to be ignored. «*Quel poète oserait, dans la peinture du plaisir causé par l'apparition d'une beauté, séparer la femme de son costume? Tout ce qui orne la femme, tout ce qui sert à illustrer sa beauté, fait partie d'elle-même.*»[†]

Vixey heard Karl playing a beautiful piece on the piano and asked what it was. Karl said, "This is Schumann's leitmotiv of his wife Clara. It's from his Carnaval collection."

"It's nice, but at the same time so melancholy..."

"Yes, it's in the minor key."

Then he tried something else in minor, a C# prelude by Rachmaninoff. This was more difficult, but he managed it.

"I like that you know how to play the piano," she remarked.

"Well, the military is not my profession, as you know. I have other interests. Practically nobody in our army is a

---

[*] Pumps, in American English.

[†] "What poet, in sitting down to paint the pleasure caused by the sight of a beautiful woman, would venture to separate her from her costume? Everything that adorns woman, everything that serves to show off her beauty, is part of herself." – Baudelaire, *Le peintre de la vie moderne*.

professional soldier – everyone comes from a diverse range of backgrounds. Do you play?"

She said yes and they switched and he stood by the piano looking at her while she played some part from Debussy's Arabesques. The graceful notes of the piece were an apt counterpoint to her soft complexion and lowered smoky-shadowed eyes. Vixey usually used black as a shadow to brush onto her eyelids, but also experimented with silver.

She said, "I know you want me to cancel that *soirée* with my friends that is supposed to be tomorrow, but I think you should reconsider. It would be too suspicious to do that so suddenly and not reschedule anything."

"That's true, but what else can I do? There are tents and military jeeps right there behind the house. Look, you can see a corner of one of them from that window..."

"But they will come at night. You can tell your men to not light any lights, not come in here, and I'll prevent anyone from going outside. I think you actually risk more from people who might randomly come here to inquire about me, if I don't see them!"

It was impossible to oppose her. Her eyes and long eyelashes were delightful enough when she was looking down at the keys, only to be strikingly surpassed when she looked up. Karl said, "How about this. Use the occasion to tell them that you are leaving to Bavaria shortly and it is the last time you can invite anyone here."

"Alright."

"I will have to be there, and Sergeant Wurzer. To pass the part, both of us would need new shoes and jackets, and he would need trousers and a shirt as well."

"I can do that! I have some clothes here. So tomorrow then. *Danke schön!*"

She had interrupted her playing, and then resumed, this time completing a soft Chopin Nocturne, while Karl admired her. It was a simple piece, not requiring a lot of technical skill, but she played it with elegance and taste.

At that moment the two lieutenants came along with a radio operator and told Karl it was time for their planned conference. Karl went with them to a large table in the drawing room, where they spread out their map under a portrait of Hitler. Out of curiosity, Vixey went too and sat down, crossing her legs in an abrupt gesture. Rather than just setting one leg over the other, she veritably threw it over, with the result that it remained swinging for some seconds from the inertia of her movement. It was almost as if she wanted to assert herself in front of the lieutenants from the conspicuous way she sat down. Landon looked at Karl questioningly but Karl shrugged, as if to say, "Why does it matter that she's here?"

Over the radio Karl talked with the colonel* in charge of the battalion he was separated from. They received updated information that they drew on the map, but their long-term plans remained the same, to stay. After conferring on some other issues with the map, they asked Vixey if she could make herself useful in judging its accuracy.

She did not know much about the location of military positions, but did see that in the area they were in, several bridges no longer existed, or the contrary – that new bridges weren't being indicated on the map. She was glad the American maps weren't accurate and said, "No, I can't do something to help your side." However, then she mitigated her refusal with a smile, one that came to her naturally when she thought how quaint it was that they should ask her for help. Her smile was one that could lighten the dismal feelings of the world, in an almost supernatural way sweeping away darkness. Nobody was

---

* Officer ranks are as follows: lieutenant < captain < major < lieutenant colonel < colonel < generals from 1-star to 4-star < field marshal. In the US instead of a marshal rank there is a 5-star general.

disappointed and the lieutenants left to have lunch, as it was already afternoon.

*   *   *

Karl lit a cigarette and offered one to her. She said she'd have one but first went to get a cigarette holder from a bookshelf nearby. She affixed the cigarette to it and leaned forward for Karl to light it, which he did with a Pennsylvania zippo lighter. Then she went to a sofa against one of the walls of the room. Karl was thinking: Everything she did made him more and more bewildered – in the sense that he could not understand how such a charming thing was possible in such a drab world and a destroyed continent. How did it come about that she is here? After all the endless mud of the war, weighed down always by idiotic orders from above, it started to feel like the whole world was a contaminated, diseased, ruined existence,- but at the end of all that, to come here..., where a pristine girl was concerned about the shade and length of her eyelashes and about her cat not enjoying a clean floor. If this isn't a dream, then how to come to terms with this unreal enchantment? For instance, it was the first time he saw her smoking, and how did she appear while doing it.......: She was lying on her back on the *divan,* with her legs over the armrest in a somewhat crooked way: knees touching but shoes slightly apart. Her beautiful anthracite-coal-black hair was thrown haphazardly over the white sofa, which was the same color as her dress. Some of her movements in settling in had caused the dress to edge a little higher, revealing some more of her slender legs. She took long hits of the cigarette and let voluminous columns of smoke rise from her mouth. She didn't blow it out but let it rise up by itself, in an opaque swirl. There was something pert and unusual about her lips. They were of average size, but the m-shape of her upper lip was more pronounced. It seemed that her upper lip extended forward a tiny bit more than her lower one, and this had an enticing effect because it looked like her lips wanted contact.

Now, she had moved her head to the edge of the divan, causing most of her hair to remain on the surface, but some to droop down, in a mass, over the edge. Through the darkness of her hair one could discern, but barely, cute parabolas of varying lengths and thickness – strands which went down the side of the divan but then looped back up, allowing her head to rest on their ends. In addition to this, a few rebellious strands simply hung vertically down, just shy of grazing the floor, outlined sharply against the white color of the sofa's fabric.

Karl went over to talk to her, bringing a chair and seating himself in front. He asked, "Where do you get all your fashionable attire from? I can't imagine that anywhere besides Paris would have things like this right now."

"You're right. Practically everything is from Paris." She got up on one elbow. "I was just there in May last time. You have terrible restrictions currently on textiles in London and New York, right?"

"Yes, clothes are being rationed like certain food is. You can only get a certain number of articles per year. It was just starting when I left for the war. In England apparently it's even worse."

"But in Paris there's none of this! It's unthinkable to do that in Paris, the capital of fashion. Now it's the only place actually designing anything! But there was some trouble in the beginning. Our government wanted to relocate the fashion industry somehow to Berlin and Vienna, which obviously would have killed it. Lucien Lelong, head of the *Chambre Syndicale de la Couture*, went to Berlin and persuaded them not to try to change anything."

"Lelong- was he not the husband of that pretty Russian princess; I forget her name..."

"Ah, yes. Natalie Paley. They separated a few years ago and she went to the US. Her early life is so sad. Her father was the uncle of the last tsar. After the revolution the tsar and all his family were murdered. Natalie at 12 years old, escaped with her mother and sister across the snows of Finland to the West. Later in Paris she started working with Lelong in his business and her glamour and taste contributed to it."

"So do you get clothes from his couture house?"

"Yes, he has a great new designer working for him: Christian Dior. I also get things from Jacques Fath, Hermès, Lanvin, some others... For hats it's Claude Saint-Cyr and I also have a few from Elsa Schiaparelli and Paulette. With shoes it's more difficult. I get a lot from André Perugia and he's the best in Paris but I'm still not impressed. I get even more chic ones from an Italian shoemaker in Zürich, Michele Ferragni. He is able to create a lightweight titanium *talon aiguille*, a long, extra-thin heel. This is essential. I would never wear something as heavy-looking as Ferragamo's designs..."

Pulling on her belt, which was tight against her waist, Vixey said, "This belt is Vionnet, but it's the only thing I have from Vionnet – I don't like those long Grecian dresses..." Then remembering something else, said exclaimed, "Oh, and about Coco Chanel – I know her personally and there's an interesting story about her. I'll tell you if you promise not to tell anyone."

"Alright."

"It's a military secret. Are you sure?"

"Go ahead," he said. "I promise."

"She closed her fashion business and started working for the Waffen-SS, for Reichsführer Himmler! She went to the British embassy in Madrid and was trying to correspond with Churchill on some kind of schemes..."

"Women make the best espionage agents. Did anything come of it?"

"No, apparently the Spanish or the British found out... But anyway, look at this: These stockings are made by Chanel, one of her rare exceptions of items produced during the war."

Saying this, she bent one of her legs to have him take a look at the portion of the dark black stocking near her ankle. It had a series of beads imbedded into it shaped into a design. Below the design was the double-C logo of Chanel, and above it was a swastika.

Karl was intrigued at why anyone would make something like this, but only momentarily. His predominant thoughts were to thank his good fortune at having an excuse to hold her leg by the ankle.

"Admit it," he said, putting down her leg back on the armrest, "You're glad there are people around to see you in all these fantastic clothes; it's not like you would've gone to a Basel *passeggiata* every day. You would've went maybe once a week and would be bored the rest of the time." He took the liberty of drawing his fingers along her leg right after he put it down, testing her reaction.

She didn't flinch; she actually laughed at his statement and said, "Maybe."

Having touched her ankle lightly, seeing her elbow and forearm tensed against the divan, hair falling over her shoulders, breasts pressing against the fabric of her chemise, Karl was overtaken by a desire for her body. At the feeling's current state of development, it was vague, unspecific. Hypothetically, if questioned at this point, he would not have been able to articulate what he wanted from her.

Meanwhile she was talking: "Style in Germany has actually regressed severely. I would dress more conservatively if I went out than I do at home. The ability to wear anything risqué has unfortunately declined since the 20s, at least from what I heard about 20s Berlin; I was born in 1926. Apparently then one could wear a skirt or dress with a hemline above the knee, for instance, but now you definitely can't. The Nazis are generally anti-cosmopolitan – there is a movement against high-heels, against make-up, even against smoking... Part of their conformist *Gleichschaltung* policy... But I try to disregard it!, whenever

I can at least. I'm not too tall – 168cm, so I always wear high-heels. To have the foot at a 90° angle is *unfeminine*."

"Unfeminine?"

"Yes; it looks strange. Whereas a shoe with an elevated heel and a small platform looks feminine – it makes my legs longer and slenderer. Besides the shoe itself looking nice, it makes everything look better – my legs, feet, posture, gait, and figure. Even my tall leather boots for the forest have a wedge heel. If I happen to wear a flat shoe I'm unaccustomed to being so low and it feels like I'm walking uphill everywhere."

"Hmm," he said. "You're an interesting girl. These shoes you're wearing now would be frowned upon by the Nazis, yet you're wearing them right below a swastika symbol. And you look like you've enjoyed that cigarette. I'd be glad to hear you explain the contradiction."

She laughed, "Oh, I don't care about their rules and politics. I'm in a position where I can enjoy a certain amount of independence, but on the other hand, I'm also tied to the State because of my father's occupation." She sat up and left her cigarette holder in the ashtray at the end of the couch. "I might as well tell you," she said, "It would come up at some point anyway. Promise again you won't try to exploit me for information?"

"Yes. I guess I have to promise."

"Well, my full name is Victoria Sofia von Isarberg. My father is Generalfeldmarschall von Isarberg, one of the highest-ranking generals."

"A field marshal! He is on the eastern front, is he not?"

"Yes. Things are not going well. The army has only been retreating and counterattacking for over a year! I'm actually due to receive another letter any day now."

"This is quite remarkable! What a coincidence that we stumbled into this house; von Isarberg's house. Although I could tell from the lavishness of its appearance that someone important must live here. I wonder: how would he feel if he knew we were here?"

"I don't know. Maybe the Americans will be defeated in France and then we will see," she said.

With that they separated to do different things. Karl addressed some logistical issues in the soldiers' tents; then he sat down at an outdoor table nearby to examine some maps and write some documents. A large, weighty bee circled above the table before buzzing towards a row of flowers by the side of the house. The mild noise of the soldiers engaged in construction or cleaning, the low unintelligible conversations, were actually conducive to Karl's work. When doing thoughtful work or reading, it is better to have, rather than complete silence, an ambiance of soft activity somewhere in the periphery – a woman applying makeup in the next seat on the train; a favorite secretary doing some filing near you in the office; etc.

*   *   *

Vixey's apparent contradictions were not really contradictory. Her individualism and averseness to *ausrichtung* (alignment; conformity) came from her patrician feeling of doing as she pleases, something she felt entitled to. As such her desire to dress contrary to prevailing social and political norms did not lead from a lack of modesty, but rather from that concept. Another factor that contributed was her appreciation of æsthetics, which made her wish to utilize and enhance as much as possible her high degree of natural beauty. "Otherwise it might be a waste of a good thing and might be perceived as under-appreciation of divine providence," was the argument she gave to her Catholic pastor when he questioned the necessity of her silhouette-defining bodices and recherché shoes. The pastor was not concerned about influencing the behavior of her private life, as he knew that that particular rôle of religion was only relevant to the middle and lower classes. He merely was worried that she would rival the Church in keeping the attention of the churchgoers, as his arguments for the deification of this or that carried substantially less force than her mere presence. (See Gautier, *La Morte Amoureuse*). Throughout Vixey's irregular Church attendance, she always brought a book of literature along to pass the time more productively.

As for her flirty nature, it was not from manipulative impulses, but due to youth and a natural goodwill toward people that led from always having been admired. She had a privileged and comfortable childhood, which was a good thing because despite her confidence and individualism, she still had too much sensibility to have survived in any situation of poverty or distress. Her trust in people resulted from being accustomed to always being in an intelligent and refined society while growing up in Berlin and Munich. Some of her character can also be explained by her predominant female influence having come from her sister Evelina (six years older) and their mutual friends, as well as influential acquaintances such as Coco Chanel.

Chanel taught her that it's pretentious and even impolite to leave one's house without elegant cosmetics. She said that it's best to be as pretty as possible always. However, Vixey disagreed on the necessity of lipstick, only using it rarely and instead focusing on her eyes. She also thought that nail polish was too ostentatious – it was unnecessary for her. After the beauty of her eyes and face, it did too little to enhance her and she thought it rather detracted from the elegance of her young, simple minimalist image. Lord Byron thought the same when describing how further enhancing Haidée's beautiful image was not possible[*]. Vixey associated bright lipstick and nail polish with the same *Belle Époque* frou-frou, the gaudy colors and frills that Chanel had opposed after the previous war. Chanel would not have approved, for instance, of Ezra Pound, who walked around 1909 London in flamboyantly-colored attire and an immense sombrero.

---

[*] *Don Juan*, III. 76.

In Vixey, Coco Chanel saw a great deal of possibilities, first of all in how she could contribute her good-looks and youth for the brand's image[*], and also in adding her taste to the creative development of styles. She saw in her a re-visioning of her own distant youth. Vixey had already impressed her, as well as Dior and Vivier with the shoes that she wore, which were custom-made as per her specifications in Zürich. But all this was put on hold because Chanel had retired during the war.

It was an encounter with a rich banker's widow in Zürich, Mme T__, that, together with re-reading Charles Baudelaire's essays on æsthetics, led me to develop a fuller insight into the underlying psychology of Vixey's fashion sense. Mme T__ is a client of the bank's investment management services, and lives in the center of Zürich on Bahnhofstrasse. Meeting her in 1943, I was struck by the extent to which she surpassed in beauty and allure various much younger girls in the same room. In her elegant appearance nothing was left to chance; «верный снимок *du comme il faut...*»[†] She was a legislatrix of parlors and halls, commanding the attention of anyone around, to the detriment of others vying for it. Much of this was based on her art of enhancing and adorning her image. She gave consideration to every artificial means that provides an æsthetic benefit – cosmetics, stilettos, jewels, regular exercise, a precise amount of exposure to the sun to provide a perfect and even skin tone, exquisite and frequent hair styling, etc. The pretty young Swiss girls, probably from somewhere on the outskirts of Zürich like Winterthur or Pfäffikon, presented a contrast decidedly not in their favor. They had agreeable features, and most were still thin, but with their simplicity, their all-natural, bland look and markedly unsophisticated dress, they looked substantially

---

[*] (As did Marie-Hélène Arnaud, later in the 1950s).
[†] Pushkin, *Yevgeny Onegin*, 8.XIV.

inferior in beauty to the elegant lady. Their youth was their only asset, and it was questionable how long it would last if they continued to neglect to enhance it.

This was what Baudelaire was contemplating when he wrote some of the chapters of *Le peintre de la vie moderne* in 1863. Baudelaire likened cosmetics and beautiful attire to saintliness, a spiritual striving towards perfection. He correctly formulated that nature is evil. Virtue, reason, philosophy, and art are all artificial concepts, all non-natural. Thomas Hobbes would have agreed with this, and even Rousseau, who differed from Hobbes on what is the best way from nature to civilization, would agree that there is no virtue or morality in a state of nature. It is an incorrect bias to assume that things that are natural are intrinsically good and things that are artificial are not. Humanity *per se* is a very deplorable creation; save a few chance exceptions, it requires artificial means just to make itself tolerable and presentable.

Baudelaire posits that clothes and cosmetics are an art,- an attempt to correct and improve raw nature. They have more value than a beauty that is only natural. «*La mode doit donc être considérée comme un symptôme du goût de l'idéal surnageant dans le cerveau humain au-dessus de tout ce que la vie naturelle y accumule de grossier, de terrestre et d'immonde.*» (Fashion should thus be considered as a symptom of the taste for the ideal,- which floats on the surface of all the crude, terrestrial, and loathsome bric-à-brac that the natural life accumulates in the human brain).[*]

As a symptom of having ideals, fashion is not materialistic but spiritual. That small *pochette* with a silver/leather intertwined chain strap and an exquisitely-crafted slide-bolt metal lock is a symbol of a sort of aristocracy of mind. Brands like Chanel are more than just a

---

[*] *Le peintre de la vie moderne*, Ch. XI, 'In Praise of Cosmetics'.

trademark of quality – they convey the noble distinction of decades of exceeding æsthetic standards of style.

Art, according to Wilde, has no practical use – hence its value. Technology improves comfort and health, but it also increases intelligence and consciousness, thus increasing peoples' discontent. Occupation with practical things is not an actualization of man's creative potential. Rimbaud, the symbolist poet, would say, «*J'ai horreur de tous les métiers.*»[*] Progress is counterproductive; life is transitory. What is its value? Who cares? But art can exist beyond the temporal – beauty is our only window on the divine. In these terms, art is the most productive thing. And within art, what could be more important than *feminine fashion*?

Baudelaire defined modern aristocracy as living according to the highest æsthetic principles while maintaining a personal originality. This includes a perfect elegance and tidiness at all times, but still a preference to simplicity rather than immoderation. These are things that have already been noticed in Vixey, but how did she arrive at these ideas herself?

She first thought about it, actually, during her incomplete Catholic education and her readings of Thomas Aquinas on the topic of Original Sin. This is a Christian notion that implies that humanity is tainted by Adam's rebellion and departure from Eden. When Adam entered into the normal world, he fell from a supernatural state to a merely 'natural' one. Consequently, humanity starts off from a position of original sin and must aim to redeem itself. Augustine of Hippo, as well as the radical Protestants Luther and Calvin, contended that the only possible way to redemption was through Christ. Vixey acknowledged this but did not understand how this by itself could be

---

[*] "I have a horror of all trades." In *Mauvais sang, Une saison en enfer*.

sufficient. She tended to include a lot of her own personal interpretation to Catholic theories. Thus she preferred Pelagius's premise that people can work towards eliminating original sin (which she equated with a state of nature) through self-improvement: knowledge, art, and beauty. As she already started off from such a high level of natural beauty, she could accrue the most advantage from perfecting that. She felt that it was a duty to use all the arts available to her to enhance her good looks and fashion – and in that way to *transcend* nature on the spiritual level. The advice that Mlle. Chanel and Evelina gave her subsequently, coincided with her line of thought.

*   *   *

After leaving Vixey and finishing his work, Karl slept and reminisced on his path through the war that had brought him here to this alluring place. Being in the National Guard, he was drafted and deployed to North Africa in 1943. The fighting there having almost concluded, he spent the next year in painfully slow advances northward through Italy, starting with an invasion of Sicily, then an attack on Salerno on the Amalfi coast. The disinterested Italians had surrendered almost immediately when faced with an invasion on their soil but the Germany army still kept up heavy resistance. It was here that Karl rose through the ranks to become a company commander.

The Germans retreated from Rome to set up their defenses further north. Karl entered the intact ancient city, along with the US 5th Army, without any resistance. Merging into a vast green-gray cavalcade of tanks, filling the air with their distinctive mechanical odor, he drove past the Colosseum and into the Piazza Venezia, beneath the massive and looming Vittorio Emanuele monument. The winged goddess Victoria, in a quadriga, looked down on the scene from atop the Corinthian-columned marble structure.

The crowds that greeted the American troops were wildly enthusiastic. Karl was kissed by more than one

Italian girl as he moved with his company down the more intimate smaller streets of the old town. Arriving at the Piazza Navona, their jeeps were filled with flowers, girls, and girls carrying flowers, maybe among them Sophia Trevesa.

Pope Pius XII met with General Mark Clark and congratulated him on taking the city. The taking of Italy's capital was symbolically a very significant event in the war effort. A year of very difficult battles had at last resulted in a worthy reward. A celebration was held at night by the officers of the division, with the girls from a top-class German military bordello:

> Many and beautiful were those around,
>> Like flowers of different hue and habitation,
> In some exotic garden sometimes found,
>> Roman, Neapolitan, Sicilian, and Venetian.

At this point the controversial invasion of southern France was being planned, and Karl's division was among those split from the 5th Army in the Italian campaign and sent to the 7th Army, making the invasion described at the beginning of the first chapter.

The American officers had supper with Vixey in the evening, and Karl noticed that she seemed to become prettier every time he saw her. She was bewitchingly dressed in a form-fitting two-buttoned jacket with a standard revere collar, in gray translucent cotton, and with three-quarter length sleeves. Under that she had an unbuttoned white plaid short-sleeve shirt, with its small soft collars going on top of the jacket. Since the shirt was unbuttoned, it kept the v-collar of the jacket open, where she had, not the amethyst necklace from the morning but a necklace with a small silver key hanging from it. The jacket was actually pieced together from various designs and patterns and there were gaps sometimes between them like in a crocheted lace tablecloth. In this way her white shirt was vaguely visible underneath the jacket, and just past the ending of her shirt's sleeve, the skin of her arm could be seen through the material, which was tight against it.

She offered them a *digestif* of *eau-de-vie*. Landon examined the sweet-smelling small glass of liquid that came from a bottle with undecipherable German words and asked, "What did you say this was, *eau de cologne*? Are you trying to poison us?"

"No," she laughed, "*Eau-de-vie*. It's like brandy. This one is *birnengeist* from pears."

Landon and the other officers drank it and commented that it was quite good.

Indicating the key on her necklace, Karl asked, "Is that a key to a file cabinet or some kind of jewelry box?"

"No," she said, "Look..." She lifted her arm to show them the steel bangle on her wrist. Hanging from the bangle, holding it closed, was a tiny, barely discernable metal padlock that Karl examined by touching it. "It's nice isn't it?" she asked.

Vixey then brushed her hands through her hair and did not notice that this action had not smoothed out all her hair but left behind a cute black tuft standing up. With her, even a bit of disorder was delectable. She said, "People make a lot of *Schwarzgebrannter* (illegally distilled liquor) currently in the Black Forest, mostly kirschwasser, to trade for food in the towns. The food situation for most people is not good, because of the war."

Karl said, "In Italy they were making a local liqueur from lemons that they called limoncello. When we were in Salerno it was offered to us every time at the end of a supper."

Vixey felt the need to stop talking about neutral topics and tease them about politics. Eating an apricot, she asked, "With all the war agitprop going on, have people in America become even more nationalistic? Are people generally impetuous nationalists?"

They were uncertain of an immediate reply. Karl ventured, "I think nationalism wouldn't be the most accurate word; it has some collectivist connotations. But Americans have a lot of patriotism and this is because the US is the best. Who can doubt that?"

"Well, I tend to see nationalism as comparable to sports fanatics – people grouping into allegiances to various teams for no better reason than having nothing to do."

"But America is a place where this is different," remarked Karl. "Americans are individualistic and have the ability the think for themselves. Over the years it was typically the most enterprising people who have undergone the emigration to get there. America does not have such long cultural traditions as Europe, but its achievements in government and democracy are unmatched. It is by far the oldest liberal republic in existence: 160 years."

"What about Switzerland?" Vixey asked.

"Switzerland was around, but it had various changes in government, such as the Helvétique Republic. Its new 1848 federalist constitution, by the way, was modeled on ours."

"But don't talk about democracy as if it's a good thing. It's certainly not."

"How so?" asked Fadiman.

"Is not Hitler a product of democracy?" she replied, throwing the apricot pit into a rubbish bin.

She continued, "Your own Hamilton and Madison write about how an unfettered democracy leads to any excesses. They would not have approved of the 'popular' excesses of Roosevelt or of Hitler. Common people can't be trusted, despite their numerical size, especially not to take precedence over the rule of law."

"What can you know about 'rule of law', or who is or isn't common?" Fadiman could not refrain from exclaiming.

"I'm speaking from a theoretical point of view. How can common people know anything about economics or governance? There are vast differences in class and race among people."

"Still," said Karl, "an element of democracy is needed in any republic."

"In the sense of an elected parliament, yes. But there has to be a protection of many layers between the people and the law. Because there are not enough layers, the fortune of all countries fluctuates, except for Switzerland, which is the most stable. Maybe your own will be undermined by Roosevelt and his friend Stalin. Everything they do is allegedly in the name of the people, even though it's only a small amount of people benefiting at others' expense."

"What about you? Do you have any national allegiance?"

"Rather than nationalism or patriotism," Vixey replied, "I prefer cosmopolitanism. Although it's comfortable to be among your own nation's people, it's even more important to be among your own class. I belong to that part of society where class is more important than *volk*, or religion for that matter. In a certain class, people will be the same no matter what country or time period. National and religious traditions mean little. Interactions between people, and money, matter more. Nor do I care about political issues unless they affect me. Since I live here, of course I prefer for something to benefit my country instead of another. Everything else is more or less abstract."

Fadiman asked, "So you don't care about things happening to people in your country?"

"I don't."

"You also don't care about what's being done in your country's name in all the places invaded outside it?"

"It's none of my business. This is how everyone everywhere feels- they just don't admit it. I have enough concerns of my own – about what will happen when the war is lost and we are occupied."

After she left Karl told the lieutenants who her father was. Landon, his Chicago bootlegging instincts rising up, jokingly suggested, "What if we were to take her hostage against them?"

"No," said Karl. "What would that accomplish?"

"Are you at least going to include this in your report?"

"I'm not. It's not necessary for our folks to know. I don't want to risk involving her in anything directly."

Fadiman remarked, "I was about to ask her what she's done, if anything, in opposition to the regime here, and it turns out her father is von Isarberg. There's now even less reason than before to consider her trustworthy and not hostile!"

"But what could she do, to oppose the regime? Not much. The most she could've done would be to transfer assets out of Germany to Switzerland, and she has that covered."

The little *tuft of hair* mentioned before contributed to making it difficult for Karl to oppose Vixey in any discussions, or to make plans without taking into account her interests and wellbeing.

Chapter IV

> She walks in beauty, like the night
> Of cloudless climes and starry skies;
> And all that's best of dark and bright
> Meet in her aspect and her eyes;
> Thus mellowed to that tender light
> Which heaven to gaudy day denies.
>
> One shade the more, one ray the less,
> Had half impaired the nameless grace
> Which waves in every raven tress,
> Or softly lightens o'er her face;
> Where thoughts serenely sweet express,
> How pure, how dear their dwelling-place.
>   BYRON

Descending to breakfast the next day, Karl was sure he would find Vixey in another new and intriguing outfit and he eagerly awaited seeing what it would be. He was not disappointed. This day she had on a tight-fitting pullover with red and blue horizontal stripes and then a simple, short white tennis skirt with pleats. Her white shoes could be called a wedge-heel – although it was just a thin hollow outline of a wedge and there was a triangle of empty space under her foot. However, she had a vacant, sorrowful expression and her eyes seemed to be glistening with held-back tears.

"What's wrong?" he asked.

"It's just this war," she replied, "Every day it seems the outlook for the future gets worse and worse. I did finally receive a letter today from my father, and... the front is already near Eastern Prussia. Romania has been taken – the last stand is taking place. Hitler is ordering no retreat, but how long can they keep them off? The front is disintegrating... I don't know at all what the country will look like after the war ends, nor who will even be still around out of everyone I know. Half of my friends are in Berlin, which is everyone's main target."

Karl could find nothing with which to reply to alleviate her concerns but sat down near her at the table. An awkward silence ensued, but then Vixey's cat approached, having felt the presence of Italian prosciutto crudo on the table. This was the cat's most sought-after type of dry-cured meat. The cat jumped onto a vacant chair and placed one paw on the edge of the kitchen table, of course not presuming to have the right to climb onto it, but still wanting to indicate its interest in the tasty pork. The cat sat back down on the chair and looked at Vixey. She petted the furry cat, who soon started making purring sounds resembling a small tractor. In her state of severe melancholy, the overwhelming cuteness of this cat was enough to trigger a streaming of tears. At first the drops fell silently to the floor, then she sunk her head on her arms on the table and wept with convulsions, no longer able to stifle her distress. The cat probably understood nothing, or at most very little; meanwhile Karl was genuinely saddened by her feelings. He reached out and squeezed her shoulder to comfort her. She looked up, eyes wet, a damp lock of hair that had been caught in her tears sticking to her forehead, and understood what he wanted to convey. She had another surge of tears, but this time mixed with them was also a pleasanter feeling: one of the gratitude that she felt at suddenly meeting with unexpected sympathy and understanding. Without looking she extended her hand towards him. He instantly met it with his and held it. At length she finally recollected and composed herself and leaned back to her chair. Karl, trying to lighten the mood, said, "Why don't we feed the cat now. Look, she's still waiting..."

"Yes, yes," she said, wiping her eyes with her sleeves. The cat savored the prosciutto and left to drink some water.

"Are you alright now?" Karl asked.

"Yes, I think I'll be fine."

"Do you want to eat something?"

"No, not really. You can go ahead and eat. I'm sorry I burdened you with all that...," she said, embarrassed.

"No, I understand... If there's anything I can do, let me know..."

"I appreciate it. Thank you."

*   *   *

In the evening of the same day, the visitors started to arrive. Most had come together from Freiburg im Breisgau, an hour's drive, and some from Basel. The Baslers used Swiss expressions such as *grützi*. One of them was a pretty Mercédès with short blonde hair, who they called in the familiar form, Sadie.

Of those from Freiburg, some came in a German military uniform. As the daughter of a field marshal, Vixey must have been well known among young officers in the armed forces and it's not surprising she would have many suitors. When Karl saw her smiling and exchanging words that he didn't hear with a young German, he caught himself thinking of jealousy even before he thought of the danger of his identity being revealed. He checked himself on these irrational feelings.

Vixey seemed to have somewhat recovered her usual good spirits. Her youthful vivacity most of the time overcame any pessimistic influences. For this occasion she did not spare any eyeliner, and extended it past her eyes in a triangular "cat eye" shape. To contrast this she just wore a simple dark gray dress that covered her shoulders, with a waist-belt, and ending in a pencil skirt. Vixey never wore strapless dresses, thinking it unbecoming and uncomfortably exposed.

She also put on black stiletto sandals with ankle straps that had large black bowties on the back of the ankle. Karl was introduced as her cousin from Amsterdam, and Andreas as his friend. He chose this cover because his German was too poor for a native and he counted on nobody knowing Dutch. Occupied Holland has close ties to Germany and could be considered almost a part of the Reich.

Karl and Vixey acting as cousins forced them to behave more familiarly with each other, with a lot more contact. He had already used the familiar German *du* (similar to *tu*, ты) earlier that morning when anything else would have been awkward. Currently that usage was established. In the evening they spent most of the time next to each other because Karl wanted to minimize the chances she had of possibly informing on their position. But she did give a promise not to, so he gave her leniency to talk to people aside. On her part, she deliberately went to have private conversations in order to test his trust in her. She thought she was worthy of having her promise believed without any proof of her reliability, and wanted to see if he would understand that.

The people and their conversations did not strike Karl as being exceptional. Some of the officers maintained a sincere confidence that the war would still be won. The Germans were conscious of their prior victories from the Norwegian mountains to the Sahara, and State propaganda continually reinforced this. This perception, as well as the Allies' unconditional surrender demand, convinced them of the necessity to not give up. One topic of discussion was whether the radical Jewish writer Kaufman and US Treasury Secretary Morgenthau were sufficient evidence of an anti-German worldwide Jewish conspiracy that had its origins before the war.

Karl was able to see the negative Nazi influence on make-up and shoes that Vixey mentioned before; also he detected in a few people an attitude of resigned submission to the State and its onerous policies of labor restriction, regulations, military draft, national service, and personal demands. Maybe they were just being guarded about what they say in public. But in contrast to this, whenever Vixey explained something to the Swiss Baslers like, "The Führer does not think it's good practice for young people to smoke," it was possible to tell from her slight sardonic smile that even if she agreed with the concept, it followed from her own evaluation of it. Other people could be saying the same thing but they made it seem as if they were speaking in earnest – that they really acted on the Führer's judgment.

To be fair, Hitler is by necessity the most important source of information to the Germans, because he controls the flow of all information. With the level of secrecy that is in place in the country, he knows the most out of anybody; he is the most informed. Thus he must unavoidably be relied upon for information. Vixey however had other means, such as access to Swiss newspapers, which deliver a critical perspective many times opposite to that of German media. She listened to what Hitler said, especially when meeting him in person at various receptions and dinners her father brought her to, but did not always agree with him.

She asked Hitler, "What is it that makes the Soviet Union and capitalist America, seemingly opposites, both allied against us?"

"Roosevelt is a tool of world Jewry, and that makes him of course aligned with the Jewish Bolsheviks," was his simple answer.

No one had offered a better explanation, so this had to suffice, until Vixey found out from the Wehrmacht that there were no longer any Jews in the Soviet ruling class (*nomenklatura*). On the contrary, they were being subjected to accelerating repression in the Soviet Union. Also, Vixey could find nothing ideologically in common between the communist Jew Trotsky and Jewish financiers on the capital markets in New York or the department store owners who were looted in Berlin in 1938.

Some of Vixey's German compatriots accepted everything they heard and assimilated to everything around them. But people of this kind exist *everywhere* and fall into the pattern of conformity regardless of the urging presence of a powerful state or religious authority. Wherever you live you will find them believing and doing things that they think are aligned with society's consensus. Often this is no more than the general consensus of their isolated, conservative social circle. These types of people typically do not travel or read to a large extent. They do not compare and they do not question.

Sometimes I would have a divergence of opinion with such a group on some topic of social mores and after learning of my disagreement they would react as if I was insane. Actually, their opinion would frequently be the one that diverges to a greater extent than mine from accepted practices across different countries and periods of time.

They belong to a broader category of people whom the Victorian writer Matthew Arnold defined as 'philistines'[*]. A philistine is a person whose mental horizon is limited by *material* interests, with a conventional morality and an indifference towards cultural and æsthetic values. They will usually be relatively wealthy because of their Protestant work ethic and serious attitude towards schooling. However, their smug, self-satisfied tastes will be of second-rate things, as opposed to nice things. A philistine will likely be indifferent to nice elements of *dolce vita*, such as a leisurely visit to a pâtisserie after lunch. They will be just as indifferent to seeing nice stilettos on their female friends as to what can be learned about society through a study of philosophy, literature, and past history.

The past not only offers a broader view to question unusual local customs, but also sometimes provides examples that challenge the most widespread of current dogmas. Take monogamy, for instance. 1820s Italy had a social etiquette that was more based on common sense, as

---

[*] Mann acknowledged their simplicity but envied them; Flaubert ridiculed them; Nabokov despised them.

was well-documented by northern writers such as Stendhal and Byron who came to live on the reverse side of the Alps. In pre-unification Italy, marriage alliances were conducted for reasons of progeny and economics, while leaving passion for other revolving affairs which were not limited by number. There was no need for secrecy and sometimes the wife's paramour was even a friend of her husband. In this way, there was less striving, as there is in current days, for a religiously inflexible exclusivity and the unrealistic expectations and restrictions carried with that.

Since Vixey travelled frequently between Berlin, Paris, and other places, by necessity she could not subscribe to the exclusivity concept. Otherwise she would never have been available, since there would always be some *ami* in another city that she had never formally severed relations with. She did not consider this damaging to reputation or against historical precedent, especially not if comparing to the far more risqué histories of people in the prior century like Mary Shelley and Lord Byron.[*]

Vixey was sitting on a divan with knees bent, her legs parallel and shoes on the floor. She twisted her legs leftward so that they were still pressed against each other but now only the tips of her shoes touched the floor and the spikes were pointed laterally, still parallel. Vixey looked down at her light-weight shoes and affectionately touched

---

[*] Mary started her relationship with Percy Shelley on a highly immodest trip to France with him when she was only 16. Byron, with true aristocratic disregard for conventional prudery, participated in numerous extra-marital affairs, incest with his half-sister Augusta, sodomy (it's vague what this refers to), and bisexual activities. Byron is noted to have sometimes exercised nonconformity as an end in itself, as for instance when he kept a tame bear while a student at Trinity out of spite for rules prohibiting pet dogs. Successfully adhering to the codes of dandyism, he lived life as a work of art, and hated mediocrity in any form.

the large bowtie on the ankle strap, saying to herself, "These really *are* nice shoes."

Among the people at the *soirée* Vixey shone like a brilliant alloy of obsidian and sapphire, not only due to her blue eyes and beauty but also from her cosmopolitan air. Her smiles and charm effected more strongly than if she had a diamond tiara in her hair. She, from her perspective, could not fail to notice how many times Karl fixed his glance on her, even when she wasn't speaking.

Towards the end a last-minute guest showed up, just to pay his regards to his new neighbor. This was Otto Abetz, the German ambassador to Vichy France, who had fled Paris after its liberation and returned to his native Schwarzwald not far from Vixey. She greeted him aside and told him not to mention his identity here.

"Why?" he asked.

"Just in case. The French are probably looking for you. Don't let the news spread that you are here."

In Paris, he had held a lavish court at the German Embassy with his French wife Suzanne. Vixey was invited to soirées there, and she would go, briefly, before leaving to find a younger crowd. Vixey had once suggested to Herr Abetz that he draw up a project proposal to opulently rebuild the Palais des Tuileries, which had been destroyed a long time ago by French communists. She thought it would be a good symbolic act for Germany to build the most beautiful structure in Paris in this empty spot in the center of the city. This was not done however.

Abetz sat down, and the conversation turned towards Paris, with people apprehensive of the possible vengeance of the French if the war was lost. Sadie said, "Aren't you concerned about your house, Vixey? It is so close to France here in Baden. Who knows what they will do?- demand reparations, turn this into part of France and make everyone leave... You should come to us in Switzerland just in case."

Vixey replied, "No, the French can't do anything to us. The UK will protect us against them. It's because they know they need us in their inevitable fight against the Soviet Union."

One of the young officers added, "Very true. And this time, not alone, we will defeat the Russians."

At a later point blonde Sadie questioned Karl with great interest on his 'career' as a Dutch lawyer, forcing him to be inventive with his replies. Also the tension of Abetz unexpectedly joining made it impossible for Vixey to enjoy anything in a carefree manner. When the get-together ended, Vixey and Karl were both were glad to be relieved of the stress of maintaining the difficult cover.

Chapter V

> She was a Phantom of delight
> When first she gleamed upon my sight;
> Her eyes as stars of Twilight fair;
> Like Twilight's, too, her dusky hair;
> WORDSWORTH

Vixey felt that yesterday's events brought her and Karl's understandings a good deal nearer. She believed in his sentiments of empathy, and also felt she could trust his word since he demonstrated a trust in her by allowing her an almost normal *soirée*. Still, she was not entirely at ease because it was a wartime situation when anything could rapidly change – unanticipated events could occur. For now, she decided to mischievously test the limits of her captivity by going out for a stroll in the woods.

The sentries knew their duties, and promptly terminated her excursion at the edge of the field. She was now seized by a desire to go walk in the forest. At once she ran into the house and went to the room where the officers had gathered for another radio communication, where she playfully demanded that Karl go on a walk with her. He was actually in the middle of a conversation over the radio and had to signal to her to calm down. When he was disengaged he asked her what she wanted so urgently.

"We'll go on a promenade through the forest. I know all the paths here. Come; *allons-y!*"

He said, "Alright. Let me get my jacket and we'll go."

They set out along a path and soon were surrounded by complete tranquility and silence. They could hear the sound of their footfalls; – the snapping of small twigs and crunch of leaves or moss. At one point a distant sound of an airplane could be noticed. The fir trees shook their tangy green scent on the two of them walking. They reached a stream and Vixey dexterously skipped over the rocks that crossed it, like a light sylph, not uncomfortable at all in her wedge-heeled, tall, brown patent leather boots. To diminish the volume of the wedge, the heel curved inward slightly instead of falling straight down. Above the boots and skirt she wore an hourglass sharply-flared peplum jacket. Occasionally Vixey and Karl heard the chirping or whistling of various birds, or a squirrel rummaging in the leaves and grass. Now and then Vixey lightly kicked aside a pine cone that lay in her path.

They began to talk about her education and youth in Germany. She had been in the *Jungmädelbund* and then the *Bund Deutscher Mädel* (League of German Girls), the girls parts of the Hitler Youth. Karl asked, "Was it voluntary?"

"Theoretically," she replied, "But all my friends were in it so I wanted to be there. Also it was a requirement for eventually going to a University and it was very good for fitness! I was actually teased for my dark black hair. They called me a *Schwarzfuchs*.* Anyway, one of the regrettable things we were inculcated with was this medieval doctrine that raising children was the top priority for women, and almost nothing else was. I have nothing but hatred for their anti-women policies. Remember I mentioned all the reversal in progress that has already occurred in this regard. The Nazis' vision is a homogeneous, anti-intellectual, and pastoral nation. And the underlying basis for their whole ideology, as I figured out, is the idea of *Gemeinnutz geht vor Eigennutz* (sacrifice for the collective) – 'duty'; 'giving something back'. As if people working towards their own interests isn't best for both the people and the nation."

"I'm impressed by what you're saying, Vixey. I was actually a student of economics back in the day and I've encountered many people in America who don't understand even just what you said now."

"I think things are easier to understand when you are inside such a system, because you can actually see it. And I have become able to differentiate what's true amongst the

---

* Black fox.

State propaganda. Reading Swiss newspapers helps. Also, my father is a friend of Bormann, the personal secretary to the Führer, so through him he has an accurate view of current affairs. Otherwise he would not be able to tell me as much because Hitler doesn't even share the full picture with his field marshals... By the way, I like that I can talk freely with you. Since you're an outsider, I can say things I wouldn't even say at a gathering of friends and acquaintances, like last night. There is a mayor of a town somewhere, who's in jail just because of a slur he made about Hitler!"

Her voice was dulcet and melodious when she spoke German, despite the possible skepticism that French demoiselles or Mark Twain* would have reading this. She had a slight Bavarian accent. There is something provokingly alluring when a lady speaks German, more so than with any other major European language.

Their path took them downstream along the creek until they reached some cliffs where the stream became a cataract. There was a bridge across the stream right before it plunged down the cliff and crossing this bridge they could stand directly above the falls. The sublimity of the rugged landscape and jagged rocks the water crashed upon was impressive to them. A sudden gust of wind almost blew away Vixey's midnight-blue-lacquered straw hat. She had to take it off to check if her bird was still in its place. The hat had a little gray silver-nitrate/glass bird-of-paradise with its tail plumage attached to it. The brim was turned up at the back, keeping the feather from sloping down.

Vixey led him off the path to show something in the forest. In one area near the cliff, the rocks had fractured in such a way that deep but narrow crevices has formed. As a result, it looked like there was a grouping of rock islands

---

* Mark Twain harshly but humorously attacked the German language in Appendix D of his famous Germany/Switzerland travel memoirs.

hanging in space, with precipices all around them. Each rock was a meter or a few meters in width and most had a tree growing on them, half of its roots exposed because there was barely any soil there. Besides trees, the rocks were covered with moss and ferns. It was possible to jump from one to another- many of them were that close. Sometimes the gaps were much wider, and the forest floor at the bottom of the cliff could be seen. The pines that were growing there, reached just high enough so that their top-most branches were at the level that Vixey and Karl were standing.

Continuing back on the path along the edge of the cliff, Karl asked if she knew of the economists Ludwig von Mises or Günter Reimann. She had read von Mises' texts from the 1920s, but nothing contemporary and did not know Reimann. Karl said, "Yes, I wouldn't expect their recent work to be well known here. They both fled out of Germany a few years ago. I met von Mises when I last visited New York and found him to be very insightful on what's going on with economics in the world. He welcomes anyone who comes to him and wants to discuss things. In economics he develops and improves on Frédéric Bastiat's classical theories. What is your perspective on the German economy of the past ten years?"

"It is a *Zwangswirtschaft* – an economy where the government has full control of the means of production even though ownership is private."

"And what specific policies do they have? I want to know what you observed, as someone on the inside."

"They have a lot of policies," she said, flatly stating the facts without any commentary. "First of all, although the Nazis call themselves a socialist worker's party and Hitler calls the country Sozialistische Deutschland, he said he doesn't follow any specific socialist program but rather whatever is practical for the moment. Originally there was an emphasis on protectionism and trying to achieve self-sufficiency: liberating Germany from the 'international capitalist network of Jewish financiers'. Specifically there are restrictions and controls on investment, foreign trade, dividends, wages, prices, and interest rates – all those things. There is exchange rate fixing and inflationary monetary policy, a program of deficit spending and public works projects (*Kreditschöpfungstheorie*), and very high profit taxes. The main thing is that the capitalists are completely removed from power – there is no question of private initiative, entrepreneurship, or the free market having any control. There is no safety of private property anymore. Companies are private in name only, they're government-controlled by the *Reichswirtschaftsministerium* and headed by people who would be better called *Betriebsführers* (operational bureaucrats) than businessmen."

"Why did businessmen support Hitler, this 'Bohemian corporal' as they called him?"

"Those of us in the conservative classes – industry, the Army, the Prussian Junkers – were pleased with his overt distance from the communists, which were the worst possible thing to us, obviously. Hitler made promises in the direction of free enterprise, but at the same time promised that class privileges would be maintained. Both these things were ignored. Fritz Thyssen of Thyssen Steelworks, one of the biggest party contributors, saw his mistake and fled Germany, saying that the Nazi regime has ruined German industry and proclaiming himself a *dummköpfe* (fool). My father owned some business enterprises from an inheritance; luckily he managed to transfer most of them to Basel early on and now he gets dividends from them in Swiss francs. For what remains in Germany, it is mainly just a bureaucratic exercise, producing what the state proscribes, how much and at what price. The workers' wages are fixed and they cannot quit. Any action requires favoritism and deal-making with the *ministerium*, and frequently bribery. Small businesses are being eliminated while government-backed cartels have gained power. The

Nazis led us to believe that they wouldn't be socialist (despite their name), but they turned out to be practically socialist anyway, with their 'new class' clique of bureaucratic managers. I'm forced to see people in society who are significantly below me in class – vulgar elements of the *proletariat* and *petite bourgeoisie* who have risen in the socialist bureaucracy."[*]

"It looks like the state here is creating coercive monopolies that are *de facto* an extension of the state," Karl said. "A blend of nationalization and private ownership."

"Hitler was actually privatizing a lot of businesses in order to raise cash for the state. But this didn't mean the state couldn't control as much as it wanted. And in fact Hitler had recently started talking of nationalizing all joint-stock companies outright.[†] Most of all, you should remember, Hitler's economic policies aimed towards the unemployed middle classes and the proletariat. He was

---

[*] Stalin's opinion is worth noting. He saw Nazism as favorable compared to other foreign economics systems because in his view this brought society closer to communism. He had a different view on historical / dialectical materialism than Marx. He envisioned that, in Nazism, the veneer of *faux* capitalism combined with the inevitable worsening of working class conditions would create favorable conditions for an uprising of the proletariat. And all the economic planning and state control mechanisms would already be in place, requiring merely a switching of personnel and terminology, and increasing the state control by a few notches.

[†] The confusion of leading Nazi members as to what should be their economic program is well known. Some had strong communist leanings, like Joseph Goebbels and Otto Strasser. Goebbels in 1926 called for nationalization of big industries, banks, and estates and wanted to expropriate property of the aristocracy. He tried to join forces with the Communist Party. Hitler managed to convince him that these viewpoints would be catastrophic towards retaining the voting support of the middle and upper classes of Germany. From that point on, Hitler steered the Nazi party towards an anti-communist stance.

seen as a champion of the 'little people', with his government spending and his utopian egalitarian *Volksgemeinschaft* (people's community) ideas. My family lost a lot of wealth, and my father had to make up for it through various unsavory or corrupt gray market ways. Much of it was somehow war-related but he hasn't told me specifics. It's hardly any kind of capitalism or conservatism."

Karl remarked, "I agree. I would say that the best and clearest test of whether an economy is truly capitalist is to see how much power is held by the market. The opposite of the market is 'planning' and this is the category of both Nazism and Bolshevism. They both clearly see their primary enemy as free-market capitalism. And in Germany's case, the economy hasn't done well. I think that economic problems were one of the contributing factors to the start of the war – the need to acquire outside resources."[*]

"That is likely... The country definitely gained much from France and from the Slavic *Zwangsarbeiters*. What about your country? What has been going on there?"

"Oh, some of the same, although on a much lesser scale," said Karl. "The market still functions. But there is a general transfer of control to the state – a drift away from capitalism. Mussolini and his system were popular for a while with our politicians. That is why our economy did not recover throughout the entire 30s, as opposed to England and France.[†] But thankfully, we have a very strong

---

[*] German propaganda portrayed the economy as greatly improving throughout the 1930s. But all the inflationary stimulus spending came with a massive government debt and deficit. Real wages dropped and raw material imports were deficient. There is evidence to suggest that the economy would have crashed severely around 1940 if not for the invasions and seizing of resources and forced labor during the war.

[†] Treasury Secretary Morgenthau, May 1939: "We are spending more than we have ever spent before and it does not work."

Constitution that prevented a total economic takeover – although Roosevelt was trying to destroy the courts. And the people would probably not have gone for it, whereas Germany had become accustomed to an increasing amount of economic intervention since Bismarck in the 1880s. That's around when my relatives left to America from Hannover."

Vixey looked at him, "You haven't told me much about where you're from – Chicago, isn't it?"

"Yes, Chicago. It's on the shore of a giant blue lake, and it has a lot of very tall buildings. Not nearly as impressive as New York, but still good. There's an elevated metro line that looks like it's going through a veritable canyon of buildings."

"And you work in real estate?"

"Commercial and industrial buildings. Office leases, for instance. But I want to work on a law degree when I get back."

They were returning towards the house by now, and Vixey asked him more about America. She had traveled a lot in Europe but had never been to the US.

The last time she was in London was in late summer 1939 – she was 13 and with Evelina and her father, and it was at the moment that a series of military excursions suddenly became a more serious war. Prime Minister Chamberlain went on a national radio broadcast, proclaiming England's formal declaration of war on Germany. She said, "I remember that we were practically allied with the Russians then and coordinating all our military actions with them, but all the invective in London was directly solely at us Germans. Stalin waited until England declared war on Germany *before* he opened his own invasion of Poland. The Soviet Union likes to consider itself neutral and peaceful before we invaded it. By that logic, Germany should also be considered neutral and peaceful when invading Czechoslovakia and Poland. Why did England and France declare war on us then?"

Vixey continued, "It was a Sunday that it happened, very nice weather. Chamberlain made his broadcast in the morning, then 15 minutes later a test of air raid sirens was conducted for some reason. It seemed quite stupid- scaring people with sirens when there wasn't even remotely a possibility or intention of Germany bombing London at the time. Electricity everywhere was cut at night, and a large number of people started immediately evacuating to the countryside.

"What was your reaction to all this?" asked Karl.

"It was surprising and confusing, but my father reassured me that it was a favorable thing for him. It provided a chance for advancements in his career in the military... I don't think he had anything against England before they declared war on us. Look- my sister has a British name – she was named after Evelina Belmont. For me and her English is practically a native language... We left back to Germany a few days later, and until the next spring, events were quiet – nothing was happening any differently in the country than before. There were some military parades though. I went once to inspect a tank procession of one of my father's divisions."

"It must have been distracting to the troops riding by on the tanks."

"It probably was..."

"And then in the spring..."

"Yes; in the spring we took Denmark, Norway, Benelux and northern France. I remember back then I spent time looking at maps, thinking about how I would reorganize them if it were up to me. Cartography, being able to draw maps, was one of the requirements in the League of German Girls. I wanted to combine the Tajik and Kara-Kirghiz Soviet states, plus Kashmir, into a *Schneeleopard Königreich* (Snow Leopard Land) – with a light-blue flag displaying a picture of a snow leopard. The capital would not be Frunze but renamed to something else."

She smiled at her own recollection, then said, "We had some air raids in Berlin as early as fall 1940, but nothing serious. The city is so big – a few small planes won't do anything. And we have good *flaktürme* like the Zoo Tower that shot down a lot of planes. But in fall 1943 some really heavy bombing began, and since it actually wasn't safe there anymore, I spent the last year of school in Munich, living at Evelina's house... Where have you been in the war up to now? Italy mostly?"

"Yes, mostly there," said Karl. "First Sicily with Patton, then Amalfi, then getting up to Rome with General Clark. That took a year."

"It would have been Generalfeldmarschall Kesselring you were facing there. He's a great general."

"He is, I suppose... I hate him, so it means he has done his job well. It was mountainous terrain, stalemate conditions most of the time. I lost a few friends there, came very close to being shot myself a few times. Probably the most interesting thing that happened was one time when we were facing a fortified German pillbox, but didn't have any mortars or artillery or tanks available. I came up with the idea of putting a lot of timed explosives and gasoline canisters in a jeep, locking the wheel in place and the accelerator, and rolling it slowly towards the building. It worked perfectly. It was mostly Germans in Italy, although sometimes we encountered Italians as well, and it was a relief to face them instead. In fact, many American and British lives were saved merely by the extremely poor quality of Italian artillery shells."

Vixey laughed, "They truly were a bad ally for us. Even neutral Switzerland and Sweden are more useful... Italy is a barbaric, backwards country; despite its past cultural achievements. Now it belongs more in Africa than it does in Europe.[*] I was on the bad side of the Alps only once; I wept

---

[*] Vixey is correct, but now, 70 years later, the contrast has increased even further (between German countries and Italy)...

from joy when I was returning and saw the train cross the border to the Reich. I would have made an exception to go the Olympics in Cortina since that's now part of Germany (it's in *OZ Alpenvorland*), but they were cancelled anyway. Who will occupy Italy? The Americans? You should definitely give back Südtirol to Austria where it rightfully belongs!*; maybe also create a separate Venetian Republic."

"Are you serious or is this like your youthful snow leopard kingdom dream?"

"No, I'm totally serious," she laughed. "But that idea is also a good one. Any piece of land taken from the Russians is an improvement."

"And from British colonies?"

"What do you mean?"

"Egypt, for instance."

"It was just because of Italy that we expanded the war to Africa and attacked Egypt. The Italians were performing poorly there (as happened in Greece too) and Hitler sent the least possible amount of help to keep Mussolini from rebelling and switching sides. However, it was Generalfeldmarschall Rommel who ended up there and with just one division he managed to keep you guys occupied for years! The desert fox, they call him."

"I thought that the Suez Canal and British colonies in the Middle East were one of your objectives."

"No, nobody ever wanted to risk extending so far. Generaloberst Halder – when he was Chief of Army General Staff – didn't want to go anywhere near the Mediterranean.

Despite having the distinction of being first in the world for fashion and coffee, Italy is more dilapidated, shoddy, uncomfortable, un-English, and bureaucratic than Eastern Europe; less economically free than Kyrgyzstan and Zambia. They lack a normal business mentality – most people think like mafioso extortionists, including government agencies and large companies.
* After the war it was not returned to Austria, destroying hopes for a unified Greater Tyrol.

We didn't even want to fight Britain initially. Hitler recognized the power and resources of the immense British Empire and wanted to come to a deal with them. After the spectacular defeat of France, we in Germany were pleased and were led to believe the war would be over, but no – it kept escalating."

They had reached the house and Karl said, "This talk interests me;- I want to talk more with you about this. Could you make some tea and we'll have it in the drawing-room?"

"Of course."

Several minutes later they had resumed their tête-à-tête about the war, over afternoon tea. While entering the room, Vixey paused to admire herself in a mirror and draw her hand through her hair. Vixey almost always stopped at a mirror when she saw one, in order to check how her hair and eye makeup looks and to delight in her image.

She had switched her boots to regular court shoes the same color as her gray wool slit pencil skirt, and settled on a sofa, one her legs folded under her, holding the tea cup on its small plate. A vase with pink peony flowers stood on the coffee table that was between them. In her hair, Vixey had affixed a small red rose in a partial knot at the back of her head. The flower primarily served to enhance her æsthetically, but it also had another use, an altruistic one. She knew that people often would want to approach her at a closer distance than propriety would allow, and the need to smell the rose gave them the excuse to do so. She didn't do it to attract people to come closer to her, but rather to make people more comfortable and grateful to her for having something that provides a convenient excuse. Lilacs worked even better for this.

At her ears Vixey had hanging earrings with crystals of pure black agate, the identical shade as her hair. Having taken off her jacket when coming inside, she better revealed her tight cashmere cardigan underneath, in a pink that was almost white, with front fastenings that were distinctive silver hook-and-eye closures. The cardigan had thick black line trim on the collar and cuffs and large solid black diamond-shaped argyle patterns running down the sleeves in one row. The diamond designs, each shape the width of the sleeve, were so visually enticing that they spurred one to touch the sleeve fabric. Doing this, one would have the pleasant delight of feeling her firm slender arm, covered by the soft layer of thin cashmere.

Karl said, "You couldn't have expected Britain to make a deal and agree to your control over all of central Europe, including France."

"True, but I think some kind of compromise or stalemate could have been reached. Of course, then there was the Russian problem." Having finished the tea, she was playing with a dagger, drawing its sharp tip pleasurably, sensuously, against her thighs over the skirt. The dagger's blade was colored black and it had the phrase *Alles für Deutschland* imbedded in it.

"Yes, how do you explain that?" asked Karl. "On our side we were shocked by that unexpected move. We still are at a loss to explain it. Opening a new front! – against such a vast country with whom you had a nonaggression pact?"

"I can explain it quite easily. Romanian oil."

"What about it?"

"Romania is Germany's largest supplier of oil. Do you know that?"

"Yes, that I knew."

"Without that supply, our ability to wage war would last no longer than a few months. In 1940 the Soviet Union invaded Romania and took over the Moldovan portion of it. They limited themselves to Moldova, but they were now dangerously close to the oil. It was discovered that they were amassing tanks there. Now we know they had something around 2,000 tanks, which at their locations were a few hours' ride from the oil fields. To compare, in the invasion of France we had 2,400 tanks."

Karl had gotten up and was pacing the room. He stopped at a large map of Europe on the wall, saying, "Interesting. Are you sure of this?"

"Yes, I of course know this from my father, but these facts are well-known in the German army."

"What kind of tanks were they?"

"I don't know."[*]

"So if they were here," Karl said, pointing at the map, "They would indeed be in an ideal position to take those oil fields. You're saying this was a reason for the attack on Russia? What about setting up a defense?"

Vixey went over to the map, saying, "It would have been substantially more difficult. To defend the oil, so close to Russia and so far from us, from a surprise attack that could come at any time,- how? And if any part of the fighting even just reached the oil fields, the supply would stop. Retaking them intact wouldn't be possible. Look what was done instead. Hitler had begun making preparations since 1940 because the threat was obvious and he anticipated that a Soviet attack might come in the course of the following year. Here through Poland, our 1st Panzer Group launched a surprise attack to the southeast, and together with a smaller force from Romania, surrounded and captured the Soviet 9th and 18th Armies right here in Ukraine." She pointed on the map with her black dagger, which scraped the paper she passed it across.

"This is quite remarkable. I did not know that Russia at the time even had 2,000 tanks it could dispose with."

"There's more to this. When our armies invaded through Poland, they found significantly more Russian tanks along the borders there. I don't know how many thousands. What's interesting is not that, *per se*, but the

---

[*] She did not know that much about tanks. Although interspersed with heavy tanks, many of these tanks turned out to be very light, with weak armor. However, this did not invalidate her point, since they were still an effective force in their numbers and mobility.

locations of all of them on the eve of the war. The Russian positions, as my father described and as General Halder described, were identical to our own positions."

"Identical! Are you quite sure?"

"Yes. Otherwise we could not have captured so much right at the start. That by itself is the proof right there. One of the Russian generals had placed his staff headquarters so close to the border that my father said he could see it from his own headquarters! On the day of the invasion, all he had to do was walk across a few meters and the HQ of a division was captured! In the first few days of the war, huge amounts of tanks, supplies, and airplanes were destroyed or captured all at once. That's the nature of lightning war. When two armies are mobilized, all the advantage goes to whoever strikes first. If we did nothing, the Red Army would have caught us with our headquarters on the border instead!"

Karl was not convinced. "But if this occurred," he asked, "Why keep going into Russia? After such a success, with the threat removed, why not build a defensive zone and offer an end of hostilities?"

"You're right; at first the plan was to go no farther than Kiev. I think they went further because they saw the threat wasn't removed. I know that we underestimated the size of the Red Army and even more so their industrial capacity to keep making tanks and ammunition."

"What about Hitler's statements about seizing *lebensraum* in the East? Was that a motivation in the war?"

"Yes, Hitler always wanted to make colonies out of the East and build German towns there. He likened it to the British colonization of India. At some point in the Reich's development, yes, but not when the Royal Air Force is making direct strikes on Berlin. Hitler said that we can oppose Russia only when we are free in the West. The Russian mobilization changed that. Then the quick initial victories in 1941 made Hitler start repeating the colonization idea, especially as he saw the need for seizing more resources to continue the long war. Germany strategy was based on lightning strikes and anything that lasted too long would fail, given our current resources. When the war continued, it became very complicated to decide what to do next. At least 700 tanks a month were coming out of Siberia alone. We have no strategic bombing aviation – unfortunately not even enough to destroy England's industry, let alone the vast Siberian plants on the other side of the world. Holding on to land proved more and more difficult, but Hitler seemed unable to cut his losses and go back... However, the attack on Russia was absolutely necessary regardless of the consequences. If Hitler had been wrong in thinking Stalin would strike in 1941, he says that the threat from the East would still be there and grow more and more dangerous every year. Probably nothing would have been able to stop them if they attacked before us, especially as the great new autobahn system over here would have favored their advance... There could have been other issues, but just what I told you is already enough to say that our strike was preventative."

"Well, given these troop concentrations," said Karl, "I agree with how it would appear necessary to strike first. Looking at the map I can see exactly what you mean. I don't know, however, how strong these Soviet armies were, how good their tanks were, and whether their leadership was capable of doing anything. Also I've never heard anything about Russian strategic interests in invading the West. Maybe in their military planning they made a series of mistakes, or maybe the Russians did not understand how war had evolved – by how much faster a penetration of the front could occur with mechanized warfare."

"I don't know. I just hope the Russians don't reach as far as here."

The map of Europe they were looking at was one of many maps that decorated the walls of the house. In other places there were also framed maps of Germany, Baden, Bavaria, Munich, Paris, and more. Aside from a few family photographs, Karl also noticed some artwork by François Flameng, a French painter who was popular in recent years. (Vixey told him who it was). There were at least four, on a variety of subjects:

'Bathing of Court Ladies in the 18th Century'
'Napoleon Ier and the King of Rome at Saint-Cloud in 1811'
'Heavy Artillery on the Railway'
'Portrait of a Girl with Toy Elephants'

There was also a copy of Couture's *Romans of the Decadence* as well as of two beautiful classic portraits, the Winterhalter one of Empress Eugénie of France[*] and the Leonardeschi profile of Beatriče d'Este. It is interesting to speculate on whether Vixey ever contemplated the latter portrait, the one of Beatrix d'Este; – what she thought of her and whether she aspired to some part of her exploits.[†]

Karl wondered why there weren't more paintings on a military subject and Vixey said there were some in her father's house in Berlin, "Too many actually. The only one I remember is Altdorfer's *Alexanderschlacht*."

---

[*] The Empress's former palace in Cairo is worth staying at if one is in the area. It is being maintained by Marriott since the 1970s.

[†] Beatrix was Duchess of Milan in the 1490s, presiding over probably the most splendid court of Renaissance Italy. She was a contemporary of Leonardo da Vinci, Alexander VI, and Lucrezia Borgia. At 18 she went to Venezia with a vexillum in the rôle of an ambassador, impressing and charming the Doge and his senators. She participated in the governance and complex foreign policy of the Milanese state along with her husband, while also engaging in revelry, designing clothes, and enhancing the court with her refined taste. The Holy Roman Emperor, Maximilian Ier, travelled down the Alps from Austrian Innsbruck to meet them and was amazed by the intelligence and judgment of the young duchess. One can imagine the Emperor's reaction at seeing her – slender, young, and pretty, enter lightly on dainty shoes into a conference hall, contributing to business matters – when he would be accustomed mostly to elderly statesmen, bankers, and councilors.

Vixey and Karl took seats opposite each other on two couches and Karl lit a cigarette. He said, "You know, I'm starting to worry a little about the Russians myself. One never knows what they're thinking. Roosevelt trusts them, but my commander in Italy, General Clark, had some unpleasant things to say about them. He wants to disregard the order to include Soviet flags along with US/UK ones in German towns we will occupy. My concern is that if the alliance doesn't hold for some reason, we'll be sent to fight them."

"Your alliance with them is ridiculous and Roosevelt's friendliness towards Stalin is revolting. Plant Soviet flags even in areas the Red Army hasn't reached? What kind of idiocy is that?"

"Yes, I recall when we first met you pounced on me for Roosevelt's policies, and I told you we often don't agree with him. What were you saying again?"

"It was a perfidy to give the Soviet Union tons of food and jeeps and airplanes when we were fighting them. That was an open act of war by the US against Germany."

"I assume that would have been to please the British, who wanted to keep Germany in the east as long as possible. It was the expediency of the moment."

Vixey said, "I don't think that anyone in America understands what the Soviet Union actually is. We Germans know, because we went in there and saw some of it. Even German soldiers who admit to being former believers in communism say that once they saw what was inside Russia they were forever cured of their communism. They say that not even the worst German propaganda about Bolshevism was as bad as the things they actually saw there – the filth and destitution everywhere, and all the killing the communists did of their own people as they retreated. Those in the Wehrmacht who were there also saw how close it was for all that misfortune to come here in 1941, if the Führer hadn't seen the threat and acted on it...

"None of this would probably influence Roosevelt," she continued. "I think he has a deliberate anti-German and pro-communist standpoint. Listen to this story. One of our spies got it from the Teheran conference. Stalin proposed to execute 50,000 German officers when Germany was invaded. Churchill was furious and left the table. As he should have. He said that he would rather be shot himself than sully his honor with such an atrocity. But what did Roosevelt do? He said, 'Let's make a compromise... How about 49,500?'"

"I expect he was making a joke," said Karl, "since no American president would be able to agree to such a crime. But still, even as a joke, I agree it's a very hostile thing to say."

"This is the thing that encapsulated for me the differences between Churchill and Roosevelt more than anything. This in particular is a very personal matter for me... To Stalin it was no joke. He already did things like this, like in Poland after the 1939 invasion when he executed all their officers. I'm sure Roosevelt knows this and knows what will happen to any place occupied by the communists.[*] And yet everything Roosevelt is doing is consistent towards making Germany completely destroyed after the war and allowing the Soviet Union to become the single and dominant power in central Europe. I can't understand why... For instance, his policy of 'unconditional surrender' and the horrible Morgenthau Plan, both of which

---

[*] She's referring to the Katyn massacre. The US actively suppressed information about it until years after the war, in order to make the Soviet occupation of Poland more acceptable to the public. As for the Soviet occupation itself and the restructuring of Poland's borders, Roosevelt told Stalin at Teheran that it must be kept a secret until after the 1944 election. Explaining to Stalin the inconvenience of frequent elections, he said that there were several million people of Polish descent in America and he was concerned about retaining their votes.

Churchill opposed but Stalin greatly favored. The Plan calls for permanently destroying Germany's industry and mines, shipping its industrial equipment to Russia, and forcing the people to a minimal subsistence.* No only would this lead to an insufficiency of food for more than a third of our population, but it would destroy the economy of all Western Europe. Also they are talking about sending five million Germans to Russia for forced labor. I can tell you assuredly that many generals in the Wehrmacht would have surrendered on the Western front already if not for these policies!"

"I heard about this Plan. The President's cabinet – Secretaries Stimson and Hull – have managed to convince him that it is completely impractical and it will be changed."

"Really? I hope that is true!"

"Yes, they are getting rid of that idea; however the unconditional surrender demands are still in place."

"But nothing different is being said by the American channels or the Swiss papers. And Goebbels, the Propaganda Minister, is still using all this to convince people not to surrender. For more than a year already, anyone with any sense knew that the war was lost, the way things were going on the Eastern Front. A war of attrition against Russia is unwinnable. To avoid a Russian occupation, many people supported a reasonable surrender to America and Britain, but Roosevelt prevented that with his unconditional surrender demand. Hitler would have

---

* The Morgenthau Plan was actually drafted by Treasury Secretary Morgenthau's assistant: Harry Dexter White, now known for being an *undercover agent* of Stalin. The benefit to the interests of the Soviet Union was brought up by Morgenthau himself. He claimed that any opposition to the Plan was anti-Soviet and was made by people "afraid of Russia." When asked about the terrible effect the Plan would have on the German population, he stated, "Why the hell should I worry about what happens to their people?"

been overthrown by now but instead the army will continue to fight back with all its strength. Look at the heavy battle going on right now in Aachen on the Dutch-German border. It's the former capital of the emperor Charlemagne's 'First Reich'. Who is there now from your people?"

"It is General Hodges. He is under Bradley's Army Group."

"Well, the Americans are seeing that with such a defense as we are making it will prove impossible to advance any further for some time. Meanwhile the only one who benefits is Stalin. With our forces tied up needlessly fighting and dying in the west, the Red Army goes further and further into Europe. Why is Roosevelt so fixated on complete destruction rather than a peaceful solution? Is he so eager to do anything his ally Stalin asks for? Already part of the Wehrmacht made an attempt to assassinate Hitler, three months ago! But still an anti-Hitler resistance is not encouraged by the West! On the contrary, the American plans came as a shock to everyone and had the effect of welding together ordinary Germans and the Nazi regime. The defense of the homeland became much more a priority than opposition to the regime. Really, one could imagine that a bunch of communists came up with the Plan and all this! The intent can only be to prolong the western front and then use total destruction and poverty to destabilize whatever parts of Germany wouldn't already be under communism."

"I think that everything will turn out alright," said Karl. "Nobody in America is truly a communist – in fact it's closer to the opposite – so I think that decisions made will be consistent with traditional American principles of liberalism and with what's best for Europe. As for the Russians – you shouldn't worry – you're about as far from Eastern Germany as you can be. You're almost on the border with France and also you have a lot of Swiss hard currency. Regardless, there's nothing we can do at this point. We'll just have to see what the outcome is." Karl got up to go, after having finished his attempt to comfort her.

Vixey said, "Annette will make schweinbraten and Bavarian knödel for supper. 8:00?"

"Very good. I hope this talk hasn't evoked too many sentiments dissonant to your well-being?"

She got up as well, "No, I'm fine. I'm actually a little relieved about what you said about that vindictive Plan being changed."

"Yes, that's right. It is not going to take effect."

"And I'll always have Switzerland in case things get bad here. As long as I have that, and also Paris (the clothes from there are essential) then I will be fine. Who knows what will happen? Maybe Bavaria will become independent again and we'll see the return of the blue and white diamond flag! That would be interesting – I'm Bavarian myself."

"There was some talk about how maybe it would make sense to combine Bavaria and Austria."

"Hmm. I wonder what kind of flag that would create... Maybe a blending of the red and white with the light blue diamonds."

Karl embraced her and stroked her ominously-black hair (making sure not to dislodge the rose). He could feel her electric warmth. When they separated he said, "I want to assure you of my ever-lasting affection and regard for your interests. I'm very glad that I ended up here."

She smiled, saying, "You have long already held my esteem."

They separated not entirely satisfied, as both were confused by what the other actually meant. At supper they were not left alone, especially after Landon had one cup too many and would talk ceaselessly about Italy until it was late at night.

Chapter VI

> [The unconditional surrender idea] is just the thing for the
> Russians. Uncle Joe might have made it up himself.
> ROOSEVELT

As Vixey indicated, eleven months prior Churchill and Roosevelt met Stalin for the first time at the Teheran conference in Persia.* At that time British and American troops were not yet in France; all they had was a small foothold in the foot of Italy. But it had already been almost a year since the Battle of Stalingrad and the advance of the Red Army was well on its way. The defeat of Germany was no longer in doubt by the Big Three leaders, but Stalin held most of the cards, as he was the only one already on a solid offensive. By this time, Churchill's greatest concern was not Germany, but what could be done to prevent the balance of power in Europe from shifting suddenly to the Soviet Union, as Hitler's power declined. In this he was ignored by Roosevelt; in fact Roosevelt sided with Stalin in every question. The biggest strategic question to decide was whether to launch an invasion through Austria and the Balkans or through southern France. Churchill was almost at the point of resigning over the repeated refusal of his plan for Austria.

Following the Teheran conference, Churchill met with George Marshall in London. Marshall was the US Army Chief of Staff, the highest ranking American general, and Roosevelt's top military advisor. An approximation of what they said can be assumed as follows, based on what is known about their other spoken opinions in those times.

"Well," said Churchill, "I hope you and Roosevelt are satisfied. Based on our recent meeting with Stalin, it seems that the Soviet Union will indeed have the ability to control

---

* November 1943

affairs in central Europe and nothing will be done by us to prevent this. With every kilometer gained, Stalin's bargaining power increases."

Marshall replied, "I think that we are taking into full consideration all the issues involved, as well as our constraints, when we plan our strategy for the continuance of the war. We need to withdraw forces in Italy to southern France in order to reinforce our upcoming invasion in Normandy. We also must have those big ports at Marseilles and Toulon, without which we can't land troops as fast as we would like. Le Havre is not enough."

"This is shortsighted. The only way to retain any influence in Europe is to have our tanks in the right places when the war ends. My strategy would do that. In fact, if we did what I proposed earlier – invading Greece *instead* of Italy, we would be in a substantially better position now. Greece was the softest part where we could have struck Germany. Once there we could have established bomber bases with which to bomb Germany's oil fields in Romania, while capturing all the Balkans. Our entry there would have encouraged that entire region to flame into open revolt against Hitler... And now it is still not too late to go in that direction, if we just continue north in Italy while landing in Croatia, according to the plan of attack developed by Field Marshal Alexander. This would ensure us being in Austria and the entire Danube area first- before Stalin gets there. I don't need to tell you that once we withdraw those divisions from Italy to France the campaign to build up a Southern Front against Germany will be completely wrecked."

"True, the southern campaign will be weakened, but that front is not part of the 'grand strategy' of Teheran that Roosevelt and Stalin support. Plus, it would be politically impossible to commit forces anywhere east of Italy. If there was then the slightest setback in Normandy, it would be a disaster for Roosevelt in next year's election. Do you want to lay our respective cases before Stalin? Ask for his opinion again?"

"No," replied Churchill. "I know what he will say. He will not favor the political implications of our troops in Eastern Europe, of course... By the way, what about this 'unconditional surrender' that Roosevelt suddenly came up with just now? We do not any longer have a chance of negotiating with the German army and turning it against Hitler. Now we have to fight even harder, all while the Russians gain ground. How many German cities will have to be bombed to the ground because of this? Roosevelt seems to be glad at finding something that's 'just the thing' for Stalin. What the devil does Roosevelt expect the political situation to look like, the ways things will develop?"

"Roosevelt feels he can negotiate with Stalin. You leave that to him. You know that Stalin doesn't like your top people. Stalin has agreed to support national sovereignty in central and eastern Europe and to seek no aggrandizement for the Soviet Union. He wants security for his country primarily. In some ways Russia's interests in foreign affairs may be not so different from our own."

Churchill had just finishing igniting a cigar, which enveloped both of them in a cloud of smoke. He countered, telling Marshall, "He does say that. You believe it? Was it so long ago that Stalin invaded and occupied Poland, Estonia, Latvia, Lithuania, and parts of Romania and Finland? Stalin seems to have you all *dans sa poche*."

"The Soviets have been our allies for two and a half years. They have endured the greatest suffering of this war. We think that they deserve some retribution and they deserve our trust. We cannot even risk offending them in any way. We still need them in the European war and especially in the Japanese war, where there is much remaining to be done."

"Do you really need them meddling in Asia as well? Can you imagine what may happen if half of Asia also falls into a Soviet sphere of influence?"

"We expect that whatever happens, the Soviet Union will be one of the great powers after this war ends. The more we cooperate with them, the more they will work with us towards peace. Roosevelt's opinion is that for this reason it is extremely important that every effort is made to obtain their friendship."

"Is that what you're after? Ha. You are in for some surprises then. The main interest of the communists is revolution. They cannot be trusted. Stalin himself built his entire political career on a history of cunning betrayal. If we fail to keep him out of Europe, which is almost certain now, we risk the entire war having been in vain."

Chapter VII

So much the rather thou, Celestial Light,
Shine inward, and the mind through all her powers
Irradiate; there plant eyes; all mist from thence
Purge and disperse, that I may see and tell
Of things invisible to mortal sight.
MILTON

Karl saw Vixey in the morning and said, "We are going to get a large box of food and supplies for the troops airlifted to us today, around noon. It will be much easier and less expensive than continually buying food in Switzerland. Do you want to come with us when we go to pick it up? It will land in the forest somewhere."

"Sure. It sounds interesting."

They prepared two jeeps and waited for the plane. In the meantime, Vixey gave the troops who were camped behind the house a phonograph and some records. She had some good and very modern jazz records. Landon voiced the strong desire of the troops to remove the Nazi Germany flags hanging on diagonal flagpoles on the side of the house close to the tent, as well as the one on a tall flagpole on the other side of the field. She agreed to remove the ones attached to the house but not the one on the vertical flagpole, saying that it was still the flag of the country.

Toward noon the plane passed overhead at some distance and they saw the package floating down with a parachute. However, a strong wind blew it further than the range in which they were expecting to collect it. Karl, Vixey, Landon, and three soldiers drove in the direction they saw it descending, at first finding a trail that led the same way, then leaving the path and traversing the red pine needle covered forest floor.

Eventually they came across the crate, which landed in a small valley about 100 meters across, with ridges on both sides. It was not heavily wooded; there were only several tall scattered firs and some boulders.

The box was surrounded with German troops.

The Germans must have seen the parachute as well and followed it. In retrospect it was foolish not to have anticipated this possibility but Karl thought they were in isolated mountains amidst only residential areas.

By the time they saw this and stopped, they were already in full view, on a downwards-sloping hill that led down toward the box. The Germans, who were obviously investigating the military supply drop, began to approach. It would not be difficult for them to see that they had encountered not fellow German soldiers but the enemy.

Karl immediately made the decision that the only choice they had was to kill them before being discovered and captured. First he told Vixey to get out and take cover behind the jeep. She did that, trying to say something to Karl but her voice completely failed because of over-excitement. Karl instructed the men to "Fire at will." Everyone either fell to the floor or crouched behind the jeeps and began firing. Vixey was sitting with her hands over her ears because the shots were being fired right next to her.

One enemy combatant was lying on the ground dead, but the rest had managed to take cover behind a rock and began firing back. The jeeps were insufficient cover so they moved to a ridge nearby that overlooked the low-ground. Those who had helmets grabbed them; also they took a mortar from one of the jeeps but unfortunately only had two shells for it. Karl made sure Vixey was in a secure spot, then fired the mortar. They missed and instead the smoke dimmed visibility around the German position. The shooting paused for long enough for them to discern an ominous grumbling sound in the distance. It slowly became louder and was unmistakable – it was the sound of a tank.

Karl ordered that the mortar be prepared again and fired as soon as the Panzer appeared. Meanwhile, the jeeps were to be brought closer in other to make a retreat. The tank emerged over the top of the opposite ridge and rolled down into the valley. The mortar shell exploded next to it but failed to destroy the cat track or cause any significant damage. Being in military engagements had become habitual to Karl, so the adrenalin on seeing the tank approach was not strong enough to displace feelings of dismay and desperation at the tide turning against him. Plus now there was also an inexperienced girl in the field who needed to be protected. Meanwhile both jeeps were stuck on the sharp hill. They had been abandoned on an incline, and now when attempting to go back up from a stationary position, the wheels dug into the soft ground in that area. There were just a few seconds available because by now they were in firing range from the tank and the increased number of troops in sight, who were running forward accompanied by Alsatian hounds. One car was abandoned; the other driver tried to gain traction by driving forward a bit and then turning around. The car was hit by numerous bullets, wounding the soldier with shards of glass from the windshield and damaging the tires.

As this was going on the tank fired on the ridge. A grove of trees was struck and exploded in a deafening noise. Karl turned and saw Vixey collapsed on the ground. Her hat was lost (a black felt hat with a wide and straight brim, trimmed with black satin ribbon). For Karl it was a terrible moment; he did not know what had happened to her,– on his knees beside her he tried to shake her by the shoulders to make her gain consciousness, but without success. Meanwhile the enemy soldiers were rapidly getting closer: only a little more time and they would be upon them. Karl would have liked to do something like try to get the nearer jeep started again or retreat on foot but Vixey was lying there senseless. He ordered his troops to surrender.

Checking Vixey's breath he was reassured to find her breathing. At the same time, being so close to her, he was struck by an intoxicating perfume, which sharply contrasted with the smell of ammunition smoke in the general area. He was also amazed at the softness of her skin when he touched her cheeks and neck, not that this took time away from his alarm at her condition,– rather these sensations were blended into one of both anxiety and intensified adoration. He noticed her jacket sleeve was torn, and pulled it up, where he found a small cut on her arm – likely from the debris of the explosion. Behind him he heard the Germans who had just arrived to the top of the ridge. He got up and threw aside his holster. He was wearing his bomber jacket, but it showed his major's insignia on the shoulders.

When he looked at the Germans closely he noticed their uniforms looked slightly different. He also saw a few individuals who were wearing odd-looking cylindrical hats from Astrakhan fur. A young but severe-looking lieutenant-colonel in a crisp officer's peaked cap with the Nazi eagle emblem approached him, yelling, "You scoundrels! Saboteurs! You should all be shot! What are you doing here?" He had dark hair and his thick black mustache was almost like a Georgian's.

Karl replied hastily but glumly, "We were sent behind enemy lines and could not go back so we stayed here. This girl is German, she's here accidentally." (Coming closer, the lieutenant-colonel had indeed noticed the girl lying there). "She fell unconscious and I'm trying to revive her. I don't care what you do after, but right now please help me."

The German officer replied, "Go with my sergeant. We will see to the girl."

"No; I won't leave until I see her recover!" Karl exclaimed as he got down to Vixey again. He unloosed the belt she had on her slim waist, checked that her clothing was not inhibiting her breathing, and examined the wound on her arm again. The lieutenant-colonel knelt down by her also to see what he could do. Karl said, "She doesn't appear to be injured, just this superficial wound. I think she just fainted from shock." The lieutenant-colonel was in a concentrated silence. He was looking at the beautiful girl lying insensible on the ground, her hourglass jacket in disorder, hair tousled. It was impossible to contemplate her beauty with indifference. He needed a moment to reset his mind, as if a circuit-breaker had been blown in it by an overload of the visual sensory channel. He then came up with an idea and brought over a canteen of water. He emptied its contents into a reversed helmet, then hurled the fluid straight at her face. She opened her eyes finally.

"Vixey!" said Karl, "You fainted during the attack. But it's over now."

She sat up, "What? I'm wet!" Her hair was sleek and wet like a *rusalka's* (naiad); her eyes were slightly more raccoon-ish.

"We poured water on you."

"What happened?"

"We couldn't start the jeeps and had to surrender. I'm sorry I brought you. I had no idea we would meet with any danger."

"I know. Me neither. But don't worry. If it's Wehrmacht let me handle it."

"Are you sure you're not wounded?"

"No, I feel fine," she said, getting to her feet.

Karl could now finally address his captor, who had remained in silence all this time, "Sir, my name is Major Karl Stevens, US Army."

The lieutenant-colonel had to restrain his anger because of the presence of the mysterious girl, who was even more arresting in her reanimated (and wet) state. He replied, with a serious countenance, "You killed one of my men."

"Yes, we did. I think we were justified to engage given the circumstances."

Vixey heard this and looked around at the site of the battle; the casualties of this simple skirmish seemed terrible to her.

Meanwhile the lieutenant-colonel introduced himself, "I am Oberstleutnant Pavel Nikitich Kirillov. We are in fact Russian soldiers in the Wehrmacht, but we have just now been made independent and are forming a Russian division. Our camp is right there behind that ridge."

This was surprising. Karl whispered to Vixey, "Russians! I don't know if this is good or bad." To Kirillov he said, "Are you the commander?"

"No. The commander is Major-General Petrovsky. He will deal with you when he arrives. He was interested in seeing captured American partisans when he found out."

In fact a *Schwerer Panzerspähwagen* (armored personnel carrier) could be seen approaching, a metal box on wheels with practically no windows. It came to a halt and the general stepped out. He was over 60, and was mostly bald except for short gray hair at the sides, but was tall and appeared vigorous. His face looked like one accustomed to conveying command. He wore an officer's hat and an imposing full-length black leather trenchcoat, lined with fur around the collar, with the scarlet lapels of a general and a heavy belt. Red *alt-Larisch* collar tabs were on his tunic.

He did not assume a wrathful tone, but simply asked, "So, these are the captured Americas? How do you do? And who is the young girl?"

Vixey answered him, "I'm a local. I live two kilometers from here."

"Oh. I'm glad you were not harmed in this skirmish, mademoiselle... I am Vladimir Maximovich Petrovsky. First of all, I will tell you that I haven't the slightest intention of capturing any Americans. We are no longer under the authority of German commanders; we have become semi-independent. But you must maintain a neutrality towards us and encourage your superior officers to do the same. Tell me why you are in Germany and how many of you there are."

Karl and Vixey were surprised and visibly relieved. Karl thanked him, explained their situation in Germany and their place of encampment, and asked, "What side are you on, then?"

Vladimir Maximovich pressed his lips together. "We have no side. Technically we are still on the German side; we fight together with them and we answer to Reichsführer Himmler. But our only true side is with whoever is fighting the Soviet Union. If you remember the Russian Civil War, we are in a few certain ways like the Russian White Army, rising once again (in the Black Forest) to fight the Red Army. Maybe one day we will fight side-by-side with the Americans. That's why we do not want to be hostile towards you, regardless of the wishes of Berlin. Are you from the US 7th Army?"

"Yes sir. VI Corps."

"They will not reach this area until after the winter, that is for sure. By that time we will have left to the Eastern Front. Behind me you see part of the 625th Panzer-Grenadier Division, soon to be rebuilt as the KONR[*] 4th Division. As a condition of our cooperation you must report all changes in American activity in Alsace. This is because we do not want to engage the 7th Army or any other US troops. We do not expect them here for a while, but if it happens, we would like to be able to move further eastward to avoid them."

Karl agreed to that, and went to pick up his pistol and reattach it to his belt. Vixey said, "General, I would be honored if you would join us for supper tonight or tomorrow. I think there is much we could talk about."

---

[*] Committee for Liberation of Russia, headed by General Andrei Andreyovich Vlasov. Often the KONR Armed Forces were referred to unofficially as the ROA (Russian Liberation Army). In this text, Vlasov Movement and Russian Liberation Movement are used interchangeably.

"It would give me great pleasure, mademoiselle. Tonight would be good."

"And you, Lieutenant colonel. Would today be agreeable?"

"Certainly, *chère* mademoiselle. Would you let us know your name?"

"Vixey von Isarberg."

"The same as Field Marshal von Isarberg?"

"Yes, he is my father."

Pavel Nikitich and Vladimir Maximovich were impressed, exchanging glances and nodding. The latter remarked, "We had met with him at the front, when we were still POWs of Germany. He did much to advance our cause and we worked with him in Smolensk."

Vixey smiled, "I'm glad you know him."

"Did you say it was Vicky?"

"Vixey; but yes, it's the same thing- Victoria... Oh, I haven't told you where to go yet. The shortest path is directly this way through the forest, but at night it would be easier to use the road going past Schönau. My estate is called Marzell. Your encampment must be very new, because I used to walk as far as here and there was never anything."

"That's correct, it was about a month ago that we set up this camp here."

The other Americans, who had been sitting on the ground aside, guarded by enemy troops, did not understand the unfolding scene since all the conversation had been in German. They were surprised by the handshakes and smiles towards the end and even more by the withdrawal of the 'Germans'. Even if their commander had decided to defect it wouldn't have ended like this. Karl explained to them that the troops turned out to be Russians. Landon had known that they were not standard German soldiers based on the inconsistency of their insignias, but up to now all the Russians in the Wehrmacht he had seen were still being commanded by Germans and there was essentially no difference between them and German soldiers. Recent events, however, had started a transition to greater independence for the Russian units and this division was entirely staffed and commanded by Russians.

Two American soldiers stayed to bury the fatally wounded Russian, replace the jeep tire, and take the supplies crate back with them. Karl and Landon returned (without Vixey- something detained her on the way), where they related the surprising story that they were assailed by a German tank, that one of their jeeps was damaged, and that the commander who captured them, instead of detaining them was going to come here on a friendly visit.

Karl explained to the soldiers that since they are undercover on the other side of the front, some unusual things may happen, including interaction with representatives from the German side, but full contact is being maintained with 7th Army headquarters.

Left by the officers, the private 1st class who had been at the skirmish was questioned by his comrades.

"Jerry beat you up?"

"Yeah, the Jerries brought out their dogs and a Panther tank."

"I bet they've been fixin' to find us."

"I bet."

"You got out okay though."

"Mhm. We had the princess with us. She talked with them."

"What about the food?"

"It's coming. We got it."

Chronic sleep deprivation and fatigue due to the long war had made the minds of the soldiers a haze. They reacted to orders and to instincts of the moment, but were removed from reality. A sickly indifference had built up.

Why devote extra energy towards caring about outcomes? To continue longer in the endless war, the drudgery of which is worse than death? They were so immersed they no longer thought about surviving to reach goals such as returning home or 'winning the war'. Apathy was the result.[*] (Of course, it was still better than being unemployed – however much they thought themselves no longer alive, they were still much more alive than unemployed civilians).

Pavel Nikitich, as they were returning to their camp, mentioned Vixey to the general, "You see, Vladimir Maximich, there are indeed красавицы[†] in Germany."

"What the devil is her name – in Russian?"

"In Russian it would simply be Vika, wouldn't it?" Pavel had already been thinking about this.

"Ah, of course, yes."

"She styles it Вíкси[‡] (*Viksy*) instead of Vicky. I suppose that 'Vixey' itself, translated to Russian, would become Викса (*Vixa*)."

*   *   *

Vixey, as soon as the tension of the past events was over, became aware of an altered mental state which far exceeded just relief. The explosion of the tank shell so near her, awful enough to cause her to lose consciousness, made her feel as if she narrowly avoided death. It was unfathomably distant from her normal range of experiences. Nothing could have prepared her for it, neither

---

[*] Visotsky—

И не волнуют, не свербят, не теребят

Ни мысли, ни вопросы, ни мечты….

From Песня конченного человека. – This poem of Visotsky is about fatal indifference.

[†] The plural form of *krasavitsa*, a Russian word meaning girl of great beauty.

[‡] The Russian i (и) is the letter used in Vika as well as the last vowel in Vixey. However, in Vixey, it would be inappropriate to enter it directly after the V as the first vowel, and there is actually no Russian letter that would adequately denote the sound. The first i in Vicky, vicar, or Dixie is needed.

hearing about it nor seeing it in a film. Overall, she actually benefited from the experience, becoming invigorated after its successful resolution.

Gradually, everything started appearing around her with a higher degree of sharpness and vividness. The soldiers moving around and preparing to go back appeared somehow more three-dimensional. She could suddenly take in details at a great distance; innumerable details overwhelmed her everywhere she glanced. The scarlet lapels of the general's coat were captivating in their color against the trenchcoat's black leather and the muted, rusty red of the ground. A bright red cardinal bird flew into the area and settled on a branch, unnoticed by anyone but Vixey. She was delighted by its cute triangular tuft of feathers on its head like a Catholic cardinal's mitre. Meanwhile Karl led her to the car and they started to return to her house.

Leaning out the moving jeep, she looked at the forest passing by. Nothing had changed in the environmental conditions; the sun and sky were the same as earlier that day. But to her the contrast was as if before a drizzling fog had swallowed up every individual color, and now a brilliant sun illuminated and colored everything to the point of excess. What she saw before in these familiar places was as from behind a wire screen and murky window, if compared to now. She opened her blue eyes wide to take in as much as possible but then had to shut them and put her hands to her face in reaction to too much brilliance.

She touched the driver's shoulder, saying, "Stop here. I want to get out." She told Karl, "I'd rather walk back. I need to talk a walk after all that."

He thought it was an irrational idea, and replied, "Why not do it closer to your house?"

"No, I want to go here."

"Do you want me to go with you?"

"No, I'll see you at the house in a short time."

Confused by the enigmatic answers, he nevertheless let her do as she pleased. She walked into the woods, a spacious forest floor of red pines and occasional groups of ferns and violet thistles. Ferns and violent thistles. She thought she was seeing beyond violet into ultraviolet, which would be possible if she could see tetrachromatically, like the *Zebrovaya Amadina* bird. Through gaps in the canopy, in several places rays of sunlight entered, creating white patches of illumination that fluctuated in accord with the swaying treetops.

Vixey looked closely at one of the pines, touching the grooves and layered flakes of red bark, which was scaled like the hide of an alligator. It seemed to her that the design of the bark was perfect, that it could not be in any other way because it represented visual perfection just as it was. She looked up at the branches hanging with green needles and pine cones against the azure sky and decided that this too, was perfect.

The forest she was in was a relatively new-growth one, only a few decades old. This is why the ground was covered in dry pine needles. As the trees grew taller, since only the top-most branches receive any light, the lower ones would become obsolete and fall off. The trees became free of branches except for at the top, while the old needles accumulated on the ground. Vixey was amused as she thought that all these trees used to be the exact same height as her! Then she contemplated how it could happen that they got so big. Energy is from the sun, that's obvious, but where does the material come from? She concluded that it must be from water, somehow changed into 'tree material'.

She sat on her knees to pick up pine cones and look at them, examining their shape and geometric patterns. After spending some time on this, she felt like lying down amidst the soft pine needles. Knees bent, she arched her back and pressed her head against the ground with pleasure. Rusty-colored pine needles were sticking to and becoming lodged in her wet black hair that she rubbed over the ground. Hopefully the reader remembers that she was still wet and with a torn jacket at this time. Her cheeks were black with her eyeliner smeared over them. Blood had just stopped flowing and was coagulating on her arm. But she was very content lying there, indifferent to the passing time, and just looking at the interplay of trees and sky above and the red squirrels running about, enormous tufts of fur standing up on their ears. One squirrel looked at her while clinging to the tree upside down. Somehow it could affix itself to a perpendicular surface like that. Then it clambered up to a branch and sat there looking intently at her past its whiskers, furry red tail twitching behind it.

She was confronted with what seemed to her the miracle of existence. She felt a self-awareness of her consciousness, a concept she could not come to terms with because it was so vast and meaningful. Familiarity with 'existence' and consciousness takes root in us from the beginning of our lives. To Vixey was revealed a glimpse into it without the built-in familiarity, and it seemed something supernatural. For her, this led to a renewal in a faith in God. She felt how everything is constituted with God, indirectly, mysteriously, similar to how the Danish theologian Kierkegaard described a subjective Christian revelation, independent of the evidentiary facts supplied by regular, common perception.

There may be readers who are curious as to why Vixey had a psychedelic episode. I will respond by saying that it is not that uncommon in situations of physical and emotional intensity that one experiences for the first time. Such events can form shifts in the mind's perception. This has been described, for instance, by people climbing and then making a first descent of a steep mountain on skis through deep powder.

Chemically, what happened to her was that the adrenalin and fainting had actually temporarily weakened one part of her mind. Our minds involuntarily filter information, memory, and thought processes in order to focus as much as possible on practical matters. This is in line with evolutionary survival but it limits the mind's full potential. Marcel Proust's recurring theme is the struggle to reconnect with former time in the mind, which is usually inaccessible. With Vixey, the events had tempered her mind's filtering function, and this resulted in a refreshing of perspective, a removal of dust, figuratively, from her sensations.[*]

---

[*] The writer and experimenter Aldous Huxley researched these topics and came to similar conclusions in the 1950s. Interference with the enzyme system that regulates cerebral functioning lowers the mind's reducing valve and permits into the consciousness things normally excluded because of their lack of biological value. However these things could have spiritual (1), or æsthetic/creative (2) value:

(1) Catholicism and visionary experience have many links. This is why such beautiful places were created for religious congregations; e.g. the prismatic stained glass windows of Sainte-Chapelle du Palais; or the intricate beauty of the Bavarian Wieskirche. Others try to make an impression rather with their grand sublimity: the Köln Cathedral; St. Peter's Basilica. The Protestants neglect this important visual feature. Meanwhile, the Jews have had the interesting idea of making wine a part of religious functions, a practice that probably strengthens their faith.

(2) The importance of perception goes far beyond spirituality and religion. Nabokov considered that æsthetic perception was the highest form of consciousness. *Id est*, practical matters like mathematics and engineering are within the category of biological functions that we are trained to do in other to sustain life, but the creative arts and abstract contemplation are more distinctly 'human'. Nabokov, as any true artist, would have had a well-developed ability to refocus his mind on the 'non-practical' without the need for external catalysts. Some artists, however, welcomed the use of chemical catalysts to even further extend

*   *   *

Back at her house, Vixey prepared for the supper by discussing the menu with Annette, and later by putting on a light-pink chiffon *décolleté** dress with sleeves at the shoulders (which suited her shapely figure as well as her Bavarian nationality), along with a silver and crystal necklace, black stockings, and platform heels. These shoes, in black patent leather, were her favorite. They were simple, versatile, and chic.† The dress's mid-length skirt was flared and had black lace lining. At the waist Vixey simply tied a black silk ribbon into a bow. Besides the enhanced perception she had felt in the forest, another thing that changed that day was that her affinity for Karl had become deeper. This was not just due to the excitement of her brush with the tank, but also how close Karl came to being captured, which made her realize how much she didn't want him to leave.

Когда гости прибыли Вікси встретил их у дверей. – Bonsoir мадемуазель – сказал Владимир Максимович, сняв шапку. Вікси сделала реверанс и приветствовала их.

Павел Никитич, увидев её вдруг в её чёрных шпильках и чёрнорозовом платьице, внутренне ахнул.

(When the guests arrived Vixey met them at the door. "Bonsoir mademoiselle," said Vladimir Maximovich, taking off his cap. Vixey curtsied and greeted them.

Pavel Nikitich, seeing her all of a sudden in her stilettos and pink/black dress, gasped inwardly.)

Vixey showed them the first floor of the house and Vladimir Maximovich commented on the volume of books

---

their insights. This was how Baudelaire developed his theory of *correspondances*.

* Low-neckline

† A similar style is now used by Christian Louboutin in his 'Bianca' design.

in the library. The Russians said they were in such need of military supplies they didn't have enough training manuals for the troops. Vixey had a stack of spare ones and gave them away willingly. Pavel was impressed with the collection of books about tanks and artillery, as well as the literature, and solicited permission to return to the library for his studies. Pavel moved with a steady and authoritative gait, despite a war-related lingering pain in his back whenever he moved. It was not due to any specific injury in the field, but somehow just came about by itself from the psychological strain of war misfortunes.

Next Vixey showed them the kitchen, where Pavel noticed a tall glass jar of fresh coffee beans and opened it. He had not seen coffee beans in years. He waited until Vixey went into another room, then luxuriated in the dusky aroma of the rare import, inhaling it as much as he could several times.

For Vladimir Maximovich and Pavel Nikitich, due to their familiarity with Soviet and Nazi society, it was immediately evident that the wealth they saw could only be a result of government connections much more significant than just the post of a field marshal that Vixey's father had.

Vixey, Karl, the Russians, and the American lieutenants sat down for supper, but as the Russians did not know English and the two lieutenants did not know German, an easy conversation was not possible and much translation was required. One thing everyone understood, however, was when Vladimir Maximovich produced a bottle of vodka and distributed shot glasses. Even before this Vixey had invited them to come again as often as they liked in order to talk at greater length, which they were not disinclined to, since the division was mostly only occupied with military training and waiting for additional recruits. It currently had 2,000 men and was intended to march to the front when it reached closer to 20,000 and was fully equipped. They would join the 1st Division under

Bunyachenko in Württemberg and the 2nd under Zverev in Baden. In addition there was the 3rd Division forming in Austria, some reserve or engineer battalions, and a small air force under Maltsev, plus other allied units such the Cossack divisions under von Pannwitz and Domanov.

Pavel was more amiable towards Karl than he had been when they met – especially after drinking together – or at least seemed to be. Fadiman was a Jew, and did not think he would be drinking with any officers associated with the Reich while the war was still ongoing.

Vladimir Maximovich ventured toasts on universal themes, because it was hard for him to come up with many on a war theme for which he could be positive everyone at the table would be in agreement. He then explained in brief what his situation in the war was, "There are significant numbers of Russians currently in the German Reich, and many of us have volunteered to fight in the Wehrmacht. This was supposed to be a fight only against Russia, but Hitler forced many of us to fight on the Western front instead. We recognize General Andrei Andreyovich Vlasov as our leader, but only now, at the current time, is he finally being allowed to take an active part in directing our activities. We are forming an independent army that will be directed towards destroying the Soviet Union."

The Americans exchanged glances, all wondering how people could not only betray their own country, but join Hitler while doing it. Fadiman turned to speak to the other Americans in English, "Look- they are evidently fascist Third Reich supporters. They said themselves that they report to Himmler. These are the same sort of Russians that fought against us so hard in France. I don't know about you but I've had enough of sitting at the same table with them."

Karl asked Fadiman to withdraw to an adjoining room so they could talk privately. Landon went after them. Karl said, "I understand your concerns, but look at our situation. What should have happened was for all of us to be made prisoner and sent to some POW camp in central Germany for the rest of the war. If they were completely loyal to Germany they would have done that, but they seem to have some of their own plans."

"Alright. But be careful about what you do and how it may be perceived back at base. There is a fine line here between interpreting our orders creatively and being court-martialed."

"The hell you say.. I'm reporting all our activity to the base. But of course, I'm being selective in what I disclose – only what I deem pertinent."

"Incidentally," asked Landon, "Why is it that we saw so many Russians fighting in the Wehrmacht? They are all volunteers, see–."

"I don't know why so many of them volunteer," Karl replied. "They seem to be trying to ignite a civil war in Russia. Maybe also Germany is agitating for some kind of Ukrainian nationalist movement?"

Fadiman had other concerns, "What about the Nazi girl, Major? You should be even more cautious about how that looks than the socializing with the German Russians."

"She's not a Nazi."

"No? She's completely neutral? Just your German *schatzi**, as if nothing was going on around us? Her father is one of the principle figures on the other side of the war! And what are the financial sources of the hospitality we enjoy? Can we honestly accept any of this without knowing where it came from?"

"I don't understand where your opposition to everything comes from. I take responsibility for everything. Now relax and come have another drink."

Fadiman declined and while Landon had no objections, he would not be able to understand their conversation, so he also retired. Karl returned to the table, where he saw that Vixey had been chatting in German with

---

* The German equivalent of *chérie*. Also termed as *schätzchen*.

the ROA (Russian Liberation Army) officers, and sat down again next to her.

Vixey put a cigarette in her mouth and immediately both Karl and Pavel Nikitich extended lit lighters to her. She smiled and took Karl's light because he was closer to her. Vladimir Maximovich observed something in Pavel's look that he was not pleased with. He had known him for a long time and thought what he saw in his face was ill-boding.

Vixey, while holding the slender cigarette in her mouth, gathered up her long black hyacinthine hair and tied it in a ponytail, as a result better uncovering the beautiful tiered chandelier earrings she was wearing.

Glimpsing herself in a mirror, she was transfixed for a moment by the rubies and diamonds on her hanging earrings because their brilliance reminded her of the visual episode she had in the forest.

At length the Russians left, promising to return. They both kissed her hand when parting. Vixey then took her wine glass and walked past Karl into a darker, adjoining salon, where she gathered her skirt to sit down, crossed her legs, and took a sip from the glass. Karl followed her and she was glad that he sat next to her on the same divan rather than somewhere else. He was sitting against the back of the sofa so was behind her.

They were alone now, and a dense stillness replaced the prior noise of the gathering. Because of the sudden change in volume, Vixey heard a ringing sound, which was gradually replaced by the ticking of a clock across the room. Her skirt rustled as she re-crossed her legs. Neither of them had anything to say. Vixey leaned back to coquettishly touch him with her pony tail. Then she turned her head to look back; he leaned forward, embracing her pliant waist with one arm, and kissed her.

For the rest of that night the rest of the world didn't exist for them. Nothing in existence existed.

Chapter VIII

> Haidée and Juan carpeted their feet
> On crimson satin, border'd with pale blue;
> Their sofa occupied three parts complete
> Of the apartment--and appear'd quite new;
> The velvet cushions (for a throne more meet)
> Were scarlet, from whose glowing centre grew
> A sun emboss'd in gold, whose rays of tissue,
> Meridian-like, were seen all light to issue.
>   BYRON[*]

Vixey thought some light, cold sangria would be good in the morning and went downstairs. All she threw on over her dainty two-piece black lingerie was a diaphanous négligée, a nominal covering. She wore her standard bedroom shoes – they were by Perugia, with a small 70mm heel, no back, a suede vamp and ocelot fur edging. To make the sangria she simply poured cabernet sauvignon into a half-empty glass decanter of orange juice.

Despite the name bedroom shoes – or alternatively, boudoir slippers – these were used rather for quick passages in between her bedroom and other rooms of the house that were relatively clean. (A garage or patio would require different shoes). When Vixey was in her room she typically wore no shoes, walking on the rugs in bare feet or in stockings, as she did sometimes in other carpeted areas or on clean dry grass in a garden park.

Inside her closet, when she selected a pair of outdoor shoes, she would not put them on in there and walk out. Wearing her bedroom shoes or stockings, she would carry the other shoes or boots to the house's vestibule, which had a mirror and a padded stool, and would put them on there

---

[*] *Don Juan*, III.67. Unfortunately, Byron died in the Greek revolution before completing this epic poem. He left off in the seventeenth canto after building up suspense over hundreds of lines of verse as to what would happen with beautiful Adeline.

just before exiting. Skirts or pants that she wore outdoors or to school were similarly limited from parts of the house. In areas that guests typically frequented, like drawing rooms and dining rooms, any kind of outdoor skirt could be used. But when sitting down in more private areas, like a kitchen table or anywhere in her bedchamber, Vixey would only use skirts designated for indoor use.

Although she was negligent on thinking about the time, it was actually quite late in the morning and Landon, Fadiman, and Pavel Nikitich were all sitting in the library reading or writing. Pavel Nikitich heard her from the clack of her shoes against the kitchen floor and got up to ask her something about the spare military books he was taking. However, the area outside the entrance to the library had a rug, and he was unable to know that she was at that moment already passing by the door when he exited and collided into her. She nearly lost her balance but he quickly supported her by her hourglass waist, preventing her from falling or dropping the bottle. He was surprised at the negligible impact from bumping into her – it felt like she had no weight at all.

Apologizes were immediately made on both sides. She had forgotten that she had given him leave to come; and indeed was not thinking about a great deal of things, as she was still in a state of sweet exhaustion. When she went back upstairs she had already forgotten too about this accidental encounter.

Pavel Nikitich, on the other hand, felt as if his whole world was turned upside down. The sudden physical contact with the beautiful girl had an electrifying effect on him. He realized that he had forgotten how lovely she was in appearance. The previous evening certainly produced a deep impression, but it was too short for him to be left with an exact memory of her features. Such an effect often happens, because the mind is incapable of accepting such memories as true, so different are they from the common reality. It requires seeing the girl again to convince oneself.

Pavel sat down again and looked at a map of Bavaria on the wall without seeing it. To outward appearances he seemed calm but inside his mind was a dazed frenzy. Sweat appeared on his forehead; the walls of the room were crushing him. He mumbled an *au revoir* to the lieutenants and went back to the base, accidentally bumping into the jamb of the passageway when leaving the room. He looked at his hand and it was trembling, something that had usually stopped happening to him even in battle. It was something that he only noticed occurring on the battlefield when death was especially close all around and only avoided by fortuitous close-calls.

Karl found Vixey sitting on the Persian rug she had in her room. The sun was hitting the waves of the half-opened red curtains. She was wearing a long white skirt which entirely covered her legs folded under it. It gave her a surreal appearance of rising out of the plush rug like some kind of nymph. Karl thought about how his affair with her would probably warrant a court-martial and dishonorable discharge from the Army but he thought it was worth the risk. It would not be discovered by the divisional staff.

Vixey's lips were open as she applied a subtle-colored lipstick, looking through a small hand mirror. She poured two glasses of sangria and they drank them while sitting right there on the rug and talking on indifferent topics. Contrasting her skirt, the rug was predominantly red although it had designs in numerous colors typical of all Persian rugs. Vixey liked to have red or wood color schemes in interior decoration. On her person she already always had blue and black colors because of her eyes and hair. With her attire, to that she most liked to add, if not a classic black or white, then pink or dark blue.

Vixey was pleased with how things had gone last night, although she was surprised with how little time had elapsed since their first meeting. She thought that she enjoys his company, esteems him favorably, and that there's nothing objectionable about him except that he is American. She enjoyed how he lost control when making the slightest touch of her, or even sometimes when just looking at her;- and she liked the sensation of surrendering to this. Some women would have placed additional obstacles in the way in a subconscious attempt to increase their implied value*, since everything risks losing value if it is obtained too easily. This line of thought did not affect her because she assumed her value to be unquestionable in the first place. The two types of women who can act with impunity are those at either extreme of reputation. At one end they are indifferent to what others conclude, and the other end they already enjoy such a level of class and integrity that they are above criticism. The ones in the middle, the majority, have doubts and need to constantly maintain their image; thus they delay and deliberate endlessly.

The class to which Vixey belonged entitled her to *set* proprieties more often than just mechanically observing them. She understood this for a long time already, ever since she heard Henry V of England explaining to Catherine de Valois, in half-English, half-French, why she should not hesitate to let him kiss her.† (Vixey laughed at their anachronistic usage of the word *baiser*). Her later readings of Nietzsche on ethics served to confirm what was already clear to her.

Although Vixey disliked conformity, neither did she like to violate society's rules and standards as an end in itself. Whatever her inclination or preference led her to do, she always maintained a conviction that she was acting according to the highest standards of respectability, and would have been innocently shocked if someone happened to question her. But she was rarely questioned because she

---

* Nothing new. This was noted as early as c.1170 by the Countess of Champagne (as documented by Louis VII's royal chaplain).
† Act 5, Scene II.

had the benefit of mostly having her acquaintances among people of understanding.

*   *   *

Towards the end of the day Vladimir Maximovich came for supper, saying Pavel Nikitich was busy but would come later. Karl went upstairs to get Vixey, finding her by her writing table. For the evening she had already changed into black stockings and a flared skirt with wide black and white horizontal stripes. She was sitting in a chair with her black platform stilettos *raised up* on the desk, legs straight and crossed at the ankles. Almost the entire length of her legs was visible due to the shortness of the skirt. Karl stopped to admire her image. What was so striking about it?, he thought. It was probably due to the novelty of the upwardly inclined position of her legs. We are accustomed to seeing stilettos relatively far away near the floor, and pointed down. But here they were elevated, beautifully out-of-place on the table – where lay papers and writing materials – a work of art whose purpose was to artistically enhance her long and svelte legs.

Vixey was re-reading a letter she had just written to Evelina and was evidently comfortable in this reclined position with her legs up. She assured Karl there was nothing compromising in the letter with regard to their military situation. He asked her to come to the dining room and she daintily took her legs down from the desk, first one, then the other, and went with him.

At the table with Vladimir Maximovich, Karl thought it was a good opportunity to ask for his perspective on what Vixey had told him about the German pre-emptive strike on Russia. Karl mentioned the 2,000 Russian tanks on the Romanian border.

Vladimir Maximovich was in his military tunic, as usual. It had a general's red collar tabs and shoulder insignia. There was also an eagle/swastika patch on the chest and an ROA patch on the upper sleeve. He said, "Yes, not only were there tanks poised to penetrate Romania in 1941, but an entire fleet of river warships in the Danube delta, air force bombers, paratroopers, and numerous divisions of special mountain troops who could secure the Transylvanian mountains that the pipelines go through. Such a strike probably would have ended any effectual mechanized resistance on Germany's part. She is right about that."

Karl asked him what other wars he had been in. Vladimir Maximovich replied, "I was in the Tsarist army in the Great War. Then I was drafted into the Red Army in 1919, where I fought unwillingly. I joined the Party and they overlooked my Tsarist military past. I next commanded a division in the Winter War. After that the war against Germany began and I was captured three months later, outside of my own city, Kiev."

"And where were you based on the eve of war? Did your battle plans have an offensive agenda?"

Vladimir Maximovich smiled, "I was not able to see our plans... Don't you think that is a little strange? I was a general in charge of a division, but in various discussions I had with my commanders I was never given an answer to probabilities or timing of a potential German attack. I was transferred to the front in a secret train and not given any plans at all, not even after the war had begun! But obviously I could see what was going on around me," he said, banging the table with his fist. "I can tell you many things about that!...

"I commanded a large Artillery Division in the Soviet 26th Army on the border when the Germans invaded. We had a large contingent of good-quality self-propelled heavy howitzers, most of which we had to abandon. It was plain to me when I got there that for a good defense of the border we needed to be at least 30km east instead... Of course for political and diplomatic reasons you can be assured that records about the placement of troops in 1941 will be destroyed*... Those howitzers that we managed to retreat

---

* He is correct. Seventy years later whatever information that still exists about overall Soviet army deployments on the eve of war and their war plans remains classified in Russian archives. It can only be pieced together from individual accounts. One researcher who has actually put together many accounts to form a bigger picture was Viktor Suvorov (a former GRU officer). Another, Mikhail Meltyukhov, managed to find an important piece: the war plan of Marshal G. K. Zhukov, Chief of the General Staff, from May 15, 1941. This was the last known version of plans by which the Red Army was supposed to be guided during the war. Below is a map of what those plans entailed, courtesy of the site «Военная литература», http://militera.lib.ru/research/meltyukhov, which contains the contents of Meltyukhov's book.

with, could barely be used. We needed maps to fire them effectively, because my reconnaissance was supposed to tell us where the enemy was and we would direct our fire there. But we had almost no maps of the area we were in! We only had a little left over from the 1939 invasion of Poland. All the new ones were of the area *west* of the border like the

Krakow and Łódź areas. Apparently nobody envisioned that we would have to operate on our own territory. They only envisioned operating on German territory – meaning a planned invasion...

"Next, about the airfields – Vixey I'm sure could have told you this herself because it was apparent from the German perspective as well. When I arrived at the front I saw that Air Force divisions and armies were located right next to me, also right on the border. But our Air Force could have covered the border very well from 200 kilometers or more inside the country, at least far enough away so that the airfields cannot be attacked by surprise! When the attack came, all the planes were caught on the ground and air superiority was lost immediately. It's well known that before the war the Soviet Union led and exceeded the entire world in the development of paratrooper corps. It was evident that an immense force had been built up, at huge expense. But it couldn't be used without air superiority! Even now when the Red Army has regained the offensive, only rarely are the paratroopers used, because they are only efficient in a surprise offensive. The Americans used them in Normandy and Belgium; the Germans in Crete and Norway – all surprise offensives because that is when their high cost pays off. If we were planning to fight on our own land, defensively, we would have needed guerilla partisans with a network of concealed forest bases – but instead of that we had exclusively paratroopers."

They had sat down a bit early and the food had not been ready yet. Now Annette brought some dishes from the kitchen and they started to eat. Various preparations of pork, and knödel were frequent items in Annette's cooking. Not just kartoffelknödel but other variations such as Tiroler speckknödel and Böhmische Knödel. Also there was relatively more game now in the markets, so she frequently used *wildschwein, hase,* and *rehfleisch* (boar, hare, and deer).

Vladimir Maximovich continued, "If we were preparing for a German attack we would have done everything differently. Troops would be digging foxholes and preparing for winter. They would be concentrating behind defensive obstacles such as rivers instead of suicidaly in front of them. They would be laying minefields and anti-tank barricades instead of building new roads. You asked me about war plans. Obviously they existed, but they were thrown out once Germany invaded. All my actions at that time were pure improvisation. The field armies to my north and south were doing the same. We simply did not have any plans for defense or retreat."

"But what about the old maxim, that no battle plan ever survives contact with the enemy?"

"That certainly turned out to be true in our case. But Stalin's favorite pastime was purging. Why did he not even reprimand the people responsible for leaving a mobilized army of millions without useable war plans or even maps of Russia? Instead their careers improved during the war and now as they advance on Budapest and Königsberg they are considered among the best strategists in the world."

"Perhaps Stalin's generals are good, but he overruled them on everything."

"Ah, but however questionable his politics, you can not often find in him an inconsistency in war strategy. He was not directing contradictory things like a lunatic. If you look at his actions, all of them fit if you consider the purpose of a surprise offensive. And they matched the things that the Germans were doing on their side as they themselves prepared an offensive. The Germans were also building railroads up to the border to create resupply routes; also putting airfields on the border to have the most possible range; they also had maps of enemy territory. We did exactly the same..."

"If Stalin *had not* thought out a carefully planned offensive – had he done nothing at all while Hitler was attacking Europe – then at least the armies and airfields would not be defenseless on the very border to be immediately captured. (And once captured- proclaimed traitors because of the fact that they surrendered)."[*]

Karl remarked, "But I had always been led to believe that the Soviet Union was entirely unprepared for a modern war at the outset. That Stalin didn't count on the importance of mechanized warfare. That's a reason we gave the Soviet Union jeeps and supplies in Lend Lease."

"Consumer goods like jeeps and food are of course the best in America. But Western investment in military technology has been substandard in the 20s and 30s. For instance, the US entered the war with just a few hundred light tanks. You have a bit more now but technologically they are still behind the ones we had a long time ago, even before the war...

"The military buildup at the frontier was massive. Of course the Soviet Union will seek to diminish reports of its military power in 1941 for diplomacy. For convincing your president that he can be trusted, it is essential for Stalin to show that he was weak and intent on peace until Hitler maliciously attacked him for no reason. But it is hard to conceal the amount of tanks that Germany captured or destroyed in the first few weeks of the war. The Soviet Union had more tank divisions than the rest of the world

---

[*] Solzhenitsyn laments the placement on the border without defensive barriers, calls it a betrayal of the soldiers, but doesn't make the connexion. (See the WWII chapter of *Archipelag Gulag*.) He is apparently unaware that just four years later Soviet armies again formed up into the same positions, with the army and supplies on the very border of an opponent. This opponent was also an Axis state with whom they had signed a nonaggression pact: Japan. They dealt a crushing surprise attack, annihilating Japanese forces in Manchuria. A historical contradiction: If the tactics in 1945 are called brilliant, then the same exact tactics in 1941 should be called brilliant as well – but then the analyst would be forced to admit that those tactics were meant to be used in an invasion of Europe.

combined. Based on the number of tanks in my division and in my field army, I estimate we had between 12,000 and 15,000. There were 7,500 alone concentrated near Lwów in former Polish territory, where I was. Presumably this would have been the main strike, a giant blow in the direction of Krakow. Meanwhile Germany only had about 3,500 in their invasion. And our T-34 tanks are the best in the world currently. Is that right, Vixey? I will ask you for confirmation of any questions of German perspective."

She replied, "Yes, Field Marshals von Rundstedt and von Kleist[*] say clearly that it's the best in the world. Other generals as well. We wanted to produce it identically the same but weren't able to unfortunately."

With her hand, Vixey flipped back a strand of hair that had fallen over her forehead. Karl, who had started to speak, almost lost his train of thought. He said, "I heard of the T-34 of course. Once in a while the Germans we were opposing in Italy had them. But did you really have so many at the start? I heard that there were many other, obsolete tanks in the Red Army at the start of the war."

"Ah, that's actually true," Vladimir Maximovich replied. "At the start we only had about 1,000 T-34s, although massive production was ongoing and it still continues. Indeed at the time of the invasion most of our tanks were of the BT series from the 30s. This tank did in fact become obsolete when the war began, but not only because of its light armor. It was actually a brilliant design and had extraordinary features of speed and range. The basis for it was stolen from the US, by Soviet military intelligence agents in New York...

"Its problem was that it was a specialty tank, and this again confirms what I have been saying about offensive plans. It was a light tank whose advantage was its speed on paved roads. It had extremely poor manœuverability, in

---

[*] The general, not von Kleist the author of *Käthchen von Heilbronn* and *Die Marquise von O*.

comparison, in any off-road area, where tanks usually operate. Simultaneously as it's an incredible waste to have them in a defensive war inside Russia where there are no good roads, at the same time they would have been a very effective tool to use on the roads of Germany. And there were several thousand just of this tank. In the invasion, most were lost or abandoned."

Karl replied, "Hmm, it's very interesting what you say about this tank. Is it conceivable that Stalin was so certain that the war would develop to the west of the border that he would have time to create so many of such specialty road tanks?"

Vladimir Maximovich responded, "I think that for Stalin, the plan became fixed once he completed the Nazi-Soviet pact in 1939 dividing Poland with Hitler. There were various military activities before then, but it was after this nonaggression pact was signed that I began to see the most intensive military build-up. For Stalin the best scenario would be a long and destructive war between Germany and the West. But the quick defeat of France was a real surprise to us. We were short on time for mobilizing...

"To go back to military advantages,– Russian tank motors are diesel as opposed to German and American ones, and this by itself is a benefit as the motors don't catch fire and explode as easily. The T-34, of course, uses this. Although its advantages as a medium tank are well-known, Russian heavy tanks have comparatively an even greater advantage against the Germans. The KV series is praised by Tank General von Manteuffel and many other commanders as a practically unstoppable tank. The Germans, unfortunately, have not a single tank they can use against it. There were 500 of them in 1941, which would have been enough to cause a lot of damage in western Poland. And I haven't seen it yet, but apparently the Russians have made an even better mammoth tank, the IS (ИС) series. We also developed amphibious tanks, which is a feature entirely absent in either the German or American army. These are the T-37, T-38, and T-40...

"You said Stalin didn't appreciate mechanized warfare? He invented it. This is not often mentioned, because it is currently a State secret, but we defeated Japan in battles in 1939. This was the first use of concentrated lightning tank warfare, or blitzkrieg, in history. Japan apparently was so impressed that the USSR became untouchable in Japanese expansionary strategy. A nonaggression pact was signed and not broken by them even to help the German invasion. They focused on southeast Asia and even attacked you instead. Once again, Stalin will control the release of information to the West only when it shows him incapable of any aggressive behavior and when it shows that there could not have been a provocation for Hitler to invade."

Karl had a few doubts building while he ate and listened to the general's discussion. For instance, he knew of the Red Army failing embarrassingly in Finland in 1940, an apparent contradiction. He started by asking, "Remember you mentioned Stalin's inclination towards organizing purges. What I heard is that in 1937, Stalin purged most of the competent command officers, about 200,000 of them. What we think in the West is that this contributed to the Red Army's setbacks in the invasion, as well as in Finland."

"I don't know where anyone has obtained such numbers. That is more than the total number of officers there were in 1937. Facts about the military purge are exaggerated. My brother was arrested in 1938, but that is a separate matter. He was in an industrial commissariat and various state committees – in the Party but not in the military. His daughter, by the way, is here in Freiburg. I'm thinking to get in contact with her soon... A large amount of officers were dismissed in '37-38, especially generals, but not all dismissed were arrested, and even some arrested were brought back, like Marshal Konstantin Konstantinovich Rokossovsky. Overall the capabilities of the Red Army command did not decline; just look at some of the brilliant and terrible victories today."

Karl said. "But if you say the army was so capable, why such poor performance before 1943, and why are there such disproportionate losses on the Russian side? I understand the setback of the surprise attack, but human losses are overwhelming even now."

"You are right that the scale and speed of the initial loss of territory and military resources was un-heard of. Russia had not known such defeats for centuries. However, you underestimate the long-lasting effects of the surprise attack. If the Soviet Union had not mobilized its resources on the border, it would not have been such a catastrophic loss. About 4,000 airplanes were lost. Thousands of train wagons filled with ammunition. Between 8,000–11,000 tanks. The supplies on the border that weren't destroyed instead aided the Germans – fuel, equipment, vehicles, trains, etc. The Soviet Union had built all of its new ammunition factories in the western part of the country. In the attack we lost 85% of our ammunition production, which means we were fighting with only 15%. Artillery remained in short supply until 1943... In addition to this there were thousands of Red Army defections, including my own. A lot of people were reluctant to fight, and this increased the number of people surrendering when they got the chance...

"Regarding the disproportionate human losses, the explanation is partly the weapons loss but also in the nature of how the Red Army fights. It does not have any consideration for loss of life. In a socialist country, no expense of equipment or resources is made if it is possible to use human life to achieve the same result. A Soviet division is never supposed to break off an attack. It keeps repeating it again and again, with waves of infantry, no matter how many are killed or whether the troops even have any weapons left. Retreats are rarely planned. Surrendering alive is forbidden, which I have obviously violated. Also, in Russia we have *Shtrafniye Batalyonii* (penal battalions)[*], which is one of the major sources of the high death rate. Soldiers and officers committing various crimes and infractions, such as cowardice or unauthorized retreat, are stripped of their ranks and sent to a penal battalion. These are used in massive infantry attacks so wasteful that few people return alive from them. They are the first ones sent against German defenses. If the attack is unsuccessful, it means certain death. That is because NKVD[†] troops are stationed behind the advance and assigned to shoot with machine-guns all Russian soldiers not moving forward. In this way Russians are forced to advance against German guns with our own guns behind them...

"Thus two goals are accomplished: discipline is improved in the entire army via terror, and Germans positions are taken without a major expense of equipment. I heard of one instance – although maybe it is only a rumor – when the Germans surrendered for psychological reasons; it became too distasteful for them to continue the battle... Mademoiselle, I apologize for mentioning such details in front of you. Is it alright?"

"You can talk freely," Vixey responded. "Unfortunately I have become accustomed to hearing about such things. The war has been going on since I was 13."

Vladimir Maximovich continued, "Well then, I wish you a few more years of war. More time is necessary at this point. We need to turn the tide, which is currently against us! As I was saying, in addition to the penal battalions in

---

[*] Visotsky—
Считает враг: морально мы слабы, -
За ним и лес, и города сожжены.
Вы лучше лес рубите на гробы -
В прорыв идут штрафные батальоны!
[†] Soviet secret police, at that time under L. P. Beria. At other times known as Cheka (ЧК), GPU, OGPU, or other.

the Red Army there are also the 'Black Divisions'. Ten of these were formed at the start of the war. I don't know how many there are now. These contain prisoners taken out of Gulag labor camps who are turned into infantry. I am not in favor of all these methods. They are what led to things like the *Rzhevskaya màsorubka* (Rzhev meat-grinder), a stalemate near Moscow where Russian casualties exceeded those of the entire US Civil War. The Soviet attitude towards its citizens, as exemplified by its treatment of its soldiers was a reason I decided to switch sides. Maybe another time I will tell you more about this. But you also mentioned the war in Finland, did you not?"

"Yes...," said Karl, "that's one more thing relating to the Red Army that seems strange. What about the fiasco in Finland?"

"Oh, do you mean in the US you still don't understand Finland? In Germany, at least in the upper command, it has been understood."

"No, the opinion in our army is that the Soviet Union in 1940 failed to occupy Finland because of insufficient military strength. Only a small territory was taken. I don't know how to reconcile that with everything you've said."

"But look," said Vladimir Maximovich, flaring up, "does it make sense at all that a former colony 1/50 our size, a country without a tank force, air force, or navy, cannot be taken? I participated in the Finland invasion, under Marshal Timoshenko. If anyone looked closely at the matter, they would immediately see that the territory we captured was the part containing Finland's impenetrable Mannerheim Line, something the Finns considered impossible to get through. Then, having taken this, we suddenly stopped when there were no more defenses in the way and when all that was left to Helsinki was a simple walk. Vixey, if your father talked about the Finland war, tell us what the high command thinks of it now."

"He told me about Hitler's discussions with Reichsmarschall Göring, which he knows from Bormann.

Hitler and Göring both stated that the Finland fiasco was an intentional misinformation ploy to demonstrate a false military weakness, when at the time the Red Army was actually at least on par with the German army. We interpreted the events mistakenly when they happened in 1940 and this caused overconfidence in invading Russia."

Karl said, "Vixey, your father tells you a lot of things. Are you sure you can't give us some current strategic information? Counteroffensives planned, for instance?"

She laughed, "You have to get it out of me. I won't tell," giving him a confusing half coquettish, half serious expression.[*][†]

Vladimir Maximovich continued, "So you see, in stopping right after breaking through the Finnish defenses, the Soviet Union accomplished three goals: We gained military experience in attacking well-fortified locations. Two- the Mannerheim Line and all Finnish defenses were overcome, leaving Finland defenseless and requiring no further effort to occupy. And third, Hitler was completely fooled about Soviet strength and his attention was diverted...

"This is not to say that everything went smoothly. We actually underestimated the Finnish defense, had some setbacks, and had to increase the allocation of force. But the Red Army pushed through and accomplished its mission despite the impossible odds. Consider – less than a quarter of days had flying conditions, and even in those days there were only a few hours of daylight in the Finnish winter. Heavy artillery was not able to approach the fortifications

---

[*] ...an expression perhaps of the kind that the 1960s Russian actress Natalie Wood was adept at?

[†] Although this is a dense chapter on historical topics, at least the author mentions Vixey occasionally. Whereas in Fielding's *Tom Jones*, where Sophia is the most important character, one could suddenly come across a vast expanse of 145 pages that are completely Sophy-less.

either. The conditions were the coldest of any military offensive in history. Usually -20° but it went even lower than -40° sometimes. Defeating such an impressive fortification line under such conditions was something no other army in the world could have done, but all this achievement was purposefully concealed from the world."

Karl reflected, "I'm impressed with the reasoning towards a Soviet offensive in '41. I don't think anyone in the US Army is aware of any of this. I was always taught to believe that the Soviet Union had neither the capacity nor desire to launch an attack. Could you tell me about their motives? Could their preparations have been a measure to restore the balance of power in Europe and protect themselves from potential future threats from Germany?"

"Ah, I see you don't understand communism! I can tell you what Soviet motives are; it's the easiest thing of all to explain. But first I'll address your theory of an offensive strike to remove a German threat. This doesn't make sense. If Stalin was concerned about Hitler, if he did not want war in Europe, he could have simply taken no actions in 1939 and nothing would have happened. Instead he signed the nonaggression pact, which established a *common border* between Germany and the USSR and established trade relations. This pact started the war, as it had a secret protocol to divide Poland and Eastern Europe between the two countries.* France and the UK declared war on

---

* In an absurd irony, Soviet judges at the Nürnberg tribunals were allowed to convict Keitel, Jodl, and von Ribbentrop of planning aggression against Poland, while it was the Soviets themselves who also invaded Poland at the same time. (The truth of the secret protocol dividing Poland was only just coming to light at that time, and the Soviet Union simply denied any evidence of this as forgeries). In this and other ways the Nürnberg tribunals were shown to be fraudulent Soviet show-trials, even acknowledged as such by contemporary observers such as the US Supreme Court Chief Justice.

Germany after the invasion of Poland, as you know. The pact, plus another trade agreement later, also provided Germany with raw materials that were essential to its war effort: oil, rubber, grain, and various metals...

"Soviet motives are important to know, because they show that the Soviet offensive preparations were not just directed at Germany, but at France and England as well. Just take a look at the official coat of arms of the USSR – you'll see the answer there. Other countries and empires typically have a shield and various symbols of their monarchy or republic. The old German, Austrian, and Russian empires liked to use eagles. The US as well. Italy and Bavaria have lions surrounding their shield; the UK has a lion and unicorn; Prince Edward Island has two black foxes [Hearing this piqued Vixey's interest]; Württemberg had a black lion and a stag. The Soviet Union, meanwhile, in its coat of arms has a picture of a giant hammer and sickle over the entire planet. Underneath is the motto Proletarians of the world unite! Their one goal, now and forever, has been world revolution...

"It is only recently, while in a de facto alliance with Germany and later with the UK and US that communists have been silent on this topic. But you should have seen the continuous slogans and official statements of the leadership before- freeing the workers of the world and reaching a glorious future of communism was the constant theme."

"Why do they need this?" asked Karl. "It doesn't seem like a sensible goal."

"It doesn't? The current momentum of the Red Army is making their goal more and more sensible. They need this for two reasons. First, adding republics to the USSR where there are still people whose wealth can be expropriated adds to the aggregate wealth of the Soviet ruling *nomenklatura*. And the more important reason is that communism cannot coexist with capitalism. Capitalist countries are an ideological threat by their very existence. A communist state must necessarily be a prison; nobody can be let out because then everyone would flee. As long as there is a possibility of comparing with other countries or escaping to them, communism cannot last and the *nomenklatura* risks a collapse of the system. The measures they take to prevent comparison with the West are truly extraordinary. All Russians having unauthorized contact with Westerners or setting foot outside Russia are liable to be arrested. This includes people surrendering during war, so it will be applied to the millions of people who have found themselves in Germany if they are caught...

"For the Soviet Union this conflict you call the second world war is just a continuation of the Communist War that started in 1917. There are really two wars going on here. One is between the Western democracies and the Axis alliance of Germany, Japan, and a few of their satellites. The other is between the USSR and the rest of the world. Currently, it suits Stalin to make it appear that the Soviet Union is simply an ally of the West against the Axis...

"If we look back to 1917, besides securing power in Russia, Lenin's main goal was to transform the first world war into a 'revolutionary war'. War is the ideal condition for revolution. The more time the better, but even the Treaty of Brest-Litovsk did not save Germany and the war ended. The next two years saw feverish attempts to start revolutions in Europe; they actually managed to seize power in Bavaria, Hungary, and Finland, forming short-lived Soviet Republics there. On the instructions of Lenin, the ones in Munich took hostages from the aristocracy and then executed them. In 1920 the Red Army invaded Poland with the aim of reaching and occupying Germany. This is forgotten because it was a failure, but they were close to defeating Poland and if they had, then Germany would have fallen because it had a weaker military than Poland at the time. After this, efforts continued to attempt to seize power in Germany, either with elections or violence."

Karl interrupted, "Was not Stalin's difference with Lenin and Trotsky that they believed in world revolution, but he promoted 'socialism in one country'?"

"Stalin differed slightly, but not entirely, in his views on world revolution. According to Lenin, revolution was even more likely to erupt in industrialized countries that have a bigger proletariat, like Germany. A revolution just in unindustrialized Russia could scarcely survive alone, thus outside revolutions needed to be encouraged with great haste. However, Marx's theories on capitalist countries turning communist turned out to be wrong. Stalin saw that Trotsky's urge to continually attack would bring more risk than benefit. Instead, he concluded that it actually is possible to industrialize and stabilize in one socialist country by itself, provided it is already self-sufficient in raw materials, as Russia is. (Lenin and Bukharin came to agree with this in their later years as well). But Stalin never changed his belief that world revolution must happen; rather he saw longer-term plans as being more reasonable towards this end."

"But why wait so long? What about the early or mid 30's, when Germany would have been weaker?"

"Trotsky would have taken such a risk, but Stalin is much more calculating and cautious. Back then, Germany was weaker, but behind Germany was France, which was formidable then and would have acted against the communists. However, Stalin did not waste time. He created the largest industrial enterprises in the world, in Siberia, which serve primarily military purposes. Meanwhile communist parties and networks of communist agents increased their presence all over the world, all under Stalin's direct control. Germany was always the main target, as it was always closer to revolution than any other large country. An interesting effect of Soviet intervention in Germany is that the German army was re-created inside Russia. The Wehrmacht you see now wouldn't have had the strength it has if it weren't for the Soviet Union."

Karl asked, "What do you mean?"

"Eleven years of top-secret Soviet-German military collaboration occurred. Consider what would have happened if a revolution broke out in Germany, and then was quickly put down by France? It would have been a waste. For the Soviet Union it was essential that Germany have an army. Weakening the capitalist order (France and Britain) by strengthening Germany was a publically stated goal of the Soviet Union for years. Did you ever wonder how Germany, a country with strict international sanctions on military development suddenly and unexpectedly overran all of Europe with a superior force? It's not just a question of weapons production, but also tactics and technology, as much has changed since the last war. This secret collaboration, started by Lenin and continued by Stalin, helped greatly. Vixey, your father started out as a tank commander, right? Did he ever say anything about this?"

Vixey replied, "Yes, he did comment how ironic it was that he got his first training in tank warfare in Russia. But, of course, in the 20s he couldn't possibly have been training here. It wasn't allowed by the Versailles Treaty. So he would go by train to Daugavpils in independent Latvia, under a false passport, and they would meet him at the Russian border and take him to the place, somewhere on the Volga. He trained there with Guderian, the famous German tank strategist. I don't know much else, or why this was organized."

Vladimir Maximovich said, "Some people said it was for mutual benefit – an exchange of technologies and developments. But the benefit was primarily on the German side, so this leads me to believe the Soviet Union's primary goal was to help the German army strengthen. I recall we received some interesting products and tools that were made by Germany, like military optics and anti-aircraft artillery, but we could have easily bought such designs from the British or Americans. It was Germany instead that was unable to get military technology from the outside world...

"Thus modern tank warfare was developed in Russia and shared with Germany. Hitler did not invent this. In addition, the *Reichswehr* established military bases, trained officers, trained more than 1,000 pilots, and researched chemical warfare and airplane design. The early development of the famous Luftwaffe Ju-87 dive bomber was done in Russia. German companies were able to produce whatever they wanted and this was shipped via the Baltic."

Karl said, "This must have given Hitler a few years-worth of a head start when he started open militarization in 1935."

"Yes. The collaboration ended in 1933 when Hitler came to power... By the way, Vixey, could you explain what happened in the 1932 elections? I have heard conflicting stories, including something from an NKVD acquaintance about communist political support for Hitler, which I would think not possible."

"I was only 6 then, in 1932," Vixey said. "But I know what happened from reading the history. It was a mess. Of course the communist party and Nazis were bitter enemies. However, in those years, especially after 1928, the communists became very big enemies of the democratic socialists. All three parties had gun battles in the streets, particularly in East Berlin. The communists called the socialists 'social fascists' and treated them as their main enemy, opposing them to such an extent that they even sided with the Nazis in certain strikes in '31-32. This may be what your acquaintance refers to. There wasn't any active support. But since the Nazis never had a Reichstag majority, only peaking at 37%, their success can be attributed to the inability of other parties to form a coalition against them. Some have blamed this on the communists refusing to join with the socialists."

"What were the percentages of all the parties?" asked Vladimir Maximovich.

"In November 1932, the last fair election, the Nazi party had gone done to 33%. The socialists had 20, communists 17, and Centre Party 12. Some pretty discouraging choices."

"It is obvious that any ruling coalition would have had to include either Nazis or communists."

"Yes. The communists you say were under Stalin's control?"

"That's true," said Vladimir Maximovich. "Anything they did would have been ordered by Stalin."

"Then given what you say about his interests, it seems surprising that the communists did nothing at that time. They could have easily gotten rid of the Nazi Party for instance."

"How so?"

"Hitler had pursued an 'all-or-nothing' strategy and this had failed. The Party was bankrupt and by November 1932 they had lost two million votes. German Chancellor Schleicher had begun to unravel the Nazi party, causing the Number Two man Strasser to leave and Hitler to almost shoot himself. By the end of 1932 nobody expected the Nazi party to survive. Everyone was saying it was finished. Later, in 1933, their political situation improved, and it was helped by them being still unopposed by any coalition. Hindenburg and Papen yielded to Hitler's demands."

"And what if there had been a coalition of the communists and socialists?"

"It could not have been more than temporary, I think," Vixey replied. "The socialists were wary of falling under the communists' control. Also, it's likely that Hindenburg and the military would have acted against any governing coalition containing communists. But still it would have been very unlikely for Hitler to manœuver himself into the position of Chancellor in such an environment."

Vladimir Maximovich gave it some thought and said, "It seems to me that the decision to do nothing against Hitler was intentionally made by Stalin when he directed the communists to oppose the socialists."

Karl exclaimed, "Why would he pursue such a policy?"

"The communists still had only 17% of the vote, despite their powerful Comintern* resources. Sizeable, but by itself ineffective to actually aid in seizing power. I think that Stalin decided to abandon democratic methods of gaining Germany, and chose the second best option. He knew that a vote for Hitler was a vote for war, and it was not easy to guess that this would start out with a war between Germany and France. As such, it would be consistent with Lenin's and Stalin's long-standing desires for renewed war between the European powers as an optimal situation for revolutionary war. What would be the worst-case scenario for Stalin? Some kind of multi-party coalition government in Germany, with moderate policies and internal conflicts. Such a government would have led to peace in Europe for many years – it would have led to a gradual strengthening of capitalism in Germany. No, it is clear that Stalin would have favored any kind of radical revolutionary, including Hitler, instead of that!"

At this point Pavel Nikitich came in. "Ah, Pavel Nikitich, just in time," said Vladimir Maximovich. "We can start drinking now."

Pavel always arrived immaculately dressed, every element of his German lieutenant-colonel's uniform perfectly arranged, well-fit, and shined. This was a contrast

---

* The Comintern (Communist International) directed worldwide communist party activity from Moscow and its stated goal was to fight "by all available means, including armed force, for the overthrow of the international bourgeoisie and for the creation of an international Soviet republic..." It was flagrantly unconcealed until 1943, then became covert.

to the Americans, who did not have the benefit of a base, nor the attention to clothing characteristic of Russians and French.

Pavel gave his salutations as he entered and placed two bottles of vodka on the table. "Two bottles?" asked Karl.

"Yes," replied Vladimir Maximovich. "We received a battalion of artillery troops today to join our forces. Something to celebrate. They were transferred from the... Lower Rhineland area."

Vixey put her hands past her neck and in one motion lifted her straight hair on both sides of her face, letting it aerate as it cascaded back down softly over her shoulders and over her breasts. For a second her neck and sapphire earrings were visible. Pavel's mouth opened in hypnotic amazement. Even Vladimir Maximovich paused. She noticed nothing.

Karl had another question, "So what does this mean, what you said about Germany? Wouldn't this suggest, also in light of the nonaggression pact, that Stalin wanted a long-term alliance with Hitler rather than war with him?"

"That is not the case," replied Vladimir Maximovich. "Hitler never ceased to be an enemy, because like the capitalists he is also in the way of world revolution. But that does not mean that he cannot be temporarily useful, because his enemies in the West are also Stalin's enemies. Stalin was an expert at using people or groups against each other. I used to think that Hitler was more of an accidental figure who Stalin later discovered might be useful when the decision to divide Poland was made. But from what she had told me about this election, I see that Stalin's influence in Germany was more than I thought. His non-use of it indicates that he did not see the Nazi party's rise as an unfavorable event for Germany, even if it meant the permanent destruction of the German communist party...

"To the few political figures directly involved in Hitler's ascension: Hindenburg and the others in the German government, one must also add one more: Stalin.

It's unclear to me how significant his assistance was, but there is one thing I am certain of. War would have been inevitable regardless of what happened in Germany! This has been building up since the 20s. If there had been no Hitler, Stalin would have found other means of making it happen, because that was the goal of helping to build Germany's army and of course the immense development of the Red Army."

Pavel Nikitich remarked, touching his black mustache, "I completely agree, *tovarishch*, but don't you think that you have talked enough? The time has come for drinking, after all."

"Very well," Vladimir Maximovich said. "But bring out the larger glasses, Vixey. This time I want to teach you how to really drink vodka."

Chapter IX

> Round her she made an atmosphere of life,
> The very air seem'd lighter from her eyes,
> They were so soft and beautiful, and rife
> With all we can imagine of the skies,
> And pure as Psyche ere she grew a wife--
> Too pure even for the purest human ties;
> Her overpowering presence made you feel
> It would not be idolatry to kneel.
> BYRON[*]

Vixey reached for a few cut-glass tumblers in a cupboard and put them on the table. "These are perfect," Vladimir Maximovich said, "they look to be exactly a quarter of a liter. Pavel Nikitich, *razlivǽ*."

Pavel Nikitich poured each glass full to the brim. There wasn't enough in the first bottle for all four glasses so he placed it on the floor and opened the second. Both bottles were dripping with condensation because they had been well-frozen before he brought them.

Vixey looked at the cups in fear, "You're pouring the entire cup full?"

Pavel replied, "Yes- for us this will just be the beginning of the night. For you, as a little girl, this 250 grams should be a good amount. But remember- don't try to have any more after this! That would be too much."

She looked at Karl, but he said, "You might as well try it."

Pavel said, "As the French say, '*Quand le vin est tiré...*'"

"We'll drink to your health," Vladimir Maximovich put in. "You wouldn't refuse to drink to your health, of course?"

It was hard to counter these brilliant arguments, so Vixey acquiesced.

---

[*] *Don Juan*, III.74.

Vladimir Maximovich got up to fill another glass for her of water that she should drink immediately after. For himself and the men, he found cucumbers. He proceeded to give her instructions, "You can stand up – it will be easier. The goal is to drink it all at once without taking your lips off the cup. Don't try to swallow too much! Take your time and continue breathing while drinking – but don't pay attention to the fumes! Resist accumulating too much of it in your mouth until you reach the end of the cup. If you do that you'll find it hard to intake any more." He said all this in a serious, almost grave manner.

Vixey struggled with the glass for some moments after Karl had finished his. She kept her eyes open, long eyelashes pointing cupward, in order to see how much was remaining. At some moments she was nauseous from the noxious liquid in her throat and thought she wouldn't be able to finish, but slowly the level of vodka in the cup diminished. The two Russians had already finished and were observing her while eating cucumbers. Vixey had a very large black velvet bowtie in her hair, and the feminine air it conveyed made her look even more out of place drinking vodka like a soldier. She finally emptied it and immediately downed the glass of water to chase the burning vodka. The fumes alone had already intoxicated her and she sat down at the table, feeling a sharply-accelerated heartbeat. But the full effect was yet to hit. She was unsure of whether to say she'll never do that again, or if she was starting to feel that it was worth it. Vladimir Maximovich and Pavel Nikitich, still sitting at the table, remained very serious; their brows were clouded but not their thoughts. Karl was in a state of restrained exhilaration, especially when he looked on and contemplated Vixey.

They talked for a few minutes on indifferent topics. Karl observed that the bottles had no labels on them and asked where they procured them. Pavel Nikitich laughed and said, "A Russian always knows how to find vodka, wherever he is... One time, as we were moving through

France, I noticed that the soldiers were constantly a little drunk, even during the day. For a few days this continued and nobody could figure out where they were getting it. The Germans were getting irritated at this inability to maintain order. But the troops couldn't be carrying it with them because the officers searched all of them and found nothing. Then, we finally figured it out. They had emptied the liquid from the water-cooling system in the trucks' radiators and filled it with vodka! To take a sip they would climb under the engines and open a valve!"[*]

This anecdote was greeted with laughter. More followed both on the stupidity of German officers, and the backwardness of Russian peasants in Germany for the first time.

Karl's chair was turned towards Vixey's and she put her shoe on the edge of his chair between his legs, resting her arms on her bent knee. She juvenilely asked people whether her hair was better arranged all tied up on her head or hanging straight down, and demonstrated different arrangements of hair. She asked Pavel Nikitich, "How do I look?"

"Very nice."

"That's it? How about now?" she said, with her hair a different way, *avec un sourire d'une douceur ineffable* (with a smile of ineffable sweetness).

"Very nice indeed."

She sat closer to Pavel and took his peaked military officer's cap, which was lying on the table, to try how that looks on her. Only the bottom part of her face was visible from under the visor; unsurprisingly the hat imparted to her a sharp, military look. To that was added the wound from the tank shrapnel she had on her arm, from her elbow almost to the middle of her forearm. Pavel noted that there was some appeal from the addition of an element of

---

[*] This is a true story, related by V. Suvorov in his Czechoslovakia memoirs, *The Liberators*.

sharpness to her overall soft, youthful image, which usually only her sapphire eyes contradict. He imagined that her loading a revolver would evoke similar feelings.

If Pavel had a knowledge of the technical structure of music, he would have seen that the same idea of contrasting features combining in an intriguing way as in Vixey, also exists in the musical notion known as counterpoint. This is the way that several musical lines, each individually beautiful, when structured together create a polyphonic whole that is more than the sum of its parts – a structure that reinforces and comments on the melodies of its underlying components. Vixey was music, of a complex but completely harmonized structure. A revolver would be like a playfully dissonant counterpoint to her delicate fairness, while her dark black hair was also a counterpoint but a more consonant one.

Her hair was so dark, in dim light it almost emanated a black radiance. It is an enticing color to touch, because so few things have such an intense, ominous iridescence of blackness. However, under the bright sun it was different – parts of her raven locks could assume a silvery or even red shine.

Pavel used the excuse of taking back the cap from her to pass his other hand through her hair. He lifted his hand through it and let the strands drop off, feeling the hair's immensely pleasurable cool texture. This was the realization of a long held-back desire. Vixey was accustomed to touching her own hair a thousand times a day, thus she wouldn't have understood why it was so important to someone else to feel and savor it. Yet Pavel had never before felt hair of such delicate silkiness. Vixey took good care of it, like the young Iberian duchesses in medieval tales.

Karl meanwhile felt slightly intruded on by Pavel's presence and his access to the house but there was nothing he could do. He was an American on German soil, after all, and had been shown leniency by Pavel's superior.

After they had eaten some more food, Vixey could no longer stand the confinement of the room and announced she was going for a walk. She went outside without putting on a jacket, hat, or gloves, and Karl went after her. Her skirt was short and flared out, with wide black and white horizontal stripes. She was visible in the night mostly from those bright white stripes. That night was moist and cold, which she felt nothing of. There was a brick-floored patio by the house, with two descending steps that ended in grass. Stumbling in the dark field under the stars, she said, "It may seem in relative terms that I'm well provisioned here, but this is far less than what I'm entitled to! My ancestors were at the court of the Bavarian Kings; I should be in a palace, in the Schloss Nymphenburg!"

Karl said, "Yes, and in the *Schönheitengalerie*."

"That's correct!" she said, and fell down, her heels sinking in the grass. She talked about how she wasn't drunk at all, just couldn't walk here. "Help me up..."

Karl picked her up and held her upright. It felt good to touch her at last, to feel her warm contact and breathe the fragrance of her neck. The entire long time they had been in the Russians' presence he had to keep a respectable distance, although there were many times when he felt a great desire to touch her hand or grasp her by the waist, if only to demonstrate to himself that she was real and actually existed there, near him in the room.

Over Karl's shoulder Vixey saw the American soldiers' tent and slipped away with the intention to go enter it. A few steps and she was there. The soldiers all looked at her in surprise. Her stability was uncertain; her facial expressions were cutely erratic. She saw that one of them was shirtless. Laughing, she said, "*Herr Major, einer Ihrer Männer ist nicht in Uniform, Sie müssen ihn maßregeln! Zumindest seine Hosen hat er an. Diese Amerikaner haben gar nicht so ein schäbiges Zelt. Es ist warm hier. Und, oh, die Männer hier spielen Karten und trinken!*"

She saw a group of soldiers playing whist with a bottle of whiskey resting on the crate they were using as a table. She remembered to switch to English, and while asking, "Do you mind offering me a drink, Herr Sergeant?," took the bottle in her hand. She was about to take a sip from it but was gently stopped by Karl, who led her back to the house.

Vladimir Maximovich and Pavel Nikitich were preparing to drive back to their base to continue drinking there. Karl parted with them and went to Vixey who was waiting at the top of the stairs. Pavel Nikitich lingered for a second looking at Vixey disappearing upstairs, and felt what can only be described as a poison flowing through his veins. The potency of this poison was enhanced considerably by its mixture with vodka, which is known to have an effect of magnifying whatever emotions we have, good or bad. Her beauty was exasperating to him, so much so that it stifled the normal thought process. And he now saw exactly where her attentions were being diverted. Vladimir Maximovich saw him still looking up at the empty space, understood what was so apparent, and severely reprimanded him.

Getting into their jeep, the black stillness of the night was broken by the creaking of Vladimir Maximovich's leather trenchcoat. "*Holodnovata* (It's somewhat cold)," he said. Pavel Nikitich grumbled an agreement, while thinking of what to do about Karl. He saw him as a blundering, naïve fool and considered Karl's only advantage to be that he had met the girl first. But he could not decide on any course of action.

"*C'est un ange,*" he thought, "*et j'en suis fou.*"

Chapter X

> My only books
> were woman's looks,
> and folly's all they taught me.
> THOMAS MOORE

Pavel Nikitich awoke relatively easily at the 4th Division officers' quarters, still thinking about Vixey as he went to breakfast. Lost in a languorous melancholy haze, he longed to contemplate her image with adoration again, as he had yesterday, when he noticed how her black-trimmed pink collared-shirt had *snaps* instead of buttons, and how the top snap out of the ones that were fastened, was barely holding because her shirt was too narrow-fitting.

The v of décolletage from all the unfastened snaps at the top of the shirt gave Pavel a guilty feeling whenever he looked at it. Speaking to her he tried to look past her bodice but always saw it anyway, and again felt as if at fault in something.

He had the chance to observe her the most when she was not facing him, and with her face in profile he could gaze on the curve of her long, blackened eyelashes; the dainty form of her nose and the delicate philtral ridges above her upper lip that gave her lips their pleasant shape. Whether or not he looked at Vixey, if she was close her closeness was felt by the effect of a dulcet fragrance around her, the origin of which was unknown. It was the combination of endless details such as this that created the sum of her captivation. Pavel consulted his book of *Fleurs du mal*, and found a description of these thoughts in the piece *Tout entière*:

> *Lorsque tout me ravit, j'ignore*
> *Si quelque chose me séduit.*
> *Elle éblouit comme l'Aurore*
> *Et console comme la Nuit;*

Et l'harmonie est trop exquise,
Qui gouverne tout son beau corps,
Pour que l'impuissante analyse
En note les nombreux accords.

Ô métamorphose mystique
De tous mes sens fondus en un!
Son haleine fait la musique,
Comme sa voix fait le parfum!*

Contrary to his wishes, the first person Pavel encountered when he returned to the house in the morning, was Karl again. He had walked into the library and Karl was already there, reading Hermann Hesse's *Narziß und Goldmund.* Karl had never had much time for literature; this was his first time reading anything by Hesse.

Because of Pavel's affinity for Vixey, everything about Karl was offensive to him – from his appearance and attire to the way he held the books from Vixey's library. Why can't he just hold a book normally- thought Pavel. Somehow the way he handled them was so coarse – creasing the spine, carelessly marring the crispness of pages – that after a few minutes it would appear more ruffled than after a full read.

Pavel started to peruse the memoirs of Fürst Chlodwig Carl Viktor zu Hohenlohe-Schillingsfürst, Fürst von Ratibor, former *Reichskanzler.* He found it tedious and instead engaged Karl in conversation: "I see that you are reading Hesse. He is from the Black Forest, as a matter of fact, where we are now. What do you think of this book?"

Karl replied, "I'm struck by the similarities between Germany then and now. It takes place in the middle ages,

---

* The poem also touches on Baudelaire's *correspondances* concept. He talks of the merging of different senses, of feeling her breath as a music and voice as a perfume. The 'harmony' that governs her is too exquisite. Similar ideas have already been mentioned in the description of her 'counterpoints' the night before.

the 14th century. And now in the 20th, we have descended again into the kind of 'total war' with so many civilian deaths, which wasn't seen in the West since medieval times."

"And once again, just as in this book, Jews are being burned throughout Europe."

"What do you mean?"

"About two months ago it was discovered that this had been going on at Majdanek. It is evidently a part of Operation Reinhard, a plan to kill all the Jews in Poland."

"There is actually such a plan?"

"Yes, I had heard rumors of it. Who could have thought. And what about the medieval-style siege of Leningrad, or the burning of Hamburg? Have you heard of these things?"

"In part, not in detail."

"Leningrad was blockaded intentionally by Hitler, a genocidal siege that was the most lethal in history. Things got so bad there were incidents of cannibalistic gangs attacking people to eat them. Meanwhile the attack on Hamburg, the third-largest German city, was the worst aerial bombing of a city to this day. The RAF drenched the city with so much incendiary that a superheated vortex was created – a 500 meter high tornado of fire with winds of 240 km/h. The inferno consumed everything in the city center. Doubtless some military objectives were also achieved, but still it reminds one of the vindictive religious wars."

Karl remarked, "And it is worse this time for the reason that it is a descent of civilization downwards. You always expect more progress, not the opposite. People expected much more from the 20th century."

"The retrogression this century in Russia has been greater than in any other place. The events of the war do not even impress me compared to what I have seen internally in the Soviet Union. I have seen a zek slave ship leaving Nakhodka bound for Magadan. That is enough. But I don't expect anything – things will always be bad; in fact I think things will continually get worse and worse until civilization is destroyed... This is not what bothers me about this Hesse book. Rather: there is an important dialogue between the thinker/theologian and the artist, when they are reunited and the latter tries to make sense of the Black Death and all the other horror and madness he has seen. He sees temporary lust as the only thing available to mitigate all that, and of course concludes that this is inadequate. I have never been satisfied with the resolution that followed, in which the thinker, Narziß, claims that the creative mind: art and ideas, are what make the world worthwhile. This is claptrap! It explains nothing."

"Well, he did put forward this one idea that has potential plausibility. Hesse himself is an artist and a thinker and it would make sense to him."

"What plausibility?" responded Pavel. "Art is just a mitigating factor that prevents total despair; it doesn't solve anything. Artists are among the most miserable of people. It's because they *see more* of the world. Not everyone is capable of seeing, and most are better off seeing less. Artists are typically outcasts; they think too differently from everyone. Read Thomas Mann's early work – he explains it all. The dancing philistines that he describes well are the fortunate ones in life. As opposed to those philistines, Baudelaire, Villiers, and Heine could do no better than illiterate mistresses. Gogol, Leopardi, and von Kleist not even that. Turgenev never did anything but admire from afar Pauline Viardot, who was married."

Pavel thought for a moment in silence and continued, "At least Hesse did didn't write something completely silly, for instance, as others have written, that 'requited courtship' is a successful counterpoint to the hell of life. Anyone over the age of 25[*] should know that this is a theoretical, antediluvian concept only existing in fiction

---

[*] Stendhal would say 30.

like *La Dame aux Camélias*[*], *Evelina*[†], and sentimental Turgenev novels. Or even worse is the solution of the religious thinkers, (to which I would add the 'Eastern' theories of Schopenhauer as well as the 'Dulçinea' concept of Cervantes[‡]). They have abandoned the physical world in favor of spirits and dreams. Camus, one of the new radical Frenchmen, correctly says that to fill the existential vacuum with a religious opiate, is essentially 'philosophic suicide.'"

"I have heard of this Camus and his ideas, but have not read his work, since it hasn't been translated from French yet."

"No need to wait for the translation," said Pavel. "Anything and everything has already been turned upside-down by the Marquis de Sade 150 years ago. What else new can be said? But I do enjoy the way Camus basically spits on culture and the classics with his wild absurdism. I also like his grand metaphor for all human technology and society: the Greek myth of Sisyphus where a man is condemned to eternally struggle to lift a rock up a mountain only to have it roll down every time he is close to the top. This is true for most of the work we have to do. Camus says that it is impossible to find any meaning or hope in the world. So it seems to me that he advocates a form of momentary living without any planning. His conclusions obviously lead him to reject an altruistic life of sacrifice and duty. So he goes to the opposite- hedonism. Omar seems to come to the same conclusion in his *Rubáiyát*."

"As long as it's combined with sound ethics, I don't see what's wrong with that."

"But how is it possible to live without planning? Even a playboy, who doesn't risk any consequences, would get bored if he just 'did what he felt like' without planning some kind of achievement of values. Look at what the

---

[*] Dumas *fils*.

[†] Frances Burney.

[‡] Dulcinea was the illusory paramour of Don Quixote.

French call *le mal du siècle*, for instance in Pechorin, the *Hero of Our Time*."

"Then why do you agree with Camus on the absurdity of the world?" asked Karl. Both of them were smoking cigarettes and sitting in armchairs at opposite walls but not too far away to converse.

"I agree with him that optimism is false and hope is irrational, but I see it a little differently. I think he is actually being too easy on the world. He doesn't think the world is absurd *per se*, just our attempt to understand and cope with it. I grew up an atheist in the USSR. Then, after what I've seen, I started to believe in God. Not for the traditional reasons of finding some kind of relief amongst a crowd of believers; no, rather from the impossibility to explain the world in any way other than divine intervention. Simply put, what else but an intelligent, malevolent deity could have created such horror? Life has become a Kafkaesque nightmare. Kafka was more an observer of reality than an fantast. The unspeakable poverty everywhere? The malicious incompatibility of men and women? The inevitable decline and extinction of the human race when people become less instinctual and start realizing what a crime it is to reproduce and thus create more and more suffering? People will die off as soon as they realize that self-preservation is an irrational instinct. The great Italian thinker Leopardi approached similar conclusions in the 1820s but he did not go far enough. Beauty is not a redeeming aspect of the world, as it may seem to some. Recall Cowley's lines: 'Beauty, thou active, passive ill! / Which diest thy self as fast as thou dost kill!' Beauty is at that simultaneous level of importance and scarcity that its effects end up negative. But what does 'negative' even mean? For Leopardi, beauty was a positive because he equated it with death and because death itself is a positive. Life he aptly termed an 'elusive and deceptive phantasm'. Anyway, such a world, with basic foundations of injustice and deception could not have been created by chance – it must have required the thoughtful construction of a sadistic divinity, an evil God. Somehow it is set up so that mankind's capacity for suffering continually increases. Over generations, man's perception of the world's evil nature becomes more acute, fuelling greater and greater disillusionment and despair. The human race will end starting with the most technologically-advanced and intelligent nations. Kierkegaard correctly remarked that every increase in consciousness is an increase in despair. One can trick or inebriate the mind, but it is impossible to be fully sober and aware and not to hate the world and be miserable. At the same time ring-fenced beauty becomes more and more *refined* while remaining inaccessible, continually increasing the contrast with the general commonness everywhere, all the hideous aspects of the world. Apparently the intent of the architects is to see at what point the pressure will be too much and the world will go up in flames. This fate cannot be changed, much like each person's individual fate. There are very few things we could do. One possible option is this: if you kill yourself, specifically with the intent to oppose the evil deity, you could then 'become God'."

"Become God?"

"Yes," said Pavel, "but the amount of time when this will occur will be a timespan of zero, so the value is nil for oneself. The only purpose is the revolt, freeing oneself from a dependence on evil."

"So, as you said earlier, you subscribe to a twisted theory of intelligent design, but coming to it from the opposite direction? What does this imply for, say, evolution?"

"Evolution is logically consistent with objective science. There has never been a *deus ex machina* event reliably recorded- nothing to show inconsistencies in natural science, as we perceive it. The question is rather that of metaphysics – if the architects are omnipotent, it is impossible to know with certainty what happened in the

past. It would not be difficult for them to create something
that has attributes of being older than it is, all consistent
with logic. But it makes no difference whether anything
happened in the past or not. Nothing significant ever
happened nor will ever happen. Everything is worthless."

"Do you think there are any solid axioms, such as the
conservation laws?"

"Modern theories of cosmology ignore them anyway,
in their description of the world's creation, so I don't see
how my theory is worse."

"Would you tell me what you think of nihilism and
Nietzsche?"

"Nietzsche has a number of interesting points and I
agree with some of them. Unfortunately, his wide-ranging
commentaries are hard to pin down and thus he is usually
misinterpreted. Often he is associated with nihilism,
although remember- he was just describing it, not
advocating it. The Nazis were able to selectively incorporate
some of his thinking into their own, even though Nietzsche
was not a German-militarist, nor is his *übermensch* concept
at all related to theirs. Like Dostoyevsky, he focused on
nihilism as a consequence of a lack of religion. From what I
see in *Beyond Good and Evil*, he noted the false ethical
dichotomy arising between altruism and selfishness. The
decline in intrinsicist, 'ends-in-themselves', religious values
(such as abstinence), create the false assumption that the
opposite is 'evil' and this confusion – the mistaken grouping
of good things along with bad things – leads to nihilism,
absurdism, and no limits. The *übermensch*, rather, is able to
surpass nihilism through the creation of his own values,–
hopefully rational, although Nietzsche didn't talk much
about objective rationality..."

"How would Dostoyevsky explain why religion by itself
is inadequate to maintain ethics? His own heroines, like
Nastya[*], are constantly at war with themselves because of

---

[*] Nastassya Filippovna, in Идиот (*The Idiot*).

the false dichotomy. The presence of religion in medieval monasteries did nothing to prevent Franciscan friars from ganging up on maidens when they could get away with it, and various other schemes of rapine – as we see from the Queen of Navarre's *Heptameron*. Nietzsche formulates an alternative – not to say that it wasn't known to many people before without them explicitly stating it – but his formulation is new. What doesn't seem new to me, however, are his anti-religious ideas in general and his famous notion of the 'will to power'. These were already among the things that de Sade discussed. In fact, de Sade may have been the first person to come up with nihilism. His thinking was a combination of French revolutionary radicalism and *ancien régime* aristocratic unrestraint. It's interesting that de Sade is still considered dangerous and is banned in the UK as of now, even though French editions have existed most of the time. Do you have him in America?"

"I think so," said Karl, "ever since Joyce's *Ulysses* became allowed in the 30s, nothing is censored."

It was evident that Pavel Nikitich liked to talk at great length. He was one of those people who have an opinion on everything. It did not matter to him that he was in the presence of his enemy. He had remained sitting in his armchair all this time, only getting up when he needed to get an ashtray for his cigarette. He continued, "What is really remarkable is that there is one thinker today who has some profound thoughts on existentialism, Viktor Frankl, but instead of working, he is currently sitting in a concentration camp! He's near Landsberg in Bavaria, right now as we speak. I read some of his earlier work during my time in Germany. It would be interesting to see what he says about the world now – if he stays alive, which isn't likely."[*]

---

[*] Frankl actually survived the camp, using the experience to write *From Death-Camp to Existentialism* afterwards.

"What did he write?"

"Many things, but one of his points was that even in the absence of any legitimate hope, there can be value in the pursuit of rational goals, or at least in becoming worthy of our sufferings. My own mission, that I have been working on continually the past three years, is the fight against Stalin."

"Hmm. But in doing so, you have to fight against your own country."

"Yes, of course. In any civil war, both sides fight their countrymen."

"In light of the fact that your country was first attacked by foreign enemies – Nazis who actually stated they want to destroy it – this is hardly a civil war. I'm sure anyone would call siding with those enemies somewhat of a betrayal of the country."

"In that case whoever would say such a thing would demonstrate immediately that they do not know what they're talking about," said Pavel, jumping to his feet.

Karl thought it best not to argue. There were several reasons why Pavel Nikitich appeared an imposing adversary: his rank and authority in Germany, large stature, impressive mustache, and- also noteworthy- his Russian unpredictability. Pavel had killed many people in close range combat in the course of the war, which was more intense on the Eastern front that it had been on the Italian. Pavel continued, "It's not a matter of military oaths. Ideologically, I can't possibly fight for communists. I took the first possible opportunity to defect. You Americans have no ideology anymore. You can do business with the communists; build industrial plants for them, give them airplanes for free, form a military alliance even! Just watch, it will end up costing you eventually. As for the Nazis, they are probably the worst possible force to be with, but there is no alternative! Nobody else is at war with the Soviet Union. Anyway, don't reply until you listen to Vladimir

Maximovich. He can explain it better than I can. I expect he'll come over today."

While Pavel Nikitich was finishing his arguments he was already engaged in scanning the bookshelves for something interesting to read. Karl willingly took leave of him and went to check if Vixey had woken up yet.

Pavel found another notable book by Hesse, *Der Steppenwolf*, and due to their discussion of Hesse that morning, was interested to compare this text and remind himself what was written here. He remembered it being a complex, Jungian-influenced novel that was also well ahead of the times with its risqué depictions of drug use (opium, cocaine, and psychedelics) and liberated, immodest relations. Reading through the middle section, he suddenly came to the conclusion that Maria was the most important aspect of the book. Why had I not realized that before?- he thought. Nothing would be possible without her. This book would not make sense without Maria. She alone is the one solution to all the problems raised – she is the most important element. Was this intentional on the part of Hesse? Or did he reveal this fundamental truth inadvertently?

It was probably the recent emphasis on Vixey in Pavel's thoughts that caused this realization. He put the book aside and took another look at the shelves. In an obscure place he happened to find a familiar Turgenev book. It was *Nakanúne* (*On the Eve*), translated into German and given the awkward title of *Am Vorabend*. Pavel was curious to see how well it was translated and sat down to look at it briefly. However, he became immersed and started reading page after page....

*   *   *

Karl, after leaving the library, went to look for Vixey and found her in her room putting on stockings. He asked, "Vix, *chérie*, how do you feel after last night?"

She looked at him, replying, "Very good, actually. Did you have breakfast yet?"

"Not yet."

"Well, I'm almost ready..." She was standing and had the tip of her foot on top of the padded stool at her dressing table. She was putting on the second stocking now, drawing it up along her leg from her foot to the middle of her thigh, securing it there with a clip from her garter. Then she slipped into a pair of Mary Jane pumps, the heels of which had a 'teacup handle' shaped like an elongated, medial S. The shoes were in white patent leather with the trim and teacup handle colored indigo. She suddenly became taller again and it was remarkable, as she moved around, how endless her legs looked. Throwing on a simple black shirt-dress with three-quarter length frill-cuff sleeves, she went out the door with Karl, only returning quickly to get an ultramarine sash belt. She finished tying it around herself as they walked downstairs.

> Give me but what this ribbon bound
> Take all the rest the sun goes round.[*]

She displayed beautiful dexterity in descending the staircase in her high heels, at some moments placing one hand on her hip. She had no need of the railing; every movement conveyed an appearance of both German mechanical precision and light airiness.

Landon and Fadiman were actually having lunch already at this time. Vixey suggested to Karl an idea she came up with: to take a trip into Freiburg. Karl liked the idea – it would enable him to spend some time with her alone while engaged in an interesting diversion. Although it was not without some risk, he thought he would be safe with her, since she knew the locality. They agreed to go

---

[*] Edmund Waller, in his poem about slender waists such as her's.

tomorrow. He asked, "What about Baden-Baden as well, or would that be too far you think?"

Vixey couldn't reply – she had stuffed her mouth full of chocolate. She just shook her head and at length said, "No, it's two and a half hours to Baden-Baden; that's too far. Swiss Basel would be ideal but they won't let you across the border with your non-German papers! So Freiburg is the best place we could go."

Chocolate for her was a staple viand. It was not plain chocolate that Vixey was eating, but criollo cacao from the cloud forests on the Colombian-Venezuelan border, in a 75% purity. In ordinary times this would be five times more expensive than medium-quality chocolate. However, since the transportation cost from Caracas to the processing plants in Zürich has gone up for everything, it has become less expensive compared to other chocolate even while becoming significantly more expensive compared to non-imported foods. The cost differential of chocolate quality had narrowed in percentage terms.

Since the war, the chocolate came to Switzerland no longer through Italian Genova, the closest port, but through Bordeaux. Then after the British naval blockade tightened around Bordeaux, it would have to come in through Lisbon or London and from there by plane.

Karl commented, "Don't you eat too much chocolate, perhaps?"

"Every once in a while, it's necessary to indulge in some good chocolate."

"Every few days?"

"No, I mean every few hours... But if I have to, I can go a day or two without any chocolate. Not any more than that!"

*   *   *

Walking through the house, Vixey heard the sound of heated arguments going on in Russian. She entered a room and saw that Pavel Nikitich and Vladimir Maximovich had opened up a series of maps and were having a sort of debate over them, probably on some points of military strategy. She wandered into another room, where she saw the Americans doing the same thing. They had spread a large map over a table and were deliberating over it. Vixey's cat lay sleeping on a corner of the map. Earlier, when Karl and the others had come in to use the room, the cat was sleeping in the middle of the table, rolled up into a ball. They had to pick it up and place it somewhere else in order to lay the map down but the cat returned to sleep on the table again, on top of the map.

Vixey suddenly recalled that she still had no access to a phone or the freedom to walk past the vicinity of the house. She confronted Karl about this. He paused at this unexpected request and didn't reply for a second. Seeing his initial reaction she crossed her arms and looked at him crossly, frowning. He laughed and acquiesced. Karl had the delicacy to realize how insulting it would be to her sensibility to even hesitate about this at this point. She was glad and left him with what he was doing before. She planned to call Evelina and other people later.

Landon asked, "What just happened?"

Karl had to translate what they spoke about, "I promised to return the phone connexions to her, and mailing stationary; whatever else we kept from her."

The lieutenants were incensed. He was placing their lives at stake as well, just based on her word. Karl reassured them and reminded them to respect his decisions.

Vixey lay down on a dark red leather divan to read *La Reine Margot*. She was lying on her stomach and had the book on the armrest. Pavel Nikitich walked in, passing through on his way back to the library. She had almost blended in to the dark divan with her black dress and black hair, except for her white shoes with those medial S shapes on the heels. It was the first time he had seen Vixey since the drinking last night. Was it really just last night? – It seemed much longer to him. He said *guten Tag* to her and she replied but didn't move from her occupation.

"How are you?" he asked.

"Good."

"These shoes are interesting," he remarked, lifting one of them by the S, causing her leg to bend up.

"Herr Oberst, I am grateful to you for the work you're doing in the Wehrmacht and in the past with my father. It's too bad our government is so antagonistic."

"I'm glad that something I do can be of service to you. And yes, our interests are aligned, indeed."

"Since you are here," she said, "Would you mind taking a look at this French text? I'm confused about the tenses in this paragraph."

Pavel drew up a chair that was nearby and leaned forward to look at the text. This required such a lethal proximity to her that for a few seconds he forgot that he knew French at all, even though it was almost as good as his German. However, he composed himself and was able to adequately explain what the specific meaning was.

"Aha," said Vixey.

As she continued to look at the pages, Pavel reached for a white chess king on a shelf right behind the divan and traced it along her back, just barely touching her with the king's cross. She told him to stop and made a movement with her hand but then immediately regretted saying anything because it felt good. She kept reading and enjoyed the subtle touch that would have been less than nothing had she done it herself, but was so different when someone else did it.

Her hair was hanging over her shoulder, leaving her neck exposed. Seeing this tempted Pavel and he started to massage her neck.

"*Que faites-vous?*" she asked.

"*Rien.*"

She put her head down on top of the pages of the book. He continued for another minute, then thought it was enough and said his *au revoir*.

After he left Vixey continued reading, then fatigue overcame her because of the late night yesterday and she fell asleep.

> ...and her face so fair
> Stirr'd with her dream,
> as rose-leaves with the air.[*]

Pavel returned to the library as he was originally planning, but was too dazed to read. The lines danced on the page. Unconditionally, he was driven outside and he *traversa au travers de la forêt* (traversed through the forest), walking for a distance of several kilometers.

He was simply staggered by her beauty, and the closeness and contact. *Elle est belle à ravir,*[†] he thought. With her hair dropped to one side, an alluring metal clip was visible on her ear, made of conjoined small silvery pieces, some shaped like almonds, some resembling leaves with acute points. It covered the entire perimeter of her ear, something extraordinary that he had never seen before.

---

[*] *Don Juan*, IV.29.
[†] Could mean something along the lines of 'entrancingly beautiful'.

Chapter XI

> The man who has no sense of history is
> like a man who has no ears or eyes.
> HITLER

A few hours later, Vladimir Maximovich came to the house and sat down with Karl, who was just about to have afternoon tea in the drawing room. Vixey awoke from her delightfully unintentional post-brunch sleep, so now she had coffee with them. Pavel Nikitich was in the library by this time and Vixey made sure to offer him coffee as well.

To have something *dolče* with the coffee, Vixey brought a plate of various berries with a good amount of *crème Chantilly* on the side. (The lace lining her sleeves was also Chantilly). The *crème* had been made from a mixture of heavy cream and confectioners' sugar, with an electric whisk. Pavel noticed that there was *yezhevika* (blackberry), *zemlyanika, brusnika,* and *golubika* (untranslatable European berries).

Incidentally, the word *ежевика, ye-zhe-vika,* always reminded him of a certain Vika Smolkina, a smoking-hot young blonde girl from Smolensk with whom he gathered blackberries in a smoldering summer long ago. Henceforth, despite the years passed, the word *Vika* still always had an arresting and magical effect on him. A melancholy effect, since that Vika had married, went to live in Minsk. There was no trace of her. The blackberries, which had the double connection of the taste and the embedded name, brought Pavel to a sudden involuntary memory, as did Proust's notorious *madeleine* mixed with tea in *À la recherche du temps perdu.*

Vixey somehow managed to drop some whipped cream on her plaited black witchwench[*] hair, where it

---

[*] Credit to Nabokov for this word.

stayed, a visible contrast to the sleek blackness of the tresses. Someone indicated it to her and she swept it off with her finger and ate it. After her sleep, she had arranged her hair in two soft plaits. Away from the city she preferred a simple style that she could do herself but in Berlin or Munich she could be more inventive with plaits, wrapping them around her head and inlaying them with lilacs and *Veilchen.*[*] Her visits to the *coiffeuse* took hours sometimes, but she used the time effectively by bringing a book. She thought it was a pleasant place to read, almost as good as a train. The acoustics of the high ceilings muted any distracting conversations that may have occurred around her. Later, flipping through pages of books, she was continually finding strands of her hair in them as a result of having read them while her hair was being styled.

To inlay a braid with a bright ribbon was another style she liked. Or sometimes she made a *chignon* with a small golden dagger gripped into it. The art of the *coiffeuse* seemed without limit. For instance, another idea was to arrange her hair in two soft, swaying loops on both sides of her face. The sleek elliptical arrangements of hair, seeming each of one piece, would reach almost to her shoulders.

Straight long hair, as she had most of the time here in Baden, was her preferred style, but even that took a certain amount of work to maintain in a perfect state. Her hair was black, but certain chemicals, applied once a month, could be used to make it even blacker. Adding various oils and running a heated metal comb through her hair improved texture and straightness. Once Vixey didn't have time to arrange a fancy style for an important state *soirée* so she went with her hair straight down and also wore a headband with triangular cat ears on it – black so that they merged in color with her hair. She caused a sensation – four marriage proposals were delivered to her father. Berlin society had

---

[*] Violets. „*Es war ein herzigs Veilchen*" – Goethe.

not seen velvet cat ears as an ornament on a lady since the 20s.

Karl asked Vladimir Maximovich to finally talk about the reasons behind his service in the Wehrmacht, since there was much he didn't understand. It seemed to him to be even more objectionable than being a regular German soldier, because those were required to fight for Germany while these Russians had to actively take steps to switch sides and volunteer.

Vladimir Maximovich began by talking about his capture in the Battle of Kiev, "An enormous encirclement had taken place, and along with my 26th Army, the 5th, 21st, and 37th had to surrender. Forty divisions in all and about half a million men. There was no other choice. I knew that by surrendering I would probably not be able to return to the Soviet Union, but actually the first feeling was relief. My brother had been arrested in '38, and although I had ties to top military and party circles and in addition a tsarist army record, somehow I slipped by the purge. From then on, however, for the next three years I expected that I could be arrested any day, at any time. Then I found myself able to escape this constant fear of arrest by surrendering to the Germans. My only worry at the time was to make sure my niece and my wife, who were in Kiev, stayed in German-occupied territory – which they did. I have no other family in the Soviet Union, so I do not risk retribution against relatives for defecting. Initially we had ambitious plans for overthrowing the USSR and discussed this with the German generals at the front. Marshals von Bock and von Isarberg sent a project proposal in fall 1941 for the creation of a *Russian government* based in Smolensk with its own army. The reply came back from Berlin: They was told by war minister Keitel that such thoughts cannot even be discussed with the Führer...

"So our troops were spread out among German commanders and later on many of them were transferred to

France, Italy, and other places, which completely destroyed their *raison d'être*. We generals and colonels went to read books and play *durak* (the main Russian card game) in various camps. We met General Vlasov and joined his conspiratorial group while at Lichterfelde, southwest Berlin – the military intelligence building at the intersection of Viktoriastraße and Sophienstraße."

Vixey interrupted, "My two first names: those two streets!"

"Ah, interesting coincidence. Sophia is your second name? Very nice..."

Pavel recollected his impressions on first arriving at the Lichterfelde compound.[*] The terrible gloom (*мрачность*) of the war and political situation was somewhat mitigated, for him, by seeing the white street sign saying, "Viktoriastraſʒe". (In Berlin signage, an "ſʒ" is used for the eszett).

It's important to have a personal æsthetic preference for names. When one deals with people one hasn't met, the name is their only aspect that differentiates them æsthetically. It has become harder in the modern age to discern class differences in names. However, national differences exist and they indicate that sensibility towards æsthetics of names can he higher in some countries than others. Thus the classic name Marguerite has the short forms Margot or Gretchen in France and Germany but degenerates in English countries to Molly or Peg. And these are not even the worst of English names; I do not even want to list some of them. Genève stays just as nice in English: Geneva, but becomes Genf for some reason in German. Livorno is called Leghorn by the British.

Veronica in Hoffmann's *The Golden Pot* (*Der goldne Topf*) is immediately charming and attractive to the reader

---

[*] It is still there, and currently houses one of the two headquarters of the BND (*Bundesnachrichtendienst*), Germany's intelligence agency.

as soon as she is introduced, and her name is a substantial part of the reason for it. Whereas Henry James' *The Golden Bowl* appears that it might be an interesting novel, but it is hard to start reading it because the primary girl's name is simply Maggie. German on average is better in terms of names than English; Russian is better but only with regard to female names (many of which are borrowed from French or Greek). Meanwhile French has the most appealing names for both places and people, for instance the beautiful name Véronique Savatier.

An appealing name adds a layer of appeal anywhere it is placed, viz. Sofia City in Bulgaria, Ada Parish in Idaho, a restaurant called Chez Severine or Chez Odette. *Ceteris paribus*, it is better to live in a County of Ada than a County of Murdock. Better than a hypothetical Church of Crucifixion or Church of St. John are the Sophienkirche in Dresden or the Sofiysky Sobor (Sophia Cathedral) in Kiev. In English countries hardly any streets are named after a Sophia but in Germany almost half of cities and towns have this. The most notable Sophienstraßen are in Dresden and in Baden-Baden. Victoria had better success in British Empire countries because of the former Empress; consequently a state in Australia and a city in British Columbia are named after her.

Pavel was understandably pleased that if he had to be confined in a military base in Berlin, that it would be at least on a pleasant tree-lined *уличка* called Viktoriastraße. However, he did not go as far as the *zdravomyslyashchevo bezymiya* (sober-minded insanity) of Sidorov, another Red Army soldier, writing letters without a recipient to an illusory Victoria. Sidorov is from the genius story by Babel, «*Солнце Италии*» (The Sun of Italy), in the collection *Red Cavalry*.

As Vladimir Maximovich spoke, Vixey was playing with her collar, which had big triangular tips. She turned it upwards and it actually was big enough to extend past her cheeks and reach just under her blue eyes. It looked *très chic* on her. She happened to make eye contact with Pavel while holding one of the collar triangles with her hand and smiling, bringing him suddenly back into the present from his reminisces. Her smile burned his soul, consuming it in flames. A moment later, when re-crossing her legs, she went a little further and double-crossed them, such that the upper leg twisted under and again slightly over the other one. She didn't know how this looked from this side – how svelte it made her legs look. During this Pavel was thinking, "This is too much!" He left the room for a few minutes on the pretext of getting something to eat, in order to try to Come to Terms with all this.

Vladimir Maximovich was continuing about Vlasov and Berlin: "After Viktoriastraße, making some political progress, we set up a camp in Dabendorf just south of Berlin, which became the headquarters of the movement. Since Soviet power solidified in 1921, after the crushing of the Tambov rebellion, Andrei Andreyovich Vlasov has been the only Russian to lead a political and military campaign against the Soviet Union. Earlier, during the war against Germany, he was a very capable commander leading the Soviet 2nd Shock Army. He was captured because he was refused permission to retreat and consequently was encircled by the Germans. From my conversations with him it is apparent he has the depth of vision, humility, and other characteristics of a great leader. Also in our group were generals Malyshkin and Zhilenkov, very interesting personalities. We created a new Russian flag based on the old *Andreyevski flag* of the Imperial Russian Navy, all white with a blue/red saltire, and hoisted it over Dabendorf. To us, the freedom of speech and ability to challenge authority that we saw in the Third Reich was an enormous contrast to the Soviet Union and we thought we could make some progress...

"Despite almost certain death if caught again by the Soviet Union; despite Hitler's reputation and sayings, between 800,000 and 1,000,000 soldiers defected from the Soviet to the Germany army. These are very significant numbers. Why were there so many? Remember what Hitler was saying, as we now know in retrospect: He talked about destroying and removing from the map Leningrad and Moscow; exploitative colonization of Ukraine and Western Russia with Germans living in separate towns and almost no assimilation; enslaving people; and destroying Russian culture and education. The majority of Slavs he considered *untermensch*. Those that didn't know or didn't believe this saw the results in practice in the occupation zone...

"What could have made so many Russians defect to Germany? Is it possible, I ask, that there were so many Nazi traitors in Russia who hated their homeland and people? Why are the traitors in Norway, England, and France numbered in the single, or at most double digits, but here a million? Or why have such vast numbers of traitors not appeared in the prior war against Germany in 1914? And in the war against Napoleon in 1812? No, what happened now was that our POWs in German hands saw that they were forgotten and betrayed by the Soviet Union – classified as criminals and left to starve. And both POWs and soldiers who were not yet captured saw something else: That Hitler's plans were already in existence in Russia, and worse! Let me explain, lest you think the Soviet Union is in any way a normal country...

"Conditions in the Soviet Union during peace were worse than the worst wartime conditions in the West. The cities are destitute and overcrowded; the countryside is even poorer and sometimes descends to cannibalism. There is a gulag labor camp population the size of some European countries (15-25 million), and being replenished as people expire. The gulag could be called 'exterminating-labor camps' and anyone can be arrested at any time for it, without a reason. (Mass arrests on the basis of race are common). Land collectivization was achieved by first putting to death millions of the most prosperous peasants and then making forced labor serfs of the rest. Sometimes 100% of their food is taken, as it was in Ukraine in 1933, where 4-7 million were killed in that one episode. (Would any kind of rumors about Germany frighten someone who has already seen that?) This is enough for a summary; I just wanted to briefly remark on what a socialist country looks like."

Karl remarked, "I knew of a few of these things because I had met and talked with the economist von Mises as well as reading some books he recommended. Still, I did not know the extent of what you described. Some of our high-ranking military officers also know a little about the Soviet Union as I do, but if you look at the common man in America, he knows nothing. I must mention a new American film that came out just now; our division was able to see it in Rome. At first I thought it was just highly misleading, but now I understand that it is simply dirty propaganda. It is called 'Mission to Moscow' and was made by President Roosevelt in order to influence people to support having Stalin as an ally. The Soviet Union is portrayed in the film as a rich, normal, free country 'sincerely devoted to world peace'. The Soviet invasions of Poland and the Baltic states in the years 1939-40 are justified as tactics for defensive reasons against Germany. Caviar and all sorts of nice things are plentiful. The victims of the great purge of 1937-38 were all Trotskyite saboteurs and agents of Germany..."

Here Vladimir Maximovich could not restrain himself. He stood up, crying, "Trotskyite saboteurs! All the millions who were arrested in that wave!?"

Karl replied, "The film doesn't mention millions, just a dozen people or so."

"Remarkable! Do you know that the real basis for arrests in those years was the assignment of numerical arrest quotas to every local NKVD jurisdiction?"

"Another thing the film mentioned was that the USSR seeks to improve the lot of the common man, just with different methods. And there's nothing objective to necessarily say that their method isn't good. Also that Stalin is misunderstood as no leader ever has been, but history will show him to be a great builder for the benefit of mankind."

Vixey said, "I always knew your president was some kind of communist. This is the same Roosevelt who won your 1940 election promising no involvement in foreign wars and then immediately proceeded to effectively ally with Russia. The same who maintains a secret correspondence with the head of the US Communist Party, with whom he discusses foreign affairs."

"I seriously doubt he's a secret communist, though," said Karl. "He has too much public exposure for such a thing to have remained unnoticed. It would look completely different if he truly were one."

"Ok, not a real communist – I was exaggerating – but at least a fascist; that much is clear. He favors state control but without a revolutionary aspect. I don't know why he's so pro-Soviet though."

"I don't know his politics," Vladimir Maximovich remarked, "but the fact that he had this film made shows he cannot be trusted and this depresses me. If this is the version of events that your president actually wants the people to believe, it means he wants to influence them in favor of policies that will be pro-Soviet! That is not good for any of us. Only for Stalin."

Karl asked, "By the way, about Stalin- I have been interested for a while in whether Stalin himself represents communism or not? This is because I've seen many Russians say that they are against Stalin but not against the Bolshevik communist system."

"Yes, even in our movement there are many young officers who say they're still committed to Marxism/Leninism and are only fighting against Stalin's tyranny. They typically owe their military careers to the Soviet Union, and have been under the influence of its propaganda their entire lives, so their mistakes in judgment could be understood. Some of them continue to have an almost religious faith in the coming of some kind of imaginary good communism. They simply do not know anything about Stalin's predecessors. It is true that Stalin is not such an ideological communist as, comparatively, the old Bolsheviks were: Lenin, Trotsky, Zinoviev, Kamenev, Preobrazhensky, Radek, etc. But that is a good thing! Stalin and Hitler both have some limits. Lenin, however, was entirely without them. He referred to people as insects. His means of control of the population of Russia included the use of poison gas attacks, military artillery, mass shooting of hostages, and widespread innovation of medieval tortures. It is unfortunate that many Western socialists, while they might disapprove of Stalin's tyranny, say his only shortcoming is his deviation from Leninism, when in fact that is his only good part! Communism means compulsion; thus the more communism, the greater percentage of people in labor camps. In the system that Lenin established, a successor like Stalin is actually a mild one...

"After Lenin and now with Stalin, at this point no regime had ever existed in the world as bloody as the USSR. I also want to emphasize that even for the majority of population that never experienced brutality or famine, the harm from the state is always felt through the oppressive poverty and ever-present control. This affects everyone – except for the *nomenklatura* and a handful of large-scale thieves."

Vladimir Maximovich's words caused Pavel Nikitich to reflect privately on his remembrances of the Soviet Union. He thought, Yes, it's true – the situation is such that you have hardworking people who get practically nothing for all the work they do throughout their lives. No accomplishment is possible. He thought of how hard it was just to secure decent housing. Since housing is determined by government 'planning', there is massive overcrowding in the cities. After all, in true socialism nothing is supposed to belong to the individual; even privacy and space must be shared with strangers. Thus nowhere else in the world do people hate each other as much as they do in the enviable brotherhood of the workers' paradise! Even more so than the dwellers of Marrakesh who are accustomed to centuries of Oriental close-living and squalor. Russians have in their own lifetime seen living spaces made for one family now accommodating three. Government agents would measure one's space, and if a person occupied more than 3 square meters, it is likely someone else would be allocated there.[*]

Meanwhile, Vladimir Maximovich was continuing to talk about the regime and the war, "In addition many people had family members killed by the state or who had simply disappeared. How can they be criticized for being unwilling to fight for the Soviet Union? Meanwhile any show of annoyance at the Bolshevik slogans or other dissent is noted and acted upon. It was not possible to revolt; the state was too firmly in place to possibly topple it. Finally with the war came a real chance! The Germans were greeted as liberators by many people. Commanders in the Red Army sometimes defected immediately. Major Kononov asked who from his regiment will follow him. Not a single man said no; the entire regiment went over to the Germans...

"The great cavalry hosts of the Cossack atamans triumphantly emerged from somewhere. Where did they get so many horses, after the destitution of 20 years of post-civil war repression? Leaders from the civil war who everyone thought were dead came out of hiding. Finally after so many long years the momentous day came at last for revenge against the Bolshevik apparatus and Stalin...

---

[*] After the war, if a family had less than 4.5 square meters per person it was entitled to go on a one or two decade waiting list for a different apartment. It was a similar situation in the occupied Eastern European cities, with most constructed housing being of the 'Soviet apartment bloc' type.

"German Wehrmacht soldiers were shocked and disturbed at the country they saw, which until that point had been completely sealed from the West. Communist agents had for decades spread the belief throughout Europe that Russia was a Workers' Paradise. The soldiers saw the opposite, and immediately understood why they were being seen as liberators by the population...

"As more and more time passed, the most absurd thing happened: the German high command themselves destroyed the favorable attitudes towards Germany. At the start of the war, few in the Wehrmacht actually knew about Hitler's colonization ideas and those that did, found it hard to believe. Then they saw the resulting subjugation of the Eastern territories by the SS and *Reichskommissariats*, far harsher than any other Reich occupation. For instance, Leningrad was besieged for the purpose of killing its population. In the countryside the Nazis decided to keep in place the inhuman collective farm system. The Wehrmacht protested: generals such as Bock, Halder, Tresckow, and Gersdorff. Even Generalfeldmarschall Brauchitsch, the *Oberbefehlshaber des Heeres* (Commander-in-Chief of the Army). General von Pannwitz, of the XV Cossack Cavalry Corps went and plainly told Hitler that he was wrong. Besides the serious ethical concerns, it was also quite counterproductive for the war effort. For Stalin, the biggest fear was that Germany would capitalize on the peoples' goodwill and spark a civil war in Russia. The Wehrmacht likewise knew that the support of the 70 or more million Soviet population in the occupied zone was essential for a favorable war outcome. Captain Strikfeldt of the Army High Command was writing and distributing articles about the need to grow that support.* But Hitler and the SS ignored

---

* Wilfred Strik-Strikfeldt, a Baltic German and a close associate of General Vlasov, left behind his memoirs, an important perspective into the Russian Liberation movement and the personal thoughts of Vlasov.

all these protests and advice. If Hitler was only concerned about the threat of Bolshevism, he would have stood aside after the preventative invasion and let the Russian Liberation Movement start a civil war, which Vlasov claims he would win with only a starting force of 200,000. Hitler simultaneously had various other motives – like securing resources, to preserve his term in power at any cost. His racist policies fit in with this. Brauchitsch was relieved from command, and Hitler personally assumed the duties of Army commander. Our hopes, as well as the hopes of German officers in the field, for a full-scale collaboration with the Russian people, faded. However, defections continued to happen. And in addition, Russian POWs were coming into the Wehrmacht because they had little other choice besides starvation. Let me explain this important point...

"A Russian soldier is prohibited from surrendering. The sentence of death in the penal code is apparently still in force. This led to two consequences for the vast numbers who had been captured: they became criminals under Soviet law and liable to be executed or sent to gulag upon their return to Russia; and they are not given food or mail like prisoners from other countries. Stalin has officially denied a recognition of their existence and refuses to abide by the Geneva Convention which the USSR has not signed. A statement came from the USSR: 'There are no Russian prisoners of war! The Russian soldier fights on till death.' As a result British/American POWs live normally because those countries and Germany follow the Convention. The Russian ones in the meantime are on the point of starvation, relying on scraps of food from Germany. Large numbers of POWs were forced to join as volunteers for Germany regardless of their political or national beliefs, because they were rejected by the Soviet Union and left to starve. Stalin already considered them to be hostile 'Germans' as soon as they surrendered."

Karl asked, "Why is it so important for Stalin to punish Russians even who are captured without any fault of their own?"

Vladimir Maximovich replied, "It has to do with preventing any possible counterrevolutionary thought via comparison with the West that I mentioned before. The measures they take to isolate people from the West are truly extraordinary. For instance, in the great famine of 1921-22, many Western relief workers came to help by distributing food. All Russians who ended up having personal contact with these Westerners were arrested because they might have become contaminated with poisonous Western influences. Note that although millions were dying of this famine, authorities still devoted their attention to finding and destroying people who had talked with foreigners.[*] If a Russian, at one point in his life had been photographed standing next to a foreigner, that would be immediate grounds for an arrest for espionage. Already Finland has returned some Russian POWs from the Winter War, and there is no information of anybody ever seeing one of them again...

"Along with POWs, I believe that the millions of civilians and refugees who have voluntarily or involuntarily found themselves outside the Soviet Union will be arrested as well if caught. This is the degree to which the Soviet Union dislikes its citizens to see the outside world...[†]

---

[*] Another irony is that the Soviet government was *exporting grain* during this famine. In addition to inducing famine in the Volga region by taking away all their food and aggressively punishing villagers for under-producing, Lenin also sold some of the food for hard currency.

[†]According to Solzhenitsyn, their chief crime was being in a foreign country outside of Soviet control. That is why POWs were treated the same as people who went to Germany and worked in their industry, or anyone else who ended up somewhere in the West. It did not matter if the POWs escaped and rejoined the Red Army, or did nothing but sit in German camps, or if they were

"Most foolish Westerners, mimicking the sayings of the communists, call us traitors. But if we manage to overthrow the communists, the perspective will change. Even now, thousands more are still joining us despite the high odds of failure and of the grim necessity to kill our countrymen, some of whom are even being forced at gunpoint to fight us. My own brother could potentially be among those forced to fight on the other side in a Black Division. But if we refused to fight for reasons such as these, nobody would benefit in the long run because the Soviet Union would still continue its wars and tyranny. Our movement is the most epic and tragic in modern history.

---

sitting in internment in neutral Sweden. They typically all got the same term: ten years imprisonment plus five years exile. Most were arrested before returning to the Soviet Union. Some managed to return to their homes, but most of these were arrested anyway later, in 1946-1949. Interestingly, under the Soviet penal code, Article 58-§1b, surrendering to the enemy should more correctly have been punished by execution. Evidently the soft ten-year sentences were a *special leniency* from Stalin. In addition, anyone who communicated with the Germans while living in territories occupied by them (e.g. all of Ukraine) was under suspicion, but only a select percentage was arrested. For instance, in 1946-47 there was a wave of arrests of former "Foreigners' Girlfriends", under 7-§35 – "Socially Dangerous Elements". Stalinist persecution was not about guilt over specific acts but about "social danger".

However, those Russians who actually fought against the Soviet state by participating in the Vlasov movement were a different matter. These received the harshest sentences: death or a term of gulag that would likely lead to death. Not only the sentences were harsh– at least 1,000 Vlasov officers "died during NKVD interrogations" (were tortured to death). Many were killed as soon as being identified, or during the transit. This is enough to illustrate what the prevailing attitudes were towards them in the Soviet Union. For decades to follow, the Vlasov movement was strongly condemned on an almost unanimous basis in the country.

Most of our soldiers would rather die than return to the Soviet Union...

"In Vinnytsa, the Wehrmacht accidentally found 95 mass graves with 100 people in each. Evidently, in the hasty retreat, Stalin was having the NKVD kill all people in prisons and labor camps who it could not relocate. Liberated prisoners would have been the most likely people to join and aid the Germans. In Lwów the NKVD didn't have much time before the Germans got there, so they resorted to the most hasty methods of killing – tossing grenades into prison cells or just throwing people into pits. Does a State that kills its own people to prevent them from potentially joining the enemy – and creates the terror of penal battalions – have any right to talk about a Great Patriotic War (the official Russian name for the war) and to determine who is or isn't a traitor?...

"Moreover, it's not a defensive or a 'Patriotic' war at all! To be more exact, it's a war of communist conquest that had a temporary setback. The interruption and the necessity to go on the defensive was caused by the unexpected speed and strength of Germany in 1939-41. But this does not change the original Soviet goals for conquering Europe. Without Soviet ambitions, there would have been no war entirely! Now the Red Army's drive west is continuing, near the same positions the armies would have started from in 1941 if they weren't delayed for three years!...

"Sometimes I recall the brutality of the invading German armies against the Russian population in 1941. But how can I hate them, without also hating my own people? Wouldn't we have done the same things to them if we had the chance? Of course! And more. It is irrational to hate only one of the two regimes: both are socialist, both seek perpetual war as a means to enlarge their power. Both are in the same category, although of course the Nazi system is a much more moderate one. (Germany still has a middle class; I have seen ordinary people with watches, automobiles, private flats and homes)...

"Recall that if the Soviet Union wanted to avoid war in Europe, it could have simply not divided Poland with Germany. It could have not created a nonaggression pact with Germany backed up with vital trade agreements. The Soviet Union also could have avoided war by not arming Germany from 1922-33 for purposes of a communist revolution. Eleven years of secretly arming Germany are not indicative of peaceful intentions for central Europe...

"As for the possibility that Germany ever had a chance of defeating and occupying Russia without the help of Russians – it is plainly impossible. The premise that we are helping Hitler win *his* war is inherently flawed because this was never a possibility. The amount of Russian cooperation that is required to defeat Russia is so large as to necessarily diminish Germany's role to that of merely an ally! Russia is not like Paris. French Provence or Brittany does not have factories churning out tanks and ammunition that constantly resupply the front. But Siberia is where the largest industrial plants in the world are located, and they are supported by vast resources of energy, metals, and manpower, plus whatever supplies America provides. Taking Moscow would do nothing, as the government is somewhere else, inaccessible. Germany's bombing capability at such distances is zero...

"But Hitler could have easily brought down the rotten structure if he compromised on his colonization goals and trusted Vlasov to act. Stalin thought the war was already over in 1941; that was why he was so despondent. He did not count on Hitler then making such a mistake: to throw away such advantages of the peoples' popular support."

*   *   *

The room had filled with so much smoke from the three men it made Vixey cough. She left briefly to get more tea and coffee. Pavel was granted a complete view of her walking away towards the kitchen – her long legs crossing with each step, beneath the flared black skirt of her dress narrowing to her svelte waist, where the ends of her black hair bounced against that ultramarine ribbon. The sight was asphyxiating.

With her gone, Vladimir Maximovich was able to talk about something he didn't want to mention in her presence in order not to disturb her. He said, "A lot depends right now on the speed of the Red Army advance. If they are too successful we will not have enough time to even mobilize our small army. I hope that the defenders in Prussia and Poland at this moment can hold their lines. Germany must throw everything into these lines if it wants to prevent a Soviet occupation of the entire country. Let me tell you what happened this very month, which I just found out. There was a temporary break by the Red Army into East Prussia, near the Lithuanian border. This is already close to the gates of Königsberg. The Soviets were later beaten back, but they had already made their first entrance onto German soil. In the villages they came upon, they murdered everyone: men, women, and children. There are also reports of civilians crucified or dragged to death behind tanks...*

"Prussia is gone as a nation if nothing is done to halt the Red Army. If we fail, it is not just Russia that is at stake, it is Germany and France, and everything in between. I anticipate that, even assuming the Soviet Union's westward movement is stopped by the US/UK, Germany will probably be broken up into small pieces like before the 19th century

---

* The subject of the immense anti-German reprisals and deportations after the war is usually ignored in traditional accounts of history, as if to make the point that ethnic cleansing is justified as long as the victims are German. They were undertaken not only by the Red Army, but by Czechs and Poles. Lately a number of scholarly books have appeared about the postwar environment, for instance Keith Lowe's *Savage Continent*.

unification, with the Soviet Union continually trying to get more that it doesn't occupy already."

Pavel Nikitich added, "Yes, the outlook does not look good. Vladimir Maximovich is overly optimistic, in my opinion. The situation in Europe is falling apart drastically. He says that the army must hold the lines in Prussia. But Soviet artillery is amassing in mammoth numbers, approaching the front in endless convoys of machinery and ammunition. The Red Army has switched over to measuring artillery strikes not in tons but in kilotons. Also, they have introduced a new and devastating weapon: the *Katyusha* multiple rocket launcher. A battalion of 48 of these truck-mounted launchers can deliver 52 tons of high explosives in less than 10 seconds! It is a more concentrated and sudden destruction than traditional heavy artillery. The rockets, when launched, make a sort of howling sound – that is the most terrible thing you can hear on the battlefield. But alas, we need to continue."

Pavel continued to reflect for a while after he finished talking and the others resumed their conversation. He recalled how a few days ago he had a dream in which he died – the dream was so vivid it made him absolutely convinced that he was dead. Then he woke up and his first immediate thought was, of course, genuine disappointment.

The situation in which he and hundreds of thousands of others in the ROA found themselves was unique among the various combatants in the war. They had the singular situation of needing to fight to the death – since they were faced with an outcome of at least death, or possibly worse, if their side loses. If caught by the Soviet Union, their punishment would be severe.

There were, at times, groups of insurgents in this war who had found themselves in such a position, but not for such a long period of uncertainty and not on such a large scale, with so many people who had no other realistic choice except to do what they are doing.

Thinking about the war in general and its effect on civilians as well as soldiers, Pavel could not understand peoples' willingness to live. One of the worst aspects of the war, because of how many people it affected, was the vast scale of meaningless work that people were overcome with. This does not just mean rebuilding or working for others, but includes an endless amount of degrading things such as dragging buckets of water from a public pump a few blocks from one's apartment because indoor plumbing has been ruined. Dostoyevsky, in his great prison memoirs (*House of the Dead*), elaborates on the idea that work acquires a penal quality when it is compulsory, but the greatest torture is from work that is both compulsory and nonsensical. (And this exists to some degree in all our lives: All the years of schooling, consisting most of the time of pointless topics, strictly enforced by incompetent lecturers. Then followed by years of nothing but futile job searching... The rise of socialism everywhere in the West, as well as ever-increasing timespans required for specialization, lead to unemployment being a default condition for most people. And then, even with a job one still might not escape work that has a heavy aspect of absurd senselessness – *бессмысленность*.)

The war was consuming entire cities, burning the production of peoples' past labor and forcing the greatest amount of unproductive or destructive work ever seen. Pavel considered that one of the reasons more people did not kill themselves was because they are so astounded by how bad it is. There is a certain pride at passing through such awful hellishness. A daze of disbelief and almost a curiosity of how bad it could get. Also, constant threats to one's life boost one's vitality. To use an analogy, these are the differences between walking many kilometers to work in a grisly November rain or a severe January blizzard. The latter is easier to endure precisely because it is so much worse according to measurements of severity and may even be a threat to one's life; thus getting through it is an accomplishment and a defiance. It is for the same reason that E.A. Poe's mariner was unfazed at the risks he took in descending into the *maelström*. He was overcome by the awful sublimity. However, there is much more of the November rain in life than the January blizzard. If the latter doesn't kill one, eventually the November will.

Solidarity with others who are in the same situation helps, thought Pavel. But a negative thing is the presence of constantly cheerful people who have, no matter what, an irrational Leibnizian optimism- as described by Voltaire. Their optimism is actually insulting to the world's suffering, as Schopenhauer would put it. Pavel considered that they may have some kind of mental differences or an animalistic chemical in their blood that gives them this instinct of hope and makes them indefatigably hardworking and positive in the face of any hardship. Those people, who are the majority, would even wake up willingly to start the daily drudgery without being prodded by reveille. Reveille – which is the ghastliest moment of existence.

When considering the daily process of awakening and revivification, Pavel considered that a more proper word to describe it would be 'resurrection'. This term has connotations of something unnatural, and thus it fits, since the torture that men endure in reveille is something that exceeds the random malevolence of nature. The mind is forcibly torn from the deepest slumber and forced to fully function at a moment's notice. It resists the resurrection, firstly because it is impossible to regain full functionality so quickly, and secondly because it knows that another wretched day is beginning. After only a few moments comes the realization that the nightmare in one's memory is merely a recollection of the prior day. Now the moment of respite is over and the ordeals are beginning anew – the mind instinctually resists the continuation of another day. The body resists as well – various inexplicable pains such as those in the back are at their worst in the morning, making any motion painful. Psychologically it is unclear how the mind can by itself create physical pain in parts of the body but the effect is real. Additionally, after suddenly leaving sleep the eyes become bloodshot red – it burns to open them. This adds to the distraught, tortured appearance of the face upon waking.

Since full consciousness is not yet achieved, the entire effect is not felt of the pain enveloping the mind like a smoldering rag. Interestingly, because memory of events during semi-consciousness are not preserved well, it is forgotten later on how much pain was experienced. However, the trauma from the resurrection results in a lingering malaise that continues for a few hours, sometimes the first half of the day. Eventually the eyes and mind recover.

It is unsurprising that the NKVD's most effective method of interrogation was simply sleep deprivation. A confession one is given to sign that condemns one to death or gulag along with a list of one's acquaintances is usually a disagreeable thing to endorse. Yet many of these were signed quite willingly, just in order to be allowed a chance to sleep.

*   *   *

When Vixey returned, Vladimir Maximovich switched from current events in Prussia to those in Poland, "Also in the past two months we have seen, quite conclusively, that the Soviet Union is no friend of Poland either. Last month Germany crushed an uprising by the Polish Liberation Army. How did it start? It was actually urged by direct messages from Moscow, which insidiously called on the Poles to start their revolt, promising support. Then Stalin betrayed them by doing nothing and keeping the army camped within sight of Warsaw. Stalin also refused to allow the West to use Soviet airfields or airspace to help Warsaw with supplies! 85% of the city was destroyed after the fighting, the resistance crushed, and a massive amount of people killed. Think of what happens when the front of a major battle envelops a city of a million people. The desperate fighting occurred not only in the streets and in homes, but underground, in the dark sewers. Stalin then stated that the uprising was inspired by 'enemies of the Soviet Union'...[*]

"Churchill proposed sending planes to help Poland in defiance of Stalin. The rift between the eastern and western Allies could have occurred at this point over Poland, but Roosevelt's reply was a negative. He wrote to Churchill that he thought it would be disadvantageous to the overall war effort, which means that he did not want to lose Stalin's friendship...

"The Soviet goal in all this was accomplished – a destruction of the Polish resistance that would have opposed the communist occupation of Poland. The Polish government-in-exile in London now has no more resources and Poland will have a Soviet government."[†]

---

[*] When Warsaw was occupied, the NKVD arrested remaining Polish insurgents, with charges such as "fascism". After the war, it came into vogue in the Soviet Union to immediately brand any opposition from the West as fascism, a sort of *reductio ad Hitlerum* that implied that since all fascists were anti-communist, the reverse is true as well. This informal fallacy worked remarkably well in the coming decades of Soviet propaganda and distanced some people from capitalism, which at a fleeting glance could not offer proof that it was indeed less "fascist" than socialism.

Stalin solidified the notion that a multi-dimensional political spectrum could be compressed into a one-dimensional line with communism and fascism at either end. For decades the crowds are still confused by the misconceptions arising from this.

[†] The wrapping up of the war became paradoxical especially for those Poles serving in the British military. As the decision to hand Poland to the Soviet Union became known to them in 1945, they realized that they were in the ridiculous situation in which the Soviet Union was simultaneously their enemy and their ally. There were Polish pilots in the RAF who were being ordered, against their will, on the mission to bomb Dresden,- the stated purpose of which was to aid the advance of the Red Army – into Poland.

Returning to the subject of the Russian Liberation Army, Vladimir Maximovich said, "Like the Poles, the Russians are also caught in between two enemies and have few options. All these years we were tormented by Hitler's and Himmler's tight rein and distrust. We were not allowed a single step. Hitler could not allow the creation of a liberal state because he was incapable of cutting his loses, giving up Russian resources, and allowing for the past German war effort to lead to the creation of a powerful pro-Western state on his eastern border. Hitler would thus have only trusted Vlasov if he became a loyal subservient Nazi. But Vlasov did not bend; he openly opposes anti-Semitism and keeps with his liberal goals consistently despite two years of pressure. Vlasov talks about Washington and Franklin as his ideals of freedom-fighters. He advocates the creation of a European community of free, sovereign nations. In the past he was sending demands through whatever military channels he could regarding the poor conditions in German-occupied Russia and the status of the Liberation movement. Vlasov never accepted subservience and wanted an alliance instead. Churchill has already set the precedent on alliances with dictators, and Vlasov has compromised no more than Churchill has...

"Some Russians, even if they are strongly opposed to communism, view any cooperation with Germany as actions furthering Nazi crimes and their war of conquest. Thus they view us skeptically. But it is precisely against the harsh treatment of Russians in occupied territory that Vlasov and our colleagues, (both Russian and German) directed our efforts. We knew that an opposite policy was needed to gain the population's support and win the war. We tried unsuccessfully to change Nazi Germany from within, for the benefit of Russia and, as a consequence, all Europe...

"It required the catastrophes on the front of 1943-44 to cause Hitler's group to finally compromise a little. The

greatest misfortune of my life has been this tragic loss of
such an opportunity because of the stubbornness of these
idiots! Even as late as 1943 Himmler was calling Vlasov a
swine for saying Russia can only be conquered by Russians.
Vlasov was ordered to stop making public appearances,
even though his speeches in occupied Russia were bringing
in numerous supporters! We couldn't understand why
Hitler and his associates would be willing to seal their own
fate – their demise was growing more and more obvious.
Now, finally – a month ago – perhaps it is too late but
Himmler accepted the reality and met with Vlasov, allowing
him to start forming the army. It was our first meeting with
the German government. But the Führer, Hitler, still
persists in forbidding this army from growing beyond a few
divisions! We had hoped to have ten! At least next month
finally we will be inaugurating the official Russian
Liberation Committee in Prague, the precursor, hopefully,
of a free Russian state. I will make the trip there. The
Cossacks and the Serbian Corps have promised to send
representatives to Prague and to join us...

"Hitler was given an extraordinary strategic advantage,
facing a country with an army unwilling to fight and
providing one million defectors. And he squandered it all
with his idiotic politics! The only thing that would exceed
the misfortune of the scorn from the Germans would be the
same scorn from the Americans and British. In our fight for
freedom we have been betrayed by Germany. Now our last
hope is to rely on America – but it remains to be seen what
America will do. I'm glad that I met you, Karl. I can see how
reasonable Americans can be as individuals, even if
questionable as a nation...

"You should not underestimate the scope of our
movement... Our numbers are quite significant already at
this point. All this, waiting to be unleashed, if nominally
backed by the West will ignite an exponential chain
reaction among Red Army troops, as well as POWs still held
by Germany, to join us. The Soviet Army will turn from Red

to White in a few moments. We have a skeleton staff of officers ready to receive troops...

"It does not matter how many tens of thousands of tanks the Red Army has now. At this point it is irrelevant: No campaign will ever be won against the Soviet Union again on a tank warfare basis. But political warfare has a chance. Entire battalions, whole divisions of tanks will reverse 180° and join our side! The war is far from lost yet!" Vladimir Maximovich struck the table with his fist, rattling the cups.

He continued: "General Patton seems to be already in favor; maybe other generals as well and maybe even Churchill. The ideal situation would be if the Americans, instead of insisting on 'unconditional surrender', allied themselves with the Wehrmacht against the Waffen-SS and Hitler.[*] With Hitler out of the picture, if someone like Patton or Montgomery, together with Vlasov, were entering Russia, millions would leave the Red Army and the tide would be turned. It would not even require a large commitment of US troops. What can we do to convince more American generals to pressure their command in Washington?"

Karl was beginning to feel the legitimacy of Vladimir Maximovich's ideas. He said, "If you want, I could put you through to General Patch via my divisional commander. He, in turn, could convey your message to Eisenhower, who is supreme commander for the European theatre, and to Field

---

[*] What actually happened was that after the removal of Hitler and the Nazis in 1945, Germany suddenly became America's closest ally. From the first day of the ceasefire, not a single American soldier was killed. This is proof that a relationship between Germany and America was not impossible. It can thus be supposed that the relationship could have been solicited prior to the end of the war – as Vladimir Maximovich is suggesting – in the form of support for anti-Hitler elements in the Wehrmacht and friendliness towards the nation as a whole. This was not done.

Marshal Alexander, commander of the Mediterranean. There is a lot of resistance in the Army to what is seen as Roosevelt's collusion with 'Uncle Joe'. Generals Clark, Clay, and Patton would probably take your side. So would possibly MacArthur and Wedemeyer, but they are in the Pacific. However, I don't think anything is possible. Nothing short of a mutiny would actually accomplish such a radical change of policy. Even if Eisenhower agreed, which is very doubtful, the highest-ranking general, George Marshall, would be passionately against this, and it would end there. The only person with more authority is Roosevelt himself. Neither the combined influence of the US/UK Expeditionary Force, nor even people like Churchill or Secretary of War Stimson, would be able to make a change against Roosevelt, Hopkins, and Marshall together."

Vladimir Maximovich said, "I could try to talk to Patch. Next month I will be meeting with Vlasov in Prague, and it would be ideal if a secret correspondence could be established directly between him and the US/UK. They need to be told of the very significant likelihood that the Soviet Union will disregard foreign agreements it has made and the Red Army will flood into France.* Maybe if they are

---

* Goebbels, in one of his last publications in 1945, came to this conclusion as well. And in Churchill's opinion, the only thing that saved Western Europe from being overrun with Soviet tanks after Germany's surrender was the deterrent possession of nuclear technology by America. Thus Vladimir Maximovich's warning that no diplomatic agreements or traditional military force would keep the Soviet Union out of Western Europe was consistent with what Churchill concluded after the war. Only the chance discovery of this new technology prevented the Red Army from being in Paris and London by the end of the decade.

Even without gaining Western Europe, it is beyond dispute that the Soviet Union caused a great deal of trouble for the world in the additional 45 years it existed since the end of the war. Five years had not passed before Korea went up in flames and Berlin, Greece, and other places had to be defended. Later the Soviet Union came

made to consider that risk they will stop to reconsider their alliance with Stalin. If they do not help our movement I guarantee they will one day bitterly regret it."

Vixey's cat came and jumped onto a table on which stood a vase with mixed equal numbers of red and white roses. The cat started to eat their petals. Pavel Nikitich asked, "Why is your cat eating roses?"

Vixey replied, "I don't know;- she likes them. I know why cats eat grass – it helps with the digestion of the fur-balls that they lick up from cleaning their fur; but the roses – don't know."

The cat finished eating the flowers, jumped off from the table and trotted to Vixey. It went under her legs, rubbing against them with its softness. Vixey petted the cat's head and then the cat climbed onto a vacant chair and rolled up to sleep. As is typical in cats with long fur, the cat had tufts of fur even on the inside of its ears and also on the bottom of its paws.

Vladimir Maximovich, pouring some more tea, asked Karl, "Why is the top leadership in Washington so anxious to help Stalin achieve full control over central and eastern Europe? Hitler's removal is already inevitable. For a long time the question has only been about what will follow him – Western capitalist influence, or communist power? We already know that British plans for invading through Austria were cancelled. We still don't know everything promised to Stalin at the Teheran conference (large portions of Germany, perhaps?), but we know Stalin returned from there very happy. What is the reason for this? Does Roosevelt actually think Stalin is trustworthy? Does Roosevelt maybe think that a massive redistribution of wealth on a continental and global scale represents justice in a Marxist way? Maybe his ideas are shaped by the infestation of your government with communist spies and

close to eradicating Israel by arming the Middle East in the wars against it.

agents? After all, Soviet intelligence is more powerful than the intelligence services of the rest of the world put together. In every major country there is a communist party and each one is controlled by Stalin. Every country has networks of agents. Besides the NKVD there is also the GRU, a separate entity whose very existence is unknown in the West even though it alone is more powerful than MI6. In a way, I'm proud of this as someone who has worked in military reconnaissance and who appreciates excellent work. Only one fact that I learned was enough to convince me of the strength of Soviet intelligence services. This was that the FBI has been learning US government secrets through its interrogation of communist agents captured in America. Thus, even random agents caught by the FBI have known more secret information about America than the FBI itself! And they do not only steal secrets. Communist agents currently sit in important posts inside the highest echelons of US government."

"Are they Russian, these agents?" Karl asked.

"No, usually not. They are Americans who had been recruited and converted to the Soviet cause.[*] Besides

---

[*] *Venona* project documents (declassified in 1995), in addition to proof provided by defectors over the years, reveal several dozen Soviet agents in federal office during the war. Nearly every department or agency had been penetrated and concentration was heaviest in international policy-making organizations such as the State and Treasury Departments, OSS (predecessor of the CIA), and FEA (Foreign Economic Administration). Among the most notable Soviet agents were Alger Hiss in State, Harry Dexter White in Treasury, and Lauchlin Currie in the White House staff. (The fact that certain agents were exposed does not mean they were the only ones). In addition to the policy decisions made by the agents themselves and their control of the flow of information, they were also in a position to influence many credulous officials such as cabinet members Stettinius and Morgenthau, as well as the president himself. ...

government, there are also a lot of agents on the Soviet payroll in your newspaper organizations."[*]

"What I think is this," Pavel Nikitich said, "I think your president has been poisoned, literally, by Stalin's people to put him in a state of unthinking compliance. He is up to his ears in Soviet agents. They are close to his person, and they would be able to manipulate him all the more if they poison him. Stalin's chemists have such drugs available. There are reports that Roosevelt looks very ill; that he sometimes doesn't know what's going on around him!"[†]

There is speculation, although no definite proof, that even Harry Hopkins was a Soviet agent. Hopkins was Roosevelt's closest advisor, a sort of Grand Vizier. He lived with him in the White House and sent orders and correspondence in Roosevelt's name. The Mitrokhin archive as well as a notable KGB defector, Oleg Gordievsky, name Hopkins as an agent. Gordievsky quotes Akhmerov, the chief NKVD illegal *rezident* in the US, as saying that Hopkins was "the most important of all Soviet wartime agents." Whether it is true that he actually worked for Stalin or not, Hopkins did influence policy numerous times in favor of Soviet interests.

[*] Their misinformation efforts were helped by the years of lies published by people like Walter Duranty, the Pulitzer prize-winning New York Times Moscow Bureau Chief. The Soviets were so good at disinformation that they once fooled US Vice-President Wallace into a favorable opinion of an exterminating-labor camp in Magadan that he toured. Wallace later admitted his pro-Soviet views were wrong. He had been shown a fake, staged production.

[†] Pavel Nikitich's claims are just speculations. However, it is a fact that Roosevelt became so ill in 1944 that many people who saw him questioned his full presence of mind. "The indispensible political direction was lacking at the moment when it was most needed," wrote Churchill in his memoirs. There were times when Roosevelt could not remember having signed important documents. One of these was the Soviet-influenced Morgenthau Plan, which Roosevelt later retracted when confronted by Stimson. At Yalta, people commented on his inability to focus on the discussions. Mysteriously, the Soviet use of German slave labor

"I do not know how plausible that is," remarked Karl.

"Regardless," said Vladimir Maximovich, "He is being manipulated by the network of agents, even if we don't know the extent of it. But this can't continue indefinitely. Eventually Soviet aspirations will become clear to all, so although a rupture between the Soviets and the US/UK hasn't occurred yet over Warsaw in recent events, it is bound to occur at some point. It would probably be a disaster for those of us in Vlasov's army if Germany surrenders before this happens. The Russians inside Germany are numerous but very spread out. Vlasov stated that the Third Reich must manage to resist until fall 1945 or maybe early 1946 in order for us to build up a truly strong power factor. Together with various small European countries, and what's left of the Wehrmacht, we would be something that both America and Russia would be forced to reckon with. If Germany collapses earlier the situation is worse. However, there would still be hope for prolonging the war. We could, in that event, join up with the Czechoslovakian, Hungarian, and Yugoslavian anti-Communist resistance.[*] Maybe these countries' continued

---

was ratified (in violation of international law), although neither Roosevelt nor Secretary of State Stettinius said they agreed to this. The inexperienced Stettinius frequently referred matters to his outspoken assistant, Alger Hiss (a Soviet agent). With some of the most consequential decisions ever faced by a president, responsible for the world war and the fate of numerous nations, Roosevelt was content relying on his weak health and an inadequate or pro-Soviet staff accompanying him to Yalta (some of whom were actual Soviet agents). The man who is consistently listed in the top three of American presidents, was *apparently heavily influenced in his actions by Soviet communists.*

[*] Germany collapsed in spring 1945, earlier than Vlasov predicted. A portion of the KONR army did end up getting involved in Czechoslovakia, with interesting results. The Epilogue will briefly revisit this topic. As for Yugoslavia, Vladimir Maximovich does not know that Stalin's powerful disinformation campaign had already

resistance would draw America and Britain into the fight, and then the overthrow of the Soviet Union would be guaranteed. Also, Greece could potentially erupt in a civil war, if Stalin decides to aid the communists there. Since Britain is occupying it, this would place Britain, and consequently the US, in opposition against the Soviet Union in Greece. If we are in Yugoslavia but see that nothing can be accomplished there, we could then arrive in Greece at the side of Britain, and the crusade could continue from there!"

Pavel Nikitich proclaimed that such hopes were way too optimistic. He remarked, "You are assuming that we are not first destroyed by our friends Marshals Zhukov, Konev, Timoshenko, Rokossovsky, and Vasilevsky. Early next year we will face them, and so far the Germans are our only help. How do you anticipate the timing of gaining the Czechs' support, for instance? We can't be with the Germans at the same time, of course. I think the range of activity will become quite limited with the Soviet and American armies closing in from both east and west. It would be highly advantageous to maintain a path of retreat towards Switzerland, if things turn for the worst! The Americans have still not reached out to the Germans even after the Wehrmacht attempt to assassinate Hitler! They still remain Stalin's allies despite the terrible thing that happened in Warsaw this summer and despite Churchill's warnings! In the event that the Americans remain allies of the Soviet Union up to the eventual surrender of Germany, we would

---

discredited Draža Mihailović and his anti-communist movement, turning US/UK support towards the communist Tito instead. (In a parallel way, the US ally Chiang Kai-shek and his interests were also destroyed by Stalin's intelligence services). On the chessboard of the world, Stalin played with world leaders as Kasparov plays with novices.

not be able to trust them and should not surrender to
them...

"Some of the Americans are such incredible fools that
they actually sent leaflets to our ROA friends in Normandy
promising (as a reward) quick repatriation back to Russia if
they surrendered! What do you think happened? The
battalion fought and died to the last man! There's an
anecdote for you! Maybe this one episode best summarizes
the West's misunderstanding of this entire war...

"My feeling is that the war will probably end with the
Soviets' triumph. Then, after the war, when people sit down
to write a history of it, I think this episode in Normandy
should be on the jacket of that book! In one image it will
show why the communists triumphed – through
unbelievable Western shortsightedness. Can you imagine
the depth of the mutual misunderstanding between the two
groups there in Normandy locked in that deathly struggle?
Those Americans wanted to do something good; they
wanted to extend a charitable offer to their opponents.
They were so ignorant of the state of things in the world, of
why the war is happening, of what the conflicting motives
of different groups in Europe are, that their good charitable
gesture turned out to be something worse than death to
their opponents!"

Pavel, in his talking had not noticed that his cigarette
had long gone out. He tried to draw on it again and realized
he needed a new one. "Can you picture the desperation
with which they must have fought, for an entire battalion to
die in combat to the last man! I wonder what conclusions
the Americans made from the result of that episode. Did
they realize that the Russians prefer to work without pay in
German fortifications in France rather than go back to
Russia? Did they make any conclusions about the
righteousness of supporting a communist state that is on
the verge of crushing all of Europe?"

Chapter XII

> Those who find ugly meanings in beautiful
> things are corrupt without being charming.
> This is a fault. Those who find beautiful
> meanings in beautiful things are the cultivated.
> WILDE

> *Wir haben die Kunst, damit wir nicht*
> *an der Wahrheit zugrunde gehen.*
> NIETZSCHE[*]

Vixey saw Annette passing, and as they had been sitting for a while and might be hungry, asked her to bring them some *hors d'oeuvre* and wine.

Vladimir Maximovich said, "Yes, to go back to Russia is the last thing we want. But not only now, but always, has existence for Russians been bleak. It is a *katorzhnaya*[†] country, where growth as an individual has always been stifled. Melancholy and pessimism are now in peoples' genetics. We came close to some significant reforms under the last Tsar, but it was too little too late. The Russian people are capable of greatness – in part because they have a drive of never settling for the mediocre – but they may end up failing catastrophically. On an individual level this means gambling, spending sprees, drinking, and dueling, but the same thing on a national level may mean the October Revolution. If the Tsar was still around, what a great country it might have been. There would have been no war, for one thing. Russia would have become like a Third Rome. The tsars already had retained Eastern Roman lineage, both by religion, and by the fact that Ivan III

---

[*] *The Will to Power*. "We possess art lest we perish of the truth." Camus later rendered it as: "We have art in order not to die of the truth."

[†] The word *katorga* means forced prison labor in far-away exile but in its adjective form, it could mean 'full of hard and fruitless labor'.

married Sophia, the niece and heir of the last Byzantine Emperor, Constantine XI...

"But currently 25 years of socialism have dramatically transformed Russian society. The Russia of before is dead: in all endeavors, viz. farming, trading, banking, literature,- typically the people of the highest quality have been destroyed or have escaped. The brutal criminal classes (*blatari*) thrive, as well as the *nomenklatura*. Rachmaninoff is one who escaped and became an émigré in 1917, but how many talents like his are being stifled before even appearing?...

"When I refer to the Russian people, I am thinking of the old days, or of the future, when hopefully the people recover from this temporary Bolshevik sewage. Essentially, the Russians are an intelligent people, and artistic as well. Æsthetics and how things look are a matter of great concern. That said, Russians hardly ever invent anything. But they study the West better than the West studies itself, copy, and make it better. Artists like Berlioz were more valued in Petersburg than Paris. Russian painting in the 19th century was only exceeded by the French; we have Repin, Surikov, Shishkin, Vasnetsov, Aivazovsky. Russian literature and poetry emerged in the 1820s with Pushkin, who was (along with Lermontov), greatly influenced by Lord Byron. Then in just a few decades it outstripped all other nations except for the English and French, who had much more of a foundation to build on...

"The themes of our literature are often reflective of the flaws and faults of the Russian mentality and character; whole novels were written just to demonstrate this. Insanity prevails in Dostoyevsky and Gogol. Could Gogol's Piskarëv have come from any place other than Nevsky Prospekt in Petersburg? And of course no consolation can be found from the climate – it is a dark, cold, gray, and oppressive winter half the year. In terms of darkness, Russian literature is only surpassed by the German, isn't that so? Maxim Gorky actually almost killed himself from reading the poetry of Heinrich Heine. There's nothing that's not bleak from German writers."

Vixey laughed, "That's not entirely true... We do have the multi-volume *Sophia's Journey from Memel to Saxony*, and some of Schiller and Hoffmann."

Pavel said, "Although even *Sophia's Journey* is not nearly as lighthearted as the British book *Tom Jones* about a different Sophia from that time period."

"Oh, you're right. I like that Sophia. By the way," she said, speaking to the two Russians, "one of your compatriots was in Berlin up until the start of the war – Vladimir Nabokov.[*] He lived near our Kurfürstendamm apartment in Charlottenburg."

"He's one of the white émigrés," said Vladimir Maximovich. "The only Russian literature now is from the émigré writers."

"Some try from within," commented Pavel.

"Some do, but look- Bulgakov and Akhmatova are censored; Tsvetaeva and Yesenin driven to suicide; Babel and Mandelstam killed directly.[†] Thankfully Bunin is not in Russia. Where is he now?

"I think he is in some village in the south of France. He's not in Paris anymore."

"Ivan Bunin," Vladimir Maximovich explained, "is the most favored writer among us émigrés. In Dabendorf we would wait impatiently for something new printed by him. In his writing he frequently went back to pre-revolutionary settings. He also published his brilliant diary from the revolution itself, from what he saw in Moscow and Odessa in those days."

---

[*] This was well before his major works, when he wrote only in Russian. At the time he would have been known by his *nom de plume* Vladimir Sirin, but here in this text it is changed to his actual name for convenience.

[†] "Only in Russia is poetry respected, it gets people killed." – Osip Mandelstam.

Pavel Nikitich said, "For me the best thing he wrote were the Sonia chapters of *Nataly*. Who would not give everything to have such a cousin at that age? Compare her to Nabokov's Sonia in *Podvig* (*Glory*). The two Sonias are complete opposites. Both are valuable artistic portrayals, though. Vixey, did you read anything by these Russians?"

"Just one thing by Nabokov – it was the only thing available translated: *Camera Obscura*. It was a glimpse into the racy former Berlin, the way it was before the Nazis took over.[*] These writers thankfully don't completely follow the modernist direction which is in fashion now, although they skirt uncomfortably near it. Ordinarily, besides some exceptions I hate modernist literature and art."

"Why?" everyone asked.

"Simply because I don't think it's the rôle of art to focus on un-artistic things, to try to seek out what is the worst. Art is a very selective portrayal of ideas, themes, and æsthetics. It shouldn't be vulgar or trivial. At the very least its subject matter should be more exceptional than the brushstroke of my simple gel liner or felt tip pen." She drew her fingers along her cheekbone to indicate her eyeliner that was just above. Her cheeks had been brushed with bronzer. Vixey also had a silvery eye shadow that day, but everything she used that was in a non-black color was always done with subtlety.

---

[*] Berlin fluctuates considerably. It has been a Prussian capital of the German Empire, progressive cabaret-full Weimar Republic center, red-flag-covered Nazi seat of power, socialist Iron Curtain city with a walled-in Western portion, reunited progressive center of techno and hipsters, and is now changing again into a start-up hub with SoundCloud and others. Berlin was first in the world for sexiness in both the 1920s and again in the 2000s, a contrast to puritanical New York. This was corroborated by Berlin's mayor himself, who said, "*Berlin ist arm, aber sexy.* (Berlin is poor, but sexy.)"

She said, "Sculptures of man should look like the classical Greek ones, like the David sculpture in Florence or 'Psyche Revived' in the Louvre. Best of all is the famous Hercules statue. I could look at that naked man all day. The worst possible art, in my opinion, is a sculpture showing man in a grotesque form. I think that is even worse than those sculptures out of urinals (excuse my language) that the Dadaists make. In painting, the equivalent is Picasso's grotesque Cubism or Dalí's macabre surrealism."[*]

Pavel objected, "In the Soviet Union, where the government is extremely socially-conservative, things like Dalí are censored for being immoral capitalist influences. When I was finally able to reach a normal place like France, these things, by their very contrast, were a relief from the stifling totalitarian atmosphere."[†]

"But I've always been acquainted with surrealism, like what you have in Jérôme Bosch from the 16th century, so there's no novelty-value for me."

"You are well aware of the war going on and what is happening in Europe. Don't you agree that if the artist is to be consistent with the world's deterioration, some of the unpleasantness and the schizophrenia needs to appear in the image?"

"No... A lot of artists have dealt with unpleasant themes, for instance Delacroix. I don't like him either, but I can say that at least he deals with everything without forgetting æsthetics like the modernists do."

"What about abstract art in general?" Karl asked her.

"I have nothing against something being abstract, if it looks pretty. Some of Kandinsky is good. And modern architecture/design is great – the Catalan *modernisme* in

---

[*] The post-1944 Dalí was not as offensive as prior to then. Maybe if she saw his future works her opinion would be different.

[†] True; every socialist/fascist state had a policy similar to the *Gleichschaltung* of Germany. Ironically, "Cultural Bolshevism" was something both Nazis and Bolsheviks were opposed to.

Barcelona or Art Deco in New York. Specifically, I could take as good examples Rockefeller Center or the Chrysler or Chanin buildings."

"That stained-glass ceiling you have over there above the hallway is nice," said Karl, pointing behind him. "It looks like it could as well have been designed by Frank Lloyd Wright."

"Yes. Indeed. The true modernists, though, don't care if something looks good. The Dadaists go so far as to call their own work 'anti-art'. So what is it then? There are so many authors who do the equivalent thing with their writing: Joyce, Hemingway, Camus, Thomas Mann (his later work), the socialists Steinbeck and Sartre, etc. Probably the worst that I've ever seen are Sartre and Faulkner. Not only is Faulkner's subject matter sordid, but since some of his character narrators are not of sound mind, their narration destroys normal composition structure, sentences, and syntax. If these writers want to, figuratively, put sordidness and vulgarity in a frame, as the artists do literally, I would agree with the Nazis that it is degenerate."

"Karl and I happened to be discussing Camus earlier today, actually," mentioned Pavel Nikitich. "Where do you get all this from?"

"I can read or buy any books I please in Zürich, regardless of them being banned here."

"Are new films shown in Switzerland?" asked Karl. "Have you seen *Casablanca*?"

"No; it's American?"

"Yes. It was made two years ago."

"Anything new from America hasn't appeared during the duration of the war. Should I see it?"

"Yes, it's probably the best film about the war that I've seen. It takes place in Casablanca recently, while it was still being administered by Vichy France. Bogart owns a saloon there. As you should expect, however, there wouldn't be any positive German characters."

"Of course. But still American films are so much better and so different than German films that it would be worth seeing them, despite the attitudes. Zürich has them, but not the newest ones."

Vladimir Maximovich mentioned, "Lenin, during his time in Zürich, was very impressed with the freedom and the libraries there. He could read his insane Nechayev's *Catechism of a Revolutionary* or anything else at leisure. That was why on the third day after he seized power in Russia, he banned all free libraries."

Vixey said, "I brought back *The Decameron* from Zürich; this is one of the books that is banned. It's interesting how even something from the Italian Renaissance, the 14th century, is considered too dangerous and too progressive in this regime because it is overly sexy. One of the stories describes a full and complete 'wife swap' engaged in by two Italian couples. In another one, a married woman is courted by a suitor but she demands a monetary payment in exchange for her favors. To avenge this avaricious insult her suitor borrows that sum of money from the woman's husband, without her knowing, and uses that on her. Afterwards, he comes and tells the husband to cancel the debt since he has given the money to his wife the other day, which she cannot possibly deny...

"The point is that even these comical old stories are 'undesirable' in the Reich. Balzac and Maupassant are likewise banned. They would ban Charlotte Dacre[*] if they knew about her. They want a pastoral, unsophisticated nation. This direction of thought leads them to forbid – or view as unwholesome – jazz, pretty cosmetics, salacious skirts, and generally anything *vice*-y, leading to too much fun. As you know, even the archives of the *Institut für*

---

[*] An author from the English Gothic age (along with Matthew Lewis and Ann Radcliffe), who created the interesting Victoria di Loredani.

Sexualwissenschaft were raided and burned, for allegedly being too un-German!...

Karl said, "You probably would have liked for things to be back again as they were in the 20s."

Vixey thought and said, "Well, not exactly. The way things were it was very unstable; it would have led to some kind of socialism or fascism eventually I think. The ironic thing is that it was the liberal culture of the 20s Bohemians that directly led to the Nazis."

"How is that?"

"Did you notice that there is this false dichotomy, I don't know why, between philistine conservatism and nihilism? Why is anyone with economic sense usually a uncultured philistine? Why are cultured people usually nihilists or socialists? Their socialism then leads to what they don't want: ultra-philistine gangsters like Lenin or Hitler seizing power and eliminating culture...

"The Nazis could not have been more opposed to the Bohemians and other liberal-minded people of the 20s. But it was not until I read Edmund Burke's commentaries from the 1700s that I understood how much the liberals also got it wrong! Like the French revolutionaries, they thought that to make improvements it's necessary to get rid of everything, acting like unrestrained nihilists. They made great things like jazz and liberal lifestyles more acceptable, but could not reject the conservatism of the previous ages without also denying classical art, economics, and epistemology, which were all sound. As a result of discarding those three things, they slipped respectively into artistic modernism, socialism, and a moral/political vacuum...

"They said they were against the logic and rationality of capitalism, which they blamed for war and injustice. And they were actually being consistent with all the German writers who kept saying that rationality isn't good and that there's no way to determine the truth or validity of any principles. It was a part of the Weimar zeitgeist. This mysticism was a thing the Nazis definitely had in common with the Bohemians. The prevailing nihilism of the times could offer nothing philosophically solid to counter any committed extremist ideology. The Nazis' dogmatic subjectivism fit into this very well, since their main point is essentially: 'There is only one rule: There are no rules'. This is exactly what the modernists were saying. But the next logical step was that since there are no objective rules, all rules, principles, and truths can only come from the Führer – this is the *Führerprinzip.*[*] The Nazis did not try to defend their conclusions logically; instead they bypassed logic with the concept of 'polylogism'. Truth was no longer correct or incorrect, it was *arteigen* or *artfremd* ('our own' or 'foreign')... In saying this I wanted to show that Hitler and the modernists are not total opposites. That is an oversimplification. The people in 20s Berlin should have enjoyed life without letting their culture turn so nihilistic, since that left everyone unprepared to counter political extremism when it came."

"Your reasoning is impressive," said Pavel Nikitich. "I may differ on some isolated points but I don't mention them, since I agree on more than I disagree. But how did you end up being so literate?"

---

[*] If her reasoning is sound, there would have to have been modernist philosophers whose ideas led them to support National Socialism and Hitler, at least in the beginning. There was one, actually: Martin Heidegger, the most influential 20th century continental philosopher. His works were praised as the philosophical counterpart of modern art. He intentionally used unintelligible sophisms and rejected traditional logical argument. But he was clear on the point that truth is subjective and unknowable by man. He wrote, "The Führer himself and he alone is the German reality, present and future, and its law."

Heidegger's ideological descendant was Jean-Paul Sartre. Is it a coincidence that while Heidegger was drawn to Hitler, Sartre was drawn to Che Guevara (another totalitarian)?

"Why should I not be?" she asked, lifting an eyebrow. "Being literate was the most important thing on Mr. Darcy's – a reference to *Pride and Prejudice* – his list of requirements for a well-rounded girl. In fact, I fulfill his entire list except that I can't sing. As for drawing – I can do simple sketches, which is enough to be very useful in describing what clothes or shoes I want made to the *couturiers*. Of course, it often requires adjusting, and re-drawing.. These shoes I have on now were made from drawings." Because her legs were crossed, one of her shoes wasn't touching the floor but was suspended over it. She slightly-upwardly moved her foot by straightening her leg at the knee. Having used the shoe in her example, she bent her leg again by untensing her muscles, and her foot continued to bob hypnotically for a few seconds.

Not able to talk about *couturiers*, Pavel asked her, "Who are your favorite authors?"

"Hugo and Dumas."

"Aha. But I don't suppose you think well of their contemporaries in Paris: Zola and Flaubert?"

"Oh no! Definitely not."

"Why?"

"They are too Naturalist. But you can't put the two of them in the same group. Flaubert had an influence on the modernists, but Zola can almost be considered a modernist himself. He was the first to have a philosophy of anti-æsthetics. Who do you like out of writers?"

"Nikolai Gogol first," said Pavel, "Then I don't know. My reading of most Western material is unfortunately limited to the year or so I spent at Viktoriastraße and Dabendorf in Berlin... But what makes you so opposed to literary realism? It's necessary and essential. It's important to have something that makes sense and is in accordance with how the world is. We talked about this before. Typically also these writers are the ones who are progressive in previously-risqué topics."

"That is true. I don't go against realism or negative endings – when it's about people or situations that have something exceptional about them. But if you go too far in realism, you have to have things that are statistically common, so it has to be vulgar or banal. In Zola each character is worse than the last. Just when you think one might be interesting, like *Comtesse* Sabine[*], Zola manages to ruin them. And it's not at all like Gogol's *Revizor*[†] or *Dead Souls*, where there are artistic explorations into totally absurd people who are amusing and comical. Zola is boredom and vulgarity at the same time. I feel that a lady ought not to even pronounce the names of his works so as not to have her mouth in any way associated with their impurity, just as with the true modernist stuff that came later on."

"Alright. What about Flaubert? You are a bit softer on him?" asked Pavel.

"Yes; compared to Zola, Flaubert is like a romanticist,- in his preoccupation with æsthetic details and pretty Emma; his description of a night promenade during a tryst; the incredibly tight structure... If only he used his skill for good!... Baudelaire, praising Emma Bovary, asked, 'Why shouldn't hysteria form the basis of a literary work?' Well my question is Why should it? Flaubert's Emma or (to use another example) Tolstoy's Anna ended badly not because of plot circumstances but because of their own stupidity and limitations, and I don't see the artistic sense of that!"

"I thought Emma's problem was in being too aspirational for her society?"

"Emma was obviously ten times more sophisticated than all the hicks and yokels that surrounded her; she did aspire to improvements. But still compared to... compared

---

[*] A secondary character in *Nana*, one volume in the series *Les Rougon-Macquart*.
[†] A play, also known as *The Government Inspector*.

to *me*, let's say, she's like a peasant. Well, not quite a peasant but merely bourgeois. She has no interests."

"But you can't deny that Anna is of higher class," Pavel said. "And Tolstoy portrays things almost as well as Flaubert."

"True, but also he was insane in his latter years. He was a complete religious nut; just take a look at his *Kreutzer Sonata*."

"Well, he slipped into asceticism. He picked up on some of the wrong things from Schopenhauer."

"Superficially, Anna is fine," Vixey continued, "She likes to dress in elegant black and occasionally has an aristocratic devil-may-care attitude. But despite this she's far below being an *übermensch*, as in Nietzsche's use of the term. Anna and Vronsky are not commoners, but their ideas and volition are commonplace. Of course Anna becomes mixed up in Tolstoy's religious theories and themes and becomes hysterical. Tolstoy intends to say that the proper way to be is like Kitty Sherbak... Shere... How do you pronounce her name?"

"Kitty Shcherbatskaya (*Щербацкая*)," Pavel said, noticing how Vixey touched her own delectable black skirt when talking about Anna in black.[*]

"Thanks. I admit that even if Tolstoy's philosophy is misguided, you still have his æsthetics and metaphysics. A modernist writer would take *that* away as well and leave nothing but banal squabbling. Thankfully there was, at least, that *fin-de-siècle* reactionary movement against Naturalism before modernism began: Huysmans, Wilde, Baudelaire, Mallarmé... Although I can't really endorse

---

[*] A lot of writers would be displeased at her remarks. Henry James considered *Madame Bovary* to be a perfect novel, and Nabokov thought that same about *Anna Karenina*.   It's unclear if the author's treatment of Vixey's comments on *Mme Bovary* is ironical, accidental, or if there is some other angle.

Baudelaire – I find some of his things too obscene to be able to read much. He has had too much of Poe's influence."[*]

Pavel replied, "Baudelaire was actually one of the refreshing foreign highlights in the library at Viktoriastraße, as well as Villiers de l'Isle-Adam.[†] We had several books brought in from Paris to augment the library.[‡] Do you read in English as well as French and German?"

---

[*] Vixey is allowed to criticize half of established literature, but what about this author's own writing? It's not that good, although it's not extremely bad for someone who does not have literature as his profession and who has no poetic talent. The lineage from Radcliffe is felt sometimes; also a bit of Victorian reticence. There is a certain degree of similarity to the concise writing and Soviet military topics of Isaac Babel (although there are many differences as well). The conciseness could be problematic – it could lead to improper transitions of pace. More importantly, it creates a situation where not reading closely enough and being slightly careless could lead to vital points being missed. Overall the structure is good; there is a historical theme as well as an abstract, metaphysical theme. Both themes, in their manifestation as plot-themes, eventually interplay with each other. There is a wealth of direct literary references. The author also seems to enjoy having Vixey dressed frequently, like a veritable doll. Etherege and Wilde did not dress their London fops as well or as often. And why did Onegin spend three hours dressing himself before going out while Olga Larina does not even get a line of description from Pushkin?

[†] Pavel's literary choices are unsurprisingly misogynistic. In Gogol, women are almost always a destructive element via their charm, if not explicitly evil spirits (*Viy*), then still unintentionally creating devastation (*Nevsky Prospekt*). For Villiers and Baudelaire, women are frequently *fleurs du mal* (flowers of evil), as in the eponymous collection of poetry.

[‡] Even in Paris, however, any edition of *Les Fleurs du mal* would still have been incomplete prior to 1949. Since the first publication in 1857, several poems have always been censored, for instance the ones about sapphism. It is unclear why this was done, since the topic had already appeared in other serious literature, viz. *Augustine de Villeblanche*, *Mademoiselle de Maupin*, and *La Fille aux yeux d'or*.

"Yes," she said. "I've read a great deal from the pre-Victorian women writers – Radcliffe, Burney, Austen, Edgeworth. More from them than any other type of English fiction." She paused to think a little. "It's interesting that among Russians and Englishmen it's quite valued when a girl is well read, but in my experience it is not usually the case with German men, especially Protestant Germans. It doesn't do much to enhance appeal. They think they must know better about everything and don't like to be corrected. They tend to be domineering in many aspects. Most people I've known have been German or French, and the Frenchmen are decidedly more agreeable and charming."

"When have you had time to form all these opinions?" Karl asked her, suddenly a bit concerned. "I mean, you're very young..."

"Not a lot of time, but it's already been three years since I've been 15.. I've never had a prolonged affair with a Frenchman, but I've known several in Paris and Switzerland... Paris is really enjoyable. It's possible to do anything; there's so much to buy and to see. The exchange rate has improved from 1/15 to 1/20.* It's the only true city in the world (although I haven't seen New York yet). People are really nice to me, despite the German occupation."

"You mean the men are nice to you?" asked Karl.

"Oh, yes. Not the women. Even if I conceal that I'm German but instead say I'm British or something else, French women are still not nice."

"So you don't get along with them?"

---

* The official rate set by Germany in its occupied areas valued the Reichsmark higher than its real market value. Thus one could make about a 16% profit by exchanging marks for French francs in Paris, then smuggling the francs into Geneva and selling them on the international market. In 2014, many countries still engage in severe currency restrictions, like Argentina.

"No, not really. Nor the Czechs and Poles, who dislike anything German. But if they are so ill-fated as to not like me,- as to live without the pleasure of liking me, then all I can do is pity their misfortune." She laughed, "I know that might sound a little conceited, though."

"What do you think of Southern men? Spaniards, Italians?"

"Hmm, I don't know. They tend to be too flamboyant..."

Vixey sharply opened a black Japanese fan with a flick of her hand and used it. Pavel Nikitich felt a bit of sweet fragrance of perfume from her hair that meandered in his direction on the air. Meanwhile Vladimir Maximovich reverted to speaking about the problems in the war which were the most vexing. Vixey was touching one her plaits, putting her fingers through the loosely interlocking tresses. She continued to use her fan, but only intermittently. Pavel stayed for another minute but then excused himself, saying he had work to finish in the library, took a last look at her, and left.

Chapter XIII

> Bavarian gentians, big and dark, only dark
> darkening the daytime torchlike
> with the smoking blueness of Hades' gloom,...
> D.H. LAWRENCE

She had gone too far, Pavel thought, even before she had finished speaking. Her one casual half-sentence about Nietzsche showed her understanding of him to outstrip his. The effect of hearing her talk about ideas increased further his regard for her, which had already reached a level of derangement just from being in the presence of her beauty. Can life accommodate such beauty? It is unreal, destructive to the repulsive reality.

"Beauty," wrote Mann, "is the only form of the spiritual that we can receive with our senses and endure with our senses."[*] Pavel agreed with the first part of this assertion but not the second. Sometimes it is too much to endure. The door to the infinite divine is opened too far – it is a pressure of divine light greater than the mind could handle.

She still had that tantalizing silvery ear clip, which was now perfectly complemented by one of her pair of soft black plaits hanging by it. At the moment when she arched her eyebrow and looked at him she decisively destroyed him. There was no going back. If he owned all of Italy and she asked to have it, accompanying her request with that enticing, unchallengeable small movement, he would give it to her without a thought.

He did not want to contradict her ideas or raise disagreements, but he would have liked to continue talking about philosophical, literary, or other topics. The prior conversations were boring to him – mostly it was Vladimir Maximovich and Karl discussing things he already knew.

---

[*] *Death in Venice*. Mann is actually quoting Plato, who is in turn quoting Socrates.

This time he was able to hear her voice for a long while. And while Pavel was speaking, he really delighted to see her attentive gaze and the corners of her mouth always on the verge of a smile. But he could not maintain a collected presence any longer; he had to leave to refocus. It was surprising that he at least managed that small discussion that started with the French authors.

He recalled Lord Suffolk's soliloquy after meeting Marguerite d'Anjou in 1444*: "...Her beauty confounds the tongue and makes the senses rough." This Margot, the future ruler of England, was a girl of 14 at the time; Suffolk was more than thrice her age. Moreover she was separated from her French court via the fortune of war and was in the power of the English commander – and yet her beauty and nobility of mind rendered him incapable of speech. Thus it is not so unusual, Pavel concluded, to have one's thoughts involuntarily constrained by the presence of a venerated and beautiful girl. It is known that semiconductors can rapidly change their electrical conductivity based on environmental factors, such as temperature. It is as if the human brain functioned by way of electrical impulses that traveled at lightning speeds when the head was cool. But a flash of eyelashes from a Vixey or a Margot could have an effect of immediately changing the electric pathways of thought from having the conductivity of metal to the resistivity of smudging graphite. Focusing all one's abilities, it is still possible to get something out, but anything said will be mediocre and the effort cannot be sustained more than briefly.

It must be noted that in Pavel's case it was not common for this to happen – most of the women he encountered bored him. An experienced, attractive, military man – not inferior in this regard to Lermontov's Pechorin,– it would have required an object of particular regard to

---

* War of the Roses tetralogy, Shakespeare. *Henry VI*, Part One, Act 5, Scene III.

cause any of the effects that have been witnessed. He had lived by Pechorin's famous aphorism, *Je méprise les femmes pour ne pas les aimer, car autrement la vie serait un mélodrame trop ridicule.* He was not approaching a lady for the first time, like Thomas Mann's Dostoyevskian *Der Bajazzo.*

Returning to *On the Eve*, Pavel resumed reading where he left off before the talk in the drawing room. It was a short book, and he was already halfway through it. He cynically laughed at Uvar Ivanovich gazing cryptically into the future of Russia. How horrible to read that now, he thought, 90 years later, knowing where Russia has ended up. How fortunate Turgenev's characters were for not knowing that even the most pessimistic of their guesses about the future would not come close to reality. Dostoyevsky took the scope of the US Civil War as evidence of how things have gotten worse, despite bloodshed having become less acceptable in a more progressive society.[*] Now, there are individual battles with more casualties. "But such is fate", Pavel thought. "Things keep getting worse. All unavoided is the doom of destiny, as Richard III said."

But all this was not the main subject of the Turgenev book. The plot was about a certain Elena Nikolayevna who was frustrated with all the Hamlets, Rudins, and Onegins in Russia – the type of men in the aristocratic circles who were unable to use their intelligence and abilities towards any committed practical endeavor. This was a theme often explored by mid-19th century Russian writers. Not finding anything to keep her in Russia, Elena Nikolayevna went so far as to marry a Bulgarian revolutionary engaged in his country's war of independence against the Turks. His stark contrast to the rest of her society impressed her. Her friends discuss this, asking themselves: When will the day come when real people – authentic and active – start to exist in Russia?

---

[*] *Записки из подполья* (*Notes from a Basement*).

Pavel stopped reading and considered this point. Pacing through the room, looking out the dark window, he suddenly had an epiphany as the thought came to him that maybe he himself was an answer to this question. Certainly it's not those Bolshevik gangsters and their *blatnoye* (criminal underground) Cheka that Russia has been lacking. It is rather the movement that he is a part of – the drastic and paradoxical, yet epic, campaign to liberate Russia and construct liberalism there for the first time in its history.

Pavel noticed a phonograph and turned it on to a record of Mendelssohn's *Lieder*. He read the book to the end, where unsurprisingly death nixes everything. Depressed again, thinking about Elena Nikolayevna, he heard at that moment the despairing *Reiselied*, based on Heine's poem. Seeking something longer, but in the same mood, he found a record of the *Winterreise*. Turning it on, he started re-reading earlier sections of the book. While doing this, as a result of the late hour and his fatigue, he fell asleep.

A little over an hour later, he awoke to suddenly see Vixey standing in front of him. "Elena Niko..." was his first startled exclamation, a Freudian slip, as he blinked looking at her. Vixey had come in to turn off the lights before going to sleep and was surprised that he was still there.

Her eyes were sleepy and half-closed, but there was enough blackness imbued in her lashes and around her eyes that they attracted attention even from far away. On the outside edges, the blackness tapered acutely like the tip of a straight apostrophe ('). It was almost a characteristic expression of her's – one eye mostly open, the other half closed; together with a slight smile – and it appealed greatly to Pavel. He thought that it conveyed a softness, a cat-like calmness, and a tinge of modesty and melancholy – although the smile tempered the melancholy. It expressed a lack of the unnaturally-frantic Protestant work ethic of those people who somehow never became tired. It was more Bavarian rather, while also conveying an aristocratic disdain for unnecessary action. Finally, her expression also had connotations related to bed – which was a place in congruence with Pavel's thoughts about desirable places for her to be imagined in. She pressed her eyelids closed twice, *сумрачно* (duskily), and Pavel imagined her waking up in a bed with her black hair on a fresh white pillow.

"Why were you listening to *Winterreise*?" Vixey asked, shutting off the machine that had just reached the end of the record. The ominous *drehleier* (hurdy-gurdy) motif was sounding as she had been walking in.

Pavel snapped out of his delirious reveries. "I don't know... Should I be listening to *Die schöne Müllerin* instead?"[*]

Vixey understood the implied allusion and did not know how to respond. Pavel was seized with a sudden energy and adrenalin, especially as he considered that he should have at least as favorable chances as 'that damn Bulgarian revolutionary' from the Turgenev book. He realized it would be weak to exercise restraint and considered that the opportunity should not be lost. He stood up to replace the book on its shelf and said, "Remember when you brought up your eyeliner when discussing æsthetics? I thought later that it's not very fair to compare things like that with art. Just looking at you, for instance, would exceed everything the musées du Louvre and d'Orsay contain."

"Are you sure you're not exaggerating to some extent?" she asked. "All that subject matter and range of themes?"

"What is that?" He came closer to her and grasped her by the shoulders, saying, "Who needs all that if one has

---

[*] Both are well-known depressing song cycles by Schubert, based on poems by Wilhelm Müller. However, *Die schöne Müllerin* is specifically about a man who comes across a house where he cannot win the regard of a girl because her affections are directed to someone else.

seen you? To anticipate the fancies and sentiments signified by your eyes makes for sufficient themes as well."

He sought her eyes' consent, thought he found it, but was mistaken. The closeness and over-familiar talk made Vixey uncomfortable, and the ensuing kiss he placed on her lips increased her unease. The fact that he had disclosed an affinity for her at this point seemed to Vixey lacking in tact. As per girlish nature, such a disclosure almost always damages one's suit, even if it had initial prospects. She moved farther away, slipping from his hold. She knitted her brows and told Pavel how opposed she was to these liberties. The conversation become more strained.

"Are you offended?" he asked.

"A bit."

"I could not help myself. I cannot continue seeing you, and – while there's such a unbearable distance between us..."

"Let us be reasonable and put aside this silliness. No–don't say anything. I understand you like me. You know I have too much common sense to be offended without an actual cause of offence, so *je ne suis pas vexée* (I'm not vexed). But currently it is getting late, and you should be on your way. I hope you will not think about this anymore."

Pavel saw that she could not understand the degree to which he adored her if she thought he could simply stop thinking about it. He left and drove off into the deepening gloom of the forest road. It was like a tunnel, as the canopy from both sides entwined seamlessly at the top. When the road went through an open field, the night sky was so bright, in contrast, that every silvery detail at the far end of the field could be seen, although without color, as in black/white cinema.

He could not understand anything and concluded in the hopelessness of *any* endeavor in the world, a feeling that always ensues after an unsatisfactory suit. There was a lot more opposition just now than he was accustomed to. But it had been a while since any attempts such as this. Had the war aged him that much? One thing he failed to realize was that Vixey was not Turgenev's Elena Nikolayevna. There was in fact very little in common between them. But the strength of an *idée fixe* (or *vixe*), as in Berlioz's meaning of the term, is that it tends to only allow one to perceive what reinforces one's existing ideas and ideals while not perceiving what is at variance. Stendhal called this mental process *crystallization*, a metaphor to a tree branch becoming covered with crystals if left for some time in a Salzburg salt mine.

*   *   *

In 1941 Pavel's time had been filled by preparations for imminent war, which did not last long when it came, as he surrendered along with Vladimir Maximovich and others at Kiev. Initial optimism faded as it turned out that simply turning the artillery guns 180° and reëntering the war on the other side was politically unacceptable. Then followed the uncertainty of the years at various camps and facilities in Germany, including Viktoriastraße and Dabendorf outside of Berlin – reading a lot, waiting for death – in a similar manner as an unemployed person waits, the hope of any future life constantly diminishing. He found his weariness articulated in the verses of Tennyson, and his hopelessness in those of Leopardi. However, the situation was better than a traditional state of hopeless unemployment, because for him the worst case scenario was merely a quick death on the barricades. Pavel had no doubt that without the help of Russian divisions, the German advance would eventually reverse. So if he stayed in Berlin, the war would eventually reach it, and then there would be a wonderful chance to leave the world gloriously, maybe helping a few civilians caught in the onslaught.

However, Pavel's fortune improved when he was able to finally leave Berlin and start doing some significant work with the Russian Liberation movement. Overthrowing the Bolsheviks was Pavel's life goal. He had even tried some careful opposition activity in the 30s, but of course it was impossible to effect any change then. The most he could do was print counterrevolutionary *samizdat*. Now there was at least a chance. It was an exciting time, collaborating with other Russian officers on practical matters, not just on paper. Some people envisioned great things, especially when imparted with energy from the vodka they consumed, even though the mission was more likely than not to be completely futile. Pavel traveled all over Germany and France coordinating regiments, equipment, and supplies, while dealing with the always invasive Nazi bureaucracy. He helped General Maltsev organize the small KONR air force. Now he was training the 4th Division and making plans for its utilization. Unlike the other officers, he did not go to the nearby towns, Freiburg and Mülhausen, to pick up girls. He did not notice there being any exceptional ones that would justify the effort and the distraction from his work. Then Pavel happened to meet Vixey, who was such a contrast, for reasons already identified. The contrast was enhanced by the fact that economic conditions and stagnant fashion design made it impossible for others to refine, to such a degree, their hair, makeup, and attire.

An army at war experiences a significant degree of what I call a "submarine effect". This is a psychological effect created by isolation from women, which would be at its highest levels on a submarine but exists elsewhere as well. The effect causes outsized, starved reactions to the slightest girl image. A sight of a few seconds of a spinning skirt, spurred on with a bit of wine, would be enough to bring tears to one's eye. For a soldier (or anyone else) away from femininity long enough, a screening of *Gone with the Wind*, with Vivien Leigh in color, is a religious experience. Pavel, not accompanying the officers to local towns, thought that he was escaping from the effect, when actually it was being delayed and focused, when he did eventually meet an interest of irresistible allure.

People not used to passion can risk it destroying the meaning of their lives. The best examples are from military or religious fields. From the former, take the example of the Cossack knight from *Taras Bulba*, from the latter, the priest from *Notre Dame de Paris*. Or, an example that is both military and religious: the Templar knight Sir Brian de Bois-Gilbert from *Ivanhoe.*[*] Contrasting this are people who continually live in the midst of passion, like Italians or certain artists. Note how Hector Berlioz was able to successfully channel his violent emotions, which otherwise would have destroyed him, into the creation of a masterpiece: the *Symphony Fantastique*. Pavel Nikitich was not such a person as Berlioz. The first thing he did on returning to the base was to down an ample amount of vodka. It is a belief among Russians that this helps clarify or renew one's thoughts. Every culture has its methods of expanding the mind via the changing of perspective, from the peyote of the desert Indians to the religious chanting of monks. Russians, if there is nothing stronger, find it necessary to make use of vodka at any decisive point.

The thoughts Pavel had were along the following lines, and ended up articulating the irreversible change in priorities that had already occurred with him. So far, the cause, the revolution, was the only thing that kept him going. By inertia he continued to work in that direction. But at the present time he asked himself what ultimate goals would be accomplished if everything is successful? He would still be in a Vixey-less world. No real advantage would occur – if measured on comparison to the advantage of gaining Vixey. Supposing, in a best case scenario, that the revolution succeeds and Vlasov or someone else becomes the leader of Russia. Pavel through his connexions would have a chance of becoming some kind of minister or ambassador. These would be substantial gains to both material and personal fulfillment. The political changes

---

[*] Novels by Gogol, Hugo, and Scott, respectively.

envisioned in Russia had been the dream of his life, and to be a part of it would have been thrilling. However, what about Vixey? The possession of the least part of her body would fill him with a joy more vehement than the conquest of any empire, (to reiterate the words of the Queen of Saba[*]). Pavel came to the realization that lately his motivations on continuing the fight were instead subconsciously based on how much a successful revolution would increase the potential for gaining Vixey. Or someone else who at best would only be an incomplete substitute for her. Acknowledging that she had become his only real goal, that even the revolutionary cause only made sense to the degree that it could help his chances with her, the inevitable conclusion was that the chance of success of the cause was too low to continue in it!

He saw that Vixey's dominance in his thoughts to the exclusion of any other considerations was a result of fate, so little did he feel he could possibly control it. He recognized that it was an abyss from which there is no escape – a bittersweet torment that cannot lead anywhere but madness – yet what could be done? – Let it take its course...

The writer Heinrich von Kleist rightly felt there was some kind of fatal mismatch between the way we are and the way the world is. That trying to fix it, to find what we are lacking in order to fit into the world, is futile. These were not always his beliefs. In the beginning of his life, von Kleist was a proponent of what he called a *Lebensplan*. He thought life can be shaped and directed with reason and with adherence to an important purpose.

It is absurdly ironic, and yet perfect, that none of this served von Kleist and he ended up finding happiness only in a bullet suicide pact with his terminally ill friend Henriette Vogel.

---

[*] *La Tentation de St. Antoine.*

For Pavel Nikitich, the counterrevolutionary plans he had continued to serve him in providing meaning and motivation, even though there was much adversity, until they evaporated and their vapor was burned up in the full glance of Vixey's eyes, like in a hot blue flame.

He recognized that he was not the first to articulate the idea that courtship replaced anything else in the world in importance. Material gains, for instance, were only valuable to the extent they could contribute to this. Similar statements were made by Marcus Vinicius in *Quo Vadis*, where he went as far as to say that all riches, glory, and power are mere smoke. The smoke that Litvinov observes in the novel *Smoke* is of a different sort, since it partly represents the political posturing of Russians in Baden-Baden, but Litvinov accepts that the reason his own life is also mere smoke is the lack of Irina. The conclusion of *Les Misérables*, Hugo's *magnum opus*, was that courtship and amorous relations were the only light to be found in the darkness of life – *On n'a pas d'autre perle à trouver dans les plis ténébreux de la vie*. Many poets (Petrarch, Donne, Cowley, Marlowe, Baudelaire) have attempted to express this and have fallen short because it is something that transcends our world. Stendhal's analysis and discourses exceed 300 pages but he only approaches the surface of the matter. Words, like any scale of measurement, lose the frame of reference that they have when applied contextually in a different realm of existence. It is like using x, y, and z to identify points not in three-dimensional, but in four-dimensional Euclidean space. In the normal world, there is no letter past *zed* to define the extra direction, which is perpendicular to all other directions.[*] How can the measurements of the normal world cope with situations

---

[*] Continuing on this line, perhaps this is why Nabokov literally placed Ada in a parallel realm, withdrawing her *iz ada* (out of hell) – i.e. out of the normal world.

where an entire physical and spiritual universe, as Hugo writes, can be reduced to a single being: the object of one's courtship?

*   *   *

At any Russian military base it is possible to find some officers who are playing cards all night and drinking. Instead of sleeping, Pavel came to watch them play, looking at the falling spades and hearts but without saying anything or listening to their conversations. Their gay laughter jarred him. What possible cause for joy can they have? he thought. Each of them will probably be dead soon. Pavel lay down on a cot next to the card table for a few hours after dawn, then washed, had a cool glass of *wein und wasser*, and drove back to see Vixey.

He found her alone. That morning she was wearing all red and blue, the Principality of Liechtenstein colors. A blue shirt with a low frilled neckline and capped sleeves and then a short red tennis skirt over which lay a diaphanous lacey layer. Between her shoes and skirt her stockings were also red. She had red André Perugia floating-heel shoes with a blue sole that extended slightly back to give balance under the arch of the foot. The heelless shoes were so intriguing and compelling that they threw Pavel off balance instead of her.

The *coup de grâce* was a bright dark blue flower in her hair – a Bavarian Gentian – that matched her eyes. She may have known of Novalis's romanticist associations with the blue flower, but probably did not suspect its associations to gloom for D.H. Lawrence and to *Sehnsucht** for C.S. Lewis.

Pavel took a few moments to study her appearance, while she looked at him quizzically, then abruptly asked her

---

* An untranslatable German term, it refers to an inconsolable longing for something, spurred sometimes by an æsthetic experience, along with a bittersweet sense of the incompleteness of life and reality.

to follow him into one of the salons where there was no risk of them being overheard. She observed the change in his behavior and attributed it to their previous talk, and this fact frightened her. She sat down and casually talked about her plans, "We are going to Freiburg for the day."

Pavel, still standing, said, "That's nice..." He paced back and forth through the room, at length asking, "Do you seriously intend to stay with this American? I think the time has come to establish that."

"I thought that we had enough such conversation the other day and that you would not so soon resume it!" she said.

"I cannot do without this. I am suffering from the worst perplexities; do you at least pity me?"

"Your perplexities, as you call them, are a creation of your own. I'm not a thoughtless coquette; I take no delight in this." Looking away, she took a moment, knitting her brows and lifting one eyebrow, to think of a historical precedent. "Indeed, I gave you less provocation even than Henriette d'Angleterre to the Comte de Guiche."[*]

"But I cannot help imagining if things could have turned out differently had not this Major Stevens entered the picture. I know that there is nothing objectionable for you about me. And I adore you. To live with an American would be boring; they have no passion. They are accustomed to boring and simple lifestyles. The more time passes, the more you will see how uncultured and petty bourgeois they are. Even if you weren't of a high class, but an ordinary European girl you would be too good for him. And remember he is also pragmatic. He may say he cherishes you but any day that an order comes from his general, whatever it may be and however it may contradict your wishes, he will follow it. His country doesn't even allow him to talk to you – whereas I no longer have a country. I am against all sides and all alliances. For me

---

[*] *Louise de La Vallière*, Dumas.

you're my *only* authority. I treasure you Beyond all limit of what else i' the world, to borrow from *The Tempest*. Beautiful, lovely tyrant; I would take pleasure in executing your most insignificant command. I would die for you; for just one night with you."

"All this is very fine, you express yourself extravagantly; but... if anything were possible, it would have already been evident even last night... I was... too sleepy to realize what you were doing. It shouldn't have happened."

"So, nothing is possible?"

"No,... and actually by continuing along some of the impertinent lines you have taken, you're only increasing my displeasure."

Pavel stopped walking and looked at her. He said, "I'm not sure what is left then to do. I don't think I'm going back to the army. I must have you." She tensed a little, opening her eyes wider. "On your own terms, of course," he added.

"Consider— to misuse me could surely only bring you remorse," she said. "You must promise never to bring this up again – otherwise how can I even receive you here?"

Pavel felt that the conversation had finished. He made no promises, saying, "I don't know what to say to that," and rushed out the door. Before leaving the house he saw Karl, who was eyeing him suspiciously as he walked from the direction of the kitchen. "You'll remember me, my friend," Pavel muttered to himself, with typical Russian bravado. He got into his jeep seething with murderous jealousy. He thought that the devil's inventions for making hell more miserable and tormenting shouldn't surprise him anymore after all his years, but they still did.

Chapter XIV

Je brûle de peindre celle qui m'est apparue si rarement et qui a fui si vite... Elle est belle, et plus que belle; elle est surprenante. En elle le noir abonde: et tout ce qu'elle inspire est nocturne et profond.
BAUDELAIRE[*]

The prior night, before going to sleep Vixey lay on her bed, on her side, reading something. Lying this way even further accentuated the curvature of her waist, because it was pressed asymmetrically into a straight line of contact with the bed along with the rest of her body. On the other side of her waist, the side that was visible, the line of curvature dipped to a greater extent than usual and then climbed relatively steeply to her hips. This produced an astonishing effect.

Besides her vertebrae and some abdominal muscles, there was practically nothing at Vixey's waist. Karl could encircle it with both hands if he squeezed it. Vixey was facing away, and Karl pulled back on her hair until he could see her face, asking something about the Freiburg trip. "By the way," he said, "how often did you go back to your hometown Munich when you lived in Berlin?"

"The whole past year I was there, and before that, every summer, at least," she replied. "My summers were typically split between Munich and Paris. In Paris I have a small apartment in the *sixième arrondissement, qui est près du* Jardin du Luxembourg. In Munich I stay with my sister Evelina on Prinzregentenstraße. And while in Munich, I sometimes go down to Innsbruck, which is one of my favorite cities."

---

[*] *Le Spleen de Paris*, Le Désir de peindre: "I burn to paint a certain woman who has appeared to me so rarely, and so swiftly fled away. She is beautiful, and more than beautiful: she is overpowering. The color black preponderates in her; all that she inspires is nocturnal and profound."

"How would you get between Munich and Paris?"

"Either an overnight train with a sleeping compartment or a two-hour plane ride."

"Did you ever see the Oktoberfest?"

"Yes, in 1938- that was the last year they had it. It was at the same time that the British Prime Minister was in town resolving the Sudeten Crisis. Wiesn is such a great holiday – it's simply the anniversary of the 1810 wedding between the crown prince of Bavaria and Thérèse von Saxe-Hildburghausen.* You wear clothes as if frozen in time from that 1810 time-period. But Munich is the best in the summer. I would go to the Englischer Garten almost every day – it has streams that are offshoots from the Isar, forests, and a lake with islands."

The lake she's referring to is the Kleinhesseloher See and the few islands in it, like the Kurfürsteninsel, are only accessible by rowboat and thus perfectly suitable for confidential summer trysts.† Spending time in the park with Evelina, she learned to easily flirt with the many other strollers, swimmers, and bikers. Evelina met her future husband there, a local Municher, when she was on a wooden raft with Vixey floating down the swift Eisbach. That was in 1940. Near the stream's beginning there is a turbulent section with rolling waves, which lifted and descended the raft wildly, requiring them to almost lay down on it to stabilize it. Then the stream divided- a left turn would lead to a small waterfall and the sunny Schönfeldwiese while the right (which they made) led to a

---

* Later on, the court of Ludwig I became very interesting in the 1830s and 40s, frequented by such notable personages as the British courtesan Lola Montez, probably the best image in the entire *Schönheitengalerie*. Others included Lady Jane Digby and Marquesa Marianna Florenzi.

† The *Bayerische Schlösserverwaltung* (www.schloesser.bayern.de) provides a good map of the park at
http://www.schloesser.bayern.de/deutsch/garten/objekte/eg_suedteil.pdf.

long shady stream through the dark trees. A man standing on a bridge that they passed under called out to the 'pretty sailing girls' on the raft. Evelina continued talking and flirting with him, laughing seductively, as he followed the quick-flowing stream on his bike. Sometimes the path would lead away from the stream, so he tried to appear at a later point or another bridge in order to encounter them again.

Vixey made a sudden movement shifting the center of balance all on one side and managed to capsize the raft, sending them both into the water with all their clothes. In Munich, Evelina has a *coiffeuse* available at whatever moment she needed, and that day Vixey had used her to make a cute *chignon* of hair in the shape of a black camellia, which was ruined. The water was deep and only Evelina was able to grab hold of something on the bank. Vixey continued to be carried by the water so the man ran a little downstream and took hold of her delicate hand as she was passing, pulling her out in one motion. He then returned to help Evelina up; – this was how their courtship began.

Over the years Evelina taught Vixey a responsible use of alcohol, mild amphetamines, and amorous relations rather than risk her being incorrectly exposed to these things by herself. Some argue that an indication of even a slight approval of these things is too radical of a lack of limitations that would create risks of escalation. But Evelina took a risk and hoped that Vixey would follow the limitations she suggested.

The reason I am acquainted with them is that as a banker at Credit Suisse, I handle von Isarberg's accounts, and have started helping Evelina and her husband as well. On a trip to visit them on business in Summer 1942, I encountered Vixey, then 16, at Evelina's house. (It was not absolutely necessary for me to go, since I could have waited until Evelina was in Switzerland, but I wanted to make the trip for the sake of such a charming client).

Managing the finances of wealthy individuals is much more than just investment allocation. These people often own companies and enterprises. Their companies need a wide range of banking services such as facilitating the sale of bonds or stock shares to investors on the capital markets, arranging syndicated loans or revolvers, advising on mergers & acquisitions, hedging various exposures via derivatives, and of course covert capital transfers and tax evasion. For Germans today, by far the most important are the latter two, as substantial illegal financial activity is necessary to mitigate the harmful effects of the Hitler regime. There is nothing illegal about this from Switzerland's perspective. The German state is the one that is violating decent standards of property rights. In Germany, any profits that still remain after taxes are subject to the State's decision on where and how to invest them. No personal or corporate property is safe in the Reich. Naturally everyone who can, wishes to get capital into Switzerland. German assets there now total around one billion Swiss francs, or 200,000 kilograms of gold.

As I was leaving Evelina, Vixey happened to be going outdoors at the same time as I was. She was taking her bike to the park on that hot day, and talked with me while I waited for my taxi. There was a copy of *Les Misérables* in the bike's wicker basket; one rarely saw her without a book in those days. Vixey touched and adjusted the soft and flexible brim of her immaculate white straw hat, which had an indigo ribbon outlining the edge of the brim and a matching one banding the crown, where it was *twisted* once. We agreed to meet again that afternoon for ice cream. She suggested, "by the lion statue in Odeonsplatz, right outside the Hofgarten." Her Cartier would enable her to know when it was time, while also serving as a subtle badge of nobility for the otherwise pastorally and youthfully-attired girl.

Attending to business matters in the Altstadt, I came to notice that I was anticipating the meeting like a stupid student. Occasionally I looked at a clock, and experienced a feeling shooting through my body similar to what one feels when realizing that one is next in line to approach the open door of an aircraft while parachuting. It was not a feeling of trepidation, since the analogy assumes that one enjoys parachuting. But still, jumping out of an airplane is a radical event way beyond the scope of regular existence, and there was something about this rendezvous that fit that description as well.

A girl on a motorized scooter shot past me down the street, a vivid and alluring image that reminded me of Vixey, except for the fact that the hair flowing back behind her was blonde not black. Of similar appeal, I thought, is the image of a girl swiftly traversing space on horseback. It has the same aspects of effortless, nonchalant speed and arrogant enjoyment.

I arrived at the lions, the site of the gun battle of Hitler's Beer Hall Putsch a long time ago; one of many places in Munich so fondly described by Thomas Mann even before that. „*München leuchtete.*"[*] Not a minute late I

---

[*] "Munich is resplendent." – The first line of *Gladius Dei* (1902). Now, in 2014, although no longer the capital of a kingdom and not as cosmopolitan as a huge city like Paris, Munich has never been so impressive. Munich is a city where space and time don't conform to conventions. It has one of the largest urban parks in the world, and also the Alps are an hour's drive away. Integrating city and nature well, it also integrates the past and present. One can see a girl in a Bavarian dirndl dress along with new Charlotte Olympia heels and a Prada handbag (possibly obtained on Pradastraße – the familiar name for Maximilianstraße). Austro-Bavaria is known for the cordiality and attractiveness of its people, and this is evident in its central city.   Compared to German states, Bavaria is the most Christian and the least socialist. Munich is the wealthiest city in Germany and a base for companies like BMW and Allianz. At the same time it is not overly focused on work and has a high appreciation for a convivial *dolce vita*. It has the Oktoberfest, probably the most significant cultural/historic

saw Vixey ride out of the Hofgarten gate, then dismount and lead her bike with one hand by the front handlebars. I liked that she didn't stop at the red crossing light over Residenzstraße, where a number of other Germans had gathered despite there being no incoming cars.

We sat down at the outdoor café and she leaned her head back, shifting her black sun-heat-attracting hair away from her neck so that it hung straight down. Looking up, she put her hands on her neck and pushed them through her hair, letting the back of her neck dry, as it was damp from being covered by the hair on that hot day. Black hair really does become a lot hotter in the sun than blonde or light ash brown hair. Probably steam would drift up from her hair if she suddenly walked into a very cold room. I recalled that there was nothing strange about this meeting – after all I was required to look after her and treat her to things as part of my business relationship with her family. So what that I notice her moist neck and long hair?

Vixey leant her bare elbows on the table's edge and thought about what to order. She sharply criticized the regime for the lack of chocolate and got ice cream made without it. Summer '42 was a quiet time and the Reich was at the peak of its conquests, but the economic situation was precarious. There were all the problems of German socialism plus additional shortages from the British blockade.

In addition to the ice cream, Vixey ordered a Maria-Tereza-café, an Austrian coffee made with Grand Marnier orange liqueur and whipped cream.

I commented, "Are Viennese products like this more prevalent now after the *Anschluß Österreichs*?"

"Just a little, in Munich."

"The Austrians are practically Germans now. But the Swiss are a completely different *Willensnation*, regardless of

---

holiday on the world calendar, and P1 – considered by many to be the best fashionable nightclub in Germany.

whether they speak a German dialect. I don't consider myself German, for instance."

"So an invasion won't ever happen?" As she ate and drank I saw that her lips were swollen and red as a result of her daytime trysts on the Kurfürsteninsel. She licked her lips with her tongue cold from the ice cream, which alleviated them. Also visible was a reddish-violet mark on her neck, caused by broken capillaries;- evidently from overzealousness on someone's part. She will be embarrassed later when she looks in a mirror and sees what was on her neck all day.

"No- besides the extreme difficulty, it would be counterproductive. Hitler recognizes that a capitalist Switzerland is needed for access to international currency and commodity markets. You also need us to provide banking services... This reminds me: you know that you shouldn't tell anyone about Evelina's or your father's dealings with Credit Suisse, right? It could lead to unnecessary questions on the basis of the monetary control laws here."

"Sure. I know."

"I recall you saying you've been to Zürich a few times. What about Berne?"

"Yes, Berne too."

"Have you seen the *Bärengraben* (Bear pits)?"

"I have. The bears are *schön!*"

"What about the Bernese Oberland? Have you visited that area?"

"No."

"You should go down there. Go all the way to Mürren. It's a town on the edge of a cliff 850m above the valley, completely inaccessible by roads."

"How do you get there?"

"Only by cable car."

"I'm not sure about this summer, but probably next I'll try to go down there."

"Very good... How is your school in Berlin?"

"It is stupid. The only advantage is to meet people. Otherwise it just takes time away from real studies."

"Like what?"

She started talking about things she had read. I was shocked to discover she had perused the Federalist Papers and the Anti-Federalist counterarguments. She also was familiar with a range of politico-economic writers, viz. Montesquieu, Böhm-Bawerk, Mises, Locke, Bastiat, Burke. I imagined what occasional questions she put to her professors,-- which would be deliberately to vex them, since she would know they wouldn't be capable of answering.

I asked her who influenced her the most and she returned, "Safie."

"Safie?"

"Yes."

"That girl from Constantinople that Mary Shelley wrote about?" Safie was a sort of early feminist fictional character in the 1700s, a young pretty brunette who escaped her native Turkish empire to come to Germany.

"Mhm. It was one of the first things I ever read and it led to everything else – to wanting to know what people outside of our one-party state have written, culturally and politically."

Most of the Federalist Papers she claimed to read during a BDM (League of German Girls) long-distance hiking trip. "Nobody else knew what was this English book that I was reading; thus they couldn't say it was necessarily un-German. First we took a fast train south to Königstein near Dresden. There were so many turns in the track, we were staggering, laughing, and falling on people when we walked through the swaying aisles. Every time there would be this rubbing, murmuring sound of the wheels pressing against the curving metal rail. From Königstein we walked and camped in the mountains for a few days. We crossed the Basteibrücke, that bridge going through those rock formations and cliffs. By the way, they don't call the area Sächsische Schweiz (Saxon Switzerland) anymore. They decided that the name of a foreign country shouldn't describe a region of Germany."

"What? They changed the historic name of Sächsische Schweiz? To what?"

"They call it Kreis Pirna... I also took a similar trip once to Karlsbad in the Sudetes. What did I take there?.. Oh, it was *Sophismes économiques*. I don't usually like overnight trips like that. I like the forest but on a temporary basis – briefly. Then I want to clean and brush my hair and go back to sterile clean comfort."

I concluded that these occupations with political, legal, and economic theory were the thing that prevented, with her, a loss of reasonableness that often happens to other pretty girls. Reason means not letting emotions interfere with evaluations. When girls have total goodwill from all sides and are helped with everything they do, not required to think for themselves, they might stifle their capacity to reason well.[*] This could be why women are underrepresented in law (despite the example of Portia in *Merchant of Venice*), even while becoming prevalent in finance and other professional fields. Law is probably the profession demanding the most reasoning.

With Vixey, none of this aptitude detracted from her emotional sensibility and æsthetic sensitivity, which are things already evident with her. They just tempered it so that it was not on the level of an Emily St. Aubert or Adeline de Montalt.[†] Emily was warned against excessive sensibility, but continued to exhibit it all throughout her misadventures in the Apennines and south of France.

It would probably not surprise the reader, after this Munich scene, if I admitted of an unavoidable *Künstlerliebe*

---

[*] "Taught from their infancy that beauty is woman's sceptre, the mind shapes itself to [that]..., only seeking to adorn its prison." – Mary Wollstonecraft.

[†] Characters in Radcliffe novels.

for Vixey, as in E.T.A. Hoffmann's meaning of the term. For Hoffmann, this represented a sort of chaste admiration of someone with the seeming æsthetic and moral qualities of a divinity. Seen through an artist's eye, her graces are so captivating that they seem to *"extinguish art"* (to borrow from *Henry VI*)[*]. Her sapphire eyes make out of all of her a blue flower, and she incites one to *Sehnsucht*. With her, cherished as an unattainable feminine perfection, any interaction is a pleasure. Anything further, is too remote to even consciously remember about and actively desire.

Returning to Karl, it may be noticed that he himself was not insensible to æsthetic discernment. His background was from the musical arts, and his ability to play the difficult Rachmaninoff piece earlier demonstrated his proficiency. He also could play guitar. The visual arts closely parallel the literary arts, but music is something entirely different and foreign to me because it cannot be explained in words. It rather has the quality of effortlessly conveying ideas without words. The *drehleier* motif thus sums up the effect of the war on Pavel, as the C-minor Chiarina/Clara piece does with the war's effect on Vixey.[†]

Music has the quality of immediately bringing the artist into a connection with the listener. I find it hard to harbor ill-will towards someone playing beautiful music. A girl who resists a man's courtship will find this resistance breaking down if he is a good guitar player.

As the reader recalls, this entire tangent was a result of Karl asking Vixey about Munich while she lay on her bed reading. Going back to that, it's essential to mention that

---

[*] Part One, Act 5, Scene III.

[†] These are from the Schubert and Schumann compositions mentioned previously. Perhaps Tariverdiev's *17 mgnoveniy vesnii* (17 Moments of Spring) motif for piano and xylophone is an appropriate leitmotiv for Karl.

one bare foot of Vixey's hung limply off the edge of the bed. While she talked, Karl examined with curiosity her delicate ankle, that odd assortment of tendons, ligaments, muscles, and joints that are so essential to our mobility. Next to the tender skin at her Achilles tendon were the excessively-protruding bones of the joint itself, which seemed so fragile that a sudden wrenching might break it. However, for her small weight, this compact ankle was sturdy enough, and served her effectively in athletic activities such as jogging or hiking. It reminded Karl of the joints of a cat's paws, which seem so small and insignificant but which enable the cat to greatly exceed the dexterity and vitality of an animal of its size.

Looking further up Karl drew his hand along one of Vixey's slender thighs, with her a feature of endless fascination, enhanced in its unworldly enchantment by the fact that, except at poolsides and athletic venues, it is something that remains rarely seen in society. (Her appeal is considered from a purely æsthetic point of view – thus it shouldn't be incomprehensible for a female observer as well). Needless to say, with Vixey's sveltness, her thighs did not touch one another when her legs were straight and knees together. Is it possible to articulate the allure of this part of her? It barrages all the senses – the sight, the feel of touching it with one's hand or one's cheek, and the smell of the unperfumed skin – each of these more intoxicating than the last.

Chapter XV

> Tower'd cities please us then,
> And the busy hum of men,
> With store of ladies, whose bright eyes
> Rain influence, and judge the prize
> MILTON, *L'Allegro*

After a late breakfast of *geröstete Knödel mit Ei*, Vixey and Karl set out for Freiburg. She checked the petrol level in the Mercedes, opened the automatic garage door, and performed the series of sequential steps required to activate the motorcar. She had claimed to have full proficiency in this, and wanted to appear as if she was doing everything nonchalantly. In actuality, her practice was not that extensive and the necessity to appear nonchalant increased her nervousness and made her forget certain steps. However, she figured it out and they departed.

The Mercedes slipped out of the garage with a silent, feline grace, and the excellent suspension made the uneven cobblestone driveway unnoticeable. It was a large and complex piece of machinery and Karl was surprised that Vixey could operate it. The keychain, hanging by the wheel, brushed against Vixey's knee as she moved her stilettoed foot from one pedal to another. She felt simultaneously the metallic points of keys as well as a velvety touch of ermine fur from an ornamental attachment on the chain.

Vixey suavely manœuvered the curves of the mountain road, one gloved hand on the wheel, enjoying the pleasure of driving with open windows, a blue sky, and warm weather. However, a couple of times she bumped into smaller cars that were stopped at an intersection in front of her, which led Karl to question her driving abilities. The owners of the other cars turned around, but did not think it worthwhile to bother anyone driving a motorcar of such relative prominency.

They descended from the Schwarzwald to the Rhine Valley, hearing all the while the sounds of artillery from the Vosges mountains on the valley's opposite side. This was an unpleasant reminder of the proximity of the front. They also passed through the Black Forest village where Chekhov died exactly 40 years earlier. Vixey's Cartier was half visible from under her left glove when she held her arm level on the wheel.

Karl asked, "What was Pavel Nikitich doing here so early in the morning? What happened with him?"

"Nothing," Vixey replied. "He seems to want to court me, but I told him that he shouldn't." Privately, she enjoyed the flattery of Pavel's attention, but knew it was inadvisable, and maybe even dangerous, to allow him so much leniency.

Vixey drove into the town center by going into the southeast tower-gate. It was a grandiose way of entering the Altstadt – driving through the *Schwabentor*. This is a large rectangular clock tower with a triangular hat and a building affixed to it that holds an arched passageway. There are many similar tower-gates in Rothenburg ob der Tauber, Munich, and Prague.

Freiburg looks like a typical medieval German town, with lots of steep-gabled roofs. Continuing on Herrenstraße, Vixey turned into the Münsterplatz, the central square containing Freiburg's preëminent building, the tall dark-red gothic Münster. She circled the cathedral on the right, and after passing through the entire square, parked at the *Historisches Kaufhaus*. This is an attractive red turreted building from 1530 that had been an important Merchants' Hall. It is bright and nicely ornamented, especially the turrets.

Vixey left her purse in the car, only taking Reichsmark notes and an identity document with her. She gave the keys to Karl. They left the car but she ran back momentarily, with an audible staccato on her stilettos, leaning down to the car's small side-mirror to check her hair and appearance before setting out. Then she led Karl on a walk through the Altstadt. He had a rakishly-donned fedora and well-fitting suit. Freiburg is the sunniest and warmest of all German cities, and the October weather was quite tolerable. Vixey's stilettos struck and knocked against the centuries-old granite setts of the pavement.

"Are you comfortable in those shoes?" Karl asked.

"Yes, I am," she replied, then later said, "But even if there was some discomfort in wearing them, the discomfort of looking bad would be inevitably worse."[*]

Vixey wore a suit consisting of a pencil skirt and fur-trimmed jacket in a reddish-brown plaid color. On closer inspection, however, it would be seen that no part of it was actually brown; rather the shade was produced by a fine interplay of black, dark red, orange, and white elements in the plaid design. A ruby and pink-sapphire brooch, not immediately noticeable, adorned her jacket.

She also had the obligatory gloves and small French hat. No ribbons and bows that she wore so often at home; out in town she was an image of sophistication. She had appeared almost maybe too young before to Karl, prior to seeing her now. (She looked especially young at those times when she was quaintly reduced in height as a result of talking off shoes and standing just in stockings).

I saw her walking in town that day. Business has been making it necessary to take many trips from Berne to Freiburg lately. Coincidentally, I was wearing my Tyrolean hat with a feather in it, even though I'm Swiss. A larger feather is impressive according to Tyrolean and Bavarian traditions. I even greeted Vixey in the Austro-Bavarian manner, saying, "*Grüß Gott.*" As expected, she did notice

---

[*] This way of thinking reminds one of Donatella Versace, who – responding to someone's question about the conservative dress code in a rehabilitation center – said, "It was harder to give up my heels than it was the cocaine..."

the feather and made a favorable comment on it. Introductions were completed and there was some conversation, but she really couldn't stay long and, after I passed my regards on to her father and to Evelina, she and the officer moved on in the town.

As she walked away, my glance lingered in her direction; it was all I could do so as to capture the last remnant details of her image before she was gone. Due to the uneven stone pavement and the thinness and height of her heels, in each of Vixey's steps there was a barely-perceptible vacillation, a slight wobble as the platform stiletto adjusted into a fully vertical position with her weight on it. All this occurred in the instant as she made the step, before shifting her weight to the front of her foot to step forward. Her tight skirt stretched with each step.

Needless to say, in a gait that came naturally to her, she placed her feet in a straight line one after the other. But sometimes she made her steps even slightly crossed over that line... When this happened, it was like an extra spark in her step -- an electricity that threatened to ignite flames over the flagstone. I felt like extolling her; commending her; of saying, "good girl..." – She knew how to do it.

I recalled Virgil's *Æneid*, "...*et vera incessu patuit dea.*"[*]

Vixey showed Karl the red *Altes Rathaus*[†] and the *Martinstor*, another tower-gate. They gingerly stepped over the numerous *Bächle*, open gutters through which fresh water continually flows.

Returning to the Münsterplatz, they entered into a *gemütlich* Viennese-style café right across from the doors of the cathedral. It was formerly a *Konditorei* (pâtisserie), but with the wartime scarcity in coffee, tea, chocolate, and *gâteaux*, it changed into serving primarily regular food. The

---

[*] This line occurs when Æneas becomes aware of the divinity of a goddess in disguise by her gait.
[†] A Rathaus is like a city hall, or a town meeting house.

wartime rationing system actually is causing an increase in business at restaurants. This is because one ration ticket could only obtain a certain small amount of food at a store, but in a restaurant it is valid for one order, only limited by cost.

The café was the best in town and Freiburg's *bon ton* would be found here. It was usually full but there were a few tables available and Vixey and Karl sat down at one of them.

*   *   *

A few minutes later, just after ordering, they saw a uniformed German Wehrmacht colonel suddenly walk in, accompanied by a dazzling blonde. They looked around for tables and chose the vacant one right next to Karl and Vixey. Due to the limited space, tables were positioned very close to each other. The imprudent sense of ease that Karl had gained driving through picturesque Baden and walking around the quaint city was suddenly dashed. He began thinking that maybe this hadn't been such a great idea.

The blonde, who was called Elena Felixovna, was drawn to Vixey's table because she had seen her fleetingly in town before. She was curious about her and this man who was with her. The tables were up against a wall such that a long wooden bench fixed to the wall could be shared amongst several tables. Karl sat there; Vixey on the chair at the other end of the table. Elena was next to Karl on the bench while the colonel, Walther Steiger, was diagonally opposite him – giving each a good view of the other. Walther took off his officer's peaked cap and tossed it on the bench between Elena and Karl. He curtly gave the necessary *guten Tag* salutation and Karl curtly replied.

Meanwhile Vixey was afforded an opportunity to examine Elena's style and appearance. She was satisfied that the advantage was decidedly in her own favor, although she had to admit that this blonde fräulein was sufficiently beautiful and stylish to present a formidable challenge.

Elena had a cinched-waist light-colored trenchcoat, cut well above the knee, as well as high-heels and an Hermès *sac à dépêches*[*]. She had an up-turned pretty nose, green eyes, and, similar to Vixey, liked to use liner and mascara. This blackness around her eyes contrasted well with her fair blonde hair. However, she did not have quite as much liner and lacked the really *winged-look* that Vixey liked. Elena's dress was in green and white silk faille with a lace-up closure and wide shoulder straps. Green can only work for a green-eyed blonde, Vixey thought, "and even then only in small amounts. But she does pull it off nicely." The lace-up was at the front and was of the type that one can pull and watch it tighten the bodice of the dress over the blouse. Vixey recalled that she had something like that too, only in black. She liked on herself the effect of tightening the laces, bringing the *décolleté* dress from a loose shapelessness to the contours of her figure.

Vixey ate *lapin aux chanterelles* and Karl had *duxelles-*coated *contre-filets de bœuf* wrapped in crêpes. They drank gewürztraminer, as there were no French reds available anymore. "*N'y a-t-il pas de vins français n'importe où?*" Vixey thought. At one point Vixey called over a passing waiter and said, softly but without a doubt of being obliged, "Garçon, change the music that's playing. I've heard this one too many times."

Karl was able to take some glances at Elena next to him and was struck by her icy, imperious look. The sharpness of her appearance was founded in a combination of features, most of all her arched, hard-angled (but not thin) eyebrows. It was further augmented by her cold bright eyes, seeming lack of willingness to ever smile, and beautiful flawless countenance. From Karl's angle, a very subtle elevation of Elena's upper lip gave an involuntary expression to her nose of vexed discomfort – how a girl

---

[*] The same handbag later made famous by Grace Kelly, Princess of Monaco.

might appear if she found herself in a crowded 2nd class train compartment where some unsavory people had occupied all corners. She thus appeared unapproachable because of the apparent scorn that one felt certain would arise and the possibility that disturbing her might heighten her expression further into a sneer. In short, she was somewhat intimidating, but this fact nonetheless made her very appealing for the reason that *if* her apparent inaccessibility is overcome and one is in full possession of her attentions, there's a constant reminder of the magnitude of the accomplishment. One could then marvel (and be sure that others are impressed as well) at how this girl who looks like she scorns everything has, despite that, an attachment or affinity towards one individual.[*]

The German colonel went to use the water closet, during which time Elena put a cigarette in her lips and turned to Karl to ask for a light, not bothering to pronounce the words clearly. He obliged her and continued his conversation with Vixey. Elena brushed back a strand of blonde hair which had fallen to the front of her face and leaned in to the flame of the lighter. She had recently had her hair styled by her Genevese *coiffeuse*, Gisèle de Crécy, who kept a salon in Freiburg.

I only mention specifically this *coiffeuse* Gisèle because I actually had the pleasure of meeting her once in Genève, at the Hôtel Bristol, Rue de Mont-Blanc. (I'm sure that at

---

[*] Pushkin ruminates on this type of woman in *Yevgeny Onegin*, 3.XXII. He ends by saying that maybe you too have seen such ladies on the banks of the Neva in St. Petersburg:

Я знал красавиц недоступных,
Холодных, чистых, как зима,
Неумолимых, неподкупных,
Непостижимых для ума;...
Над их бровями надпись ада:
Оставь надежду навсегда...
Быть может, на берегах Невы
Подобных дам видали вы.

least some readers would be interested in a longer version of my interaction with her, but I will limit the description here to the following. I advise those who want more to meet me for café and we would be able to talk then). Gisèle thought I was British, because we spoke mostly in English, with a little French mixed in. Her English was almost as bad as my French. When we parted, I kissed her twice on the cheek as in France but she made it thrice, saying, "*Trois, en Genève.*" This I will always remember because I never met a nicer French girl. Living in Berne, I'm frequently ashamed at not knowing the French language, but like all Bernese I use it whenever I can, since I know the correct pronunciation and a few dozen words. Writing and thinking in English as opposed to French is an unfortunate necessity.

To return to Elena:

At that moment Vixey and Karl were discussing the Russians. Elena suddenly remarked to Karl, leaning her head closer and touching him by the arm, "Are you referring to General Petrovsky? Vladimir Maximovich?"

"Yes," Karl said. "Do you know him?"

At that moment they both noticed that Walther had already returned and was standing by his chair. "Don't let me prevent your conversation," he began, sitting down.

"I was just asking for a light," Elena replied sharply. She had her own specific reasons for not discussing Vladimir Maximovich in the presence of Walther and was angry at the interruption.

Walther was often suspicious of Elena, and not without reason, due to her many infidelities that came to be revealed. (He had no problem, though, with using her for swap transactions with his close friends, when an attractive arrangement could be had). He recalled the fact that she had chosen this table herself, when others were available. Perhaps she knew this man from before? Perhaps it was the same Ticinese from Lugano that he had discovered but never was able to come across? He engaged Karl in conversation, at length asking where he was from.

Karl said he was Dutch, as usual, so that there would be a reason for his non-native German speech. Walther asked, "So how is Holland faring with the famine ongoing there right now?"

Like most people, Karl was completely unaware of this fact, and his lack of a natural reaction was evident. "The famine there is severe. In fact, that would be one of the reasons why I am in Germany instead of there. I'm staying with my cousin," he said, indicating Vixey.

Walther replied, without concern if anything he said may be offensive or caustic, "The Dutch are bringing it upon themselves. Why did they have to initiate a railroad transport strike? And now Montgomery has failed in his attempt to capture Arnhem. Undoubtedly you and your countrymen are hoping rather for Montgomery's success. If you are really from there."

"It is as I said. Where else could I be from?"

Setting down his table knife and shrugging, Walther said, "I don't know, but we are very close to the front here, as well as to the Swiss border. There is all manner of various traffic in this corner of Germany."

Walther's table manners made Vixey cringe. They were not the most outrageous but still weren't pleasant. For instance, he chewed very audibly, banged utensils loudly on the plate, and used them to point at things. With this example serving as a contrast, Vixey saw Karl as definitely *not* being of proletariat origins.

Karl did not enjoy playing the farce with the colonel. He decided to simply tell the truth and hope it would be seen as sarcasm, since nobody would envision someone saying such a thing earnestly. Also he felt overconfident because Vixey was with him. He said, "You have guessed it, colonel. I'm actually an American Army officer. I am charged with disrupting supply lines to Alsace."

Vixey laughed out of necessity, but otherwise continued eating and drinking nonchalantly; she was unconcerned and felt she could take control of the situation at any time if it got out of hand.

Elena gave a sort of snickering laugh, amused at the ironic statement. Walther, meanwhile, was irritated at what he perceived to be jesting made at his expense. He said, "A fine excuse for traipsing around Germany you seem to have, being Dutch. I take it you are not enlisted in any of the Reich's armed services?"

"No."

"You should have been drafted, along with all Hollanders, for the common defense of the Reich. It was a mistake from the start not to annex the Netherlands to Germany, as was successfully done with Austria."

"I agree with that," said Vixey.

"Yes," continued Walther. "It is a fine country, and as soon as it was *Judenfrei* (liberated of Jews), it was just as ethnically sound as Germany. Plus there were few countries where the Jews had accumulated so many assets. Not only real estate and currency, but all sorts of tangible and intangible assets like artwork and patents. All this now became available for the benefit of the people, as well as a few enterprising Party members, such as myself, who managed to secure a substantial profit."

"Was it just for economic gain that you participated in expropriating their assets?" asked Vixey. What he was saying was reminding her a little of Bolshevism.

"Primarily, yes. I've always disliked them personally, but not any more than the French, Poles, and Soviets. The Poles and Ukrainians were only too glad to get rid of their Jews. That's where they were the most numerous. In Odessa we found that they had been urged to stay while other people were being evacuated. There was a great deal of money to be made from transferring workers from the east to German factories and construction sites, Jews at first, then Poles. All of this is within the rights of exercising strength for the greater good of the Reich, and its Nordic race. Essentially, it is the mark of a superior mind to be able to transgress former social boundaries in the pursuit of one's goals."

"Now you are starting to sound like the Marquis de Montalt," Vixey remarked.

"Like who?"

"Never mind. It was an Ann Radcliffe reference."

Walther was interested by this sophisticated and attractive dark fräulein next to him, and he falsely assumed the allusion she made to be a favorable one. He continued, seeking to ascertain her own viewpoints. "I would go even further to say that ethical values are illusions. Nature is fundamentally indifferent to man's comforts. In fact it tries to thwart man whenever it can. Why oppose it then? Nothing we can do can offend nature, as it has already created fundamental inequalities among men. Philanthropy or mercy towards the weak is wrong; it helps them and thus goes against nature's process of Darwinian competition. Rather, it is the exercise of power over others, that is in line with nature – otherwise it would not have the incredibly intoxicating characteristics that it does."

"So anarchy then?"

"Anarchy would be Rousseau's state of nature. Jean-Jacques Rousseau believed that inequalities become institutionalized as society advances and as controls become more centralized. But while he thought it's a negative, I see it as a positive. That is why I am not an anarchist like Nestor Makhno[*] but a fascist. It provides opportunities for the advancement of those groups that are naturally meant for it."

---

[*] In addition to the Red and White Armies in the Russian Civil War, there was also the Black Army, opposed to both. It was led by Makhno, sometimes called Bat'ko Makhno. They were based near Zaporozhye and their flag resembled a pirate flag, with a skull and crossbones on a black background.

"These are sophisms," Vixey said. "For instance, social Darwinism doesn't say that the 'fittest' are necessarily the strongest or cleverest. Well-meaning cooperation, for instance, should end up being more beneficial and thus more competitive in the long-term. Who do you associate with, I wonder?"

Irritated by the disagreement evident, Walther nonetheless replied, "I find it better to be among acquaintances who think the same way. They are at least honest, and one knows in advance what to expect from them. One won't be surprised at an awkward moment. Nobody can claim to be completely 'good', especially in these days when necessities force people to desperate measures. *Schadenfreude* is in everyone. Take as an example French guillotines in the Place de la Concorde or de la Roquette: the joy of people attending them proves the underlying animosity of everyone towards everyone. It is precisely the taking of a human life that interests them in the spectacle so much. Unfortunately in Germany it is mostly secretive and in France it was stopped during the *Deuxième empire* in 1870."

Elena interrupted, "In France they had those spectacles up until 1939 actually."

Walther whispered angrily at her, "Don't correct me in public." She did in fact make the statement in public, but had it been otherwise Walther's reaction would be similar. He could never imagine himself to be wrong in his views or his factual statements- that was inconceivable. He had a tendency to perceive any kind of analytical discussion as an insulting disagreement. To him all of his own opinions were fact, and thus he spent much time criticizing everything around him, from politics to other peoples' personal preferences.

Vixey diverted the topic to a comparison of party membership advantages in Germany and the Soviet Union. Walther explained, "Bolshevism offers more comparative rewards for top party members but the risk is greater. Spies are everywhere. In fact the higher you go, the more visibility and danger there is. Against that I have to conclude that our system is better. Then there's market capitalism, as seen in the most complete form in America in the previous century. That has failed and has led to plutocracy. The transition from capitalism to plutocracy has been amply proven by German theorists. In it the same kind of opportunists are free to profit by plunder – they were known as robber barons. But the opportunities and wealth are controlled by only a very small number. In fascism, at least a decent standard of living is guaranteed to everyone. Production is not left open to haphazard, uncoordinated whims, nor to external financial markets. Meanwhile there is a vast amount of profit to be made from administering the system, as well as redistributing from those elements that are *unerwünscht* (undesirable) for the future of the Reich."

Vixey was confused by some of Walther's logic and stopped trying to understand his philosophy. Karl still had some questions though, "So you view fascism as the best means of providing egalitarianism to the majority? While keeping a sub-class at the bottom? You assume that each system has class conflicts that can only be resolved by force?"

Walther, enraged just at these discursive questions, sneeringly remarked, "You're disputing what I have said?! Who would you rather have control everything then? The communists; or perhaps the robber barons?"

Karl found it necessary to reply to this, during which Walther became increasingly astonished at his speech. He said, "I would differ in my view of the 19th century American businessmen. The ones that were true capitalists were not as you described them. How did they gain their wealth? By way of people voluntarily giving money to them. This happened because of their continual effort to provide better products at lower prices. By necessity, they could only have gained personal profits after having first provided a disproportionately large value to society. For instance, Vanderbilt defeated the government-backed steamship cartels, permanently reducing costs to consumers on all steamship lines he entered. The investors he is accused of ruining on the NYSE[*] were corrupt politicians short-selling his stock. Then there's Rockefeller, who fought the Russians in an international oil war. He increased efficiency of production so much he was able to beat the Russians' natural resource advantages and sell oil at prices lower than ever to people worldwide...

"The famous first transcontinental railroads were all built with government subsidies and support. They all failed due to inefficiency and bad construction. The only success was the privately-financed Northern Railroad to Seattle, built by James Hill. So, as you can see, even government help to industries ends up detrimental in the long run. Whereas the private entrepreneurs are the ones who create technological progress and efficiency that everyone benefits from. But there are certain lunatics who would rather destroy an economy with controls, and then try to make up for it by exploitative colonization."

Walther was incensed, "Are you referring to the Führer, perhaps?"

"No, not the Führer. I was referring to lunatics."

Vixey suggested, "That's enough, Karl. You're forgetting where you are." She was mindful of the risk of Gestapo or SS people being nearby.

---

[*] To note an interesting coincidence, in 2011 an ETF started trading on the NYSE with a ticker called "VIXY". It is based on short-term futures contracts on the CBOE's VIX – Volatility Index. VIX, in turn, is a derivative of prices of 1-month plain vanilla puts and calls (*id est*, straddle options) on the S&P 500. It's relatively well-behaved because it keeps reverting to a base price range; thus it is easier to profitably trade this derivative than any other major derivative.

Most of Karl's arguments were lost on Walther; Karl merely aroused his intense animosity. Walther thought there was definitely something strange about this person, and did not see the need to spend any more time talking with him. Elena urged that they go and Walther said to her, "Yes. It's time we went already."

Karl was relieved at this pronouncement. Walther left money on the table and stood up to gather his things.

*　　*　　*

Around them other people were reading newspapers or eating. There was a hum from the conversations of people and the activity of the waiters, but nothing too loud to prevent one from reading. All the interior elements in imitation of a Viennese café were there, including the familiar wood paneling and Thonet chairs. Many people were there to use the space as a sort of second living room.

Elena fumbled for something in her handbag, then got up. Unseen by Walther, when she only had one second, she dropped a card to Karl and winked with a significant but silent air. That was all. Walther took her arm and they left.

As they were walking out Walther was already taking out his antagonism to Karl on her, "What was he bringing up all those capitalist monopolists for? What is their relevance now?"

"Maybe he was just trying to make conservation. In Holland maybe they have a different merchant viewpoint and..."

"Don't seek a justification for him!" Walther interrupted with irritation. "You're always taking someone else's side!"

"I'm just trying to suggest why..." this continued in a typical manner as they continued to argue.

The card that Elena gave Karl was the business card of a hotel in Freiberg. On the back she had hastily written her name, Elena, as well as "17:00", two hours from then. Karl and Vixey were bewildered at to what this meant.

"Who is she? What can she have to say?" wondered Karl.

"And why this secretive rendezvous? Why not tell us here?"

"Maybe it has to do with the colonel."

"Should we go meet her?"

"Yes, why not?"

Since two hours remained, they stayed to eat dessert with *ersatz* coffee, then walked around to various places, including the inside of the Münster. The cathedral's stained glass windows had already been removed in anticipation of potential RAF bombing raids.[*] They took a drive through the hills outside the city and then returned in time to pull up at the hotel at 17:00.

There was a marble staircase at the end of the lobby which went up several steps to a platform before turning 90 degrees and continuing further up. At the platform was a full-length mirror, before which Elena stood without a hat, adjusting her hair.

She had changed into narrow-fitting pants and a short jacket and while waiting, was standing with her legs crossed, still wearing heels. In the immediate area this constituted a singularity, in the mathematical and mechanical sense of the term. A singularity is an unmanageable part of a continuous function, where things are nondeterministic and the rules of physics may be distorted. An example of it in mechanics is when rotational axes are driven into a collinear alignment, resulting in an undefined instability. When a girl who looks like Elena, dressed like her, happens to stand in that way, a similar effect occurs to the world in the immediate vicinity. Contemplation of such a singularity, admitting it into one's mind, could be disruptive to one's well-being. She did not

---

[*] Which would happen only a month hence.

reflect upon any of this; it appears that such poise came instinctually to her. She transcended the vulgarity of the typical unrefined means of standing in whatever way it happens, the familiar shape of two legs at an acute angle planted haphazardly on the ground. Instead she formed an hourglass X shape twice: first at her slim waist, then a longer and narrower X centered at her knees. Her long legs seemed to intersect at a single point. At her knees, one leg was behind the other; thus it created a wondrous optical effect whereby her body seemed to come to a single point of practically no width. Looking further down, one could observe her right and left foot inverted from the usual placement. This lent her an air of girlishly-vulnerable instability on her high-heels, even though she was actually more stable and comfortable than she would be in the next-best stance: one where the legs are straight and the feet close together, shoes touching. Both stances benefit from their appearance of compactness, a positive feature for a lady. But one further advantage of the crossed-legs stance is the warmth it generates as a result of the close pressing contact between both legs, something that can't happen when they are un-crossed. This has pleasanter associations than coldness.

To recapitulate: form-fitting attire, slender legs, soft blonde hair falling over her back; an attractive face reflected from the mirror. Elena's pants were tailored with a slightly longer length so that they ended at the exact midpoint of her stilettos. In this way only a part of her shoes was suggestively revealed,- the lower part of the heel and the front of the vamp on its centimeter-high platform sloping inward subtly. At the top the pants were tighter, but became less so further down from the knees, allowing for a sharp ironed crease at the front and back to be visible. To compete with Vixey, she had chosen her best short jacket – it was in white and sapphire checked tweed. Under it she had a blouse that exactly matched the interior jacket lining visible on the revere.

The effect of the total image, even if an undefined singularity, would vary by the person. Pirogov, the carefree tsarist officer, could have been in the lobby reading his *Сѣверная Пчела* (*Northern Bee*), and he would do nothing upon noticing her except be impressed and make a mental note to find out who this fräulein/*devitsa* is. The singularity would have rather the most dangerous effect on the opposite kind of person: the lonely artist type. To him it is not just a fräulein but a sylph. Someone like that would have cause for an immediate temptation to find a gendarme in the street, seize his pistol, and shoot himself. One would have a disbelief of ever again seeing such a sight, which would be a terrible thing, impossible to come to terms with. To see such a vision would make one imagine that this is the peak of æsthetic experience and everything will be downhill from here. It is like finding a diamond in the ground and, right then and there – as soon as touching it – learning that one must give it away almost immediately. A voice of reason might persist, "No, it's not the only vignette that could be glimpsed, nor even the best. In a year's time it's quite possible that two or three similar or even better flashes can be seen, also of Elysian visions." But what to look at in the meantime? Leaden skies; beneath them dirty tenements, degenerating from a lack of plumbing, electricity, and rubbish collection; the populations they contain.. These things are nauseating for anyone who is æsthetically sensitive. Nevertheless a man can become accustomed to seeing such 'commonness' continually all the time, accustomed to anything that lasts long. Severe grief or happiness can occur at a change, but after time the change is adapted to. Well, here one can drag along his weary way, having learned indifference to the daily realities of life, and glad for the fact that, at least, things are not worsening at a rapid pace. And then such a sight! All of a sudden, unexpectedly, such a jarring reminder of everything one lacks. A jab to the face, waking one up to the fact that one is not actually living. A brief anguished glimpse into another world, a vignette of angels and paradise. It is neither *devitsa* nor *videnye* (apparition). But she must be something transcendental, sylph- or nymph-like, since what else can so harness the elemental power of beauty that it creates a veritable singularity? What else can change the world just through the force of *appearance*? Simply the outrage over the devil mocking and taunting one with such a wildly inexplicable vignette is enough to run to find a gendarme's gun in madness. How can one force oneself to continue toiling through life, having seen something like this? Why work — what for? No amount of work could make a difference in bringing one closer to this. Comparable would be a half-starved *zek* (inmate) of a concentration camp coming across a deliciously smoky barbeque feast happening on the other side of the barbed wire, forever inaccessible. To the *zek*, food is an *idée fixe* – he knows of no other goal, he sees it in his sleep, and almost tries to eat the pages of books where he sees fine food described. To the hypothetical unfortunate artist described above, susceptible to abstract synecdoche, accustomed to tying abstract ideas to visual representations, it is the same with beauty. – In this case, a potent example of it in the seemingly-impossible curves shown by the way Elena Felixovna was attired and standing.

I'm sure that more can be written about her stance – this still doesn't seem sufficient – but on with the story! Elena saw Vixey and Karl approaching and said, "Ah, there you are! Will you tell me now who you are? We're alone."

Karl and Vixey looked at each other. Vixey said, "Why don't you tell us who you are."

"You know Vladimir Maximovich somehow. I'm his niece."

"Oh yes," said Karl. "He did mention his niece is in Freiburg. Nice to meet you. I actually did not expect his niece to be so young." (She was 21). They all shook hands and told their respective names. "Why the secrecy with this meeting?"

"It's simply because I'm afraid of what Walther might do if he knew Vladimir was here. The two of them have sworn to kill each other."

"Really? Why is that?"

"Come, let's sit down," she said, walking over to some armchairs in the hotel lobby where she had left her hat. Sitting in the chair, Karl explained that Vixey's house was right next to the Russian division's base, and as a result of a chance acquaintance formed, they saw Vladimir Maximovich quite often when he visited.

Elena asked, "Do you think you can take me there tonight? You see, it was actually this very morning that I found out that Walther is to leave today for a week to his HQ. If I hadn't met you I would have to telephone Volodya[*] tomorrow and wait until he could have time to visit me here."

Karl said, "Yes, of course we can take you back."

Vixey added, "But I don't think you would want to go to the base. Imagine what kind of living conditions they have there. Why don't you stay in my house?" Aside to Karl, she said, "She can take the room you have. You don't really use it, right?"

"Your house is close and he can visit us there?" Elena asked.

"Yes."

"Well, alright! Just give me an hour to gather my things... As for my story, I can tell you more later, but the short version is that I was affianced to a Russian, Andrei, but he was captured at the front. A German officer started

---

[*] This is a more familiar form of Vladimir. There are many standard variants of Russian names. Pavel Nikitich sometimes calls the general Maximich, a shortened version of his patronymic. Elena would be called Lena most often, while the pet form of the name is Lenochka.

courting me in Kiev- Walther Steiger. Things had gotten so bad at that point in Kiev that I practically didn't have any other alternative. Then Andrei ran into him at a POW camp. They fought a duel and he lost and was killed. Such is life- *c'est la vie*. Nothing can be done about it now. For some reason, Volodya could never let it be settled with that. After he switched to the Germans, he met Walther and they had an argument. People separated them but they made some serious threats against each other. Since then they luckily haven't met, and I have kept it a secret that I am still seeing the German colonel. I thought about it, I really did, after the duel, but he has too much money to consider leaving him for someone else."

Vixey was initially uncomfortable at these admissions of the mercenary way of life Elena engaged in, but assumed it was unavoidable for her due to circumstances. "When was the duel?" she asked.

"April '42."

"And you've been in Germany since then?"

"Since the summer of that year, yes. So it's been more than two years already. I was also in Paris and Bruxelles for a bit."

Vixey was glad she herself had money of her own, since even in Germany basic essentials like food was becoming scarce for most, not to mention Ukraine- where Elena was from.

*   *   *

Elena needed to go to make some final arrangements, so they planned where to meet in an hour. Again with some excess of time, Vixey and Karl had a drink at the hotel lobby bar, then walked around the Altstadt looking at the evening colors. Vixey sheltered herself from a gust of wind with the fur trim on her collar. She was uncomfortable in wind.

Karl asked her, "Were you in Berlin at the time of the Olympics there?"

"Yes! It was a great event. It was started the next day after my tenth birthday. There were so many things built in preparation – the *Olympiastadion*, the *Waldbühne*. Don't forget that before that, in the February of the same year, there were also the Winter Olympics in Garmisch-Partenkirchen. I was there too, and it was a smaller, more intimate thing, so I was able to see everything up close."

As an aside, I must mention that I was there as well, just after starting to work in Berne, and was able to see Vixey. For the first time, I think it was, and she was already starting to become impressive with a black on black style: black whirl of hair against black coat and white snow. I told her the same thing that the Prince de Condé told Angélique in 1649: that he would wager that when she grows up men will hang themselves for having met her.

Vixey said to Karl, "Then, four years later in 1940, the winter games were again supposed to be held in Garmisch, but they were cancelled because of the war. And now in February of this year, 1944, they were planned to be in Cortina d'Ampezzo, but the war *still* is going on and again they were cancelled."

"I'm sorry that we could not finish it on time for you, so that you could watch the skiing," Karl said sarcastically, but immediately regretted it because, on second thought, it sounded extremely harsh.

She wasn't cross; but she did feel the need now to emphasize how much she would have wanted to go, "I had it all planned out what clothes I would bring and wear. For instance, a nice headband of fur and a short, tight little fur-lined coat from Révillon Frères of Paris. I spent a lot of time on finding a perfect pair of boots for snow conditions. I know that just the word boots doesn't sound good, but you mustn't think I would wear something like a cheap pair of army boots. Let me explain...

"In the winter the question comes up of how to differentiate oneself from others – in terms of thinness – while still wearing a lot of voluminous clothes. Of course my coats are tight at the waist, but that's not enough. I came up with idea of making leather boots that are really high and really tight. I had my *cordwainer* in Zürich make them, custom fit. They are up to here," she said, indicating her leg right above the knee. "On the back, however, they end a little lower, so that they don't prevent me from bending my legs to sit down. It's a really cute effect when I do sit down, because the material in the front of the boot rises higher than my leg." She lifted her leg with bent knee and indicated with her hand where the flap of leather material would be. So doing, she started losing balance and this required Karl to take her arm. He thought she was done, but there was more to say. Typical of an American, no matter how recherché and stylish an article of clothing, he would still prefer her without it rather than with it.

She continued, "The heel was obviously not a stiletto, not to sink in the snow. It is a square stacked heel, about 110mm. Most boots that ladies wear are very wide around the calf – there's extra space there, which looks really bad! I specifically had these made to be as tight as possible. They have a steel zipper along the entire length of the outer side and it's not that easy to zip it up; the leather has to stretch a little for me to be able to close it. Then there's a buckle at the top to ensure that the zipper stays in place."

"Does this allow your blood to circulate?"

"Yes, of course. It's pleasurably-tight, like a well-fitted corset. It feels really pleasant. It's not like any loose piece of clothing I have on – it feels like it's an extension of me. One that makes me taller and accentuates my thinness. When I walk in the boots I feel that my gait is even more neat; maybe I should say more deft and precise. Oh, there's more; I forgot one thing. They're each made from two pieces of leather, with the zipper dividing them. The front half is black, but the back half is dark gray. This creates an appearance of even greater slimness, because whenever you look at a length of something divided vertically in two shades of color, it appears narrower than it is....

"A corset is another great thing, but obviously for different situations- preferably for when I'm indoors and don't need to move around a lot. I can only take short breaths in it, so this precludes any kind of activity or much eating. But that's fine, since a lady shouldn't be seen eating anything more than 'lobster salad and champagne' at a *soirée*, according to Byron...

"Also I can't lean forward with a corset on. Once at a fashionable French *soirée* the shoelaces on one of my heeled Oxfords came undone. I saw a dandyish fellow who I nevertheless suspected of being in *la Résistance – les fifis*[*] – and bluntly told him, '*Monsieur, binde meine Schnürsenkel – mes lacets. Je ne peux pas les atteindre.*' Then I placed my foot several steps up on a staircase – sideways."

"Why sideways?"

"Um, I don't know – to be more coquettish.. He had to reposition my foot to be upright, then tie the laces – all the while behaving as if *I* were doing him a favor – and thanking me afterward. I attribute this to my good looks and of course the corset – otherwise why would he thank a German for letting him tie her shoes?"

Karl was slightly overwhelmed with the chatter of information about her boots and corsets but liked to have her talking about anything.

*   *   *

At length, it became time to meet Elena and go with her back to the house. When Elena saw the Mercedes she was surprised and impressed, since only the higher political or military hierarchy had anything at this level. When they got in Karl and Vixey kissed, then smiled, then kissed at further length. Elena hit Karl's shoulder playfully from the back seat, saying, "You're so affectionate with your cousin. I like it."

---

[*] This diminutive nickname came from FFI – *Forces Françaises de l'Intérieur*.

They laughed at the misconception, Karl explaining, "It's only a false identity that I have been using that I am her cousin from Amsterdam. I'm actually a US Army officer, as I said in the café."

"But how is that possible?" she asked, lifting her sharp, dark eyebrows.

"I'm with a small company of soldiers. We got lost in Germany and commandeered her house. We're just waiting for the front to reach us."

Vixey, behind the wheel, just smiled and shrugged, as if to say 'That's how it is. I didn't have any say in this.'

Elena was confused. There were now just too many things going on in this war to understand. And she was a little worried, because it was the first time she had seen the enemy. What could Vladimir Maximovich be doing associating with enemy Americans? Vixey calmed and reassured her and they talked about their respective histories while driving up the mountains to the Black Forest.

Meanwhile, as should have been expected, Walther had engaged a spy to look after Elena's movements while he was away. This soldier followed them to the house, escaping detection by turning off his headlights. Walking through the brush, he detected the American troops camped behind the house and returned to town. He could not contact Walther by telephone, so had to travel to reach him, which took some time. He gave a description of Karl and Walther remembered him from the café.

Chapter XVI

> "I'm confident of the future, and reasonably
> sure about the present, but the past
> seems to be constantly changing!"
> A joke in the Soviet Union*

Elena, as already related, was Vladimir Maximovich's niece, and he considered her almost as a daughter, since he had no children of his own. Their family came from a line of

---

* An accurate version of history could not be written right away because of many things kept confidential and numerous disinformation campaigns. Some secrets were quickly revealed: The 1939 division of Eastern Europe in the Nazi-Soviet pact was discovered in German records in 1945. The Katyn massacre was not known for a fact until the US stopped suppressing evidence about it after the war. The forced repatriation of Soviet citizens remained unknown until the 1970s, when writers such as Nikolai Tolstoy had to rewrite history. Usually attempts to do this are derisively called revisionism, but there is nothing negative about it if history could not be written correctly the first time. George Orwell, in 1945, stated that the refusal of the press to report on the forced repatriation issue had the appearance of a conspiracy. Later he was shown right. Significant evidence about earlier theories continues to emerge slowly – for instance the declassification of the Venona spy documents in 1995. Some secret codicils to the Yalta agreement were kept secret until the 90s, but many other US/UK files remain confidential. Much has been discovered in the USSR's archives since its demise, but information about Soviet history and its vast gulag system will forever remain incomplete because a lot of it is lost or destroyed. The most negative things remain top secret, such as whatever facts relate to 1941 military preparations. It seems that the past will continue to change in the future!   The author would not have known any of this since he was writing in 1944. Why then, did he include this epigraph at the beginning of this chapter? It is reasonable to suppose that when it was put here, it was not meant to refer to these things but rather to Elena's changing history, which forms a large part of this chapter.

prosperous merchants in Kiev. Both Vladimir and his brother Felix joined the CPSU (Communist Party) early on, sensing that this was the way to get ahead. Vladimir continued his military career, while Felix worked in local government bureaucracy, consolidating the rule of the Soviets in Kiev after the end of the Civil War. He rose in the ranks quickly, ending up in the Kiev District Committee. After a while, his friendship with Stanislav Vikentyevich Kosior, Head of the Central Committee of the Communist Party of Ukraine, helped him secure a post as chief of the Ukrainian State Board of Glass and Ceramics Industries. In this rôle he was tasked with the construction of new factories in the Kiev and Cherkasy regions and their associated Dnieper River hydroelectric plants, for which slave labor was provided by the OGPU.

His daughter Elena was brought up in relatively wealthy conditions compared to the rest of Ukraine in the 30s. The family had a house in Kiev, a flat in Moscow, access to a well-guarded resort complex in Crimea, and an automobile. All this, including the furnishing of the houses, did not cost any money – it was provided for free. Elena went to exclusive schools and shopped at special stores reserved only for the *nomenklatura*. They had products never seen by ordinary Russians, at least not since the revolution.

Elena would spend every summer in a *dacha* – a traditional Russian summer house, usually grouped with other such houses belonging to city-residents. There she grew up with her friend Andrei, two months spent outdoors in the fields and forests every summer, in between going to school in the city. The place was called Nikolska.

(The subject of the *dacha* in general is a very emotionally complex one and warrants an entire book on its own).

Elena's dacha was close to Sofiyivka, a remarkable park and arboretum, which they could visit often although it was closed to the general public.[*] In this amiable summer environment they agreed to become affianced and to get married when they reach 19. However, this did not occur.

In 1937-38 the Party experienced a large purge. First came the downfall and arrest of Stanislav Kosior himself.[†] Shortly after, Elena's father was arrested, apparently while he was at work, and she never saw him again or heard anything about him. She did not find out that the arrest had taken place until NKVD men came to meticulous search her house and all her intimate possessions, taking everything apart, while she stood looking on for six hours.

The arrest immediately ended any advantages Elena enjoyed and she fell into the ineffable destitution that was all around her in Kiev, but with which she never came in contact before this point. The squalor and sordidness was like an unimaginable nightmare to her that could not be awakened from. This is the worst of all kinds of poverty – one that comes suddenly after a decline from prosperity. If one becomes accustomed to certain comforts and customs all one's life, one can't endure without them. Elena moved with her mother to a poor, cold, apartment with a faulty stove and was entirely reliant on some help Vladimir Maximovich or Andrei could provide. Vladimir

---

[*] The Bolsheviks gave it the dreadful new name Park of the Third International, which thankfully was only temporary. Sofiyivka had been built by Count Potocki in 1796, a 15 million złoty gift for his Greek wife, Zofia, or Sophie. It was named after her. Zofia Potocka was notorious throughout Europe for her affairs and was of unparalleled beauty according to contemporary accounts. She also participated in diplomacy, for which Catherine II of Russia once gave her diamond earrings as appreciation for her services.
[†] Kosior somehow managed to withstand various NKVD tortures and refused to sign a confession or name "accomplices". However, he finally submitted when his 16 year old daughter was also brought to the interrogation chamber and callously abused there.

Maximovich, although a brother of a convicted anti-revolutionary, was not dismissed or arrested, possibly due to his friendship with Lev Mekhlis from Odessa, then Deputy People's Commissar of Defense.

Soon Germany invaded the Soviet Union and Andrei, by that time an officer in the Red Army, was captured in 1941. Elena's beauty was spotted by Walther on Khreshchatyk, the half-bombed out main street of Kiev and he courted her without much difficulty because of her desperation to get out of that degrading poverty. The rest of the story is already known, at least from Elena's perspective. Vladimir Maximovich's perspective, which is different, remains to be seen.

*   *   *

By the time Vixey, Elena, and Karl reached the house in Marzell, it was late evening. Elena was genuinely impressed with the well-furnished interior: the number of rooms, the stained-glass ceiling over the staircase; and expressed that to Vixey. However, the well-stocked kitchen, which she hadn't seen yet, was what distinguished the house the most from the rest of Germany. If Vixey lived farther than she did from the Swiss border, even banknotes secured by gold reserves wouldn't be able to procure some of the rare items she had in large supply, like coffee.

Karl moved his things from his room into Vixey's. It may be recalled that he entered into Germany with very few articles of clothing, so mostly it consisted of things that she had lent him. When she saw him just before the *soirée* a few days ago, she had asked, "What is that you're wearing?"

"What do you mean?" he replied.

"You can't appear in those pants. Here.. let me give you something else..."

Fadiman and Landon were introduced to Elena but they did not have a language in common as she only knew German and Russian.

Karl informed the lieutenants of the situation and Fadiman was disturbed at what happened, "Why would you even speak to a German colonel?"

"The Germans have a practice of seating people at cafés and restaurants very close to strangers," Karl explained. "He sat next to us and then we unavoidably began talking."

"The whole trip to Freiburg was 'avoidable' in my opinion," Fadiman retorted.

"I will put it in my reports as a reconnaissance mission. It's useful to know what the Germans are doing in their towns. In fact, if we hadn't taken a look around we could be accused of inactivity. Landon, what do you think?"

"I'm thinking about something else, see–. I can't decide which doll is more smoking."

Karl laughed, "Vixey, I think."

"I don't know; I actually like blondes more."

"Ok, but don't flip. She doesn't even know English. And you won't afford her. This one won't belong to anyone unless he has a large bank account."

Fadiman again brought up a concern, "Say, what about the German? Won't he come looking for her?"

"No," Karl replied. "She said he's gone to his military headquarters for a week."

Karl went outside and found the German-speaking sergeant, Andreas. He sent him to the KONR army base to ask the major-general to come.

Returning inside he encountered Elena and told her to expect Vladimir Maximovich tonight. They sat down in a salon and talked more about how Karl came to be in Germany.

She said, "Vixey is sweet. Are you going to marry her?"

"That would be good. It remains to be seen how it could be done."

"What do you mean?"

"While the war is going on, there's not a chance that the Army would allow me to do this.* Comparatively, I would expect less resistance from her army – from her father who's a Field Marshal. – Unless we lose the war and are pushed out of France and Italy – that would end everything. But I'm assuming we'll win and I was already thinking about how interesting it would be to send a letter to him about such a proposal. She would have to write it, and I could add a note as an attachment. If he's reasonable, I do not think he will deny that in a situation of an occupied Germany, it would not be a bad match for her to marry an American rather than a German."

---

* In fact, marriages between Army personnel and German fräuleins were not permitted until December 1946, a year and seven months after the end of the war. Or two years, two months from this point when Karl is in Germany. Austrian fräuleins were allowed much earlier.

Of course even casual interaction well before marriage was *verboten*. The issue of preventing fraternization, especially with fräuleins, was a great challenge to military planners. It was seen as most egregious while the war was still in progress, due to security concerns. But after the war ended it was still against policy. Back in the US, there was much disdain, especially among women, when reports started coming back about the soldiers' liaisons. Soldiers, often greeted civilly, naturally came to treat Germans as a liberated rather than a conquered people. Fräuleins were more charming and forward than what the Americans were used to, and wore "remarkably short skirts" according to *Newsweek*. They were better in general than the French and Italians, and certainly a contrast to back home. (This is according to contemporary reports. However, the contrast has actually *increased* now, 70 years later. In the 21st century, American women have abandoned any attempt of dressing presentably, even presenting themselves on Manhattan streets in abominations such as 'flip-flops'.)   It is not surprising that many violations of the German fraternization policy were made by the occupation forces. The highly unpopular policy was revoked about four months after the end of the war, in September 1945.

"Are you sure he doesn't have any specific intentions for her?"

"She hasn't mentioned anything about that."

"Who is her father?"

"Generalfeldmarschall von Isarberg."

Elena looked at him, expressing surprise with her eyebrows. "I've met him. A few times. In fact we know each other quite well."

Karl wanted to ask more but she avoided the subject. However, she felt more affection for Vixey now that she knew who she was.

Shortly thereafter Vixey came downstairs, holding in her arms the fluffy gray cat, *le chat gris pelucheux*.

"*Schätzchen*," Karl addressed Vixey, "You told Annette that we have two more for dinner, right?"

"Yes, I did."

She dropped the cat onto a chair and herself sat on a divan. She brought her feet up on it as well to sit in a more relaxed way, hair cascading down the side of the divan; spikes of her shoes pressing against the cushion of the opposite armrest. Elena's Russian instinct was disconcerted at this apparent disorder but Vixey said, "It's alright – these are house shoes. I don't go outside in them."

It's unlikely she would have ventured to take them outside and get them dirty, as they were court shoes with the surface covered in delicate lace, and tassels on the vamp. More interesting, however, was the rest of her attire. This was a style that she came up with herself but it was one that she couldn't take outside because it was too unconventional. Stay-up opaque black stockings went to just above her knees, with small pink ribbons at the top. The hemline of her narrow black dress could not practicably be any shorter. Owing to this, the upper part of her legs, still tanned from the summer, were left exposed. It was very avant-garde to leave the lower part of her legs covered, but not her thighs.

Her short sleeves were trimmed with silver. Above her décolleté v-neck collar she had a narrow 2-cm-wide black lace necklace conforming to her neck's circumference. In addition to that, she had a silver cross on a low-hanging necklace. The cross necklace had multiple uses – for instance in Church at a holiday it prevented anyone saying she is dressed un-Catholic. Then after Church, it became an adornment with ironical value, because it functions to alluringly draw attention to the place where it is situated, touching the top of her breasts. Also, when combined with a coquettish all-black attire (and especially that lace necklace), it brought to mind a neo-Victorian chic with nuances reminiscent of Gothic vampire stories and Bram Stoker's sirens.

Elena was impressed and jealous, since Vixey's dress and stockings were not *prêt-à-porter* things and could not be obtained easily. (Elena's own shoes, mentioned earlier, were also very stylish but this was her one and only pair that actually had a *talon aiguille*; she got them in Genève). Karl meanwhile was impressed that Vixey still had a lot of capacity to be so fascinating after he had already seen so much of her attire. The other day he had walked into her closet and was curiously looking through items it contained when he discovered a headband with small wooden deer antlers, and something that looked like a black fox's tail. Vixey was in the bedroom and he asked her about this. She said, "That's from a costume party during last Carnaval! I combined the antlers and the tail to be a mythological *Schwarzfuchs-Hirsche*." So saying she put on the antlers, fluffed up her hair to cover the headband, and cutifyed her expression even further by moving her pressed-together lips to one side. She also showed him a pair of high-heel shoes that she had used once on New Year's Eve. Below the sole at the heel they had ruffled *pompons* of silvery tinsel completely concealing the spike. It created an effect, looking at her, of impossible lightness because it looked like she was walking on those ethereal strands of tinsel foil.

*   *   *

Elena was watching Vixey's cat, which at that moment was moving about in order to take a break from sleeping and reposition itself for further sleep. The cat rolled onto its side, stretching its paws to full length. Then it rotated so that while still lying on its side, its ears and the back of its head were against the chair and its chin was facing up.

Elena petted the cat, drawing her hand and the delicate inner side of her forearm through the cat's soft fur, feeling the *mgnoveniye koshkino roskoshnovo prikosnovenye*. (In English, but without the poetic flavor: '...moment of cat's luxurious contact').

Soon Vladimir Maximovich arrived and was led in by the sergeant. He embraced Elena, saying, "I haven't seen you since Berlin. I forgot how beautiful you are – a *Yelena Prekrasnaya*[*]. But you used to have a чёлка (*cholka*)."[†]

Elena said, "Yes, I ended that practice because it looked too Russian. I did not want to appear any more Russian in Berlin."

They talked in Russian when by themselves. He last saw her when they met in central Berlin a year and a half ago, 1943.

Currently Elena had her hair tied into a knot at the back of her head, with some strands haphazardly hanging down from there. It was a loose tie, with enough remaining at her sides to cover her ears. She also had a long ribbon tied into the knot and hanging down, which was of the blue/black/white colors of the Estonian *tricolore*. She did not know that it was Estonian, she just chose it because it contrasted well with her blonde hair.

It was a joy to look at her hair – the depth of all the different hues and shades contained within it ranged from

---

[*] 'Elena the Fair', a stock character in old Russian fables.
[†] He is referring to the bangs of hair descending to the eyes that many Russian blondes have, especially at a young age.

cream yellow to dark goldenrod and all the subtleties in between. To have so much of this silken material of such an extraordinary color was something to be cherished.

When Vladimir Maximovich entered and saw Vixey, he was at first uncomfortable and confused, as if he accidentally walked into where he oughtn't have. Was she interrupted mid-way while getting dressed? At length, he became convinced that this is what she's wearing for that evening and he became accustomed. He thought that, after all, what could he understand of European fashions from his time in the backwards isolated USSR and Third Reich?

Dinner consisted of spätzle, schnitzel, and Dolcetto, a Piedmontese red wine. Vixey held her glass up for Karl to pour into. She exclaimed her appraisal after tasting it, "This wine is so good... It may even be better than all the Provençal and Bourgogne reds."

Elena, in describing how she met Karl and Vixey in Freiburg, mentioned she was still involved in her affair with Walther Steiger, which disturbed Vladimir Maximovich. She said, "I don't know what you have against this. I never understood. You know how limited my options are. My country is completely gone to me. All I have is Germany, where I am treated as a stupid foreigner. Sometimes I thought of going to Switzerland, but always reconsidered it."

"I thought that you were working somewhere," Vladimir Maximovich said.

"You thought I was working in Berlin?; or in Freiburg? Could I have afforded these clothes and this easy life from some random work? Do you really think that *I* would work? How absurd- the very thought of it!"

When first in Germany a few years ago, she submitted to the change in her situation with extreme distaste. Then after a while, like with Chekhov's Anna (*Анна на шее*), it started to suit her, despite some unpleasant things.[*]

Vladimir Maximovich said, "Since I see how things are, I will tell you something now that I was planning not to reveal until I had finished my business." He went into detail about things that happened after his defection and during his travels and meetings in Reichskommissariat Ukraine. It can be summarized thusly: Andrei was a POW near Kiev and repeatedly challenged Walther to a duel when he found out that his fiancée Elena was seduced by him. Walther initially refused, then finally accepted because he decided to give Andrei a pistol with a *blank* charge instead of a bullet.

They met in the middle of the Russian prisoner compound. Both fired at each other and Andrei was killed. The German officers all laughed about it because they didn't even consider Andrei as having had the right to challenge Walther. The story became well known among the Germans and they praised Walther on his efficient handling of the situation.

However, Walther didn't count on any Russians being in a position to intervene. Vladimir Maximovich came to his office, dressed in his general's uniform, alleging to be a friend of notable Wehrmacht officers such as Field Marshal von Bock and General von Gersdorff. He confronted Walther to determine the truth of the rumors, and when receiving confirmation, swore to give him the pistol shot that he did not receive earlier. He demanded a meeting in a secluded place where they would stand at the same distance

---

[*] It's also interesting to compare the present text to *Дым* (*Smoke*), which likewise combines political themes with a plot involving Russians in Baden. The main character Irina, although having some similarities in her history, is nevertheless a much more complex character than Elena or Anna. Irina is one of Turgenev's greatest creations.

as at the original duel and Vladimir would deliver the shot that was due.

Walther protested that the circumstances would be different than the prior duel; he did not know how good of a marksman the general was; plus without a danger to oneself the hand is more steady and there is a much greater chance of hitting the target than in a regular duel. Vladimir Maximovich cast aside these excuses, saying that the treachery of Walther's false duel was such that only to receive one shot at the same distance is actually a leniency.

Walther knew that from a legal point of view no case could be brought against him- even the commander of the POW camp had supported his plot. He rejected Vladimir Maximovich's demands and ordered his sergeants to escort him from the building. Vladimir Maximovich promised that he would reappear, perhaps at a most unexpected time, and deliver the missing shot that was owed! But in the meantime, circumstances prevented the two men from meeting again. Vladimir Maximovich was planning the formation of a Russian Army with General Vlasov in Dabendorf while Walther was transferred to the Western front.

Elena listened with absorbed attention to the developments Vladimir Maximovich described at the dinner table with Karl and Vixey, which revealed to her how she had been deceived for so long. She was galled and outraged in silence during the account, but after the initial confusion and shock she was surprised to find herself glad to hear what he said. It put the decision out of her control, leaving her no options and no room for any worried indecisiveness that may have remained. Most of the time uncertainties or excessive options trouble us more than actual facts. A conclusive end to either can bring relief. Elena's eyes glistened with tears at the legitimate ire she felt, but then this subsided.

Elena said calmly, "This certainly changes things. I'm not going to see him again."

"And you haven't any objection to his death?" Vladimir Maximovich asked.

"No, quite the contrary;- you can go ahead – as long as there's no danger to yourself." Her eyes, even sharper than usual, expressed her vengeful vexation.

"What are you going to do now?" asked Karl.

"I guess I'll go to Switzerland and try to get a counterfeit passport there. I've long been considering it."

"What about the border – will they let you across?"

"Oh – I forgot; my visa expired! I went to Switzerland before on a visa but it's not valid anymore!"

Vixey said, "If you know how, it's actually easy to get in without going through a border checkpoint. I'll show you." She brought a map and laid it on the table. "Everywhere in this area the Rhine divides Switzerland from Germany. Except right here, in the outskirts of Basel. [She pointed at the map]. You can drive up this road, cross the border on foot, and then past this small forest, about 200 meters and you will find yourself in Basel. From there you can take a train anywhere in Switzerland." Elena was pleased with this scheme and thanked her.

"Can I take this map?"

"Sure!"

Karl had an idea. He said to Vladimir Maximovich, "You can give her the documents and letters you wanted to address to the American commanders. I can arrange a US Army courier to meet her in Zürich. This is actually the best way we can get documents confidentially out of the Reich."

"That is a good idea. Let's discuss it in more detail later. Ideally I would want Eisenhower, Alexander, and Montgomery to get my messages. Lenochka, you could become instrumental in changing the outcome of the war by delivering secret correspondence."

Vixey added a suggestion, "You should also write to the Swiss government in Berne. Remember that Roosevelt is still ultimately the decision maker in America. Supposing the US snubs you in favor of continuing to support the Red Army. You would want to have at least the protection of a neutral state like Switzerland. You might not be able to go anywhere else."

Elena said, "Yes, it's such a pristine island in the midst of the war. When I was there I was impressed by the contrast. Zürich has business almost as usual – only a few disruptions to imports like less gasoline for cars and all that. Compare it to Warsaw or Kiev, changing hands several times and completely destroyed."

"Switzerland is small, however," said Vladimir Maximovich. "If things do turn for the worst in Europe, for the long-term we would need to establish a Russian émigré center in a place more suitable for receiving a large number of people. Perhaps in Victoria?"

"Victoria is good," Vixey replied, "But Sydney is the best place to be if you are in Australia. Or think about Argentina or southern Brazil. A lot of Italians and Germans have gone there."

As they finished their supper and drank more wine, they turned to more agreeable topics of conversation, like clothes, cats, and the Schwarzwald natural scenery. Vixey described how she came across a large *Stachelschwein* (porcupine) in the forest the other day. It was sitting in a tree and she was able to come close to it and touch its paw. As Vladimir Maximovich was leaving, he remembered to ask if anyone had seen Pavel Nikitich, since the lieutenant-colonel had completely disappeared from the base. They said they hadn't, since that morning.

Vixey and Elena were left alone, as Karl went to check on something. They had switched to Riesling after the end of the dinner and went to the salon, putting the wine glasses on small tables near the divans. The thickness of the glass was minimal at the top of the wine glass where one's lips touch it, which enhanced the texture of the wine. It was also at a perfect temperature because it was allowed to warm a few degrees after being taken out of the refrigerator.

Vixey asked Elena more details about the coterie of acquaintances she was among the past couple of years. Elena, eating a peach, explained that Walther was involved with government corruption at a high level, and would invite all his close associates to various decadent *soirées* they would have. She described them as being scenes of obscene revelry, lust and abandon. Still, she hadn't said anything specific.

Vixey inquired further, "What specifically?"

"Pretty much anything you can imagine," Elena replied. "Why? You don't like such things, do you?"

"No, I prefer more traditional things," she said, which was true, but she still wanted to hear about it.

Karl came downstairs and joined them, getting his glass from the supper table. Elena finished her wine and decided to go to sleep because it was very late and she was tired. She said good night, kissed Vixey, and retired to undress.

Vixey could still taste the peach in her mouth a few minutes after she had left.

Chapter XVII

> *C'est la Mort qui console, hélas! et qui fait vivre;*
> *C'est le but de la vie, et c'est le seul espoir*
> *Qui, comme un élixir, nous monte et nous enivre,*
> *Et nous donne le coeur de marcher jusqu'au soir;*
>
> *C'est un Ange qui tient dans ses doigts magnétiques*
> *Le sommeil et le don des rêves extatiques,...*
> BAUDELAIRE[*]

Pavel Nikitich awoke, the sun blazing above him. He looked around and saw that he was lying on the forest floor. Pines swayed in the wind on that brisk autumn day, clumps of needles floating down. He did not know where he was, but saw an empty vodka bottle lying next to him. He stood up and suddenly a flash of memory erupted in his mind – memory is horrible at times like this, when it brings one back to the living nightmare. Day brought back his night. Better never to wake at all, he thought. It was so painful, had he another bottle he would have drank its contents, if only to delay a little longer in the stupor of forgetfulness.

No, there was no way to end it. What else to do? He wanted to hurl his head against the rocks on the ground to stop the inflammation. He wished that the earth was a hollow sphere filled with gunpowder, so that he could throw a match on it. *Alles ist todt, und wir sind todt.* He felt utter disgust with the worthlessness of life; ineffable, hopeless desolation. Desolation was the dominating pain; it would have made no difference if he were in this forest, in the conclave of the Vatican, or among his closest comrades. Always the same thought, the one overriding concept, one individual fräulein.

He struggled to reconcile the dichotomy between hating her for destroying him, bringing him to this state;

---

[*] *Fleurs du mal*, La Mort des pauvres (Death of the poor). This is about the consolation brought by death.

and the worship and admiration he couldn't help feeling. Simultaneously as he feared to cause her the slightest unease or discomfort, he wanted to drink the sweet nectar of her blood and watch her pretty face contort in pain.

Horrified at the feelings he found in his soul, he thought of alternative lines of thought. Of course, she had nothing to do with anything – she has the best intentions always – it is the fault of fate; or rather the devil, which is the same thing. He was not in the situation of Shakespeare's Cloten, who could enjoy himself in forming merry and elaborate plans to ravish Imogen, thinking specifically about how to "vex her" the more.[*] Then Pavel thought that he was thinking too much. All thought is futile; progress futile; the only advantage is that it could lead quicker to death, which is a positive. Animals are the envy of mankind, for the far lesser amount of thinking, and thus suffering, that they experience.

Pavel wandered through the forest, oblivious to the spectacular scenery in abundance. He saw some of it, but tried not to. Unless one is happy, or at least moderately contented, the natural beauty of the world causes pain. He recalled a simple poem of Heinrich Heine from *Die Heimkehr*, which seemed to him to be about Vixey:

> *Saphire sind die Augen dein,*
> (Sapphires are those eyes of yours...)
> *Die lieblichen, die süßen.*
> *O, dreimal glücklich ist der Mann,*
> *Den sie mit Liebe grüßen.*
> ...[†]

He considered taking some kind of action – would she enjoy that? Girls like action, not words which he mistakenly

---

[*] *Cymbeline*, Act 3, Scene V.

[†] Praising a girl's eyes and other aspects, the poem ends with an intent of revenge against the man benefiting from all this, preferably in an isolated forest.

used first; they admire the aggressive exercise of power, which countless examples throughout history have proved. Only it was definitely not the right time for that. Shouldn't he rather shoot himself? He did not know what to do, and continued to wander in the forest, since motion was at least more bearable than being still. He passed by the site of the small skirmish, where he first saw Vixey, Vixetka, Vixette lying in the red pine needles amidst lingering ammunition smoke.

Sometimes when Pavel recollected something specific about her, especially (and these were the most vexatious recollections) something sweet that she did such as letting him touch her hair or approaching him to offer a coffee, he wished he could just dissolve in grief from the burning fever of that image in his brain.

Suddenly his thoughts dallied on a wisp of hope – what if she would forgive his indiscretions? What if time would pass, the American major elsewhere and forgotten, while Pavel would accomplish some great deeds to make him worthy of redeeming his mistakes. Would she perhaps be receptive towards a courtship, let him start over? No. The ridiculousness of his thought struck him forcefully. These things did not happen on the earth.

Nature creates everything, he thought, to be subservient to the overall process of life's recycling. The Second law of thermodynamics, which Sir Eddington considered one of the fundamental laws of nature, describes the irreversible dissipation of everything towards entropy. But only humans have the consciousness to become aware of the evil embedded in the order of the system. Pavel recalled Schopenhauer's aphorism, "All the cruelty and torment of which the world is full is in fact merely the necessary result of the totality of the forms under which the will to live is objectified, and thus merely a commentary on the affirmation of the will to live." That is the very thing that makes hope so nonsensical. Evil is not accidental; it is embedded. If, remarkably, a person escapes the scourge of unemployment, if he somehow enjoys fortune in all his endeavors, he is struck down by sickness or age, or sees the untimely deaths of others. Health is a precipice that our fragile bodies can tumble down at any moment. Or, if enjoying health, one is brought to a downfall by women or some other misfortune. Or, to use a historical analogy, if Hitler had never existed, a German communist counterpart would have led Europe to war. The war and all its destruction, its rivers of blood, was inevitable.

Even the most successful of the *Anna Karenina* characters, Konstantin Levin, the rural landowner who married Княжна[*] Kitty, came to similar conclusions as Pavel. This was the inevitable consequence of him having a lot of free time to think and philosophize about life. He saw the transience, the meaninglessness, and the suffering, and "he concluded that to live under such conditions was impossible; that one must either explain life to oneself so that it does not seem to be an evil mockery by some sort of devil, or one must shoot oneself."[†] Tolstoy's solution was of course religion, but that is like using duct tape to seal the gaps in philosophy.

One feature of life's structure is the occasional creation of positives that are very momentary but which increase desires and expectations while actual means and prospects are continually decreasing. This was Emma Bovary's soirée at the château of the marquis. This can also be found in a marvelous encounter with a girl who gives promises but then disappears and doesn't reply to letters. The fact that this tendency is hard-wired into them is an example of the world's malevolence. Women are like indifferent cats; and their beauty like a cat's paw. The paw, in that soft, velvety

---

[*] Knyazhna, a Russian title that is something between a duchess and princess.
[†] Part VIII, Ch. 12.

exterior conceals dangerous, diligently-sharpened claws that will rip apart one's soul.

The best metaphor for Hope was written by Baudelaire: he compares hope to a bat in a humid dungeon, bumping its head against a rotten ceiling. Meanwhile a dark, sad rain makes immense streaks that resemble the bars of a vast prison.*

Baudelaire also wrote one of the best descriptions, in one line, of life: A desert of ennui with oases of horror. Pavel looked around at the world and saw nothing but hostility around him – a schizophrenic nightmare vision. Memories of ancient happiness one may have known in early youth only serve to make more heartbreaking the limitless darkness presented now. One of the symptoms accompanying his thoughts was an extraordinary aversion to "doing anything" – an epic lethargy that required a painful concentration to make the slightest effort of action. In amusements, distractions, he saw extreme tedium and pointlessness. In any kind of real concentration of work he saw such torture that he would have preferred to tear himself apart.

Auguste Villiers de l'Isle-Adam's jaded Axël and Sara made a good point by rejecting all aspects of the world even at a moment of prosperity, preferring to preëmpt the moment when their fortune will eventually reverse. In their embraces they had already achieved the height of what is possible on earth, and in an expression of *Weltschmerz*,

---

* *Quand la terre est changée en un cachot humide,*
Où l'Espérance, comme une chauve-souris,
S'en va battant les murs de son aile timide
Et se cognant la tête à des plafonds pourris;

Quand la pluie étalant ses immenses traînées
D'une vaste prison imite les barreaux,
Et qu'un peuple muet d'infâmes araignées
Vient tendre ses filets au fond de nos cerveaux.
Spleen IV.

decided to quit while they're ahead. «*Vivre? les serviteurs feront cela pour nous*»[*]. This is allegorical (Villiers was a decadent-symbolist) since almost nobody reaches such a success in fortune. But the hope of someday reaching it is the primary motivation of most people, who do not question whether it is worth it or even remotely possible.

Pavel considered whether there were any forces that were 'good'. Aphrodite being placed among the evil, he saw that Death was the only such thing. Nothing else could reduce suffering as permanently and as assuredly.

Time is either a scythe or an acid; better for it to be the former.

He thought of the scythe-carrying Grim Reaper, the Black Angel of the Abyss, and he imagined Death appearing, under the old, dusty black hood, as a lovely maiden of incomparable beauty. Flowers in her auburn hair, a gentle affectionate smile, and only the bright red-violet of her eyes marking her as not mortal. *Devushka s'kosoi*, because the word for braid and scythe are the same in Russian, simultaneously means Girl with a braid and Girl with a scythe. Her divinity would make her know one and understand one like no person in the world. Desolation would be eased finally. The pleasure of spending a minute with her and feeling her delicate compassion – which exceeds that of the human pity shown by all the people one has ever encountered – would bring one to tears if she existed in a real and not a figurative sense. But her final action – in severing one's head with her scythe, releasing one's soul from the material world and letting one blend with her in infinite nothingness – would indeed exceed the aggregate sum of goodwill from the world and from the wolves of humanity. Pavel wept thinking of this – at the sadness and absurdity of the world being like this, – a world where life is something to be gotten rid of and nihility is the highest hope.

---

[*] "Live? The servants will do that for us."

In extreme situations, it is not hard to fall into temporary insanity. An abnormal reaction to an abnormal situation may be, in fact, a normal reaction, according to the Austrian psychologist Dr. Frankl.

Some have argued, in discussions of *Die Leiden des jungen Werther*, that it was not just Goethe's Charlotte that drove Werther to desperation – that there was something in his underlying situation that preconditioned him to such a 'response'. This is usually the case, to varying degrees, and in the example of Pavel Nikitich the unsettling factor was the previous several years. Things started going on a downward trajectory ever since that disillusionment with regard to Vika from Smolensk mentioned earlier. Then the war began in the birch forests of Poland, and continued from there. Tarnopol, Dubno, Lwów, Borislav, Brody, Zhytomyr, Kiev, Rowno, Berlin, Dabendorf, Smolensk, Vinnytsa, Westphalia, Normandy, Baden. Years of struggle, sometimes a period of heightened expectations, always ended and submerged under a wave of the ever-rising inevitability of death. «*Quoi que je fasse, elle est toujours là, cette pensée infernale, comme un spectre de plomb à mes côtés...*»* From all Pavel's calculations, due to his opposition to the Red Army he should be seen as a hero by the world and getting widespread support. After all, the Red Army was still the same army as in 1918, when the British Empire, US, France, and seven other countries sent expeditionary forces against it. Churchill was one of the world's biggest proponents of sending and arming troops to fight against the Red Army when he was War Minister in 1918. But Pavel and his colleagues were intertwined with the Germans and this would make any overtures to the Western Allies futile. And what help have the Germans been? Of all, they at least

---

* "Whatever I do, it is always there, the hellish thought is always at my side like a leaden spectre..." Hugo, *Last Day of a Condemned Man*.

should have seen the great importance of building up an anti-Soviet Russian power. But they refused to cooperate until now, when it is probably too late.

With the knowledge that one is fighting for the right cause, to be universally regarded as a traitors, to have the entire outside world bristling against you: the Red Army flooding in from the east, a Germany locked into an irrational course, and the Western Allies short-sighted and traitorous beyond comprehension – all this was enough to have an unsettling effect.

When one is in the midst of such a nightmare, it feels like a monstrous load overbearing on one from all sides. This happens, not as dramatically but with just as serious results, in life outside of war as well – for instance when one is in the midst of a grave legal process that could determine the outcome of one's life. (Actually this is an even worse situation just because it is so banal). The forces irreversibly moving against one are like a juggernaut machine that cannot be reasoned with. The fatal uncertainty weighs one down as if all the air around one had been changed to lead.

In the midst of this adversity Pavel clung to his conviction that he was working in consistency with his values, doing all he could towards the accomplishment of long-standing goals. It was with this unstable set of affairs that Pavel had to cope with the effect that Vixey had on his priorities, namely the quick realization that it is ridiculous to think of any priority or meaning existing besides her.

Chapter XVIII

> What Time would spare, from Steel receives its date,
> And monuments, like men, submit to fate!
> Steel could the labor of the Gods destroy,
> And strike to dust th' imperial towers of Troy;...
> What wonder then, fair nymph! thy hairs should feel,
> The conq'ring force of unresisted steel?
> POPE, *The Rape of the Lock*

As this is the last chapter, I will take the opportunity of wishing the reader adieu. I heartily wish you well, and am grateful that you have undertaken to read as far as this point. Hopefully, at least *some* parts were of interest, if not the shoes that Vixey wears, then maybe the literary or foreign policy discussions. Apart from scenes where I was present myself, like the Munich reminiscences, my favorite scene was the one where the Russian army officers force Vixey, who is wearing a black velvet bowtie in her hair, to drink vodka.

The revelations about C. Chanel would have been kept discrete, but I believe that the matter will have become public knowledge anyway by the time that this goes to print.

If someone thinks that Vladimir Maximovich was allowed too much space to talk about the war, I must counter that even to concisely explain the context of the events and his motives would require no less. The information he relates is necessary for a complete understanding of the position of the Russian anti-Soviet movement. A key piece of the context is that the Soviet Army's *raison d'être* appears to have been a goal of communist control of Europe, and going on the defensive against Germany during 1941-43 was merely an interruption of aggressive plans existing before and continuing after.

*   *   *

In the morning Vixey had to change her bed cover because of spilt syrupy *crème de cassis* (blackcurrant liqueur) from Luxembourg *(parce que la nuit précédente, ils avaient bu la liqueur sirupeuse directement à la bouteille alors qu'ils l'utilisaient comme lubrifiant). En plein acte, elle goûta et avala quelque chose d'autre aussi, remarquant «c'était pas mal, à l'exception de la texture».*

Il est jugé indiscret de mentionner ouvertement tous ces détails à propos de notre héroïne. Cela reste uniquement pour les lecteurs les plus perspicaces.

This day she wore ankle-high black velvet small boots with heels. The boots had bright gold zippers with large slider tabs that clinked with an agreeable sound as she walked. She also had a silk-chiffon skirt: mid-length to the knees but light, such that if she happened to spin around in a pirouette, the entire length of her legs would be seen up to the garter. She tied a pink/blue ribbon into her untied hair.

As evening was falling, Oberst Walther Steiger drove up the road towards the house with a few platoons of troops. He took enough men with him to be sure of having a numerical advantage against the American troops that his sergeant described encamped here. They encountered Pavel Nikitich randomly sitting on a tree stump by the side of the road, who came down and approached Walther, asking, "Where are you going?"

Walther saw he was speaking with a lieutenant-colonel of a Wehrmacht auxiliary, so he replied earnestly, "There is a company of American soldiers lodged in these woods. Judging by this map, we are presently approaching the place where they supposedly are. Who are you?"

"How do you know this?"

"My sergeant described their position to me. He observed them two nights ago."

Pavel considered what to do. He only had a brief moment to decide what to say to the colonel. Perhaps this unexpected turn of events could help him if it eliminates

Karl from the scene. However, if they arrived and encountered the Americans they would have no other options than to attack them immediately. All he could picture from this unexpected event was that the ensuing conflict would put Vixey in too much danger. Thus Pavel thought that he had to do something to prevent the Germans from storming the Americans' position. He came up with a way to equalize the situation a little in the Americans' favor, while giving him time to get his own battalion just in case it was needed. He told Walther, "Your man was mistaken. There is a large ROA base here. He must have confused our slightly foreign uniform insignia for an American one. Come inside to the house a little further up the road, our general staff headquarters, and you can take a look at our orders, signed by Reichsführer Himmler himself."

The name of the Reichsführer had a convincing effect. Walther said, "Very well."

Leaving the troops on the road, only Walther and a lieutenant entered the house. They noticed that Pavel disappeared as they walked in, like Pierre Gringoire en route to the storming of Notre Dame. Pavel realized that he shouldn't be seen with them, lest Vixey suppose that he had a rôle in bringing them here. Thinking about the situation in retrospect, Pavel thought that it might have been better to inform Walther of the true situation – that this was a German girl's house that a company of Americans had commandeered. Then it may have led to favorable results if they agreed to attack them in a delicate manner not to endanger the girl. But they might also have not agreed to take her safety as a consideration. Regardless, Pavel thought, what was done was done – the Germans would be isolated from their commander who would presumably be captured and held. Meanwhile Pavel would get a battalion of his own to restore order – and possibly assume command of the Germans himself.

Walther turned through a few doorways inside the house and happened upon Elena in the large drawing room, actually the original purpose of his visit here. She stood up suddenly, shocked at seeing him here. He confronted her, "What is the meaning of all this? Is it an affair or some kind of espionage? I can't decide which is worse."

"It's actually neither. I don't know what to say but..." She could not finish.

"You are always ending up with some kind of suspicious affairs... Let's not forget that you're a kept woman, and you have to subordinate yourself to my wishes or you'll lose your livelihood."

"True, but it's contemptible of you to point it out in this way and remind me... Anyway, I can get by without you."

As she spoke Walther glanced over to a picture of Generalfeldmarschall von Isarberg on a bookcase by a window. He walked over to take a look and recognized his former commanding officer and close business associate. Vixey's father, the field marshal, was instrumental in setting up the various schemes and projects that had been so profitable to both of them, the biggest of which was providing *zivilarbeiter* and *ostarbeiter* to the Ford-Germany and Opel factories. Simultaneously as seeing the picture, Walther saw the troops behind the house, unmistakably an American company. He turned to Elena, "What is going on? Von Isarberg, the Americans?"

At this moment Karl, Vixey, Vladimir Maximovich, and two of Karl's sergeants entered from another part of the house. "Aha," said Walther, seeing the Russian, "Why not another add another aspect to this? But I should have known you'd be here when I heard there was an ROA base. Are you working with the field marshal?"

Vladimir Maximovich was also surprised at seeing him. For three years his intention had been to kill Walther whenever an opportunity presented itself but they hadn't met until now. Walther's tone irritated him and he replied, mirroring the speech of Macduff confronting Macbeth, "I see you still do not take the situation seriously. I have no more words – my voice is in my sword." So saying he directed Andreas to detain the German lieutenant and to disarm Walther.

Walther said, "So, Elena, I see why you are being impertinent. He told you about the duel, didn't he? But the two of you [pointing at Vixey and Karl], how are you involved? I will capture and interrogate every last American caught here!"

Vixey responded, trying to keep calm and decisive although she was a little worried, "This is my house. I don't want anything to happen. If all of you can just work something out, maybe? I really don't think that you can just execute someone for a crime committed long ago."

"Long ago?" said Elena. "For something to that degree it's not so long ago. But everything since then, what about that? Based as it was on such a deception?"

"Wait, you live here?" asked Walther of Vixey. "Who are you?"

"Vixey von Isarberg."

"And the field marshal is who,... your father?" he asked, pointing at the picture on the shelf.

"Yes."

"Ah; I knew he had a daughter, I just didn't know you were grown up already... I am at your service and will wait for the orders you give me." He then explained his connection to the field marshal after her inquiries.

While they spoke Andreas was leading the German lieutenant out to the American camp. Vladimir Maximovich at this point apologized to Vixey, saying that it's not an execution, just the return of a dueling shot that was never received. His tone was firm; he left no room for counterarguments. He then forced Walther at gunpoint to walk with him out the back of the house.

As they were crossing the threshold, a blast of gunfire erupted nearby, allowing Walther in the confusion to turn a corner of the house and get away from Vladimir Maximovich, who pursued. A few minutes earlier, the German lieutenant had succeeded in escaping from his captors and reaching his side. The information he had gathered led him to relate to his troops that a company of American saboteurs had occupied a German girl's house and that they were intending to shoot the German commander this very minute. Taking over command of the platoons, he ordered an immediate assault, but with the care in mind not to put in danger the fräulein who lived here, and another blonde miss he also saw.

Karl ran to take charge of his troops as they rushed to reinforce their defenses, pausing only for a moment to tell Vixey to stay in the house. The Americans were not entirely unprepared for an assault and had some defensive barricades and small trenches in place that they retreated to.

Vixey's thoughts were in a turmoil due to the sudden events. The gunfire, shouting, and some reverberating explosions occurring directly on her property was something too dire to even accept as reality. But the exigency of the situation left no time for negative emotions or apprehensive contemplation. She acted on impulse. The only other person left in the room was Elena. Vixey told her that she would go find Walther and tell him to go to his troops and order them to withdraw.

Elena, perplexed at this, said, "What are you talking about?" As Vixey was already turning to go without thinking of answering, Elena clutched her long hair to hold her. At being thus roughly stopped in her movement, Vixey's reaction was to grab the arm holding her hair while lightly hitting Elena with her other hand. However, she was incapable of hitting anyone with sufficient force to hurt them. Elena let go of Vixey's hair and pushed her against the wall, pinning both her arms flat against the cold, polished Venetian plaster. They both calmed down. Their perfumes mingled from their closeness.

"I need to go," Vixey said. "It's the only way to stop all this."

"What? Do you actually think he'll do what you say?"

"Yes, of course. Why not? He knows who I am, so he has to."

"You're wrong. Don't you think it's too late to stop anything?"

"No, I have to go try."

"But it's dangerous out there." The sound of automatic gunfire was continuing, combined with more and more frequent explosions, probably from mortar grenades.

"I'm going to go."

Seeing she was determined, Elena let go of her arms and Vixey started to turn towards the room's exit. Elena stepped towards her again, saying, "Wait.." and embraced her before she left.

Karl found his lieutenants at the far end of the field, and they were already appraising the situation. "There are too many of them. We cannot hold out indefinitely."

Unexpectedly, Karl saw Pavel Nikitich, who had emerged from the path leading out of the forest. When Karl questioned him, he said, "I have an entire armored battalion ready on call. I don't intend to use it. It is only in case things get out of control and the girl needs to be protected. But she seems to be safe in there."

"What? What about helping us? Can you see how outnumbered we are?"

"So? I haven't the slightest desire to help you. How could I possibly even consider such a thing? The simple fact of the matter, and I think this summarizes the fatal flaw with the world, is that... you are in my way, and I am in yours. This is what no theory of economics, or philosophy, or existential psychology will ever solve."

Pavel, smoking a cigarette, seemed to be in a detached, philosophic mood, talking unhurriedly in the midst of the din of ammunition being fired, and the smoke-filled darkness around them. "Recall the writing of Lev Shestov: He thought rightly that the true, the real problems escape the philosophers. What they do actually is obscure the real issues, which cannot be reconciled by any theory or thinking...

"Dostoyevsky had a ridiculous phase towards the end of his life when he actually started to contemplate ideas about utopias. He thought that they might have some kind of relevance. But even if you indulge in an assumption that one day technology could create a material sufficiency for everyone, does that somehow alleviate the natural inequalities between people? Material sufficiency removes one problem, but it does not remove the inevitable competition and hatred between people. Jean-Jacques Rousseau wrote a lot about the hierarchies modern society has created that have led to disparity and conflict; see his *Discourse on Inequality*. Again, however, he focuses on material and political hierarchy. Economists and philosophers have spent centuries debating the problems of scarcity of economic resources. Yet what significance is that, compared to social scarcity?...

"Compared to that look at how easily the distribution of material resources is solved. Someone discovered that resources are not static, that wealth can be created from nothing via work, then accumulated as capital and redistributed through the capital markets. You are American; you must know these things well. Although there is competition, on the large scale one's success adds to the overall economy and often contributes to others' success. Knowing this, it's simply a matter of creating a legal system of property rights and so forth that doesn't discourage people from working and trading. *Raz plyunut'* (A walk in the park) compared to the problem of social scarcity – I'm referring to social relationships, courtships, the unsolvable scarcity of beauty. Here there's a fixed amount! A zero sum playing field – here is where you truly see cutthroat competition. It is impossible to get through life without either being trampled or trampling over someone else. Anyone who wants to avoid either of those two things must die immediately, since one of the two must happen. The most well-intentioned person destroys hundreds of others if successful. And, don't think that success means success. No! It's only temporary. It has to be short-lived because the problems of hierarchy always come up. People are only interested when in the company of those who are their betters – not their equals or lessers. Thus all society and relationships are like a house of cards. Competition for the attention of the most attractive and most pleasant leads to inevitable, endless conflict. This is a hierarchy that overcomes class, national, or material differences. The Church has deluded people with a promise of a perfect state of heaven, but these are difficulties that even the concept of heaven can't solve. The same problem would even exist in there. What do you do when two people want the same thing and are ready to die for it?"

"I see where you are going with this,- you could have come straight to the point," said Karl, irritated. "You are practically calling me out for a duel. But I'm a little busy at the moment."

To return to Walther:: his escape from Vladimir Maximovich was ineffectual because he was stopped and captured by the American troops outside the house. Vladimir Maximovich now had to reappraise the situation. A serious assault of the German platoons had started against the Americans entrenched at the far end of the field by the Nazi flagpole. His first priority was now to prevent any possible danger to Elena and also Vixey. He left Walther with the Americans and went to the radio in his jeep in order to call a few armored cars over from the nearby base. A lieutenant answered him that a battalion-sized group had already been called out, by Pavel Nikitich.

At this point Vixey found Vladimir Maximovich, by his jeep behind the furthest end of the house. She asked him, "Where is the German colonel?"

"The Americans are holding him. Why are you here and not with Elena? But actually, it's fine. Can you stay here with the jeep while I go get Elena? It's best to move a little away from this conflict."

"And leave my house, in the midst of all this?! No, don't you realize I have authority to command the whole German company? But I need to find the colonel for that." She ran off. Vladimir Maximovich, seeking to surround himself with an entourage of his own well-armed people so that he was not at the mercy of various events, skirted the edge of the dark field to its further end where he expected to find the Russian battalion.

The Germans attacked relentlessly and would not have accepted a surrender if it were offered, unless they saw that the opposing force was already decimated. The lieutenant believed that his commanding officer, Walther Steiger, had already been executed by the Americans after their deceitful way of capturing him. The plight of the German girl also motivated the troops, and the thought of liberating her gave a significant emotional impetus to the vigor of the attack. They believed that she would stay inside the house, and thus no harm would come to her from the battle, which was focusing on the entrenched American position at the edge of the field. Finally, the Germans felt they had the justification to kill any saboteurs under Hitler's Commando Order, which overruled the traditional rules of war in special circumstances.

Walther imagined himself like a Javert bound in the enemy camp at the 1832 Parisian *émeute*. He was mortified at the fiasco he was inadvertently involved in regarding Vixey. If anything happened to her he would be blamed and his career would be over. If, on the other hand, he protected her, he could gain many advantages, the biggest being a possibility of courting her. He wished to stop his compatriots under his command immediately, and shouted to the Americans, "Idiot fools! Let me go and I'll right away call a ceasefire!" However, they did not understand German so his arguments were futile. The deaths continued to mount.

Karl and Pavel and were still talking at this time. Through a gap in the shooting, Karl heard Walther arguing with the other Americans and left Pavel to go to him. Hearing Walther's demand to be released, Karl had no reason to doubt his intentions, but still asked, "How can I risk trusting your word?"

"What other choice do you have? You are outnumbered; you are losing the battle as we speak. Maybe you should call the girl here- she can tell you what you should do... Oh, there she is, in fact. There, by the house. What is she doing outside?"

Vixey, in walking back found herself in between two groups of American troops, one which was by the barricade, and another which was grouped by the side of the house. They were dying now and then from MG42 machine gun fire and the occasional mortar round. The mortar is a very effective weapon. It is light, inexpensive, and not complicated. A mortar grenade is capable of reaching over barricades since it flies up in an arc and then descends.

Karl saw the mortar projectiles shifting closer to the house in order to strike the soldiers gathered there. Terrified of the danger Vixey was in, he first cut Walther's bounds, enabling him to go for his lines, then ran to Vixey.

Walther got up but his movement was perceived by Landon and he was shot to death by him. Landon was at some distance, had not understood what was going on, and thought he was escaping.

Pavel, meanwhile, was circling around the field in order to reach the house. He intended to look for Vixey there. On the way he ran into Vladimir Maximovich, who had made contact with the significant force of Russian troops just beyond the field in the forest. He exclaimed, voice elevated because of the noise of the explosions that had intensified, "Where have you been the past two days? How have you come to be involved here?"

Pavel replied, "I was the one who called for the troops just in case. I saw the Germans approaching on the road."

"What are you thinking? Why an entire battalion? We can't afford any kind of incident. It would jeopardize the entire movement!"

"First of all the girl. Then I will think about the war."

"What?"

"I need to find her. In the event that..."

"What is wrong with you? You look unwell. She's probably with my niece. They brought her here from Freiburg. Let's take an APC to the house and get both of them."

"Wait, isn't that Vixey there near those tents?"

*   *   *

The majority of this chapter was written in a cellar underneath a café in Freiburg. I was sitting in the café when the planes arrived to bomb the city, and had no choice but to descend to the cellar to wait to the end of the air raid. It has been a heavy one, and it looks like the building on top of us may actually collapse. The air is practically unbreathable; it seems there are fires in some surrounding buildings. It is like some kind of toxic smoke. I will try to finish what I can.

*   *   *

As he got closer to Vixey, Karl noticed a mortar projectile being fired, and from the trend of the previous trajectories, gathered some sense of its direction. He reached Vixey and grabbed her away from the house, just before a shell exploded where she had stood previously. Glass windows shattered and shards fell upon the troops building a barricade there.

She barely had time to thank him when another shell exploded, this time closer. It killed him and threw her into the pit made by the first explosion. She spit out some blood and was too dazed to move, so continued to lie there, her back against the diagonal surface of the pit. She heard nothing but a heavy ringing sound. Gradually it transformed into a more agreeable sound of violas and timpani. She couldn't understand where that was coming from.

After what seemed a long time to her, she thought about getting back to the house. "I'll climb out of this pit, then just a short walk and I'll be back home," she said. "I'll try turning around first. That wasn't hard. Now that I'm on my knees I can easily climb out and stand up. It seems pretty dark around. I can see my house but why are the lights off inside it? Let's walk there. Am I out of the trench yet? Oh, yes, I'm almost at the door."

Who she is talking to, is not clear.

"I will get out of this Freiburg air raid and you will get clear of that shelling, and then Paris?"

"How nice... That would be splendid."

"You would need to figure out what to wear first."

"Not a problem. I'll just go to my closet and try on a few things and pick a few combinations and look at the mirror and see what to take."

"You will need Swiss francs. How many do you think will suffice?"

"Oh, I forgot that Paris has been lost already! I can't use Reichsmarks. It will be hard to stomach their victory festivities but it doesn't matter. It would be a good place to wait out the rest of the war. I just have to remember this time to use French only!"

"Or use English rather."

"Yes. Where's the light switch for this hallway?"

She was still lying in the pit, actually, not having moved from her original spot, delirious from loss of blood.

Pavel found her there. By the light of a broken, sad-looking lamppost he perceived the black tears etched over her face because of eyeliner mixing with them as they flowed down. He touched her neck and her head rolled to the side involuntarily, blood pouring from her mouth. He shut her eyelids and wiped the blood from her chin. It tasted good as expected. Pavel did not hesitate needlessly like Heathcliff; he promptly shot himself with his pistol, as the world now fell within his definition of being impossible to exist in.

Vladimir Maximovich came in an armored car and took Elena to the Russian military base. Most of the Americans were killed; the rest captured. One character is still unaccounted for:: the cat.

Vixey's cat slept through the lulling battle but then awoke from the onset of silence, as Grantaire at that same 1832 *émeute* mentioned earlier. She surveyed the scene was disappointment, thinking *c'est la vie,...*[*] Then she departed for Evelina's house in Bavaria on Prinzregentenstraße, near the Englischer Garten. I wish I had been this cat, more than anything in the world.

The cat was not at the intellectual level of Hoffmann's scholarly Tomcat Murr, but I'm sure she would have no problem finding Prinzregentenstraße. The geography of Germany was one thing she knew well, seeing it from the car a few times crossing with Vixey.

---

[*] This sentence is unfinished in the manuscript.

Epilogue – A footnote

> [The moment of victory in the war] was to me a most unhappy
> time. I moved amid cheering crowds ... with an aching heart and a
> mind oppressed by forebodings.
> CHURCHILL, *Triumph and Tragedy*

Part 1: Vixey

The narrative ends here, and it is obvious that the last thing written was in November 1944, during the bombing of Freiburg. It remains in the epilogue to describe what happened after in Europe and to suppose how this would have affected the remaining players.

Records show that there was no General Vladimir Maximovich Petrovsky at the time; possibly he was a stylized combination of other ROA generals. The narrator must have been acquainted with one or two, possibly Bunyachenko or Zverev, who were both in Baden-Württemberg then with their divisions. This must have been the basis for all the facts about which Petrovsky speaks. As the editor, I verified all the information – everything that relates to historical figures or events is true. For instance, the descriptions of various things done by Generals Vlasov, von Pannwitz, von Bock, and others; Hitler's discussions with Göring about the Finland invasion and Romanian oil threat; Vixey's story about German tank generals training in Russia; von Rundstedt's opinion on the T-34; etc.

If one has doubts about the severity of the ending, one merely has to read the rest of the epilogue to see that it is the only direction that the plot could have taken in order to be consistent with what is going on in reality. Anything less severe would be implausible because of its sudden inconsistency. It would be possible, but then the plot would be of the kind no different than one about nymphs, naiads, Freyja with the chariot drawn by cats; the boar Hildisvíni, Pegasus, and Psyche.

Or one can compare elsewhere in literature; A young man reading *Notre Dame de Paris* may be resentful of Agnes at the gallows as the ending, only to realize later on in life that Hugo got it right – the plot/themes/setting leads inevitably to this.

Or elsewhere in history;- Marie Duplessis, one of the most beautiful ladies of Napoleon III's Paris (of all Paris, not just the *demi-monde*), succumbed to a very untimely death, as is known through the writing of Dumas *fils*. The illustrious Beatrix d'Este, mentioned already in one of the footnotes, lived only until 21. Her demi-goddess magnificence was merely a flash of lightning in time, leaving behind decades of mourning for all who had known her. Then the Italian Wars began and what was left of her court became a black inferno, in the words of her secretary Vincenzo Calmeta.

Incidentally, if comparing Vixey to one renaissance Beatrix, it brings to mind another interesting comparison – Beatrix Portinari who inspired most of Dante's writings, even though he only saw her briefly a few times.

It's apparent that the narrator, although he lived in Berne, travelled frequently in Germany and was casually acquainted with a real Vixey, the acquaintance going back as early as 1936. Seeing her at occasional points, some of which he mentions throughout the plot, he developed a fictional story based around her. A *Künstlerliebe* element is obvious, even if it hadn't been mentioned by the narrator.

Perhaps Vixey was real completely as described. If she wasn't stylistically enhanced, then she would have been quite exceptional for 1940s Germany. Even in 1960s Paris her style would be above par. Naturally, I am skeptical that everything about her was real. She is too good. Perhaps, like Dante's Beatrix, she developed (or crystallized) from a potent *idée vixe* of the author's abstraction, one based on a temporal paragon – an ideal, but not, before the synthesis with art, a transcendental ideal.

*   *   *

Part 2: Vistula

The Russians who found themselves in Germany as the war was drawing to a close faced a lot of uncertainty, but they had differences in their expectations and hopes: some were more optimistic while others were completely discouraged.

Neither could anticipate what would happen to them as a whole. The optimistic were obviously wrong. The grim pessimistic ones, even the ones reconciled to death, were wrong as well. The reality turned out to be even *worse* than their fears, because they couldn't imagine that the Americans and British would consent to forcibly transport all the two million that ended up in the Western occupation zone, *including* women and children, at Stalin's request to be killed/enslaved in the Soviet Union.

But that was yet to occur; the war was still on. While Vlasov and his divisions were still in the process of preparation and mobilization, the Reich suffered critical defeats in January 1945. In the West, Hitler's Ardennes counteroffensive failed, leading to a practically unobstructed path into Germany for Bradley, Patton, and Montgomery. In the East, Zhukov and Konev's Army Groups had been sitting by the Vistula River in Poland for half a year. In January, they broke through with all the mammoth numbers of tanks and artillery that they had amassed there. Losses were significant, but the stream of weapons from the bottomless factories of Siberia resulted in the army still expanding as it moved with speed to the West, soon to bristle at the gates of Berlin with a veritable forest of artillery.

This was the collapse of the eastern front – the realization of citizens' worst fears. Last desperate efforts were all that remained – the roads became filled with people trying to reach the west on foot. Grand Admiral Dönitz ordered the evacuation of all northern coastal areas

– one of the largest emergency evacuations by sea in history. Soviet submarines hunted the refugee ships, resulting in immense losses in the January icy waters, but still, more than a million escaped the Red Army in this way.

Lev Kopelev, then a Red Army officer, was imprisoned for his opposition to the degraded Soviet acts against civilians in Germany. Solzhenitsyn witnessed the Vistula offensive also, and wrote *Prussian Nights* in reflection. This significant historical event that affected millions of people (women, mostly), was suppressed for decades in the media. Even now many people, for inexplicable reasons, believe that the attacks do not deserve criticism.

At this time the picturesque city of Dresden was destroyed by the RAF and USAAF. It was done so late that it was largely irrelevant to the outcome of the war. But if there was a military benefit, it would only be to quicken the Red Army advance. This was a political goal, as Eisenhower explained: the late aerial attacks on Berlin and Dresden were important to demonstrate "Allied unity".

*   *   *

Part 3: Prague

During this period some ROA units saw action against the Red Army, attracting some amount of defectors even now, but at length they had to face facts and retreat to Czechia.

Bunyachenko's 1st Division was near Prague at the time the Czechs rebelled against Germany. Heavily armed Waffen-SS units moved in to crush the uprising, and would have done so, destroying large parts of Prague, had not the ROA entered into the conflict on the side of the Czechs. They successfully defeated the SS regiments, fighting on streets such as Pařížská in the *vieille ville*. Bunyachenko was thanked for saving the city but told the very next day that he had to leave, as the Soviets would soon be entering. He had initially been led to believe, incorrectly, that the US would occupy Prague. Thus the 1st Division had to escape

out of Prague, along with some remaining SS troops, to flee
the encircling Red Army. History rarely credits the Russian
Liberation Army with the liberation of the Czech capital.

Meanwhile Patton's 3rd Army was actually within hours
of Prague, some units just 20km away. But Berlin and
Prague had been promised to Stalin by Roosevelt (without
consulting Churchill). Patton was thus subjected to the
embarrassment of being forced to stop so close, powerless
to do anything. During the uprising the Czechs implored
for help but Patton was forbidden to advance. Allegedly,
Patton was so enraged that he cursed out the government
and top command for the length of an entire hour without
stopping. It was a shame to let such an intact, undestroyed
city, behind only Paris and Venezia in beauty, go to the
Soviets.

Vlasov and his associates could not expect much from
the relatively weak Czechia. The Czechs limited their rôle in
the days after German surrender to violently killing or
deporting German civilians living in Czechia.

Poland, a large country which had never surrendered
to Germany but kept up a resistance for four years, was now
finished. The army destroyed, army officers shot by Stalin,
interests betrayed by the West, it was now totally
controlled by the communists and was also involved in
revenge against Germans. Belgrade, Budapest, Bucharest,
and Sofia were under communist control as well.

Athína (Αθήνα) did not fall to the Soviet Union.
Churchill clearly indicated his interest in Greece;
subsequently Stalin ordered the Greek Communist Party
not to seize power in Athína, which it could easily have
done. Vladimir Maximovich correctly surmised that a Soviet
takeover of Greece would cause a rift between the US/UK
and the USSR and would be advantageous to the Russian
Liberation Movement. Stalin was too wise to allow this to
happen. He backed down from Greece in order to keep the
façade of good relations with the West and secure greater

objectives in central Europe. Milovan Đilas, the vice-president of Yugoslavia, quotes Stalin's reasons in his *Conversations with Stalin*. Theoretically, the British might have accepted the help of Vlasov in fighting the Greek communists, but there was no way for the ROA to arrive there without crossing Tito's Yugoslavia.

In Lithuania (as well as on a smaller level in the other Baltic states), a desperate and courageous resistance against the Soviet Union continued for years. Besieged partisans almost always fought to the death in order to avoid the torture of those captured alive. They fought with the hope that the West would eventually aid them but it never did. The ROA would have had little information about this resistance movement and would not have gained much from joining them.

Some Russians, trapped in Eastern Germany, had no alternative but to put up a last stand of defiance. Anatoli Granovsky, an NKVD officer who defected to the West, writes in his memoirs how Breslau was defended by a garrison of Russians. The town held out against the Soviets for 78 days, at the end of which not a single member of the garrison remained alive. Granovsky, who has seen much in his life, notes how extraordinary this incident was and expresses his surprise that so little has been said about it in history.

For the Russians still outside of the reach of the Red Army, it only remained to go over to the US/UK. Even if the fight was over for now, thought the ROA generals, at least there could be a chance to form a separate Russian state to perpetually challenge the illegitimacy of the USSR, or to form a considerable émigré community somewhere. But this is laughable to someone who knows the Western political climate of the times and how much it was subordinated to the fear of being insensitive to Stalin's desires. Stalin merely had to proclaim any resistance against him to be Hitlerite fascists and the whole world would immediately strive to destroy them.

Germany surrendered in May 1945 and that war ended. Forced repatriation of Russians in the West had already begun earlier, but now it was to begin in earnest.

*   *   *

Part 4: Repatriations

Nikolai Tolstoy wrote the definitive historical analysis of the repatriation fiasco. Not Lev Tolstoy the old novelist, but a British descendant of his. A concise overview of the matter must be given here, enough to give an idea of how the war ended for the Russian Liberation Movement once it had depleted all possible alternatives, and the tragic consequences of its failure.

Some information given here is widely-known, and some is directly from Tolstoy's research in *Victims of Yalta*.

In total some 5.5 million Soviet nationals were repatriated back to the Soviet Union from territories outside it. 3.2 million of these were captured by the Soviet Union itself and 2.3 million were transported by Western states. An unknown number, possibly as high a half a million, escaped repatriation entirely. (However, often the relatives of those that escaped were arrested instead).

Out of the total 5.5 million, 15-20% were allowed to return unscathed to their homes, although these remained under suspicion and may have been arrested later in 1946-49. The remainder were executed, entered the gulag, or were exiled to frontier areas of Siberia.

Some repatriates had been in England for some time under lax controls. Seeing a prosperous country must have appeared wondrous to them and the contrast in subsequent gulag all the more terrible.

The Soviet nationals in Western Europe consisted of four main categories:

1) POWs

2) Vlasov divisions, Cossack divisions, other anti-Soviet forces, or Wehrmacht conscripts

3) a large number of Cossack civilians who retreated along
with the German army out of the Soviet Union
4) other civilians who were either taken by Germany for
labor (*ostarbeiter*) or who fled the Soviet Union voluntarily
(for instance many Georgians)

By far the majority of the 2.3 million repatriated by the
West were quickly transported in the summer of 1945
without much resistance. They were mostly *ostarbeiter*
civilians and inmates of POW camps, many of whom
probably did not expect to be sent to gulag. Soviet
representatives (NKVD) had immediately been dispatched
everywhere to trick people into believing they would
receive a good reception and welcoming back home.

For the West, the problem was with the groups who
desperately did not want to be sent back: the ROA soldiers,
Cossacks, and others. The transfers continued through
1946.

In the very beginning, some were able to slip through
by surrendering to the Americans. Patton was able to save
General Maltsev's Air Force men (although not Maltsev
himself). The military's sympathies were often with the
anti-Soviet Russians, but ultimately they had to respond to
their orders from above.

The Cossacks are a sort of Ukrainians with a long
tradition of horsemanship and warring. The Germans
helped the Cossack nation retreat with them away from the
Soviet Union. In a large group, with all their belongings and
farm animals, they resettled in Belarus, then moved to the
Italian Alps, then were forced to cross into Austria. Some
Cossack soldiers were already in Germany and working with
Vlasov, such as the XV Cossack Cavalry Corps. When all the
Cossacks were encircled in Austria, the British Army was
treated to the last scenes of massive cavalry formations in
history – tens of thousands of mounted riders parading in
front of the mountains of the Austrian Alps.

They were forcibly transferred to the Soviet Union, an action which would be comparable to transferring escaped Jews to Nazi Germany. And there were many other groups repatriated besides the Cossacks. In general, giving credit where it is due, the Americans were decidedly less eager at their task than the British.

Sometimes trickery and lies were used to convince troops that they will be treated as allies, until they gave up their weapons and agreed to enter trains to be transferred somewhere. The trains were routed to the east, however, to the Soviet NKVD.

Naïve British soldiers at first supported the repatriation policy, accustomed as they were via British wartime propaganda of perceiving the Soviet Union as a great country of justice and progress, a socialist utopia. This is how Western media colored the Soviet Union. The soldiers couldn't understand why the Russians, in such large numbers, were proclaiming that they prefer death to repatriation, pleading for the British to just shoot them rather than send them back. (Petitions were written and signed in Cossack camps, stating, "We prefer death...").

Soldiers had to use bayonets, clubs, and tear gas to get people on to trucks and to prevent suicides. Still many suicides occurred. Families killed their children as well, a preference to this rather than having them grow up in a concentration camp. Sometimes learning the fact of repatriation came suddenly, and people were forced to resort to all sorts of awkward objects to assist their suicide: small rusty knives, shards of glass from a window, jumping off a truck head-first in a way to break one's neck, etc.

Equality under the law is a fine thing, but as early as 1861 Dostoyevsky, in his penal memoirs, wrote about how the same punishment to all is actually a different punishment because people are different. For instance, to have the ribs broken of an 18 year old girl recaptured back into the Soviet Union, on the floor of an NKVD interrogation chamber, is worse than the same is for an experienced soldier or a criminal recidivist, who may survive it. But Stalin demanded all civilian Soviet nationals, not just volunteers who fought in the Wehrmacht, and the West had to comply. It was an unprecedented situation in the West- to actively collude in extrajudicial reprisal on such a large scale. People found out what it actually meant to be in an alliance with a communist state. Many American and British soldiers who were forced to participate were appalled, brought to tears, and suffered psychologically for many years hence.

So far this has only described measures against Soviet citizens who had left during the war. In the official agreement with Stalin, there was nothing about sending back any 'old émigrés' – the numerous Russians living in the West who had left Russia or the Soviet Union *prior* to the war. It is apparent that a special request was made secretly, and fulfilled by elements in the British government (probably Foreign Office) with a great desire to do something further to please Stalin. As a result, the White Army Generals Krasnov and Shkuro, allies of the British in World War I and the Russian Civil War, were forcibly delivered to their deaths – along with a few thousand other old émigrés. This again shows the strength of Stalin's foreign influence.

The British also delivered the German General von Pannwitz and his *German officers*, just because they had commanded divisions of Cossacks. This is comparable to a US general surrendering to Germany and then being sent to Italy to be executed without trial because Italy didn't like the fact that he had Italian-Americans under his command. Of course Germany and Italy never did such things. Helmuth von Pannwitz was one of the noblest generals of the war. In the end, he saw a chance to escape but did not take it due to the solidarity he felt for his doomed troops.

At first the Soviet Union had the delicacy to conceal from the West the fate of the returned citizens. For instance, in Odessa a squadron of airplanes would circle over the Western ships in the port that had brought repatriates. They would conceal with their noise the mass shooting going on out of sight. Then the Soviets realized that Western politicians actually knew what was going on and they stopped caring about concealment. Thus there are British soldiers who report witnessing, in Germany, how people were shot or hanged at the transfer point. Frequently in that category of immediate execution were ROA soldiers, or old people and hospital patients unfit for work in gulag.

Although many files related to repatriation activities and the Yalta conferences have been released by the US government, some still remain classified. The British are even more concerned; they released little over the decades and they also deliberately *burned* a set of related documents in 1969. How the transfer of the old émigrés happened is still a guarded British government secret.

If no person responsible for forcible repatriation (especially of civilians) was brought to trial for war crimes, then no Nazi official should have been charged for crimes such as transferring *ostarbeiter* to German factories. Likewise, no French collaborator should have been charged for capturing Jews for the labor camps of the *Deutsche Wirtschaftsbetriebe*. After the war 48,000 collaborators were incarcerated for various reasons just in small Belgium alone.

Wearing a German army uniform entitled the wearer, regardless of his Russian or other origins, of the rights of a German POW and protections of the Geneva Convention. Sending such people to execution during the war, as Britain did, violated Germany's rights and actually entitled Germany to maltreat British POWs. The SS were waiting for an excuse to do this. Had they known about the repatriations and retaliated, the results would have been the moral responsibility of the British, who were instigating the law-breaking.

After the war ended, even if disregarding the dilemma with the Geneva Convention, sending the Russians to their fate was still unquestionably a violation of the Hague Conventions of 1899/1907. Note that the Geneva and Hague Conventions are fundamental components of international law while the Yalta agreements of 1945 were handshakes between heads of state.

The uniqueness of the Yalta Conference was that because of expediency, broad executive powers were permitted without regard for consistency with international/domestic law as evaluated by the courts. However, the fact that an agreement made with Stalin calls for some action should not remove the taint of illegality. Post-war trials such as the notorious ones at Nürnberg did not allow German defendants such as Keitel, Jodl, von Ribbentrop, and Dönitz the legal defense that their actions were excusable based on commands from their government.

Ultimately, most repatriation actions, while acknowledged to be insupportable by law, were dictated by motives of the British Foreign Office. The motive, which was the same as that of the now-late Roosevelt, can be summarized thusly: It is a small sacrifice to make in exchange for gaining the goodwill of the Soviet Union. Stalin's intentions towards the West are benevolent and it is essential to cooperate fully with him.

*   *   *

Part 5: Vladimir Maximovich, Elena, and the Cat

Now it is easy to see why in retrospect, Vladimir Maximovich's relative unconcern with personal consequences was misguided. He was concerned about the success of the movement, but always considered that if all things failed, at least he could surrender to the West. Whatever their attitudes could turn out to be, he thought, he would be treated no worse than a German general, which is what international law demanded.

If the plot continued, he would probably have followed through on his plan to surrender to the Americans once there was no other alternative. They would detain him, have pleasant conversations with him, and once the order came they would hand him over to the Soviets to be executed. Of the ROA generals ending up in the Soviet Union, only a few had been actually captured by the Soviets themselves: notably Vlasov and Zverev. All the rest ended the war in the custody of the Americans and then were handed over: Bunyachenko, Vlasov's close associates Zhilenkov and Malyshkin, Maltsev, and several others. They were all executed in Moscow.

The soldiers in the ROA divisions, except for a few chance escapes, would either commit suicide, be shot or hanged immediately on delivery, or continue on to NKVD interrogation. If they survived that, they would be sentenced to execution or to exterminating-labor.

Vladimir Maximovich's wife, it was mentioned, was also in Germany. As a Soviet citizen, she too would have been subject to involuntary repatriation. However, in her old age, it is likely she would have died in transit before reaching the prisons. Conditions on the stiflingly-overpacked cattle cars were so bad that many arrived with a percentage of people dead.

Poor Elena would have avoided repatriation, as she would have easily entered Switzerland incognito, as planned, and obtained a false Swiss passport. There, it is easy to imagine her marrying a rich banker or lawyer in Zürich. It is also easy to imagine complications arising with inheritance issues, if the gentleman already has a son and/or daughter the same age as Elena. Going even further, suppose that the step-daughter is married herself, and finds her husband and Elena flirting with each other?

Complications like that seem likely to follow Elena wherever she goes. But in most cases it is reasonable to suppose that she would be able to advantageously resolve the situation through the effect of her attractiveness.

Another possibility is that von Isarberg, the field marshal (who was absent from the story and whose daughters were Evelina and Vixey), would want to cross into Switzerland to escape likely prosecution for war crimes by the occupation forces. The most likely place for him to go would be Zürich, the largest German city, and there the chance would be high that he would run into Elena eventually. If this happened, then they might have reconnected, having in common the fact that they both like Vixey. Historically, there was no von Isarberg in the German army, but the author may have changed the real name of a different general.

It was seen that Karl had not had time to arrange the US Army courier to meet Elena in Zürich, so Vladimir Maximovich could not use her to deliver the planned documents about the ROA. If they had reached the intended people, they could have helped explain a great deal to many US/UK generals on the front line who were largely ignorant of the Russian Liberation Movement. The overall political situation could not have been reversed, but still some positive effect would have resulted from more military commanders being aware of the full picture. Perhaps, at least, more of them would have acted to provide captured ROA soldiers a convenient chance to escape.

The cat would go east until reaching the recognizable Lech River, at which point she would be in the *gemütlich* town of Schongau in Bavaria. Here she would undoubtedly be offered cheese and various provisions for the journey by the hospitable residents. The cat would realize that she could not travel during rainstorms – she has to wait for them to pass since her fur was very long and would take too much time to dry if soaked.

But from here it would not be far- she would find the Loisach and follow it to Wolfratshausen, a town whose name must be frightening for a cat, but in which she would finally reach the Isar River. This she would follow a short distance straight into central Munich, and when she would see the Friedensengel (Angel of Peace) monument, she would know she is on Prinzregentenstraße, Evelina's street.

*   *   *

Part 6: Liechtenstein

There is no need to describe what happened next in Europe. All this can be read in historical accounts, the ones that don't skip over the facts. They describe in detail how East Germany changed from Nazi to Stasi. Meanwhile the homes of 11 million Germans were taken away, sent to live elsewhere. This included the old German city of Königsberg in East Prussia, given as a gift to the Soviet Union and renamed Kaliningrad. And the beautiful spa town of Karlsbad, renamed Karlovy Vary by Czechoslovakia.

Churchill fought against Stalin's new demand to give Pomerania, Silesia, and parts of Brandenburg (with the cities of Breslau and Stettin) to Poland, thus displacing millions of Germans. But he was not supported by Truman and was even on the verge of being replaced as Prime Minister. Earlier, he repeatedly asked the Americans not to withdraw from vast portions of Saxony and Czechia that they occupied at the close of the war. But Truman and his advisors gave up those lands and that leverage as an act of good faith – They wanted to accurately comply with the agreements with Stalin, without waiting to see whether he would comply with them first.

Nazi concentration camps in Poland were kept open by the NKVD, working with the Polish communists. Some were filled with German civilians who were being expelled from their lands. The NKVD made sure to have them run by sadistic Poles whose specifically stated goal was to exceed the torture of the Nazi camps. Unbiased researchers like

Keith Lowe have documented this and other things that have long been unknown or inaccurate in the history of postwar Eastern Europe.

At the time Poland was also the most dangerous place in Europe for Jews. It was there that mob attacks on Jews such as the Kielce Pogrom of 1946 occurred. Very little was known about this new Poland in the West. Churchill apparently had no independent source of information from British Intelligence (MI6) about the state of affairs there, relying only on information from Stalin's people as he negotiated over Poland's future. On the contrary, Stalin's network of espionage and political agitation in Europe was significant. Communists held 20% of the postwar vote in Italy and 30% in France.

Three million German military POWs were kept by the Soviet Union for forced labor, another illegal decision of the Yalta Conference. One-third died; most of the rest were held until 1950. Part of Austria was occupied by the Soviet Union for ten years until 1955, despite Otto von Habsburg's prior warnings.

All this is important to know in order to be able to assess the consequences of the US/UK war strategy. It was no accident that the war ended with the Soviet Union seizing half of Germany and half of Europe, and emerging as a superpower to plague the world for the next half-century. It was achieved through the consistency of Roosevelt's decisions, all of which favored Stalin, and which amounted to a collusion. Roosevelt was of course helped in this by the host of Soviet agents in the West, and also the pro-socialist attitudes of many functionaries in Western governments. The desire to please Stalin extended to repatriating more than two million refugees, some of whom were armed and ready to fight to the death rather than go back. Just two years later, during the Berlin Airlift when the Cold War was in full swing, did they remember their betrayal of this large movement that wanted to ally itself with the West?

While undoubtedly one of Roosevelt's goals was the destruction of Hitler, simultaneously he actively fought for the advancement of a second goal: the establishment of Stalin's power over central Europe. The US must be blamed (not only Roosevelt but the people who voted for him) for maintaining communism in Russia and spreading it to half of Europe. Fighting Hitler did not automatically mean Stalin had to be supported. The two could have been allowed to collide, while invading the Balkans through Greece as Churchill proposed, supporting the Eastern European nationalists, using the Wehrmacht against Hitler, and using the ROA against Stalin. The ROA, if allowed to act, could still have succeeded against the Soviet Union even in spring 1945.

To end on a positive note, one country will be mentioned which did not agree to cooperate with the Soviet Union. That was the *Fürstentum* Liechtenstein, with a total population not even bigger than that of the nearby town of Feldkirch in Vorarlberg. Compared to Swiss cantons, it is only larger than two: Uri and Appenzell Innerrhoden. Using the Swiss franc and with an open border with Switzerland, it might be considered a *de facto* federal canton, if not for the fact that it is still a constitutional monarchy. In this way it is between Switzerland and the Holy Roman Empire, a remnant of the days when there were many German principalities and duchies. Currently, it has the distinction of being one of the last remaining tax havens that refuses to cooperate with larger states, such as the US, hunting for their citizens' earnings.

General Smyslovsky was a White Russian émigré who commanded the *Sonderdivision Russland*, one of the Russian divisions in the Wehrmacht that was not associated with Vlasov. The division was a mix of old émigrés and defectors from the Red Army. As the war situation deteriorated, he retreated through Austria. Failing to join up with the 3rd ROA division, most of his troops dispersed and only about 500 remained, along with a few dozen women civilians. With Germany's surrender ending the war, Smyslovsky entered Liechtenstein, seeking asylum. Passing the summer there, he and his troops would have learned of the policy of forcible repatriation in effect in occupied regions all around them. Kempten in Bavaria was just over 100km away. It was there that Americans, under observation of NKVD officers, forcibly subdued a group of Russians who had hidden inside a church, and dragged them out to be repatriated.

Soviet delegates presently came to Liechtenstein to try to arrest the Russians there, but the governing Prince firmly refused to allow this. The Soviets persisted, but the refusal was still given, with the citizens of Liechtenstein in agreement with their government. Eventually the Russians emigrated to Buenos Aires. In this way, meeting with a principled show of resistance from the West, the Soviet Union did not resort to force and backed down. If it happened more often, much could have been avoided in the 20th century.

Fin

APPENDIX

Acknowledgements
P1 Club, Munich
(and other places throughout Austro-Bavaria, for providing inspirational feminine fashion and æsthetics rarely available to see on the streets of New York).

Typeface used for the text:
Constantia

A note on sources
I used a range of various sources, including the experiences of relatives in the war. Specific books for further detail on certain topics are listed as follows:

Latter part of the war from the British prime minister's perspective:
Winston Churchill, *Triumph and Tragedy*

American foreign policy:
George Crocker, *Roosevelt's Road to Russia*

Soviet government and foreign policy:
Michael Voslensky, *Nomenklatura*

The war from perspective of certain Wehrmacht generals:
B. H. Liddell-Hart, *The German Generals Talk*

Evidence for 1941 Soviet offensive plans against Germany:
Viktor Suvorov, *The Chief Culprit*
Mikhail Meltyukhov, Упущенный шанс Сталина (*Stalin's Missed Chance*)

The repatriation fiasco and the Vlasov movement:
Nikolai Tolstoy, *Victims of Yalta*
Nicholas Bethell, *The Last Secret*

A summary of the Vlasov movement:
Gen. Wladyslaw Anders, *Russian Volunteers in the German Wehrmacht in WWII*

Vlasov movement from a participant:
Wilfried Strik-Strikfeldt, *Against Stalin and Hitler*

Soviet history, labor camp system, Vlasov movement, etc.:
Alexander Solzhenitsyn, *Archipelag Gulag*

Third Reich economics:
Ludwig von Mises, *Omnipotent Government*
Günter Reimann, *The Vampire Economy*

Nazi Party history, including economics:
William Shirer, *The Rise and Fall of the Third Reich*

Hitler's perspective on the Eastern War, etc.:
Adolf Hitler, *Hitler's Table Talk 1941-1944* (compiled and edited by his private secretary Martin Bormann)

Post-war disorder, including anti-German actions:
Keith Lowe, *Savage Continent*

Soviet influence on US government during war:
Evans and Romerstein, *Stalin's Secret Agents*

Fashion during war:
François Baudot, *Fashion: The Twentieth Century*
Danièle Bott, *Chanel: Collections and Creations*

A brief chronology of the historical context

1917 – Lenin comes to power in Russia

1922 – Stalin succeeds Lenin

1933 – Hitler comes to power in Germany

1939 August – Treaty of Non-aggression between Germany and the USSR, dividing Eastern Europe

1939 September – Germany and Soviet Union invade Poland; UK declares war on Germany

1941 June – Germany invades Soviet Union

1941 December – United States formally enters war

1943 February – Soviet Union switches to the offensive

1943 July – US/UK invade Italy

1943 November – Teheran Conference (1st meeting of Roosevelt, Churchill, and Stalin)

1944 June – US/UK invade France (Normandy)

1944 August – US invades southern France (Côte d'Azur)

1944 September – KONR (Russian Liberation Committee) begins to form an independent Russian Liberation Army

1944 October – *Vixey and events in Schwarzwald*

1944 November – Official inauguration of Russian Liberation Committee, in Prague

1945 January – Red Army begins Vistula-Oder offensive

1945 February – Yalta Conference (2nd meeting of Roosevelt, Churchill, and Stalin)

1945 May – Surrender of Germany

1945 July – Potsdam Conference (Stalin, Truman, Churchill, and Attlee)

1947 March – Truman Doctrine (an anti-communist policy)

1947 July – Severe restrictions on West German economy eliminated

1948 – Berlin Airlift (first major political event where the US fully sides with Germany against the Soviet Union)

Map of Europe, 1944
(Courtesy of Dept. of History, US Military Academy at West Point)
The thick line marks position of the fronts as of December 1944.

The dotted line going through Romania and below Luxemburg through Metz, also shows the fronts' positions as of September 1944. The star indicates the location of the Black Forest.

EUROPE, 1944
ALLIED GAINS IN EUROPE
6 June - 24 July 1944
25 July - 14 September 1944
15 September - 15 December 1944

SCALE OF MILES
0   100   200   300

About the author

Ron Cogan is a New Yorker who has at times lived in Germany, Italy, Florida, and the Catskills and has origins in Rīga. He works in banking and capital markets in New York, after previously working in bond insurance.
www.linkedin.com/in/roncogan1

The first picture above was taken somewhere off the Ligurian coast in the Mediterranean, June 2012. The second is from Salzburg, January 2013.

Idée Vixe was finished in October 2014. Some of the research was done in the palatial Beaux-Arts library building in Bryant Park. The only writing done outside of New York was a bit in the coffeehouse of the University of Florida library.

A potential future project would have the tentative title *Émigré Dacha* and would be set in the Catskills dacha scene of the late 1990s/early 00s.